PRAISE FOR
## *A Nail Through the Heart*

"Hallinan scores big-time with a fast-moving thriller set in Thailand. . . . Dark, often funny, and ultimately enthralling."　　—*Kirkus Reviews*

"[A] tale of blackmail, extortion, and revenge . . . spinning along at a speedy clip."　　—*Washington Post*

"Excellent. The rich depictions of Bangkok's seedy side recall John Burdett's visceral mysteries."　　—*Publishers Weekly*

"Excellent. This is a twisted story. You can read and read. And never imagine the end."　　—*Contra Costa Times*

"*A Nail Through the Heart* is a haunting novel that takes place way out on the fringe of the moral landscape. It's fast, bold, disturbing, and beautifully written. Hallinan is terrific."　　—T. Jefferson Parker

"Don't miss your chance to read *A Nail Through the Heart* before it starts winning all its awards. Timothy Hallinan deals in a profoundly serious way with important themes and terrible depravity, yet his touch is so sure, his humor so mordantly pungent, his dialogue so pitch-perfect, and his humanity and intelligence so self-evident that every page shimmers with life and light. Hallinan is a writer's writer, and this is great stuff!"　　—John Lescroart

"If this opens a new series, Hallinan is off to a sure-footed start with a supporting cast (including Poke's precocious, pugnacious, almost-daughter Miaow) well worth getting to know."　　—*Booklist*

"Definitely worth a visit. Will keep you on the edge of your seat and clamoring for Hallinan's next book."　　—*Montgomery Advertiser*

"Well constructed, lively . . . full of misdirection, surprises, humor. It is the respect [Hallinan] has for his characters that ultimately makes reading *A Nail Through the Heart* more than just a quick and scary ride. A well-paced thriller."　　—PopMatters.com

"Exhilarating."　　—BookCrossing.com

"Brilliantly conceived and beautifully rendered . . . artful, compelling, and entertaining. Kudos to Hallinan for an exceptional story."

—PerfectText.com

"A page-turner."                                    —Bookgasm.com

"Timothy Hallinan is a tremendous writing talent. There is plenty of mystery in his story to keep the reader engrossed and some very colorful characters to make this novel an entertaining read."

—BestsellersWorld.com

"Rich with detail and sympathetic characters. . . . A very talented writer."

—TheBrownBookLoft.com

"A page-turner. It's the closest you'll get to going to a strange land without actually visiting. Dark, thrilling, and unforgettable, *A Nail Through the Heart* is a journey you won't soon forget."

—PopSyndicate.com

"A haunting read. . . . Goes deeper than the usual thriller in giving you a sense of Bangkok. Hallinan is an author to watch."

—BellaOnline.com

"This dark and captivating story isn't an easy one to put down. It moves at a swift pace, with a horrifying new revelation around every corner. Hallinan skillfully blurs the line between good and bad. It's sure to keep you guessing—and it'll leave you wanting to read more from this talented author."                                    —NightAndWeekends.com

"*A Nail Through the Heart* is a terrific opening to this new series, one that has the potential to captivate readers for a long time to come."

—*Mystery News*

"A well-written, fast-paced, beautifully drawn thriller."

—*I Love a Mystery* newsletter

"In the first of a truly remarkable series, Hallinan takes you to Thailand with a vengeance. This [is] one of the best novels I have read in years, and it will be a true, long-lasting favorite."

—BookSense.com (monthly pick)

Munyin Choy

## *About the Author*

TIMOTHY HALLINAN divides his time between Los Angeles and Southeast Asia, primarily Thailand, where he has lived off and on for more than twenty years. As a principal in one of America's top television consulting firms, he advised many Fortune 500 companies and pioneered new methods of making quality television programming accessible to teachers. He has also taught writing for many years. He is married to Munyin Choy.

# a NalL
# THRoUGH
# the HEaRT

## A Novel of Bangkok

# TIMOTHY HALLINAN

HARPER

NEW YORK · LONDON · TORONTO · SYDNEY

MYS HALLINAN

HARPER

A hardcover edition of this book was published in 2007 by William Morrow, an imprint of HarperCollins Publishers.

A NAIL THROUGH THE HEART. Copyright © 2007 by Timothy Hallinan.

FIRST HARPER PAPERBACK PUBLISHED 2008.

*Designed by Laura Kaeppel*

The Library of Congress has catalogued the hardcover edition as follows:

Hallinan, Timothy.
    A nail through the heart / Timothy Hallinan.—1st ed.
    p. cm.
    ISBN 978-0-06-125580-9
    1. Travel writers—Fiction.   2. Bangkok (Thailand)—Fiction.
I. Title.

PS3558.A3923N35  2007
813'.54—dc22                                                2006047085

ISBN 978-0-06-125722-3 (pbk.)

11 12  DT/RRD  10 9 8 7 6 5 4 3

For Munyin. Again.

PART I

RaISING the HaMMER

## The Blue Rises Up

For the thousandth time in twelve weeks, the blue of the tsunami rises up—now safely contained behind the glass screen—and breaks to pieces on the trunks of the palms. At this point, as everyone in the world who has a television knows, the horizon tilts to a forty-five-degree angle. Then the camera moves back, herky-jerky to the rhythm of the cameraman's steps, and another wave rushes forward to devour the one before it and shatter itself against a low wall, and the small figures resolve into running people, and for the first time you can hear the shouts and the occasional scream.

And around the camera now, as it turns to show us the single street of the village, awash with the detritus of deck chairs and plastic bags, more water surges ashore. You can no longer see the running people.

# The Most Famous Invisible Jewels in Southeast Asia

**M**oon and river. House and trees.

The hard line of the roof lops the lower half from the rising moon. Across the river, the city of eight million shimmers like the ghost of a brushfire.

In the dark trees at the river's edge, a rustle of birds. In the palm of Tam's hand, the sudden spark-red pain of a splinter.

The shovel he has driven deep into the mud strikes something hard and stops. The laws of physics force Tam's hands down the wet wooden handle and drive the sharp fragment a full inch into his lotioned and pampered palm.

It is a measure of the care Tam takes with his hands that his first thought is, *Thank God it's the left,* giving him approximately one-fifth of a second of gratitude before the second thought lights up the night: *The safe.*

He straightens slowly against his aching back, hoping the water in the hole has muffled the sound of metal striking metal, but the man above him, the man holding the flashlight in his one good hand, has seen Tam's hands skid down the handle and bends forward and says, "Something?"

Tam wiggles the blade of the shovel. The surface, whatever it is, is smooth and slick, not a rock.

"A rock," he says. Then he says, for the third time, "I hate this water."

Not that hating it does any good. Even in a hole less than four feet deep, the water seeps in and saturates the dirt. It turns it into a sluggish, heavy soup, precisely the old red of dried blood, that slops over the sides of the shovel and splatters back down. And rises up from below: For every shovelful of mud Tam throws over the side, a pint of warm, muddy river water seeps into the bottom of the hole.

Bangkok is a river town, built around a network of canals radiating off the Chao Phraya, the silt-saturated River of Kings. The city's office towers, roads, and palaces float queasily on a tropical floodplain. Even in the dry season, the water is always there, pooled just beneath the dirt, just beneath the pavement. Waiting for some fool with a shovel.

But now the fool has struck gold. No, not gold. Jewels.

Tam leans on the shovel and gazes down into the hole to hide the elation in his face. There must be a way to get rid of the man above him for a minute. A minute is all it would take.

The moon has lifted its dappled face another fraction above the house: old Thai style, graceful angles of dark, heavy teak. Large and sprawling, it opens to grand verandas that gaze down across a sweep of grass to the river. In Bangkok only wealthy people have room for grass. They surround it with high concrete walls topped with shards of broken glass to keep people like Tam and the other man at bay. The house is unlighted. According to the other man—who says his name is Chon, although it is not—it is empty.

The emerging moon sharpens the house's shadow across the lawn.

The empty house, the glass-topped wall, the jewels: Chon had known many things. Not until this moment, though, leaning on a shovel up to his hips in muddy water, with his palm bleeding, does

Tam actually believe that Chon knows the location of the most famous invisible jewels in Southeast Asia.

Okay, so maybe Tam can't make Chon leave. Time is still on his
side. If he can slop around in the hole for another forty minutes or so,
they'll have to fill it in, and then he can come back on his own. Chon
has arranged for the watchman to disappear for only ninety minutes.
When he made this point, Chon had pointed at the face of his heavy
watch, gleaming in the moonlight above the ruined left hand with the
crushed fingers on it.

The hand had made Tam think of a swatted spider the first time he
saw it. The second time he looked at the hand, he noticed that three of
the fingers had no nails. After that he stopped looking at it.

If Chon is right about what's in the safe, Tam will never have to
open another one.

"So who is she, this woman?" he asks as he slips the shovel aimlessly into the mud.

"A general's widow." Chon is bent forward, beaming the flashlight's yellow cone straight down, trying to see through the reddish
brown water that swirls around Tam's legs. Looking for the straight
lines, the edges of the safe, that will announce that the hole is in the
right place.

"What time?" Tam asks, just to make Chon move the light.

"Twelve twenty-two," Chon says, beaming the flashlight at the
watch. "Jewels won't be much deeper." Is there a note of suspicion in
his voice?

*The jewels.* Like a magic spell, the words ease the pain in Tam's
back. Even his palm stops hurting. In 1987 a Thai servant, returning
home after a long period of service to the Saudi royal family, brought
with him a suitcase full of jewels that belonged to the princess he
worked for. Prodded by the Saudis, the Bangkok police arrested the
servant and held a press conference to let the jewels dazzle the cam-
eras. After an unexplained delay of several months, the jewels were
shipped back to Saudi Arabia, where they were promptly pronounced
to be fakes.

The entire population of Thailand immediately concluded that the police had commissioned the manufacture of the fakes so they could either sell the real articles or give them to their wives. Since then the Saudi jewels have been the object of feverish speculation among Bangkok's jewel thieves. So when Chon told his story in the jail cell where he and Tam met, Tam's interest was fully engaged. A lifetime of relative virtue, he thought, was finally being rewarded. A policy of nonviolence. Stealing only from the rich. Gifts to monks. Pleasantries to his in-laws. His wife, the great treasure of his life, would be so happy.

"I thought you said she was a policeman's widow," Tam says at last, sluicing mud over the side of the hole.

Chon wiggles the flashlight back and forth, a negative. "Who cares? Just dig. Once you hit the safe, we have to pull it out, open it, put it back—"

"Yeah, yeah." The shovel slices through the water and probes soft mud, a good foot from the safe. Tam steps off the shovel carefully, lifts it, and dumps a streaming load of mud over the side of the hole. "How are we going to clean up all this mud?" he asks, keeping his voice light.

"Don't worry about it," Chon says.

"I wasted five minutes cutting out that square of lawn to hide the hole. What good is that going to do if the lawn is covered in mud?"

"I said don't worry about it."

"Right. You're not digging." Tam slides the edge of the shovel through the mud. The safe seems to be about eighteen inches long. "How big is this thing?"

"It's a cube," Chon says grudgingly. "About two feet on a side."

Tam has located the corner of the safe. Turning his back to Chon to mask his actions, he slips the shovel down along its side and uses the handle as a lever to worry the safe free of the mud's grasp. It gives a few inches, and Tam wiggles the shovel around to scoop up some of the mud, which he tosses over the edge of the hole.

"About the mud on the lawn," he says. "You didn't answer me about the mud. Look at it, it's everywhere."

"Oh, fuck the mud with your grandfather's dick," Chon says. "I'm going to hose it into the hole. The guard's getting paid, but there's no point in leaving a mess that he'd have to be dead to miss, is there? You want the cops asking him questions and knocking him around, or you want some time to sell the jewels right instead of throwing them away for a few baht just to get rid of them fast?"

"Maybe we're digging in the wrong place." Tam does not dare to pry the safe loose, so he drops his shoulders and strains again, filling the shovel for what seems like the thousandth time. The splinter drives a nail of pain into his palm.

"Another six inches or so," Chon says. Then his expression changes. Something reserved and watchful comes into his face. "I'll dig."

"But your hand—"

"Don't worry about my hand," Chon snaps, watching him closely. "I'll dig."

"Forget it," Tam says, giving up. "I can manage another six inches."

Chon looks at his watch as ten pounds of mud land next to his shoes. "Manage it faster," he says.

"Another six inches," Tam repeats. "Not very deep."

"You want it to be deeper?"

"Just, you know, to protect these jewels—"

"She's not depending on the safe to protect the jewels," Chon says. "She's depending on being the scariest fucking woman in the world."

"She's *what*?" Tam asks.

"Hmmm?" Chon's eyes come up from the hole to meet Tam's. He looks surprised at the expression on Tam's face. "I meant him, not her. When he was alive. Very scary guy."

Tam continues to look at him. Chon looks up at the trees.

"Listen," Tam finally says, "when I find this thing, I'm going to need my stethoscope. In my jacket." He gestures toward the dark shape on the lawn. "In the left pocket."

After a moment Chon grunts and goes to pick up the jacket. He pats it and makes a little inquiring sound. "What have you got?"

"A can," Chon says. "With a little . . . ah, something like a straw, coming out of it."

"That's good, too." Tam puts his hand out without looking, and Chon plops the can into it. "And the stethoscope."

Chon gives the jacket an impatient shake and flips it upside down. He says something sharp-sounding in a language Tam does not understand and then says, "There's nothing else in the jacket."

"A stethoscope," Tam says. "It's got two earpieces—"

"I know what a stethoscope is," Chon says. "I have a heart and a doctor, same as you."

Tam does not look up. "Then it's in the boat."

Chon processes this for a moment and looks back down into the hole. "You get it."

"Don't be silly. I can dig while you're gone. What can you do while I'm gone? Walk up and down? Wave the flashlight around? You said it wouldn't be much deeper."

Chon watches him for a moment and then turns off the flashlight and jogs off toward the boat.

Immediately Tam squats into the warm water, which comes up almost to his chin, and slides his hands around the edges of the safe to free it. Then he slips his arms under it and lifts.

At first he thinks it won't come. The mud sucks at it, and Tam curses quietly and works his arms back and forth in the mud, trying to break the vacuum, hitting his precious fingers on stones and roots and something sharp that cuts into the back of his hand.

He knows he is bleeding, but something pleasantly tight has begun to build in his chest, and he can almost feel heat coming from the safe, flowing into his arms and giving him the strength he needs. With a deep grunt, he pulls the safe free of the mud's grasp and straightens, standing in the hole with a dark cube in his arms, streaming water and mud.

A sound like crumpling paper as the birds desert the trees overhanging the river. Chon must be at the dock.

Moving quickly now, Tam slips the safe over the edge of the hole and examines it.

He sees a black plastic bag tightly knotted over a cube. He tears it open to reveal thin steel, irregularly scratched, dented, and pocked with rust. A long crimp creases the top where his shovel hit it, and rust reddens the hinges of the door. It looks cheap, and he is vaguely disappointed; he had been looking forward to a challenge.

No time now. Pulling a slender penlight from his pocket and cupping a hand around it to shield the light from Chon's view, he takes a quick look at the combination dial. *Junk*, he thinks. He picks up the aerosol can, shakes it twice, and places the tip of the thin tube that comes out of the can's top against the edge of the dial, where twelve would be on a clock. He pushes the button on the can, and it emits a sharp hiss. Tam pushes the button three more times, placing the thin tube at three, six, and nine. Then he puts down the can, picks up the shovel, and taps the end of the handle against the dial three or four times, hard.

"*Mai*," he says. It is his wife's name and the only prayer he ever uses. Suppressing the shaking that has seized control of his fingers, he turns the tumblers.

Within fifteen seconds he has the safe open. He risks a glance over his shoulder: no Chon. He reaches into the safe.

And finds nothing.

He has expected a soft bag with the stones inside it, or perhaps the jewels themselves, loose as pirate's treasure, sparkling in the moonlight. There is nothing.

No. There is a plastic bag, flat as cardboard, with a knot tied in the top. He tears it open, hurrying now, and finds an envelope.

Tam pulls it out, laying it flat at the edge of the hole. The envelope is rigid manila with bruised edges, the size of a large piece of paper. Its flap is secured by a piece of twine twisted many times around a clasp. It takes Tam almost as long to open the envelope as it took him to open the safe. The papers in the envelope are slick and cold and stiff beneath his fingers, and he knows what they are even before he pulls them out. Photographs.

The top sheet has eight small pictures on it, each framing a person's face. All but one of them are male. They seem to be in their late twenties and early thirties. They stare unsmiling from the page, dark-skinned and wearing identical dark shirts and caps, standing in front of a bare wall. The lone woman is extraordinarily thin, with sharp features and the enormous, lustrous eyes of a starvation victim, but she does not look like a victim. She has the face of someone who chewed her way out of the womb.

Eight small pictures fill each of the other three sheets as well. These are not faces, though. In these pictures, taken from farther away, people bend forward, focused, doing something. Work of some kind. The photos are small, and the moonlight is not bright enough for Tam to make out what is being done. He aims the penlight at them and pushes the button.

His blood shrieks in his ears.

"You shouldn't have looked," Chon says behind him.

Tam wants to turn, wants to face Chon, but he cannot.

He sees what the people are doing in the photographs, sees it but does not believe it, and sees it again. Believes it. His eyes slam shut.

"I *am* sorry about this," Chon says sadly. Tam turns to catch a quick glimpse of the man. A silvery edge of moonlight gleams on the thing in his hand, and then Tam hears a muffled little sound like a cough, and something punches him very hard in the chest, dead center, and his knees go loose beneath him. He tries to grab the side of the hole, but his hands—his trained, sensitive, responsive hands—won't do what he wants them to, and he feels himself start to fall very slowly as the light shines into the hole, and he sees Mai's face looking up at him, and she smiles the way she always does when she sees him, and he realizes it is his own face, reflected in the water. He starts to say her name again. And then his head hits the water and he is gone.

The man who called himself Chon stands over the hole, looking down, waiting to shoot again if he must. The flashlight is gripped beneath his left arm, and the right hand holds the silenced pistol. His mouth is a sad, tight line. Tam lies facedown in the muddy water, one arm raised, caught against the side of the hole, the fingers extended like someone waving good-bye.

When it is evident that Tam is not going to move, the man who calls himself Chon puts the gun in his pocket, skirts the hole, and picks up the envelope and the photographs. Without looking at the pictures, he slides them back inside the envelope. Then he lays the envelope on top of Tam's jacket and jumps into the hole.

It takes him a minute to wrestle Tam out of the mud, rolling him onto the lawn before he climbs out himself. He lifts Tam by the shoulders and drapes him over the safe on his stomach, his arms and legs splayed out. The man studies the effect for a moment and then picks up the envelope and slips it into the front of his pants, flat against his stomach. He bends down again and grabs Tam's jacket and spreads it out on the lawn several feet away, in the direction of the house, making it as big as he can.

He does not fill in the hole. Instead he lays the shovel down so the cutting edge is pointing like an arrow toward the dark opening.

Twenty-two minutes later, when the guard returns, he first sees the great splash of mud around the hole, then the shovel, and then Tam's body. He stops where he stands as though listening for something; then very slowly turns in a full circle, scanning the grassy area, washed by moonlight, and the deep shadows beneath the trees. When he has completed his circle, he moves, as tentatively as someone who expects the ground to give way beneath him, up the lawn toward the house.

At the border of a flower bed, he stoops and comes up with a large, smooth, white stone, the size of a small coconut. He takes the stone in both hands, raises it high, and brings it down with all his strength on the top of his own head.

His knees soften and he staggers, but once he has regained his equilibrium, he raises the stone again and brings it down once more, striking the same spot on his head. He reaches up to the wound. When he brings his hand away, it is slick with blood. He smears the blood on his face and shirt and then walks, as carefully as a drunk man, down to the edge of the pier, where he drops the stone in the grass, where he is sure it will be found. His story will need all the support he can provide. As he works his way back toward the house, wobbling on legs that will barely carry his weight, he paints himself with more blood.

At the back door, he pauses and listens, although he knows the place is empty. Logically, he knows that the woman who owns the house can't be in two places at once, but after working for her for twenty years, nothing about her would surprise him. Squaring his shoulders, he goes inside.

The door closes behind him, and the moon shines down on the empty house and the dark figure sprawled on the lawn, the corona of mud surrounding the hole like the ring around a target, and the jacket empty and open like a signal. Empty and open like a flag.

## All the Mass an Eight-Year-Old Can Muster

A blur at the edge of sight, a blue blur across the sidewalk, and Rafferty feels Miaow stop in her tracks, yanking him back with all the mass an eight-year-old can muster. The blur collides with a stout woman, knocking her sideways. Hands grab at her to keep her from going down. The blur pauses just enough to resolve itself into a running child, and then Miaow drops Rafferty's hand like a stone, all but pushing him aside with a shriek that scrapes the upper limit of the audible spectrum.

The blue child launches itself off the sidewalk, splitting the distance between two cars, aloof as a subatomic particle, and vanishes into traffic. Miaow, her pigtails flying, has covered half the distance to the curb before Rafferty can get his body organized, but then he sets off at a dead run, without even scanning the crowd for Rose, who is somewhere ahead of them on the sidewalk, on her way to buy the evening's dinner.

Silom Road is jammed this late Sunday afternoon with shoppers and tourists threading between the sidewalk vendors' booths.

Rafferty shoulders past several of them, earning a shout of warning in some unknown language, and then slams his hip against a rickety plywood booth piled with hill-tribe souvenirs as he sees Miaow leap from the curb and into the path of a battered taxi. More shouts as the booth splinters to the concrete behind him, the taxi swerves right, and then Miaow is gone, too.

*When in doubt,* Rafferty thinks, *stop.*

The sky is low enough to scrape a nail against, that peculiar sullen gray that usually precedes one of Bangkok's frequent rainstorms. Rafferty is aware of the livid greenness of the trees, of the wind that has kicked up to make the empty plastic bags dance on the pavement, of his heart hammering in the vein at the side of his neck. Aware that both children have disappeared.

The taxi that stopped for Miaow is stalled in front of him, and Rafferty skirts it at a trot, looking for anything that could be a running child. He hears another shout, across the six lanes of Silom this time, and the blue blur reappears and disappears in a blink around the corner of a narrow *soi,* leaving Rafferty with a mental snapshot of a dirty blue T-shirt and baggy, low-slung blue trousers, torn and flapping below the child's right knee. Hair, long and knotted, bounced over the blue shirt as he—she?—ran. Behind the ragged child, in full charge, is Miaow.

Spaces open between the cars in front of him, giving him just room enough to dodge between them. Miaow lived most of her eight years on the sidewalks of Bangkok before Rafferty found her, but he chases after her, weaving suicidally through traffic as though she were a rich, pampered preschooler wandering outside the family compound for the first time.

He gets across the street and under the elevated track for the sky train somehow—later he will be unable to remember any of it—but by the time he makes the turn into the *soi,* she is gone. The sidewalks host a few harried-looking pedestrians, all adults. There is not a child in sight.

The other end of the *soi*—one of the countless small streets branching off Silom—is too distant for Miaow to have reached it. The buildings are raw, shiny apartment houses, too new to have acquired the city's distinctive petrochemical tarnish. Their doors are guarded against unattached children. A third of the way down the block, he sees a driveway, leading to an open underground garage. He takes off at a run.

The driveway slopes so steeply that he has to lean backward against the incline. The afternoon sun has dropped behind the building, darkening the interior of the garage, and he slows to a walk, waiting for his eyes to adjust.

Thin, watery sunlight leaks through small, sidewalk-level ventilation grilles, casting elongated patterns on the concrete floor. The far corners fade into gloom. Fewer than twenty cars occupy a space big enough to accommodate a hundred.

"Miaow?" The name ping-pongs off the walls. Rafferty can hear his fear in the echoes.

Nothing. His pulse bumps beneath the skin of his throat like someone tapping him with a finger. Moving slowly toward the right side of the garage, where the majority of the cars are, he quiets his breathing so he can listen. Horns from the street, the catch of an engine. Outside, a woman laughs.

A scuffling sound off to his left terminates in a fierce, choked whisper.

Rafferty goes on the balls of his feet, moving faster. A cluster of dusty cars looms ahead, four or five of them. One of them rocks suddenly as something slams into its side. Rafferty starts running again, and when he rounds the car's rear fender, he sees Miaow planted on her backside on the cement floor, her feet wedged against a tire, both hands wrapped in the blue T-shirt of the other child, who is straining to pull away. The second child—it is a boy, Rafferty sees, with sharply angled cheekbones beneath a mat of filthy hair—flails at her arms with clenched fists.

The boy's back is to him. Miaow's eyes come up to meet Rafferty's, and he sees her shake her head *no*, although he's not sure what the no means, and the boy's head snaps around. When he catches sight of Rafferty, his eyes narrow so far they almost disappear, his lips peel back from his teeth in an animal snarl, and he screams, so high it goes through Rafferty's head like a bullet. It caroms off the walls in all directions, a human distress siren.

The boy kicks out at Miaow with new urgency, the torn trouser leg flapping against the thin calf, and Miaow dodges the kicks left and right, and then, as the boy raises his right foot to kick at her head, she whips her own leg around and sweeps his left foot out from under him. The boy goes down on his back. Miaow scrambles up onto him, straddling his chest and sinking her knees into his shoulders. They fight in complete silence. The boy batters at her back with his legs, so hard that Rafferty can hear his knees strike, but Miaow bears down, and Rafferty suddenly realizes how much weight the child has gained since she started living with him. The boy, whose elbow joints are the widest part of his stick-thin arms, cannot throw her off.

Rafferty approaches from behind her and looks down at the boy's face. Confronted by an adult at such close range, the boy goes limp, a trapped animal giving up hope. He stops kicking, and his head rolls to the right. He is completely still. He seems to be studying the car's tire. His face is filthy beneath the shock of knotted hair. The eye Rafferty can see seems to be infected; it is red and swollen. Automatically, Rafferty reaches down, and Miaow slaps his hand away.

"He bites," she says in English. The boy's head rolls around at the sound of a foreign language. When he sees Rafferty's face, he freezes. Even the damaged eye looks confused. Rafferty's native English and half-Asian looks, courtesy of his Filipina mother, have bewildered the Thais since his arrival in Bangkok. "Back up." Miaow doesn't look up at him. "Not so close."

He retreats four or five steps, enough to give the boy some room but close enough to get involved if necessary. Miaow leans forward and whispers for several moments. The boy shakes his head violently, and Miaow leans in and looses a torrent of Thai, too fast for Rafferty to follow, although he can make out *jai dee*, which translates into "good heart" or "good person," one of the language's supreme compliments. The boy looks up at her for a long moment, the left eye swollen almost shut, and then snarls a short, bitter question. Miaow shakes her head in the negative and waits. After a good ten seconds, the boy lifts his head, and his eyes go past Miaow and settle on Rafferty. They look at him and through him. Once, for an article he was writing, Rafferty interviewed a monk who had just emerged from four years of solitude. Except for the moment when that man's eyes fell on him, he has never been looked at like this in his life.

At last the fierce eyes release him. The boy lets his head drop back on the concrete. Then he makes a minute nod, not so much assent as surrender, looking at neither of them.

Miaow slowly lifts her hands from his wrists and, keeping her eyes on the boy, climbs off. With one hand behind her, she waves for Rafferty to come closer. He does, but he is careful not to get too close to either child. The world they have inhabited for the past few minutes is not his.

Looking over Miaow's shoulder, Rafferty sees a boy who could be ten or twelve and who probably weighs less than sixty pounds. The injured eye is as red as a geranium. He has a short, broad nose; heavy, unnaturally red lips; and tight-lidded, enraged-looking eyes. A bruise, not a new one, swells on his right cheek. The neck of his T-shirt is twisted, revealing a shoulder with a bone structure as delicate as a bird's. The shirt may once have been sky blue, but now it is dark with grime and pitted with holes big enough to push a finger through. A red, irregular *S* has been scribbled with some kind of marker on the front of the T-shirt.

The boy glares up at Rafferty. His broad nostrils flare like those of an animal smelling blood. Rafferty thinks he should have known that the boy bites even without Miaow's warning.

Miaow steps away and offers the boy a hand up. He ignores it and stands on his own, the furious eyes still fixed on Rafferty. Miaow looks up at Rafferty, and he can see the urgency drawing tight the muscles of her face, but he does not know what it means. Most surprising, tear tracks glisten on her cheeks. Rafferty knows she could survive a cataclysm dry-eyed.

She indicates the thin, dirty boy with one hand. "This is Superman," she says. Her voice comes from a throat as constricted as her face. "He's coming with us."

## 3

## There's Something Between Them

The boy's glare says, *This close but no closer*. Every minute or so, he turns back to look at Rafferty. If the distance has narrowed, the boy speeds up, as though he is keeping an iron rod between the two of them. Miaow has her hand on the boy's elbow, which startles Rafferty; Miaow does not touch people often.

Dusk has fallen, a wash of gray tinted with the cold, electric spectrum of neon. People glance at the thickening sky, at their watches, at the lighted shop windows. Groups of foreign men plow the sidewalk, beginning the long nighttime prowl that will take them to the girl-packed bars of Patpong Road, dead ahead.

Seen from Rafferty's perspective, six feet back, the children look like a cautionary UNICEF poster: the well-nourished child and the starving one. Superman probably weighs twenty pounds less than Miaow, even though he is two inches taller. The skin on his neck and arms is mottled with camouflage patches of dirt and an irregular pattern of bumpy, red irritation. With a rush of irritation of his own, Rafferty thinks, *Scabies*.

He feels a cool hand on his arm.

"What's this about?" Rose asks. He looks back to see an unanswerable argument for the effectiveness of evolution: six elegant feet of perfectly assembled Thai womanhood. She wears one of Rafferty's white shirts, blindingly clean and as unwrinkled as an angel's robe, a pair of faded jeans, and the inevitable outsize pink plastic watch. She looks as though she has never perspired in her life. Her eyes are on the children.

"He's coming with us," Rafferty says, unconsciously mimicking Miaow's tone. They are speaking Thai.

Rose nods once. "I see." Her tone could cool the entire block. She is extremely choosy about who comes into the apartment they sometimes share.

Rafferty looks down at the bagful of vegetables and noodles dangling from Rose's hand and changes the subject. "You did the shopping."

"Someone has to." She has removed her hand from his arm now, and they walk on together, maintaining their distance from the children and a proper separation from each other. In public, Rose is always proper. "Especially if you're going to bring home someone new every time you go out," she says. When Rafferty does not reply, she adds neutrally, "He's extremely dirty."

"It's Miaow's idea. I thought I'd stop at Siam Drug and get some shampoo for lice and some skin ointment. See if we can't get rid of whatever's hitching a ride."

"I'll do it," Rose says. Her tone does not invite discussion. "You just take them home and get him into the tub. Burn his clothes. Don't let him sit anywhere. He's riddled with bugs."

"I think it's better if you do it." Rafferty lowers his voice, although there is no sign that the children are listening. "He doesn't like me."

Ahead of them the boy turns back again to check on Rafferty and does a literal double take when he registers Rose. He looks away for a second, like someone trying to shake off a mirage, and, to Rafferty's surprise, Rose slips her hand into his, in defiance of her own rules. The boy looks back again and gazes at them for a long moment, letting Miaow guide him. Some of the rigidity goes out of his face. His shoulders drop a full inch as his spine relaxes. In place of the "stop right there" glare, there is assessment. He says something to Miaow, and she hits him playfully on the head, a mock insult. For the first time, the boy smiles. He socks her on the shoulder, and she grabs her shoulder and hops on one leg, pretending it hurts.

"What's all that mean?" Rafferty demands. Miaow doesn't jump up and down on one leg and hug her arm when *he* pretends to sock her on the shoulder.

"He's afraid of men," Rose interprets. "He looks at you and sees you with me, and suddenly you're not the kind of man he's afraid of. What do you *think* it means?"

"Oh," Rafferty says. Even after more than eighteen months in Bangkok, he still fails to see things that are obvious to Rose. In her twenty-three years, she has been a village child, a grade-school student, a Patpong go-go dancer and prostitute, and now a hopeful businesswoman who is trying to set up an apartment-cleaning service while refusing support from the foreigner—Rafferty—who loves her. "But he's just a kid." Even as he says the words, he knows how stupid they are.

"There's something between them." Rose is watching the two children, who are whispering now, Miaow's shiny-clean hair next to Superman's snarled thatch. "She's deferring to him."

As Rafferty follows Rose's eyes, he can see that Miaow has curled her spine and drawn in her head to make herself shorter. He can hear only snatches of what she is saying, but she has pitched her voice slightly higher, emphasizing its girlishness. The charade puzzles him; she has plucked the boy from the street, but she is apologizing for it, exaggerating the boy's dominance.

The crowd of pedestrians parts momentarily, and Rafferty spots a boy to their right. Since Miaow came into his life, he sees street children everywhere, but they have multiplied since the tsunami ravaged Phuket and Phang Nga three months earlier, a wave of children washed all the way to Bangkok, leaving behind an island many Thais believe is now haunted by scores of anguished ghosts. The boy to their right wears the threadbare, oversize uniform of the street, stained as brown as a used tea bag. He sags against a building as though it is the only thing holding him up. Rafferty watches as the child notices Miaow—as always, he wonders, does this child know her?—and sees him look beyond her to Superman. The boy straightens instantly, a single, electrified movement, and cranes his head forward, narrowing his eyes. Then, very slowly, he begins to walk, parallel with Miaow's path, his eyes glued to Superman. When Superman senses the scrutiny and glances over, the boy freezes. Then he turns and runs as though all of Phuket's ghosts are after him.

With profound conviction, Rafferty says, "Oh, shit."

"He's terrified," Rose says. She turns to watch the boy run. "What are you getting us into?"

Patpong Road opens up on their right, the neon signs above the bars just beginning to snap on. The young women who dance in the clubs push their way up the street in jeans and loose T-shirts, their black hair wet and gleaming. "Get them home," he says. "I'll go to the pharmacy here and pick up the stuff. Can you think of anything else we'll need?"

"Shirt and pants," she says, sizing the boy up. "Size ten." She gives Patpong an unfriendly glance; she was once the top girl at the King's Castle bar, probably the most famous of them all. "Blue," she adds, glancing back at the children.

Above them the sign for yet another bar blooms bright pink with a sizzle of juice. "Only shopping, right?" Three girls shoulder by them, laughing their way to work, two of them giving Rafferty a practiced eye. "No bars."

"Of course," Rafferty says. "No bars." He gazes at Superman's bruised and sullen face, and the child turns away to stare into the traffic.

"On the other hand," Rose says, "the bars might be safer than this boy."

## 4

## You Are Being Sought

In the light of day, Patpong Road is slow, even sleepy, a short block of closed doors and open pharmacies. On a map of Bangkok's population density, Patpong at 3:00 P.M. would be a watercolor wash of pale gray. By 7:30 on any given night, it would be solid black, the bars and sidewalks crowded shoulder-to-shoulder with perhaps twelve hundred young women and the men who come to rent their favors.

Like most male expatriates, Poke Rafferty arrived in Bangkok alone, and like most of them he found his way to Patpong, but not for the usual reason. He came to write a book, *Looking for Trouble in Thailand.* The first books in the series, *Looking for Trouble in the Philippines* and *Looking for Trouble in Indonesia,* had done well enough to earn him an attention-getting advance for book number three, and the money took Rafferty to Thailand.

The readers of the *Looking for Trouble* books are males in their twenties and early thirties, obsessed with knowing things like how to beat official foreign-exchange rates, how to spot fake amber (hold a match under it), how much to bribe a cop, how to recognize counterfeit tens (look for the number 28 on one corner of the back of the bill), how to identify a transvestite before it's too late, and how to know, within an hour of arriving in a strange city, where to find the best bars, the best clubs, the best food, the best clothes, the dodgiest entertainment, at the best prices. It's a small niche, but Rafferty owns it.

By the time he finished the book, he was also finished with Patpong. He'd asked his questions, gotten his answers, written his chapters, and departed from professional objectivity to take home more dancers than he can comfortably remember. He knows now how the machine works, knows how coldhearted are the mathematics behind the smiles. Whatever tawdry allure the street may have possessed has evaporated.

On the other hand, he'd met both Rose and Miaow here, so he feels he owes the street something. He can't bring himself to hate it with the same intensity Rose does, but like her he has used the street up. His heart now is entirely with her and Miaow, the family he has cobbled together with a former go-go dancer and a child selling chewing gum from a box, one of the heartbreaking legion of sidewalk sparrows who haunt the Bangkok night. Slowly, by keeping faith with them, by making promises carefully and meeting them, he has begun to make it work.

Miaow does not trust easily. In her short lifetime, she has been betrayed, abandoned, cheated, and probably abused in ways he has never dared to ask about. Even with Rose's help, it has taken him months to win her confidence. He has given her much, while she has asked for nothing.

Cartier, Rolex, Louis Vuitton, Gucci, Armani: watches, purses, blouses, scarves, all of them lacking the only accurate label: "Fraudulent." Stale sweat, cheap perfume, cigarette smoke. Frying garlic. The thunk of big-hair eighties rock and roll from the bars. A bottle hitting the pavement. He picks his way between the bright lights of the Patpong night market without registering the glitter of the jewelry and sunglasses, the colors of the textiles, the sweating crowd, or the broken-record calls of the touts pushing Ping-Pong shows, razor-blade shows, and other improbable vaginal feats.

The boy can't stay with them.

Two children will be noticed and misinterpreted, perhaps officially. At this moment, with Rafferty on the verge of making the moves that will legalize the bonds among him, Rose, and Miaow, that kind of trouble would be unendurable. If he succeeds, they will legally be a family. If he fails, he will have lost the center of his life. He can't let that happen.

But Miaow has finally asked Rafferty to do something for her. On one level, he supposes, it's good news. She has developed enough faith in him to ask the impossible.

So what does he do? Think short-term: Get rid of the boy's scabies.

Rafferty is edging his way toward one particular stall when he turns at the sound of his name being mispronounced.

"Poque." The voice, a theatrical basso profundo, belongs to an elephantine man in a flowery shirt as big as a fumigation tent. He somehow manages to insinuate several redundant European vowels into the single syllable of Rafferty's first name. "A word or two?"

"Leon," Rafferty says. On the very long list of people he would rather not see right now, Leon Hofstedler occupies the top position. "Is the bar on fire? Are they renovating your stool?"

"American humor is the envy of the world," Hofstedler says solemnly.

Hofstedler imagines himself as the heart of a small group of permanent sex tourists—Rafferty thinks of them as "sexpatriots"—who spend most of their waking hours in the eternal twilight of the Expat Bar on Patpong 1, solemnly swapping lies and denying that they buy Viagra in bulk. The bar is probably the only place in Thailand where the television has been unplugged to avoid the endless repetition of the huge waves sweeping away so much of the south. Mass death dampens the patrons' libidos.

"That's six or seven words already, Leon." Rafferty resists the urge to shift from foot to foot. "I'm kind of on an errand here."

"Ze beautiful Rose." Hofstedler puckers his lips for a whistle and then, wisely, thinks better of it. "I would be busy, too, if I were so lucky as you. But zis—*this*—is about someone substantially less alluring."

"Everyone's less alluring, Leon. But who specifically?"

"You are being sought." Hofstedler's voice drops an impossible octave. He occasionally claims to have spent his youth carrying a spear in some of the world's longest and murkiest operas, and he retains an impressive bass range and a Wagnerian sense of drama. "Sought," he repeats, "by a woman of mystery."

"Okay," Rafferty says.

If Hofstedler is disappointed that Poke fails to clutch his chest and stagger backward, he doesn't show it. "She does not wish you to know you are being sought."

"Well, closing right in," Rafferty says, glancing at his watch. "Thai? *Farang?* Japanese? Eurotrash?"

"Australian," Hofstedler says, sounding dissatisfied with Rafferty's reaction for the first time.

"I don't know any Strines," Rafferty says. "I mean, not of the fair sex, so to speak. Just out of curiosity, how fair?"

"Not so very," Hofstedler says with a connoisseur's confidence. "In her thirties, I would say, the most tragic period in a woman's life . . ."

"I know, Leon. The decade of decline, and all that." Like most of his circle, Hoftstedler expends his enthusiasm exclusively on bar girls in their late teens and very early twenties. "So, anything that might help me identify her other than the ravages of time? You know—hair, height, weight?"

Hofstedler's mouth contracts around something sour. "Plump, blondish, frizzy all over. Not happy. She smelled of angst."

"I've got all the angst I need at the moment. And I really have to get moving."

"She comes in the bar several times," Hofstedler plows on. "And always she sits beside me and drinks many glasses of tomato juice." He shudders as though the drink had contained eye of newt.

"Leon," Rafferty says, "life is short."

Hofstedler waves it off. "So we talked. She wants to know how long I am here, who my friends are. And always she keeps coming to you, Poke. 'Do you have any artist friends?' she asks. 'What about writers?' she says. 'Do you know any writers?' So naturally I tell her about you, and she says she knows your name, that she has read all your books."

"A woman of taste and discretion," Rafferty says.

"But as interesting as you are, Poke, you are not enough to keep a conversation alive." Hofstedler nods energetically, agreeing with himself. "So I attempt to move on, but always she comes back to you. Where does he live, Poke Rafferty? Is it true that he sometimes helps people find other people?"

Rafferty resists an impulse to spit on the sidewalk. "And I hope you said it wasn't."

"Naturally, I reminded her that you were only a writer. But it seems she read the little thing you wrote for that throwaway."

"'Going Native,'" Rafferty says between his teeth. "I never would have written the goddamn thing if I'd known anyone would read it."

"And, of course, one presumes you were paid something."

"One may presume what one likes."

"Still," Hofstedler says grudgingly, "I have to admit, it was tidy, the way you found those men."

"Leon. A thousand guys a year go missing in Thailand because they want to. A Cub Scout could find them. There's probably even someone who wonders where *you* are."

"She certainly does," Hofstedler says.

"So anyway, this woman in the bar is taking time out from the decade of tragic decline to ask about me."

"Yes, this is the refrain: When do you come into the bar? She asks several times, when do you come into the bar? I say I have no idea, but I will be happy to tell you she is seeking you." Hofstedler simulates a smile to demonstrate how happy he would have been. "And she says, 'Oh, no, no. I'm not looking for him. I was just curious, that's all.'"

"Golly," Rafferty says, "maybe that *was* all."

"No," Hofstedler says. "She was lying." His eyelids drop to an eloquent half-mast that owes much to the early Lauren Bacall. "Regard this." He slips fat fingers into the pocket of his shirt. "She smoked, did I say that? And when she went to the bathroom, I discovered I also wanted a cigarette, so I borrowed one of hers and used *these*."

Rafferty would not be surprised if Hoftstedler's hand came out of the pocket holding a half-eaten pork chop, but instead it is a book of matches. He gives it a little magician's flourish and then hands it to Poke. On the outside it says CHAMPION SNOOKER, with an address in Sydney. Rafferty opens it and finds himself looking at a very neat, formally uniform handwriting that says *"Expat Bar, Patpong,"* and, below that, *"Poke Rafferty."*

For a moment Rafferty thinks he recognizes the handwriting, but then it eludes him and it looks like it could belong to anyone.


IN THE GATHERING dusk, the early shoppers flock to the stalls of the street vendors, adding the vigorous push and pull of capitalism to the similar but more primitive dynamics of sex.

"Sweatpants and shirt," Rafferty says in Thai. "Blue, child's size ten. And a couple of pairs of underpants."

"For you, special price," the woman says automatically. Then her eyes reach Rafferty's face, and she reaches out and slaps his forearm, quite hard. "*Khun* Poke," she says, smiling broadly. "I give you number one deal." Tik is speaking Thaiglish, the official language of Patpong. "How's the baby? She's size ten already? Big, *na*?"

"They're not for her, Tik," Rafferty says. "They're for a friend of hers. Another street kid."

Tik gives him a knowing nod. "Be careful with your heart. They look different when they're clean." Her eyes drop to the clothes in front of her, and for a moment her mouth goes slack and she stands perfectly still, as though she has forgotten he is there.

"Tik?" Her gaze comes up and skids past him, avoiding the contact. "Are you okay, Tik?" He asks the inevitable question: "Did you have family or friends down there?" "Down there" means only one thing in Thailand now.

"Sister's son," she says, finally meeting his eyes. Rafferty registers the smudged-ash rings beneath her eyes and the lines around her mouth. "Him, him . . ." She squints toward the term. "Him *beach boy*. Bring chair for *farang*, sell cola, sell cigarette." She blinks several times and looks down again, then busies herself straightening a plumb-straight stack of T-shirts.

"How old?"

"Seventeen. Good boy. Go school. Sometimes." She is curling her fingers into a tight fist, crumpling the T-shirt on top of the stack.

Rafferty touches the back of her hand, and the muscles in her arm jump, but she relaxes her hand. "I'm so sorry."

"Not only me," she says. "Everybody. All same-same. Have brother, sister, mama, papa. Everybody."

Rose had a friend working the bars on Patong Beach in Phuket, swept away now with dozens of other night flowers, leaving impoverished families grieving on the thin-dirt farms of the northeast. "How's your sister doing?"

"How doing? She working, same everyone." She tilts her chin toward a stall across the way that sells enormous spiders and scorpions preserved under glass. A woman sits in front of it, hands cupped in her lap as though she is trying to hold water. "We lucky," she says. "They find him. Can take him to temple, let him rest. Now so many ghosts down there, people nobody find."

"That's the worst part," Rafferty says.

She shakes her head. "Hungry ghosts. Very terrible."

The Thais share the world with a whole pantheon of ghosts, a taxonomy of the dead, and not only in the less-cosmopolitan villages. The prime minister's official residence is said to be so haunted that no one spends the night there. The new Suvarnabhumi airport, not even complete yet, is crowded with spirits. But hungry ghosts—people who died suddenly, sundered from their lives without any kind of grace or completion—are the most horrifying. Incapable of rest, they wander the world on winds of rage, eating life where they find it, unable either to return to the lives that were stolen from them or to move on. Rose fears them completely and uncritically, just one of the many ways in which she and Rafferty, despite all their efforts, inhabit different worlds.

"I'm sorry, Tik," Rafferty says again. The words are so insufficient he is not even sure they reach her. "There's not much anybody can do."

"They can live," Tik says. Then she says, in Thai, "Life is a gift. If we don't live it well, we are being ungrateful. And we have to love the ones who journey with us." She leans her head to the left and then snaps it to the right, cracking the vertebrae in her neck. Rafferty has seen Thais do it many times, but every time he tries it, he feels like he has dislocated his head. Tik shakes her head experimentally and blows out a breath. "Boy or girl?"

"Sorry?"

"The child. Miaow's friend." She has her business face on, willing away tragedy. This is another thing Thais have that Rafferty doesn't, this genius for inhabiting the present moment.

"Boy."

"Size ten, blue, *na*?" As fast as a gambler's shuffle, she flips through the clothes and comes up with two garments.

Rafferty glances at them and visualizes the filthy rags they will replace. "How long have you been on this street, Tik?"

She pauses halfway through slipping the clothes into a plastic bag and narrows her eyes. "Four . . . no, five years. Why?"

"Maybe you know the kid."

She shrugs. "Many kids. Now even more." Her eyes go past him and settle on something, and Rafferty half turns to see what it is. "You very handsome tonight," Tik says.

"Clean living. What were you looking at?"

"She gone now."

He turns to survey the street. "Who?"

"Lady," Tik says. "*Farang* lady. She look at you and look at you. Because you so handsome. You almost look Thai."

Rafferty, whose straight black hair and smooth features mirror his mother's, knows this is a high compliment. "What did she look like?"

Tik shakes her head. "Not so good. Too fat, *na*? Too fat, yellow hair, big nose."

Hofstedler's mystery woman. "All *farang* have big noses."

"This is why you good-looking," Tik says. "You almost got Asian nose. Also, black hair and eyes. Right color, very nice."

Rafferty turns to scan the crowd behind him. "And she went where?"

"Toward Superstar Bar. She go fast when you turn around."

"Life is more interesting than I'd like it to be," Rafferty says. "So the kid. He's ten or eleven, real skinny. Got hair that looks like a hundred people spent a year tying knots in it."

Tik's mouth widens in distaste. "Not know." She shakes her head and extends her hand to give him the bag. Her eyes fall on the fold of the sweatshirt and then come up to Rafferty's. There is a crease between her eyebrows. "Blue?" she says. She shakes the bag as though the child is in it. "He wear blue?"

"Blue as the sky, but dirtier. Head to . . . um— What in the world is wrong?"

Tik has stepped back, shaking her head vigorously. "Thin, *na?* Blue clothes. Here, on the front—" She sketches a loosely shaped zigzag on her chest.

"That's him," Rafferty says.

"No." She holds out the bag to him as though he has something communicable, not meeting his eyes.

"What do you mean, no?"

"No. Just no." Her arm remains stretched out, her hand clutching the bag, forgotten.

"Can you be a little more specific?"

"This boy. No good. Him . . . him . . ." She extends her right hand, index finger pointing like the barrel of a pistol, and lets her thumb drop. "Bang, bang," she says. Then she says, "Him kill."

## 5

## Then We'll Start to Ask Him Questions

The guard's head breaks the surface, spouting pints of muddy water. His jaws have been clamped open with a stainless-steel device designed for root canals. When it was forced into the guard's mouth, it dislocated his jaw, which sags to the side like something in a funhouse mirror.

The largest of the three shirtless men ringing the hole in the lawn puts a hand the size of a badminton racket on top of the guard's head and pushes him back under.

One of the other men laughs.

"I'm glad you find this amusing," says the lady of the house, and the laughter stops as suddenly as though someone had shut a door on it.

The guard surfaces again, and the big man slams him on top of the head with the broad side of a brick. Red brick dust settles on the surface of the water. His arms flailing, the guard tries to get a grip on the grass fringing the hole, but the man who laughed puts the edge of his boot heel on the closest hand and grinds down. Whatever it is the guard is trying to say, the dental appliance turns it into one long, agonized vowel.

The biggest man picks up the garden hose that they have used to fill the hole and wields it like a whip, the metal at its tip opening cuts in the guard's scalp and face. Water spouts out of the hose in lazy arcs, sparkling in the late-afternoon sun. The guard goes underwater, this time on his own, trying to dodge the hose, and the man lashes at the surface of the water, splashing the thick liquid everywhere.

The lady of the house moves her chair back so she will not get mud on her shoes. She says, "Give him another drink."

When the guard surfaces again, one of the men grabs his ears, tilting his face up, and the big man thrusts the end of the hose into the guard's mouth and six or eight inches straight down his throat. Then he pinches the guard's nostrils closed. The guard begins to spasm, thrashing, striking out with his arms, spouting water like a fountain. After ten or fifteen seconds, the big man pulls the hose out, and a spurt of water gives way to a ragged howl loud enough and high enough to lift the birds from the trees and send them skimming over the placid, coffee-colored surface of the river.

"Two more times," says the lady of the house, settling herself in her chair to watch the hose snake once again into the wide mouth. "Or maybe three."

The scream is cut off as abruptly as it started. "Then we'll start to ask him questions," she says.

## 6

## A Cool Heart

Silhouetted against the setting sun, Miaow squats on the little balcony overlooking the Chinese cemetery eight floors below, staring a hole in the fire as she feeds the blue flames their blue fuel. The sleeve of Superman's filthy sweatshirt hangs over the side of Rafferty's rusty hibachi. A fine edge of flame licks its way down. With a long-handled barbecue fork, Miaow spears the sleeve, lifts it, and drops it into the center of the flames, raising a small puff of smoke and ash. The sliding glass door between the balcony and the living room is open, and Bangkok's March heat and the throat-scratching smell of burning cloth fill the room.

"Miaow," Rafferty says. She turns her face fractionally farther away from him. "Miaow, we have to talk."

"After," Miaow says in English. She does not say it loudly, but her tone is final.

The plastic bags hang heavy in his hands. "Fine. But not *too* much after, okay? Where's Rose?"

"Using all your soap," Rose says in Thai, coming into the living room. "This boy has so much dirt on him I'm not sure there's anyone underneath." Her sleeves are rolled up, and soapsuds gleam on her dark arms. An archipelago of splash marks decorates the front of her shirt.

"He doesn't have a *house*," Miaow says fiercely to the fire. "How clean would *you* be if you had to wash yourself on the street and they chased you away all the time?"

"We get the point," Rafferty says. "Nobody meant that he—"

"*I* was dirty," Miaow snaps. She still has not looked at them. In the rigidity of her back, Rafferty sees the fury of the powerless. She knows that the decision, whatever it is, will come from the adults.

"And look how nicely you cleaned up," he says as Rose rolls her eyes. "Here's some special shampoo," Rafferty says to Rose, pulling the bag open to show her a bottle of Kwell. "There's some . . . ah, salve in there, too."

"For *bugs*," Miaow says disdainfully in Thai, without a glance. "As though bugs matter."

"Bugs do matter," Rose says sharply.

The words bring Miaow's head around sharply. Rafferty is startled at the fury in her face. "What's more important?" she demands. "Not having bugs or not letting people . . . *play* with you?"

"We're not fighting with you, Miaow," Rose says.

Miaow shrugs and folds herself into an even smaller knot, hunkering down over her knees. Sharp shoulder blades protrude on either side of her spine, curled back like stunted wings. The movements of her hand as she stirs the flames are short and jerky. Misery emanates from her like a fog. The sky darkens behind her, its lower edge torn jagged against the silhouettes of buildings as the night skyline of Bangkok blinks into being, rectangle by rectangle, one office block of lights at a time.

"I bought him some new clothes," Rafferty says helplessly. Female unhappiness is as mysterious to him as plant disease. He knows it when he sees it, but he has no idea what to do about it.

Miaow sniffles, and Rafferty takes a step toward her, but Rose grabs his arm.

"You're being stupid," Rose whispers in Thai. "She's manipulating you." She yanks at his arm, not gently. "In the kitchen."

He follows her, still lugging the plastic bags with their bottles of medicated shampoo and whatever else the lady at Siam Drugs foisted off on him. He drops them onto the counter, and Rose puts an exploratory hand on the bags and the other on her hip. "You're both acting like children."

"One of us *is* a child, Rose."

"Not the way you mean. Miaow is short and she has a high voice, but she's not anything you mean when you say 'child.' She can take care of herself better than you can." Rose swipes her forehead with the back of a long brown forearm and leaves a lacy pattern of soapsuds in her hair. "You can't let her act like a baby all of a sudden."

"So what am I supposed to do?" Rose's eyes widen at the frustration in his voice. "Explain the laws of adoption to her? Maybe bring in a lawyer? Run a spreadsheet to show her how much the kid will cost? A pie chart to illustrate what I have in the bank? How exactly do you think I should deal with this, Rose?"

Rose puts her fingertips against the front of his throat and begins a gentle downward smoothing motion, the Southeast Asian remedy for unseemly emotional displays. Thais take equanimity very seriously, and no one loses face faster than someone who gets angry. "You deal with it the way you should deal with everything," she says, soothing him. "With a cool heart. You look for what's best for everyone. You create a situation where you can earn merit."

"So we don't just clean the kid up, dress him in new clothes, slip him a twenty, wish him luck, and put him back on the street."

Rose looks past Rafferty at the balcony, where Miaow has let her head fall all the way forward onto her chest. "You can't," Rose says. "I think you'll lose Miaow if you do."

The words straighten Rafferty's spine. "You don't know what I've heard about this kid. Tik says he killed someone."

"That wouldn't surprise me," Rose says.

Rafferty abandons the rest of his speech and stares at her.

"I can see it. When I was dancing, there were men who came into the bar, and I knew immediately I shouldn't go with them. They hated women, and the hatred steamed off them like heat from a road. It rippled. I knew I shouldn't let them buy me drinks, shouldn't let them talk to me, shouldn't give them any reason to think they were going to get me out of the bar. I tried to tell the other girls, but some of them went anyway. They came back with cigarette burns on their arms, a missing tooth, a broken nose, razor cuts on the webbing between the fingers. And those men only *shimmered*. This boy's aura is a very dark red. It boils the air around him. He's like a cat that's gone wild again and can't decide whether it wants to kill or be fed." She holds out her arm to display a red crescent of bruising, not bad enough to break the skin but bad enough to triple Rafferty's pulse. "He bit me," she says.

Rafferty slaps a palm against one thigh. "That's that. He's gone."

A hand on his arm. "Miaow will go with him."

"She won't." He is whispering, and he can see Miaow straining to hear him. "She's not going to run away with a killer."

"Even if he is a killer," Rose says, "we don't know who he killed."

"And?" Rafferty says. "If we knew, that would make everything okay?"

"There are people who should die." Rose might be discussing the price of milk. "Americans have a hard time with that, because they think everyone who is bad got broken somehow and someone else is at fault. Whoever broke them. But in the real world, people know life would be better if some people were removed from it."

"Jesus," Rafferty says. Her face is calm and clear. "I feel like I'm back in the States, listening to talk radio."

"I don't know what that means. But I know you'll lose Miaow if you don't keep your heart cool. Learn what you can. The boy has been hurt terribly. Just listen and go gently, and look for a chance to do something good." She leans forward, kisses his cheek, and taps the nearest plastic bag. "And give me the shampoo."

He hands it to her and watches her straight back as she leaves the room. The kitchen is immaculately ordered, everything part of a set, everything in the right place. If anything broke, he thinks, it would create disorder and incompletion as obvious as a missing tooth. But, of course, there's nothing in the kitchen that couldn't be replaced.

"UNLESS MY EYES deceive me, we're burning clothes." Framed in the doorway, despite a yellow polo shirt and a pair of checkered slacks loud enough to draw stares even on a golf course, Rafferty's friend Arthit still looks like a cop. "Are we trying to make someone disappear?"

"Actually, we're attempting a rebirth," Rafferty says.

"If you figure it out, let us know," Arthit says. "There are a few hundred thousand people who'd give their all for it." He looks hollowed out, almost to the point of transparency. Total exhaustion identifies honest cops in the days following the great waves, in stark contrast to the sleek cheeriness of their corrupt colleagues. The tsunami has made many of them extremely rich. "How are you, Miaow?" Arthit calls over Rafferty's shoulder. "If you sit all bent over like that too long, you'll fold your lungs." Miaow does not answer, but she straightens a tiny amount and stirs the fire. Arthit brings his eyes to Poke's and says, "I'd love to come in, thanks. And did you say something about a beer?"

"Sorry, Arthit." Rafferty steps aside and lets Arthit in. The trousers make him look like a giant Scotch tape dispenser. "Take whatever's in the fridge."

"We all aspire to the manners of the West," Arthit says, stepping past him. "'Take whatever's in the fridge.' In those few words, you can hear generations of breeding. Do you want one?"

"More than I should. So, no."

Arthit disappears into the kitchen, trailing a blur of plaid, and Miaow follows him with her eyes, seeing a possible ally.

"You're obviously off duty," Rafferty calls. "At least from the waist down."

"Noi says I'm dreary." Rafferty hears the pop and hiss of a can being opened. "Do you think I'm dreary?" Noi is Arthit's wife, grappling with the early stages of multiple sclerosis. Rafferty suddenly sees the pants differently: Arthit would report for work wearing an ostrich-feather peignoir if he thought it would make Noi happy.

"No drearier than any of my other friends."

Arthit emerges from the kitchen, a can of Singha beer in hand. "Not the ringing endorsement I had hoped for. I personally think I'm intriguing." He is speaking British-accented English, a legacy of long, cold, miserable years spent as an exotic brown boy in one of the United Kingdom's better schools. "There's more to me than meets the eye. The younger Claude Rains comes to mind."

"I always thought Claude Rains looked like someone who secretly kept small animals in a dark room."

"Aren't you cheery. I see Miaow, pooled in misery out there, but where's Rose?"

"Doing some washing." Poke and Arthit are friends, but he does not want to talk about the boy until he's figured out how to present the topic.

"She's washing my friend," Miaow volunteers from the balcony. "He's dirty."

Arthit's eyebrows go up, and Poke says, "Later, okay? It's a little complicated."

"Not complicated," Miaow says stubbornly. "He's my *friend*. Poke let me bring him home."

"Poke's heart is bigger than his head," Arthit says. "But if the kid is a friend of yours, he has to be okay."

This is met with silence, even from Miaow.

Arthit says, "This is what's known in the interrogation room as a pregnant pause."

"Like I said, *later*," Rafferty says. "And maybe you do resemble Claude Rains."

"So." Arthit upends the beer and lowers it again. "Dreary as the movie might be, let's cast your life story. If Claude Rains plays me, who do we give to Sydney Greenstreet?"

"Oh, for Christ's sake," Rafferty says as Hofstedler, in his flow-ered fumigation shirt, lumbers into his mind's eye. "That was *your* handwriting. Leon calling her a woman of mystery—was that your idea, too?"

"Not at all. He probably just forgot her name, what with her being in her thirties and all. On the other hand, Leon could spot a conspiracy in a water-gun fight."

"You sent her to the bar. Whoever she is."

"She's a perfectly nice Australian woman named Clarissa Ulrich whose uncle has gone missing. And I'm sorry about the indirect approach. I've been busy, and I ran into Leon, so I offered him something to do besides throwing money at bar girls. I didn't want to give Clarissa your address."

"Was he down there?"

"The uncle? That's my first guess," Arthit says. The can goes up again, and he swallows longer than Rafferty could hold his breath.

Rafferty waits until the can has been lowered. "And this has what to do with me?"

"Well, on one level you wrote that piece about finding foreign men in Thailand who didn't want to be found. I gave a copy to Clarissa, and she thought it was very interesting."

"But you know it was silly. I asked you where they were, and you told me."

"Our little secret," Arthit says. "On another level—a much more important level—it's an opportunity to do me a favor." He drinks again and smooths his hair with his free hand. "At a time when it might be a good idea for you to be owed a few. We both know how much you hate to ask for favors, so I thought this would make it easier."

"The adoption." The process of a Westerner adopting a Thai child—as Poke hopes to do with Miaow—is an endless minefield.

Arthit pats his belly. "Testimonials from four or five of Bangkok's finest, so to speak, would smooth things considerably."

"What's this Australian got to do with you?"

"Nothing personal," Arthit says. "She was getting passed around among some of my hungrier colleagues. She arrived a week ago with about six thousand in traveler's checks, and she's down to three thousand now. With nothing to show for it. So I thought, let's snatch her from the jaws of the wolves and turn her over to someone who's going to need a few favors. Do a little something for both of you."

"I wish I could say I appreciate it."

"Just talk to her." Arthit lowers his voice. "I'll get you into his apartment, which is something my brother officers couldn't be bothered to do, and you'll probably find something that shows he flitted down to Phuket or Phang Nga. You're a reporter, Poke. You know more about how Thailand works than any other *farang* I know. A couple days down there, you'll have it wrapped up."

"He looks much better now," Rose says, coming into the room. "It's amazing what a little soap will do. Hello, Arthit. How's Noi?"

"She's fine, thanks," Arthit says automatically. It is the lie he always tells.

Rose turns to the balcony. "Really, Miaow, he's almost handsome."

"I know," Miaow says. She throws a look at Rose and then turns away again.

"I'm in your way here," Arthit says. He reaches into the pocket of the plaid pants and pulls out one of his business cards. On the other side is the name "Clarissa Ulrich" in that same disciplined handwriting, followed by a phone number. "Promise me you'll call tomorrow?"

"Promise," Rafferty says, but Arthit is looking past him.

Rafferty turns to see Superman glowering at them from the door to the hallway. He is shining clean, his gleaming straight black hair falling below his shoulders. Except for the one swollen eye, Rafferty would not have recognized him. He glances sharply at Arthit, and his nostrils flare as he smells cop. Just as quickly, his eyes skitter away toward the balcony.

Miaow takes one look at him and bursts into tears.

The boy drills her with a glare and crosses the room toward her, his posture rigid. If he had spines, Rafferty thinks, they would be bristling. But Rose was right; he *is* handsome, even though the new blue clothes hang on him in folds. He steps out onto the balcony, and Miaow straightens without rising. He sits beside her, only inches away. Miaow wipes her face fiercely with a palm and resumes poking at the fire. The two of them sit identically, knees up and narrow backs curved, with six inches of air between them. To Rafferty's eyes, something about the effortless way they share the space suggests an old married couple.

"I know that kid from somewhere," Arthit says. He's wearing his policeman's face.

On the balcony Miaow curls herself against him as though he were much larger than she and she could shelter herself beneath his arm. Rose watches them gravely, doing emotional arithmetic in her head. Whatever the answer might be, Rafferty knows he has no chance of reaching it on his own. It's a calculus he hasn't mastered.

Arthit touches his arm. "Call Clarissa tomorrow," he says again. Then he turns to study the boy.

"HE'S FINE WHEN he's with me," Rose says in Thai. They are sitting in the living room, surrounded by the ruins of a dinner that even Rafferty, who cooked it, has to admit was appalling. The children had sat shoulder to shoulder on the balcony, talking in whispers while Rose carried on a bright stream of chatter, not one word of which Rafferty remembers. When everyone reached a consensus that the endless evening could be abandoned, Superman retreated into Miaow's room without even saying good night.

"He *bit* you," Rafferty reminds her.

"Only once. He was just keeping in practice." Rose rummages through her enormous leather handbag for the ever-present Marlboro Lights. She pulls out a fresh pack of the local bootlegs, complete with its oversize black death's-head, and uses a disposable plastic lighter to burn off the cellophane at one corner of the pack. Then she worries a tiny hole in the foil and taps out a single cigarette. It is an extremely labor-intensive process.

Rafferty watches the routine for the thousandth time. "Half the Thai women I know open cigarettes that way," he says, "and I've never been able to figure out why."

"When you arrived here, you smoked," Rose reminds him, lighting up.

"I actually recall things that far back, Rose," he says. "It's the short-term memory that's going."

"And when you went into a bar, you put the pack on the table in front of you, wide open the American way, with a great big hole in it. What happened then?"

"Women hit me up for cigarettes," Rafferty says.

"Every girl in the bar. Even the ones who didn't smoke. It's all part of getting as much as possible from the *farang.* That's what that whole life is about."

"But the way you open them—"

"It just makes it harder for people to take them away from me," she says. "These things cost money."

Money is a sore subject with Rose, whose earnings took a vertical nosedive when she quit dancing go-go and went into cleaning apartments. Now she is trying to start a cleaning business, recruiting women from the bars who are either too old to attract customers or just want out of the life. It's slow going. The women may want to quit the bars, but for years most of them have never washed anything but their hair. Even with occasional help from Rafferty—he put up eight hundred dollars, one-fifth of his savings account, for 20 percent of the business—Rose has intermittent bouts of despair.

"So the boy only bit you once," Rafferty says, changing the subject. "I suppose that's encouraging."

"It's not women he has a problem with." She blows a funnel of smoke with enormous satisfaction.

"Who *knows* who he has a problem with? Given that he's probably killed somebody and he's alone with Miaow in her room right now."

"They're friends," Rose says soothingly. "You think too much."

"The inevitable Thai response. My daughter's shut up in a room with an incipient homicidal maniac who's got an aura like a forest fire, and you tell me I think too much."

"Miaow is tough," Rose says. "She got along without you for

years, and now you're right here in the next room with your ears pointing up like a guard dog. Just sit back and relax."

"Did he say anything at all to you?"

"It seems to me," Rose says, folding her long legs under her, "that the one who owes you an explanation is Miaow."

"Later," Rafferty says. "That's what she said: 'Later.'"

"It's later now," Rose points out.

"It sure as hell is," Rafferty says, getting up.

Rose gazes up at him in mock adoration and bats her eyelashes, which are lush enough to kick up a breeze. "You're so masterful."

"I really don't know what I'd do, Rose," Rafferty says, "without you on hand to supply the play-by-play."

"The what-by-what?"

"American expression." He crosses the room. "Play-by-play. It refers to one big, slow, dumb guy and one little, fast, dumb guy who tell you what's going on at sporting events."

She lifts a hand to slow his exit. "While you're feeling so chatty, what did Arthit want?"

"He wants to owe me a favor. There's an Australian woman who's lost an uncle here in Thailand."

Rose taps the cigarette once, and the ash falls dead center in the ashtray. "Is she a blonde?"

"She's a blonde in the same way Miaow's a child. Do I hear an undercurrent of jealousy?"

"Thai women don't trust their men with blondes."

"I'm *your man*," Rafferty says. "That sounds nice."

"Don't change the subject. You were going into Miaow's room, remember? I'll clean up," Rose says, doing a languid rise from the couch, "while you lay down the law."

The Crayola frowny face is hanging on the doorknob of Miaow's room, usually a sign that entry is strictly forbidden. She designed both it and its counterpart, the smiley face that means "Come right in," shortly after moving into the room that had been Rafferty's office. Rafferty pauses at the door, listens and hears nothing, and then knocks softly.

He waits a moment, opens the door a few inches, and peeks in. Miaow sits on the lower bunk with Superman's head in her lap. He is fast asleep. One arm dangles down to the carpet in graceful, tapering planes. It looks like Michelangelo's *Pietà* would look if the *Pietà* depicted two small brown children.

Miaow gazes up at him as though from a great distance. Her eyes are shining with happiness. They seem to look through him. Very slowly, she lifts a hand from the boy's head and places an upraised finger to her lips. "Shhhhh," she whispers, more a breath than anything else.

## 7

## Not Anyone Anymore

The man who called himself Chon sits alone at a table. The open-air restaurant is dim and deserted. His shiny new watch—bought to help him track time on the night he and Tam dug up the safe—says 3:48 A.M., and even Bangkok slows down to catch its breath at that hour. The single waitress is asleep on a chair, and he sees no reason to wake her. He isn't hungry. He just needs a smooth, horizontal surface for half an hour or so.

A pad of blue-lined paper lies open in front of him, and a clutch of cheap ballpoint pens bristles from his pocket. He had been worried that he would write so many drafts that his pen would run out of ink, so he went to two stores, buying the pens in one and the paper in the other, at the busiest time of day. A black three-ring notebook sits beside the paper.

In the end, though, the note has proved very simple to write. He has copied it twice to make sure it is legible, because his nervousness makes his hand shake. Even writing her a letter frightens him.

Or perhaps he is just tired. He has not slept in the same room twice since the night of the buried safe. For the first few days, he stayed in the Chinatown district, but the noise in the narrow streets made it impossible for him to sleep, not that he sleeps well even when it is quiet. He has not slept well for almost twenty years. Now he makes his futile grabs at sleep in firetrap fifty-baht flophouses, one more anonymous pauper.

Other than a thin sheaf of Thai money, he carries nothing but the pens, the paper, and the notebook. If he is killed, as he almost certainly will be, there will be nothing to say who he was. Just as well, he thinks, because he is not anyone anymore.

What is left of his life, his reason for being alive, is in that notebook.

He regrets having shot Tam. If the man hadn't looked at the photos, he'd be alive now. Once he saw them, though, he couldn't be allowed to live. He might have tried to play the angles. He might have gone to *her*.

Still, Chon has relived many times the moment when the gun coughed in his grip and Tam dropped into the water, one hand uplifted for help. The hand haunts Chon. Although he has seen thousands of deaths, although he is saturated with death and can sometimes smell death on his skin, he has never killed before and never thought he would.

If a fortune-teller had told him twenty-five years ago—when he had a home, a wife, children, a violin, and two good hands—that he would now be planning the total destruction of another human being, he would have laughed out loud. But he couldn't have known then that there would come a time when destroying someone would be all he had in the world.

He knows who he is now, but he has no idea what has become of the man he was. It seems to him that man is dead and he is the ghost that remains.

From the notebook he takes a copy of one of the photos from the safe. He puts it behind the letter and aligns them, tapping the edges on the tabletop. He realizes he has forgotten to buy a stapler. Unbidden, the thought washes over him: *What else have I forgotten?*

Contemplating the next part of his plan, he breaks into a sweat even in the cool evening air. He will have to get close to her at least once. It will be very difficult for him to force himself to be anywhere near her. She is terror itself to him.

But he had believed the letter would be hard to write, and it was easy. Maybe the rest of it will be easy, too. It will have to be.

In ten days, by the twenty-sixth of the month, either she or he will be dead.

He looks down at the note one last time. It says, in Khmer, *"I KNOW WHO YOU ARE."*

## 8

## Mommy's Little Surprise

He awakes to the familiar gloom. The bedroom's only window is blocked by an asthmatic air conditioner that drowns out the noise of the Bangkok streets eight stories down, as though to compensate for its failure to cool the room. Four or five beams of light penetrate the ragged seal around the air con and pick out objects at random, like bad stage lighting: his shoes on the floor, a paperback of Conrad's *The Secret Agent* splayed open and facedown, the towel Rose folded at the foot of the bed when she came in from her inevitable bedtime shower, the shower every bar girl takes before slipping between the sheets to go to work. His efforts to convince her that he actually prefers her own taste to that of soap have not been successful. In her mind, the bar may be behind her, but the body retains its habits.

So: the towel, the book, the shoes. A harmonica Miaow briefly tortured them with, discarded now, that somehow crawled out of the closet under its own power. Pieces of the life he has made here. A life, he thinks, that could shatter into its component pieces as quickly and senselessly as the lives broken by the great waves.

Midway through his first stretch of the morning, he remembers the boy, and his stomach involuntarily contracts.

And then he puts out a hand and realizes that Rose is not beside him.

Wrapping himself in the ersatz-silk robe Miaow bought him for his birthday, an unsettling pink the color of healthy gums and adorned on the back with a fey dragon lisping fire, he pads into the empty living room and then the empty kitchen. Morning light slants into the room, throwing the remains of their dinner into unappetizing relief. No Rose: an early-morning start for the new businesswoman. Trying unsuccessfully to smooth his hair, he goes down the hall to Miaow's room.

The children are seated on the pink rug he bought Miaow when she moved in. The boy averts his face the instant Rafferty looks in. Miaow is rebraiding his hair with such intensity of purpose that she does not even turn at the sound of the opening door. Eight or ten brightly colored rubber bands circle her wrists, and several others are already wrapped around the ends of the boy's new braids, a style that owes something to Snoop Dogg and Thai MTV. Rafferty thinks briefly about Having Their Talk and then looks at his watch: almost ten. He has promised to call Clarissa Ulrich. But before he can do much of anything, he needs coffee.

He has caffeinated, showered, dressed, and set his appointment with Clarissa when the door opens and Rose comes in. As always, when he first sees her each day, he feels the same jolt of electricity that straightened his spine when she stepped onto the stage at the King's Castle bar the evening they met. Then she had worn a black bikini and a badge with her number on it, the number customers used to buy her drinks or order her for the night. Today she wears jeans and a carefully ironed T-shirt. Plastic shopping bags hang from her arms where the gold bracelets—now long sold—used to be. One bag is full to overflowing with shoes.

He toasts her with his third cup of coffee. "If those are for me, I generally wear higher heels."

"So do I." She drops the bag where she stands. It must be a scorcher outside, because her upper lip is damp, Rose's reaction to weather that would melt most people where they stood. "I've got two maid interviews today. My girls have promised to do their job, which is to dress down and not plaster on the makeup. My job is not to tower over the women who want housekeepers."

Rose has been trying to build her business for several months now, and she has learned the hard way that most women, especially married women, aren't eager to hire someone who looks like she earned an advanced degree at Pussy Galore. Some of her corps of former flowers are still beautiful, while others are well past the point at which they would be assigned to dance at the front of the bar, visible from the street. By and large they are not convincing housemaids. Something of that other world clings to them, some kind of glimmer that can't be washed off like makeup or hidden beneath baggy clothes. More than anything else, it's a physical attitude. People who have danced naked in front of hundreds of strangers present themselves differently.

"You shopped yesterday," he says, looking at the bags.

"Seems like a week ago." Rose blows upward at her damp bangs. "These are the things I'm going to need for the next few days."

"You're going to stay here?" A basic plank of Rose's declaration of independence is her reluctance to spend more than one night at a time in Rafferty's apartment. Most nights she sleeps in a sweltering ten-foot-by-ten-foot concrete box near Convent Road, splitting the rent with two women who once danced with her at the King's Castle.

"You have to go running around for Arthit, storing up favors," she says. "We've got a guest. I thought you could use the help." She bends down and rummages through the bags while Rafferty tries to think of some way to express his gratitude that won't embarrass her. "This blond woman," Rose says, both hands in one of the bags. "Is she pretty?"

"Not particularly."

"Would she, as you say, turn heads?"

"Only on very loose necks."

She straightens up with a brush in her hand. "Then do something about your hair," she says. "No point in frightening the poor thing."

"WE TALKED ONCE a week for fifteen years," Clarissa Ulrich says without moving her lower jaw. Her lips work fine, but her teeth might as well be wired together. Tension creates vertical bands down the sides of her neck. "It's been more than two months since I heard from him."

If Rose had seen this woman, Rafferty thinks, she would have combed his hair herself. Clarissa Ulrich is no threat. A long peninsula of sweat extends down the front of her blouse, and her pale, flyaway hair catches the rosy light from the window of the coffee shop, creating the pinkish aura of an igniting match. She is clearly not enjoying Bangkok's climate. She has the look he has come to recognize on *farang* who are new to Bangkok, a steely conviction that life will go on if they can only survive the next five minutes. And Hofstedler is right: She reeks of angst, both metaphorically and physically. He smells sweat, cigarettes, and fear.

"Have there been lapses before?" He blows on his coffee, keeping his eyes on his notebook. She is uncomfortable being looked at.

She folds her hands in her lap like a child being reprimanded. Her plumpness is watery and unhealthy-looking, as if a finger pressed into her cheek would leave a dimple. The front of her blouse sags beneath a wilted silk flower that strikes him as the most metaphorical fashion statement he has ever seen.

"We've never missed a talk." She lifts her cup. Her nails are bitten to the quick, the cuticles ragged as torn paper. "We're much closer than most uncles and nieces." She sips the coffee and winces at the burn. "My parents," she says, as though he has asked a question. "They're both surgeons. They never had much time for . . . um, anything but their work. Everything was life and death except, you know, actual life. Everything was a distraction."

"Everything." He writes *"surgeons,"* mostly to keep his gaze off her.

"Well, I was *certainly* a distraction." She wraps her damaged fingers around the cup, although he knows it must be burning her. "I was a . . . a piece of furniture they hadn't ordered, something they stumbled over in the dark. My mother told me as much. 'You know, dear,' she said, 'you weren't planned. You were Mommy's little surprise.'" She registers the heat in her hands, puts the cup down, and blows into her palms. "So Uncle Claus stepped in."

Rafferty suddenly recognizes the bitterness in her eyes. He has seen it in Miaow's. "He took care of you."

"He took me in. It started with visits when my parents were on vacation, and the visits got longer until finally I was living at his house. Nobody ever said much of anything, but when I went home one day, my mother had rearranged my room. I always slept under the window, because light came through it and I was afraid of the dark. My mother had pushed the bed against the wall. 'It looks much bigger this way,' she said. I was fourteen, and I said, 'It looks bigger because I'm not in it.'" A strangled laugh, rocks rattling in a can. "So I went back home. To Uncle Claus."

"Okay, so you're living with Uncle Claus. What took him to Bangkok?"

"He worked in oil in Saudi Arabia when he was young. He'd work there a few months and then spend a month here, decompressing, he said. He loved it here. When I went to college, he came to stay."

Rafferty hesitates for a moment, but he has to ask the question. "People usually stay in Bangkok for a reason. What was your uncle's reason?"

"I just told you. He loves it."

Not very specific, he thinks. "And what did he do here?"

"What *does* he do here, you mean." Her eyes roam the room, taking in the clientele, mostly affluent young Thais wearing designer clothes, some of them in the head-to-toe black of the world's terminally hip, although until recently Thais associated black primarily with funerals. "He helps out. He works with groups that do volunteer work with the homeless, especially kids. That's why that nice policeman thought you'd want to help, because of your little girl."

Thanks, Arthit. *"Groups that work with kids,"* he writes. "Okay, so before he stopped calling. Did anything seem different? Did he talk about anything new?"

She studies the tabletop for a moment, then wipes her side of it with a napkin. "There was a maid. He hired her not too long ago. His calls were full of her. Doughnut was her name. Doughnut this, Doughnut that. He was crazy about her."

"There can't be that many girls named Doughnut." He doesn't even bother to write it down.

"I sort of hope not," Clarissa says. "But it's funny, because she hasn't answered the phone in his apartment since his calls stopped. She always answered before."

*Doughnut,* Rafferty thinks. "Two months ago the waves hit. Do you think there's any chance he went down to the coast?"

"That's what everybody asks. No. Uncle Claus is enormous. Not the bathing-suit type. And he burns in five minutes. I can't imagine why he'd go down there."

Rafferty can think of several possible reasons, all of them in the raunchier areas of Patong Beach on Phuket. "I'll check anyway. Have you been to his apartment?"

"I don't have a key."

She has turned to stare out the window and into the glare of the day, as though she hopes she will see her uncle stroll by.

"Somehow," Rafferty says, "I don't think that will be a problem."

## 9

## A Triumph of Veneers and Inlay

Closets are always a good place to start. Claus Ulrich's closet contains a great many linen shirts, every color of the rainbow and a few that got left out in the interest of good taste. The labels proclaim that they are size XXL, ordered from an expensive catalog that pretends to sell clothing to the fashionable world traveler, the kind who puts on a bush jacket to watch the Discovery Channel. Ulrich has arranged the garments to hang bright to dark, a dandy's spectrum. To the right are ten or twelve carefully folded pairs of pleated linen slacks, waist size 46, all beige. Rafferty hears his mother's voice: *Beige goes with anything.*

But it had not, apparently, gone with Claus Ulrich when he passed through the front door with its surprising assembly of locks. Nor had the open suitcase containing a week's worth of lightweight clothes, stashed in the back of the closet. In writing his travel books, it has never once occurred to Rafferty to remind people not to forget their suitcase.

An hour in the apartment tells Rafferty several things. First, he is the only person to enter it in weeks. The air conditioner has been off all that time, letting the heat and damp attack the rug and drapes and corrupt the foam-rubber cushions of the couch. The smell is as dank as wet leaves, and the heat gives Rafferty a blinding headache.

The headache leads to a second discovery. Looking for an aspirin in the medicine cabinet, he finds a trove of painkillers that, taken cumulatively, could prepare an elephant for surgery. He swallows a couple of ibuprofen the size of jawbreakers and surveys the remainder of Claus Ulrich's pharmacopoeia: prescription drugs for indigestion, powerful antihistamines, and, most interesting of all, three bottles of nitroglycerine tablets, one of them with the protective seal broken. Claus Ulrich has a heart condition and he keeps the emergency remedy right at hand.

So why are the tablets here when Uncle Claus isn't? Rafferty goes back and rifles through the suitcase. An unopened bottle of nitroglycerine, sealed in a Ziploc bag, is folded carefully into a shirt.

In addition to chronic pain, indigestion, allergies, and an erratic heart, Claus Ulrich has both money and taste. It's terrible taste, and there's a lot of it on view. Ulrich's eye runs to the rococo: Wooden objects tend to be heavily gilded and intricately filigreed with curls, gewgaws, and little bulbous tumors that might be either bunches of grapes or the scrotal sac of some alien organism with ten or twelve testicles. The ornate furniture sits beneath walls that are heavily hung with massive gilt-framed mirrors and hand-painted reproductions of dark museum oils. Rafferty looks more closely and sees filmy nymphs of indeterminate sex, cavorting on swings in some sylvan setting that's probably slated for development. Taken *tout ensemble*, the room has the cosmetic appeal of a fever blister.

The only exceptions—the only things in the place Rafferty would allow within ten feet of his own front door—are two remarkable Khmer apsarases, winged angels, carved in sandstone and maybe eight hundred years old. They're ethereally beautiful, and Rafferty makes a note to talk with a dealer in Cambodian antiquities who works out of the Oriental Hotel.

Not exactly Aussie taste, Rafferty thinks. In his somewhat limited experience, Australian men run more toward dark hardwood and leather: Cut down some trees, skin a few cattle, hammer together a living room set, and hope it doesn't sprout branches. See if your dog tries to herd it.

There are five rooms, four of them twinkling densely with frou-frou and bric-a-brac: living room, kitchen, den, and two bedrooms. In the den Rafferty learns that Uncle Claus is au courant with the computer age. A 1.8-gigahertz Dell with a flat-screen monitor sits incongruously on the nineteenth-century desk, a triumph of veneers and inlay. When Rafferty boots the machine, it defaults to Netscape, and a dial-up connection stakes out the screen and demands a pass-word. Stacks of CD-ROM disks, Bangkok counterfeits of popular software programs, are slotted in a four-foot-high plastic storage tower. There's a lot more software, Rafferty thinks, than most people would need: four word-processing programs, two spreadsheets, three graphics suites, several project planners, even two programs for writ-ing screenplays. About fifteen games. He pokes the storage tower with an index finger, making it wobble. Why would anyone need four word-processing programs?

He turns off the computer and gives the desk's single drawer a cursory rummage. Uncle Claus is a neat freak. He bundles business cards with a rubber band, alphabetized by company. Paper clips are segregated by size. Forty or fifty sheets of blank letterhead proclaim something called AT Enterprises, but there is no correspondence. His monthly bills are tied neatly in annual bundles. The bills are moder-ately interesting: He's spending a fortune on the phone but not calling long distance, so either he's incurably chatty or he spends a lot of time online. There's also an invoice from a company called Bangkok Do-mestics. Rafferty puts that one in his pocket.

In the far corner of the office stands a filing cabinet, a three-drawer beige rectangle that looks vaguely hangdog at being so proletarian. It is locked, so Rafferty gives it a pass.

Entering the master bedroom, Rafferty feels as though he has stepped into a painting on velvet or a malarial fever dream. Crim-son carpets support a canopied bed, gussied up with a tasseled satin spread. Looking around, Rafferty feels that Elvis might appear at any moment, sheathed in an unearthly light. On the table next to the bed is an expensive wristwatch, a gold Vacheron Constantin no thicker than a quarter.

Another thing Rafferty rarely suggests to his readers: Don't forget your watch.

Beside the watch are two photographs. One is of a fat man with thinning hair combed forward in a sort of Bill Haley spit curl above the apprehensive expression of a man who is the last in the room to get a joke. He has a pale mustache trimmed too short over full, sensual lips that look oddly naked. The other is of a young girl, whom Rafferty recognizes as a young and even unhappier version of Clarissa. Rafferty takes the portrait of Uncle Claus to send to Arthit.

The second, and smaller, bedroom breaks the mold. Tucked away at the rear of the flat and lacking an air conditioner, it contains nothing but an unpainted wooden dresser and a narrow bed, just a thin mattress atop an iron frame. The gray concrete slab of the floor is bare and looks recently scrubbed. The grit of a powdered cleanser scrapes beneath his shoes. Rafferty is willing to bet that this was the room that housed the oddly named Doughnut.

In addition to its spartan simplicity, it is different from the rest of the flat in another way: It has been completely emptied and then scoured. Not one trace of its former occupant remains. So if Uncle Claus and his wonderful new maid left together, only Doughnut knew she was going.

10

## The Living Map of Expat Bangkok

**N**ever heard of him," Leon Hofstedler says.

"Oh, come on, Leon." Rafferty shamelessly signals for the Expat Bar's ageless barmaid, whom the regulars call Toots, to top up Leon's vast stein. "You're the living map of expat Bangkok. You know everybody."

"Nice of you to say so, too," Leon says comfortably, watching the foam rise. "But this is one German I don't know."

Rafferty holds up the photo, but Hofstedler's eyes slide over it without recognition. "He's not German, he's just got a German name. He's an Aussie."

"Claus the Aussie?" Hofstedler packs the words with irony leaden enough to deflect gamma rays. He is playing to the house, which is to say to the collection of aging sex addicts who call the bar home. Rafferty mildly enjoys them individually, but as a group they comprise a new paradigm of what he doesn't want to be when he grows up. On the other hand, they collectively know more about one aspect of Bangkok than Rafferty does, and that's the aspect he thinks might have drawn Uncle Claus to desert his life in Australia—niece and all—and live here.

There was a time, if he is honest with himself, when this room could have been part of his future. Had he not met Rose, had he not seen through the rented smiles, had he not found himself focusing on the bewildered eyes of the girls who hadn't yet learned the game, he might eventually have been sitting here. In his heart he knows that the gulf separating him from these men can always be crossed. Bangkok is packed with men who have crossed it.

Hoftstedler lifts the stein to eye level and regards Poke around it. "There is no Australian called Claus anywhere, and certainly not in Bangkok. Australians have names like Hughie and Paul and Geoff."

"I didn't name him, Leon. I'm just looking for him." This earns a snicker from the Growing-Younger Man, halfway down the bar. The snicker barely sends a ripple through facial muscles so saturated with Botox that Rafferty wonders how the man chews his food. New plugs of hair dot the previously barren area above the Growing-Younger Man's forehead like a failing crop. He has spent a small fortune on cosmetic surgery, trying to appeal to bar girls one-third his age, and the result is a sad little froth of Brillo above a face as mobile as the mask of Agamemnon.

For a moment Rafferty thinks he will speak, but Hofstedler plows over whatever he might have been going to say. "You will have to look elsewhere," he says. He lifts the stein to his lips and puts a pint of Singha into the past tense. Then he belches, pats himself on the chest, and leans toward the dim end of the bar. "What about you, Bob?"

Bob Campeau, sunk in permafrost gloom at the far end, says, "He go to any clubs? Patpong? Nana Plaza? Soi Cowboy?" Campeau is the resident expert on Bangkok's more garish red-light districts. The others in the bar may cherish the occasional romantic illusion about the women they rent for the evening, mistaking really creative avarice for affection, but not Campeau. The man is a walking catalog of girlie bars; he can rattle off the specialties, merits, drawbacks, costs, and take-out policies of every joint in the city. He has never completely forgiven Poke for removing Rose from circulation.

"Not that I know," Rafferty says.

Campeau lifts his glass and eyes the bottom, apparently in the hope it refilled itself while he wasn't looking. "Then I don't know him, do I?"

"And he has been here how long?" Hofstedler asks.

"Decades," Rafferty says. "That's one reason I figured you might know him." There is a brief silence as Hofstedler ponders the improbability of his not knowing someone who has been in Bangkok such a long time.

Campeau chews ice. The Growing-Younger Man fingers his hair plugs and sips his green cocktail, made from some obscure age-reversing algae he imports by the carton from California. Everyone except him gets a minute older.

"Is your missing friend gay, Poke?" Mac O'Connor asks from the isolation of his accustomed booth, the Expat Bar's version of the back of the bus. "There's a Claus who pops up at Narcissus occasionally."

"I suppose he could be gay. He's unmarried," Rafferty says. Hofstedler gives a disapproving cluck on behalf of the room's heterosexual population. None of them is married, the better to pursue their obsession with the go-go dancers for whom they uprooted whatever lives they had to move to Bangkok. "What's your Claus look like, Mac?"

O'Connor tents his fingers and peers through them. "Dishy in that kind of seedy way that suggests piercings in unexpected places. About twenty-four or—"

"Wrong Claus, Mac." Rafferty displays the picture again. "This guy's in his fifties and big as a house."

"*Definitely* the wrong Claus. Not likely to be at Narcissus either. If you're over thirty these days, forget it. It's getting so they barely let you in if you shave."

"Such a life," Hofstedler says unpleasantly. "Such values, yes?"

"I don't notice you taking home any matrons," Mac says from the safety of his booth.

"Okay," Rafferty says, getting up. "He keeps a low profile, doesn't mingle with the European community here, he's probably not gay, he doesn't go to clubs, and he's got an awkward name. I guess that's information. Sort of."

"He is not leading an open life," Hofstedler observes. "Do you know what kind of a man he is?"

"A small-time saint, from what I've been told, although my source is biased."

"I doubt he's a saint," Hofstedler says.

"Why? Because he doesn't troll the bars?"

"One reason people come here, as I believe you said in your book," Hofstedler continues comfortably, "is that here it is possible to behave openly in ways that one would hide at home."

"I wrote that?" Rafferty says.

"It makes you wonder, does it not," Hofstedler says, "what kind of behavior one would hide in Bangkok."

## 11

## Not Big Enough to Sell Gum

I was really little," Miaow says without preamble. She is speaking Thai. "Maybe five or four." Miaow has no idea how old she actually is, so they took a vote and decided she's eight, although she could be a big seven or a small nine. "I slept under bridges. There were rats there that bit my fingers. When it rained, I slept in the doors of stores that were closed. Men came around all the time to chase us away. At night I went behind restaurants and waited for them to close. They throw away a lot of food, did you know that?"

"I wouldn't be surprised," Rafferty says. On his lap is a plastic bag containing a bright pink T-shirt, which Miaow bought for him on the sidewalk. He is perspiring against the plastic, but he doesn't want to move the bag.

"Well, I didn't know it until some other kid told me. We had to keep changing restaurants. If a place threw away really good food, the big kids would learn about it and take it all." She looks at a large spot on the carpet for a moment—a spot Rafferty and Rose have been battling for weeks—and then out at the balcony. "Kids can be mean, you know. Some adults think all kids are cute, but we're not. Some kids are as mean as adults."

"I'm sorry, Miaow." She rarely speaks of her life before he met her. Much of what he knows about it he has learned from the pictures she draws, Crayola nightmares of children huddling together on sidewalks surrounded by adult knees. Once in a while, there's an adult face with big, sharp, white teeth.

"No problem," she says. "It's the way it was." She brushes a stray hair from her face and runs her palms over her head to make sure her part is straight. It's an aspect of the world she can control. "I wasn't big enough to sell gum. So I just asked people for money. But most days nobody gave me any. I was really, really hungry. It was all I could think about."

"Poor baby," he says without thinking. She usually meets pity with scorn, but today she lets it pass.

"It's hard to sleep when you're hungry. You know you're going to wake up hungry. You know you'll be hungry all day. Sometimes I got so hungry I fell down."

"That should never have happened."

"It happens to lots of kids. It's happening right now. Out there." She lifts her chin to the glass doors and the city beyond.

Rafferty pats her hand, feeling the insipidity of the gesture all the way to his bones.

"It's hard to make friends, because kids come and go. They get taken by the police or something. So you stop trying. You think it's better alone. But then there's nobody to tell you things, like new places to sleep or which men are bad. I didn't know who I should run away from."

He has never asked her about this. They have never discussed whether she was abused sexually, in part because he doesn't know how to ask and in part because he isn't sure he could handle his rage if she was. He knows that an act of sudden physical intimacy—an unexpected hug, for instance—makes her go rigid, and sometimes she strikes out reflexively with fists and fingernails.

"I was frightened all the time," she says. "I *hurt*. I remember when I lost one shoe in the summer and my bare foot got so burned on the pavement I couldn't walk. There were holes in my skin. I found a piece of wood in the street and put it under my foot and tied it with a plastic bag. It made me limp because it didn't bend, and people thought I was crippled. I got more money then, so I put a cloth around it, like a bandage." She breaks off, listening to herself. "It was a pink shoe," she says regretfully. "I looked everywhere for it."

She rests her hand on his forearm and keeps it there, fingers open and palm up. She rarely touches him. Her voice changes and softens. Up until now she has been talking to the room; now her words are aimed directly at him. "What I wanted then was to sleep at night and have food and a place to get clean. I was dirty all the time. Just like Superman. I never thought I would live this high above the sidewalk. In the air. I never thought I would go to school."

Rafferty does not trust himself to speak. Finally he says, "You deserve everything, Miaow. You give me more than I give you."

"Nuh-uh," she says, and adds in English, "I make problems for you."

"I love you," he says. "You make me happy."

For a moment she leans her head against his arm, and Rafferty feels as though his heart will dissolve. It lasts only a second or two, and then she is sitting upright again, and he can hear her swallow.

"One day this boy came up to me with a handful of flowers, and he said, 'Come with me.'"

"Superman," Rafferty says.

She gives him a long look. "His name then was Boo."

"Okay, Boo."

"He took me to a room," she says, "on a little *soi*. There was a big woman there, a really fat woman. She had gold bracelets. And a whole bunch of little kids on the floor, making garlands out of the flowers." She pauses, working out the order of the story she wants to tell.

"So you sold the flowers," Rafferty prompts. Bangkok's garland sellers, children of five and six, work the city's busiest intersections, approaching drivers at stoplights to sell the fragrant loops of flowers offered at shrines. It is filthy, dangerous work. The children breathe carbon monoxide all day. Occasionally they are hit by cars. "For how long?"

"A long time," Miaow says.

"And were things better then?"

"I had some money. I could eat every day, and I had a place to sleep. But then—" She withdraws her hand. "Then everything was bad again."

"What happened?"

She takes the bag from his lap and pulls the T-shirt out. She looks at him and then at it. Very carefully, she folds it into the smallest possible square. Then she unfolds it slowly, as though she hopes to find some answer written on it. "What happened," she says, "is that Boo went crazy."

## 12

## We've Been in Worse Garages

Miaow sits bolt upright as a key turns in the lock. The T-shirt is twisted between her clenched hands, her knuckles pale in the dark skin.

Rose comes in with four large bottles of drinking water clutched to her chest. She stops, looking from Rafferty to Miaow and back again. "One minute," she says in English. "I put water and go."

"No," Miaow says, looking up at her. "I want to tell you, too."

Rose colors with pleasure. "She likes us both today," she says, and Miaow produces a low-wattage smile. "Why is your friend downstairs?"

"Downstairs where?" Rafferty asks.

"In the garage," Rose says in Thai. "Asleep in somebody's jeep, with his feet out the window."

"He's waiting," Miaow says. "We've been in worse garages."

"You and Superman?" Rose settles cross-legged on the floor with her back to the glass doors. The sunlight on her hair is dazzling, a knot of rainbows.

"When I was little," Miaow says, "he found me and took me to a place where kids were making garlands. My first day I made thirty baht. Almost a dollar. I could eat. Boo—that was his name then," she informs Rose—"Boo showed me a good place to sleep. There was a number hotel that was closed. We could sleep in the garage, behind the curtains. We were dry when it rained." Number hotels, indispensable to Bangkok's sexually furtive, have curtained garages to allow customers to get out unobserved.

"We started every day at five in the morning. We sold flowers until it was dark. Boo already had four kids with him. They were my first real friends, ever. When some older kids tried to chase us out of the garage, Boo took a big piece of wood with nails in one end and hurt two of them until they ran away." She pauses for a moment to swallow. "He took care of us.

"I sold flowers every day for almost two years," she says. She is looking straight in front of her, seeing her own life unspool like a film. "Boo was always there. One night a man called me to come to his car. When I got there, he reached out and grabbed my arm. He tried to pull me into the car, right through the window. Like a bag of rice. Boo ran up and bit the man's arm. He wouldn't let go. The man dropped me and drove off, with Boo hanging from his arm, biting him deeper and deeper. We were running behind, screaming for the man to stop. The man was screaming, too. When Boo let go, he fell on the road. He got up with blood all over his face and shirt and on his elbows and knees from where he fell. He was laughing."

"Fierce heart," Rose says.

Miaow falls silent. Rafferty can see her struggling with the next words. Rose pulls a pack of cigarettes from her purse, looks at it, and drops it back in.

"Then some bigger boys showed him about *yaa baa.*" *Yaa baa* is a cheap, potent variant on amphetamine that is widely sold on the streets of Southeast Asia. "Then he wasn't Boo anymore. People who smoke *yaa baa* don't want to eat, so he stopped helping us find food. He got mad all the time. If you smiled at him wrong, he got mad. He hit one of the girls so hard her nose broke. He was sorry later, but we were already afraid of him. One of the kids left, and then another one. After a while it was just me.

"He smoked it every morning. He smoked it all day. His hands shook. He screamed at people who didn't buy a garland. Drivers closed their windows when he came up to them, and he spit on the windows. The police got him, and I didn't see him for two weeks. When he came back from the monkey house, he took away the money I had made so he could buy *yaa baa*. I gave him the money when he asked, but he hit me anyway. Two days later he came again, and this time he cried and said he was sorry. He said he wasn't going to smoke anymore. The next time I saw him, he was so crazy he didn't know me."

"He was how old then?" Rafferty asks.

"A year before I met you," she says, working it out. "I was about seven. He was maybe nine or ten."

Rafferty blows out a breath he hadn't known he was holding. "Miaow," he says, "*yaa baa* is cheap, but if he was smoking so much, he had to have money. Where did—"

She stops him by raising the hand with the T-shirt in it, sees it, and drops it into her lap. "I'm telling you." She squares her shoulders like someone who is about to pick up something heavy and sits forward.

"He joined a bunch of boys. They stole things. They smoked and ate pills and stole things. Maybe from a food vendor or even a beggar. Sometimes they beat people up. Ten or twelve boys, who would fight them? They were bigger than Boo, but he was smarter. So he had an idea. Those men—those men who want little boys. Before, they were around Soi 8, Soi 6, you know?"

"I know," Rafferty says.

"So one of the boys would pretend he was going with the man and leave the door unlocked, and the others would all come into the room and hurt the man and take his money." She looks from Rose to Rafferty. "That was when they started to call him Superman. Then I stopped hearing about him."

"What happened to him?" Rafferty asks.

"He told me last night he went to Phuket." Her eyes come up

to Rafferty's, as if assessing the impact of what she is about to say. "Phuket is full of boys."

It's not Pattaya, Rafferty knows, but it's bad enough. "What brought him back to Bangkok? The wave?"

"He won't tell me," Miaow says. "But he said it was worse than the wave."

ROSE GETS UP and crowds onto the couch beside Miaow and wraps her in dark, slender arms. Rafferty wants to hug her himself. She could have stopped long minutes ago, with the rescue from the man in the car. She could have left the boy a hero. She didn't have to talk about the drugs. He knows what she wants, and she knows that every word she speaks makes it harder for him to say yes.

Miaow gently disengages herself and takes Rafferty's hand in her right and Rose's in her left. "After it happened, Boo ran back to Bangkok. He's too old to beg now. He sleeps in the street. He says he hasn't smoked any *yaa baa* in a long time." She stops, breathing heavily, as though she's just run up the stairs. She wraps her fingers around Rafferty's thumb, gripping hard. "I want him to stay with us."

"Oh, Miaow," Rafferty says, although he knew it was coming.

"He can sleep in my room," Miaow says, talking faster. Her hands are tight fists around theirs. "I'll sleep on the floor. He can have half my allowance. He doesn't eat much. He can wear my extra shoes. You already bought him a pair of pants and a shirt. I'll make him stay in the other room, out of your way, when you're home. He can help Rose." She has squeezed her eyes shut with the effort of dredging up argument after argument and also, Rafferty thinks, because she is afraid to look at his face. He presses her hand to stop the flow.

"He can fix the faucet," she says. "You always say you'll fix it, but you never do. He can get that spot out of the carpet. He can— "

Rose says, "Miaow, did he tell you to ask Poke if he could stay with us?"

Miaow's eyes open. She looks surprised. "No," she says. "I don't even know if he will."

"It's just not a good idea, Miaow," Rafferty says. "I'll try to find someplace else for him."

She drums her feet against the sofa in frustration. "That will take weeks. And he won't stay there. He needs to be here." She looks at Rafferty with an expression he has never seen on her face before. "He needs *me*." She brings her hands up, head high, in a prayerlike *wai* of supplication. "This time *he* needs *me*."

Rafferty looks at Rose, and Rose looks at Rafferty. Rose closes her eyes, seceding from the discussion. Rafferty sits back, feeling the "No" rise up in him. And then he sees Miaow being lifted through the window of a car.

"Not for long," he says. "One week, two weeks. Until he feels better and we can find a place for him to stay."

"Really?" Miaow's eyes fill half her face.

"Go get him," Rafferty says. "Let's see if we can talk him into it."

## 13

## Nickname Doughnut

**M**r. Ulrich used us both times," the lady behind the desk at Bangkok Domestics says in crisp English.

She is in her forties, clinging grimly to twenty-eight. Her face is white with powder, and her hair has been dyed blacker than a crow's wing and lacquered into a rigid little wave in front that would probably shatter if touched. Her uniform is a frilly lavender junior-miss business suit that sports buttons the size of the doorknobs. It looks like something a small girl would wear on Take Your Daughter to Work Day.

The wall behind her is a panorama of past glory. The anxious woman sitting at the desk is pictured in happier times with some of Bangkok's most media-hungry socialites, faded snap after faded snap attesting to a once-thriving concern, supplying domestic help to the wives of the rich and—given the topsy-turvy world of Thai politics— the occasionally powerful.

But now she sits behind a scratched wooden desk in a room barely big enough to exhale into. On the desk, facing Rafferty, is a file, topped by an official-looking form adorned with many impressive seals. One of them, Rafferty notices, is a United States Boy Scouts seal. In the blank for NAME, he reads: Miss Tippawan Dangphai.

"Doughnut," Rafferty says. "Any idea why Doughnut?"

The woman barely shrugs. "Who knows? We have one girl nick-named Pogo and two who call themselves Banana. Several years back we had one named Aspirin. Girls," she says, as though this explains everything, which it probably does.

A passport-size black-and-white photo has been stapled to the form, next to a blank space where a fingerprint should be. Despite the frivolous nickname, Doughnut is not a particularly blithe-looking girl. She faces the camera glumly, with the attitude of one who knows the picture will not come out. The camera has been kind to the large, beautiful eyes, but it has muddied the dark skin of Isaan, in the north-east. Aside from the eyes, she is not a striking woman. Her face is as wide as it is long, her lower lip too full, and her nose has virtually no bridge to it. It is a face Rafferty sees everywhere in Bangkok, the face of refugees from Isaan's broken villages and barren farms and no rain. On the basis of the photo, Doughnut would be difficult to pick out of a lineup.

"So the first maid stayed with him for ten years?"

"Or more." She makes a patient show of checking a piece of paper in front of her. "Ten years and seven months."

"And then he called you for a replacement."

"Nine weeks ago." She pauses. "As I said."

He feels a flare of irritation. "So you did. And, as *I* said a minute ago, the man's disappeared, and so has the maid. The maid you se-lected for him." He sits back, watching her, and then puts out an index finger to move the Bangkok Domestics business card he took from Claus Ulrich's desk. "The maid whose fingerprint you forgot to get."

She straightens, and laces her fingers together on the desk. "Surely there's no question that the maid had anything to do with it."

"Isn't there? Do you know where she is? Has she called to say she's available for work again?"

The air-conditioning unit kicks out for a moment and then kicks in with a depressed hum, something it does every forty seconds or so. However thriving it may once have been, the present Bangkok Domestics is a one-room operation, housed in a deteriorating four-story walk-up in the Pratunam area of the city. If the firm is profitable these days, it is saving a fortune on office space.

"Has she?" Rafferty asks again, since the woman has apparently slipped into a meditative trance, staring down at her file.

"No," she says, without looking up. A furrow appears between her eyebrows, and a fine snow of face powder sifts down toward her lap.

"Right," Rafferty says. "Tell me what the police will say. A missing *farang*, a missing Thai maid, who cleaned out her room before she left. A *farang* woman who's come to Bangkok to try to find him. Tell me what the police will say."

"The police are not involved," she says, tidying the piles of paper on her desk.

"Not officially," Rafferty says. He holds up his cell phone. "But perhaps they could be helpful." The woman blinks twice. He begins to dial.

She tells him what he wants to know.

What Claus Ulrich requested—what he had requested both times from Bangkok Domestics—was a relatively young woman, in her early twenties, who could cook and clean and who had at least one strong reference.

"And she had a reference?" Rafferty asks.

A hesitation. The woman's eyes drop to the file again but don't focus on it. "Yes."

"I want to talk to the reference."

"Oh, no," the woman says immediately. "Out of the question."

"Not really," Rafferty says. "Not when you think about it."

She pushes her chair back from the desk very quickly, as though there might be a snake beneath it. "Please, no. This woman is a *very* good customer. Also—how can I put this?—she is not someone I would want to make angry. She is *formidable*." The French pronunciation.

"She'll get over it."

The chair is already pressed against the wall so she can go no farther, but she flutters her hands at him, making him feel like a bird she is trying to shoo out a window. "Please, let me explain. There are people you meet who, you know at once, will make a good friend. I'm sure this has happened to you. And then, much more rarely, there are people who you know immediately will make a bad enemy." The fluttering turns into a fanning gesture, as though her face is hot. "A *very* bad enemy."

"This is a woman you met on the phone," Rafferty says, "not on a battlefield."

"I was called to her house," the woman says, as though this will make it all clear. "I spent time with her. She is . . ." She searches the air above Rafferty's head, looking for the words. "She is not easily forgettable."

"Well, I'm sorry, because I'm going to have to talk to her. In fact, I need a photocopy of the reference she wrote."

"This is very bad." She is fanning herself again.

Rafferty smiles at her reassuringly. "Oh, come on. What can she do to you?"

"I don't want to know," the woman says.

Three minutes and one more mention of the police later, he has a copy of the letter of reference and a pair of fuchsia-colored sticky notes with Doughnut's address and the number for the sole telephone in the village she left behind. Halfway to the door, he turns back.

"It might be a good idea to talk to Ulrich's first maid, too."

A pause, during which the woman seems to be framing her reply. "She's dead," she says at last. "Motorbike accident. That's why he needed a new one."

Rafferty takes another look at the cramped little office. "Where do your girls come from?"

She blinks surprise at the question. "The northeast, mostly."

"Do you have any former go-go girls working for you?"

The heavily powdered upper lip rises a scornful quarter of an inch. Compared to the dead white of the powder, her teeth are yellow. "Of course not."

"Why not?"

"They're liars and thieves, every one of them. Liars and thieves."

"Really," Rafferty says, thinking of Rose's roomful of scrubbed hopefuls and then the scrubbed room Doughnut had left behind. "We couldn't have that, could we?"

## 14

## The Only People in Bangkok
## More Dangerous Than the Crooks

The maid's address is the Bangkok Bank Building," Rafferty says into the cell phone. He has ducked into the bank's deep doorway to escape the setting sun's final attempt to incinerate the city before giving up for the night.

"Maybe she sleeps with her money," Arthit says.

"And the telephone number is not in service."

"Careful girl." Arthit covers the mouthpiece and says something to someone else. "I'm back," he says. "Maybe she was planning to steal something and disappear."

"And maybe she got caught," Rafferty says. "And overreacted."

"And maybe it has nothing to do with anything. Maybe she was living on the street. By the way, thanks for the photo. I faxed it down there and asked a couple of guys to check the hospitals and compare it with the boards." The "boards," at least one in every community struck by the tsunami, display the photos of corpses that have washed ashore. A crowd gathers to study them each morning, all hoping to find, and hoping not to find, someone they love.

"So I don't have to go down?" He tries to keep the relief out of his voice. It is after five o'clock now, and it has been a long day: the meeting with Clarissa Ulrich, Uncle Claus's apartment and the Expat Bar, the scene with Miaow. The sneer from the woman at Bangkok Domestics.

"Probably not. There's no Ulrich on the hospital lists, although it could be that he's unconscious and didn't have any ID. The picture will help there. He's not on the computers of any of the hotels whose computers weren't destroyed."

"Your guys ought to show the picture to the people from the other hotels."

"Really." Arthit sounds like he's rolling the word uphill. "We never would have thought of that. Where there *are* people from the other hotels, they'll talk to them."

"This guy is not a beach bunny, Arthit. He weighs three hundred pounds, and according to Clarissa, he burns faster than bacon. And you should see the apartment; it looks like he roomed with Ludwig of Bavaria. No one with taste like that goes outdoors if he can help it. And the only thing I can see him doing with a coconut palm is eating it."

"So what's your guess?"

"I think it has something to do with the maid. Her name is Tippawan Dangphai."

"Dangphai," Arthit says with the tone-deaf inflection of someone who is writing and talking at the same time. "Nickname?" All Thais have nicknames, a necessity in a country where a name can have six to eight syllables.

"Doughnut."

Arthit sighs. "Sometimes I think we Thais carry this merriment thing too far. I'll run the full name through the databases." He clears his throat, usually a sign he has something to say and he's not happy about it. "Poke, I'm afraid Clarissa did something stupid."

"I'm not going to like this, am I?"

"She very politely called the two cops who had been taking her money and told them she wouldn't be bothering them again."

"And you criticize Western manners." Despite the sun, the temperature suddenly seems to have dipped.

"She told them I'd put her in touch with someone."

"Just 'someone'?"

"Well, no. You impressed her quite a bit. She apparently went on at some length."

"And they're not happy." Rafferty finds himself scanning the street.

"No," Arthit says. "I think it's accurate to say they're not happy. They were already spending the rest of her money."

"This is great, Arthit. The only people in Bangkok more dangerous than the crooks are the cops."

"*Some* of the cops." Arthit can be touchy about police corruption.

"And these particular cops?"

Arthit says, "They're in the *some* category." Then he says, "I faxed their names and ID pictures to you. You might want to keep your eyes open."

"Are you in any danger?"

"I laugh at danger," Arthit says. "But lock your doors."


OKAY. COPS AFTER him. If anything happens to him, Arthit will know where to look. The thought is not particularly comforting.

As long as he's standing in the shade, he pulls out the letter from Doughnut's dreaded reference. He privately dismisses Arthit's suggestion that Doughnut was a thief, because a woman who strikes terror into people, as her previous employer apparently does, would not be likely to recommend a servant with large pockets. He unfolds the photocopy and starts to punch the tiny buttons, then thinks better of it. One does not, he thinks, call a *formidable* woman, one who apparently has quintillions of baht, from a noisy sidewalk at 5:00 P.M. It isn't done. People don't like to be disturbed at the end of the day, especially when they're rich and old and the evening's pleasures beckon, whatever they may be. Cocktails, perhaps. Bloody Marys with real blood, if the woman at Bangkok Domestics' description was accurate.

Much better to call from his apartment in the morning, at the start of a bright new day. The sun will be shining, the sky will be blue. The day will vibrate with promise. She's just an aged lady, he thinks. She will refuse him nothing.

## 15

## The Familiar Wall of Female Solidarity

No," says the man on the phone for the second time.

"I only need a few minutes," Rafferty says for the third time.

"She will not see you."

"Then I'll talk to her on the phone."

"Madame does not speak to people." It is an older man's voice, stiff as wire. They are speaking Thai. Rafferty has a vision of a sort of Southeast Asian Jeeves, tall and long-fingered and immaculately shaven, possibly even wearing a morning coat.

"You haven't asked her."

"I am not paid to ask her."

"Then let me leave my number," he says. "Tell her I'm investigating a disappearance here in Bangkok and I need ten minutes of her time. It's important. I'm trying—"

"The number?" the man interrupts.

Rafferty recites his phone number and says, "My name is—" He is talking to a dial tone.

"Thanks for your time," he says, hanging up.

The day is, inevitably, bright and hot, with so much light pouring through the glass door that Rafferty has to squint against it. Rose has trudged off somewhere, visibly depressed by the failure of yesterday's potential clients to hire any of the faded flowers in her labor pool. Her despondence worries him. He suspects she has been lending the women small amounts of money to keep them from going back to the bars.

*She should know better*, he thinks, and then mentally slaps himself in the face. Like *he* knows better. Like he's a shining example of knowing better than to try to help people who probably can't be helped.

For example, Superman.

The events of the previous evening, welcoming Superman provisionally into the family, were bad enough to make Rafferty wish he could reformat his memory. He was up half the night trying to think of something, *anything*, he could do with the boy that won't break Miaow's heart.

AFTER MIAOW BROUGHT him up from the garage, the boy had greeted without visible enthusiasm the news that he could stay with them. He had gazed at Rafferty through the good eye and the swollen eye as though Rafferty were a dirty window with nothing interesting on the other side. When Rafferty had finished his little speech, Superman had waited to see whether there was going to be more talk, then turned and stalked down the hallway to Miaow's room.

Rafferty hadn't said anything, but his big, scrutable half-Anglo face evidently had, because Miaow said, "He's happy."

"Give him time," Rose said.

"That's exactly what I *am* giving him," Rafferty had said. He thought that both the words and his tone had been reasonable, but he saw from their expressions that he was facing the familiar wall of female solidarity, rooted in some profoundly obvious emotional reality that was completely invisible to him.

"You have to give it from your heart," Rose said.

Rafferty said, "I'm having trouble getting my chest open."

That exchange had been the high point of the evening. It had been, on the whole, an evening to be forgotten as quickly and completely as possible.

"If I were Claus Ulrich," Rafferty asks himself aloud, "where would I be?" He crosses to his desk and idly opens and closes the screen on his laptop. "Or," he amends, "if I were Claus Ulrich, *who* would I be?" He lifts the screen again.

As he sees it in the highly overrated light of morning, the errand he has undertaken can have five outcomes: (1) He can find Uncle Claus alive and make Clarissa happy. (2) He can find Uncle Claus dead and make her unhappy. (3) He can find an Uncle Claus who is radically different from the one she thinks she knows, and break her heart. (4) He can fail to find Uncle Claus at all and leave everything unresolved.

Or (5) Arthit's renegade cops could kill him.

The dinner with Superman—the First Supper, as he's beginning to think of it—had been well beyond grim.

The children had sat on one side of the table and the adults on the other. Rose had talked enough for four, and Miaow had eaten enough for two. The boy, for the most part, had stared at his food as though he expected it to start wriggling on the dish. At one point Miaow had broken a spring roll in half and reached over and put it in his mouth, and he had removed it and dropped it on her plate as though it were a stone. Rafferty had fought the impulse to pull the cloth off the table, dishes and all.

"You have to eat something," he finally said. "Rose cooked this food for us, and you have to eat something."

The boy had looked at Rafferty for a good count of ten and picked up the half a spring roll and put it in his mouth. Then he had chewed it, noisily and deliberately, for at least five minutes. He had swallowed it three times. Then he pushed his chair from the table and sauntered down the hallway to Miaow's room.

This performance had been followed by a long silence. Rose ate as though nothing had happened. Rafferty counted to a hundred. Miaow stared at her lap.

"He wants to show you he won't eat much," she finally said.

"He's smoking *yaa baa*," Rafferty replied.

"He's just confused," Rose said placidly, helping herself to some more noodles. "He doesn't know what he's supposed to do, and that makes him angry. He needs time."

"Not smoking," Miaow said very softly.

"How do you know?" Rafferty had asked.

"Not smoking," Miaow repeated more loudly.

"Fine," Rafferty retreated. "He's not smoking. Tell him he has to eat, Miaow. It's the only way I'm going to know."

"He's not smoking," Rose said. "He just doesn't know what he feels."

And they left it there. The boy had slept on the couch in the living room, with Rafferty rejecting Miaow's repeated offer to give him the top level of her bunk bed, and when Rafferty woke up, he was gone. Rafferty secretly hopes he won't return.

He has started a game of solitaire on the computer when the phone rings.

"Poke," Arthit says. "Do you have a pencil?"

"Of course," he says. "I'm a writer."

"While you try to find one," Arthit says, "here's an update. No results on the photograph yet in either Phuket or Phang Nga. There are four guys working on it now, but there are a lot of people to talk to. So far, though, no one recognizes him either alive or dead."

Rafferty is opening and closing drawers. "That's because he wasn't down there."

"Maybe not. Got the pencil yet?"

"Yeah, yeah." The one that has come to hand is dimpled with the tooth marks Rose always puts into it when she subtracts her assets, little indentations of anxiety.

"Here comes the first part of your favor: 555–0475. That's Hank Morrison's number. Do you know Hank?"

"Pilot or something. Runs that school for street kids."

"He puts the kids through a few years of basic schooling," Arthit says. "He—what's the word?—*socializes* them. You know, teaches them not to kill each other over who gets the first helping of noodles. And then he arranges their adoption. I've told him to expect your call."

"Adoption? You mean, like *adoption*?"

"Have some coffee," Arthit says sympathetically. "Crank up those verbal skills, then give him a call. And keep working on Claus Ulrich."

Rafferty is already dialing when he realizes he hung up on Arthit without saying good-bye. The phone feels slick. His palms are sweating.

After two rings the telephone is picked up. Nobody says anything, but Rafferty can hear the shrieks of what sound like a million children on a roller coaster. "Hello?" Rafferty says. The squeals rise in pitch as the roller coaster, or whatever it is, reaches the top of its arc. "Hello?"

On the other end of the line, somebody laughs. From the sound of the laugh, its possessor is less than three feet tall and easily amused.

"Is Hank there? Khun Hank, is he there?" Rafferty asks in Thai.

After a deliberative pause, the person on the other end says, "Yes," and hangs up.

Rafferty counts to twenty to give the child time to become interested in something else and wander away, and then he dials again. Four rings this time, and then a deep male voice says, "Hello."

"Hank Morrison? This is Poke Rafferty."

"Hey, Poke. Did you just call?"

"Sort of."

"Natalee said someone had called. She's got the basic idea, but she's a little shaky on the drill."

"You're training them early," Rafferty says.

"You don't have to train them at all. They fight to help out. One thing about kids, they like to feel useful."

"Hank, I need to ask you a couple of questions."

"This is about what Arthit mentioned."

"Actually, the first thing is business."

"Fire away. Listen, if you hear me drop the phone suddenly, hang on. It just means I'm intervening in one of the day's near-death situations. We've got prospective adoptive parents coming through today, and it gets the kids kind of worked up."

"Okay, the business. I'm looking for a guy as a favor for Arthit. He's supposed to be active with kids here. Do you know anyone named Claus Ulrich?"

"Claus . . ."

"Ulrich."

"Can't say I do. What organization does he work with?"

"I have no idea."

"Might help if you could find out. But I've never heard of him, and I think I know most of the folks who are really doing something. Maybe he's an angel."

"An angel?"

"You know—doesn't do the work but gives the money. Is he well-off?"

"Seems to be."

"Okay, I'll ask around and get back to you. Now, what about the child Arthit mentioned? How old?"

"She's eight," Rafferty says. "I think."

"A little girl," Hank says carefully.

"That's right, Hank," Rafferty says, suddenly angry. "An eight-year-old female is often called a little girl."

"Sorry, Poke. It's more . . . complicated with girls. How did you get involved with her?"

"I met her in Patpong, selling gum. She didn't have a place to live, and I didn't want her on the street. I put her in a rented room for a while, and I set her up in one of the international schools. After a while I cleared out my office, here in the apartment, and she moved in."

Morrison clears his throat. "Is she still in school?"

"Yes, and she's doing great."

"Poke, what did you tell the school about her? What have you been telling people in general?"

"Not much. It doesn't come up that often, actually. I have a long-time girlfriend who's here a lot, and that sort of takes some of the curse off. When someone asks—at the school, for example—I say she's my adopted daughter."

"Mmmm," Morrison says. "You want to be careful with this."

"I know. I worry about it." The person he worries most about is one of the people who lives on his floor, a Mrs. Pongsiri. A regal-looking lady of a certain age who works very peculiar hours, leaving in the afternoon and coming home late at night, Mrs. Pongsiri never misses an opportunity to gaze speculatively at Miaow. She has demonstrated a vast repertoire of ways to purse her lips. Since she is essentially the central switchboard for the apartment house's gossip network, her interest is disconcerting.

"You *should* worry about it. And for the meantime you want to avoid rubbing people's noses in it. What's your girlfriend's name?"

"Rose."

"Well, it would be a good idea to take Rose along when the two of you go out. This is a serious relationship?"

"I'd marry her in a minute. She's the one with reservations."

"Well, good for her. Marriage is supposed to be for life. But adoption *really* is."

"Yeah, I know. That's fine. I mean, I want to see her grow up and everything, while I get old, just like I'm supposed to. I want her to have some kind of life. She's an amazing kid, Hank."

"They're all amazing," Morrison says. "That's the hard part."

"So, then, what? I mean, what do I do?"

"Are her parents dead?"

"She doesn't know. She's been on the streets practically her whole life."

"That makes it harder. Normally, to qualify for adoption you need to be able to demonstrate either that both parents are dead or that they've consented to the deal."

Rafferty emits three frustrated little pops of breath. "Well, we can't do that."

"Probably not the end of the world." Morrison puts a hand over the phone and calls out to someone, using a tone that has a lot of military starch in it. "Listen, don't take this wrong, Poke. Arthit says you're a good guy. But before I can do anything at all for you, I have to see you and her together. And I have to spend time with her alone. At least a couple of hours."

"Do you really think you can do something for us?"

"It's possible. But one thing at a time. Before we can do anything, I have to talk to both of you."

Rafferty is up and pacing the room. He feels light enough to float. "Jesus, Hank. Thank you."

"I'll need some money. The paperwork isn't cheap."

"How much?"

"The low thousands."

"Is that all?" Rafferty asks, and then realizes that his total net worth at the moment can be placed in the very low thousands, especially with the drain of Rose's business. And Miaow's school claims a chunk every month, too.

"That's it. But don't get your hopes up too fast. It's a bumpy track. We'll talk in a day or so."

"Hank, one more thing. There's another kid."

"Poke, are you writing books or doing day care?"

"This is a boy, about ten. He took care of my little girl for a few years, starting when she was four or five, and now she's trying to return the favor."

"What's his problem? Because there is one. I can hear it in your voice."

"Amphetamines," Rafferty says. "And violence."

"What kind of violence?"

"Ganging up on pedos who like little boys, which I can live with, actually. Stealing. And biting."

"Oh, good Lord, Poke," Hank says, "we're not talking about Superman, are we?"

"Um . . ." Rafferty says.

"Because if we are, forget him. He can't be helped. I know that sounds cold, but I learned early on that you have to conserve your strength. There are a lot of kids to take care of, and you can't burn yourself out on one. That boy is a black hole."

"I don't have a lot of kids to take care of," Rafferty says stubbornly.

"And you don't want him around your little girl either. He's a terrible influence on everybody he gets close to."

"Does that mean you wouldn't take him? If he cleaned up his act, I mean?"

"I wouldn't have him here under any circumstances."

Some of the lightness goes out of Rafferty's spirits. "Do you know anywhere else?"

"No. The toughest place in town wouldn't take him. Listen, the would-be parents are due any minute. Is that everything?"

"When will the parents be gone?"

"Couple of days."

"I'll call then. And thanks, Hank. More than you know."

"Oh, well," Hank Morrison says. "I think I probably know."

Rafferty puts the phone down, and the room is suddenly too small. He feels a need to be outdoors, but more than anything he needs someone to whom he can tell his news. He knows he should be concerned about Superman and Uncle Claus, but all he can think about is the possibility of adopting Miaow. Not worrying about the cops or the bureaucrats or even Mrs. Pongsiri. Knowing that Miaow is his, and he is hers, by law.

It's almost—but not quite—enough to send him to Hofstedler and the others at the Expat Bar. He wishes he weren't so solitary by nature, that he had a dozen friends he could call with the news.

But the person he most wants to tell is Rose.

Rose, who adopted him as he staggered his way through the go-go bars of Patpong. Rose, who taught him the first rules of Thai life he learned. Rose, whose little sister Lek he and Arthit had rescued from one of the seamier upstairs bars on Patpong and frightened all the way out of Bangkok. Rose, whom he has come to love.

And the thought strikes him, not for the first time since the tsunami stretched out its careless blue hands and slapped thousands of lives to tiny pieces: *We can be a family.*

He has to do something, and it might as well be something to earn the favor Arthit promised. He grabs his wallet, a few hundred baht, his cell phone, and a pair of sunglasses and checks the apartment for anything he has forgotten. He will go see Heng, an antiques dealer. The man is certain to be in his shop in an arcade at the Oriental Hotel, doing a brisk trade in Khmer treasures that have been chiseled off the walls of Angkor or other, less-well-known temple complexes in the dead of night. If Claus Ulrich was seriously in the market for black-market art, Heng will probably know.

As he opens the door to leave, the phone rings. Rafferty deliberates for another ring and then double-times across the room to pick it up.

"Your name," says a voice on the other end. A demand, not a question.

"You called me," Rafferty says. It is a woman's voice, deep, but definitely a woman.

"Your *name*," she repeats impatiently. She speaks Thai, with some kind of accent.

"Why don't we start over?" Rafferty says. "You made the call. You probably know who you want to talk to."

"You're the investigator," she says.

Under other circumstances he would correct the assumption, but he knows who it is.

"My name is Rafferty," he says.

"You want to see me."

"You changed your mind," he says.

"That does not concern you. Come here now."

"Where is 'here'?"

"My home. Give your name at the gate."

The *gate*? "I need your address."

"If you need my address, I do not need to talk to you." The woman hangs up.

Rafferty grabs the letter of reference with the address on it, folds it, and puts it into his pocket. Then he goes out into the promise of the bright new day.

## 16

## Madame Brings Her Chair with Her

The guard at the gate has a tommy gun slung over his shoulder and the flat, unreflective look of someone who would enjoy using it. The guard station is twice the size of a telephone booth and sits beside the only break in a twelve-foot concrete wall, brightly whitewashed, that stretches half a block. Beside the booth is a sliding gate of black wrought-iron rods, sharpened to wicked points at the top. Broken glass dazzles atop the wall.

The guard studies the photo on Rafferty's passport and then Rafferty's face, as though he is waiting for Rafferty's disguise to melt. He reluctantly picks up a canary-yellow telephone, grunts into it, and hangs up.

They stand there. The guard looks at Rafferty, and Rafferty looks at the guard. "Get a lot of trick-or-treaters?" Rafferty asks.

"Don't talk to *her* like that," the guard says. "She'll have the skin off you." His English is accented but serviceable. The gate begins to slide open.

Standing on the other side is a man, possibly Thai, who looks almost startlingly like the individual Rafferty envisioned during his first telephone call to the house. A slender sixty, with steel-gray hair plastered to a narrow skull, he is immaculately dressed in a suit and tie, even in this heat. He has the erect carriage of a soldier and the eyes of a man who could watch colon surgery for laughs.

"You will follow," he says, turning away.

Rafferty does as he is told, trailing the man up a long curve of blacktop driveway toward one of the most beautiful houses he has ever seen. Huge, rambling, built in the old Thai style, it is shuttered against the heat and light of the day. Rafferty has studied Thai houses, and he guesses this one to be at least a century old. Banks of pale flowers foam up against its wooden sides, and an ancient tamarind tree shades the front. Half an acre of immaculate lawn creates a clean green sweep down to the swift, coffee-colored flow of the river. The house has a private pier with a speedboat tied to it, dragging against its rope on the downstream side. For some reason a hole has been dug in the lawn. As beautiful as the house is, it has a brooding air; as he approaches, Rafferty sees peeling paint and sagging steps. Looking at the roofline, he has no problem imagining bats flying out of it. The disrepair of the house surprises him, given the investment in the wall, the guard, and the gate.

The person who lives here needs serious security.

They walk—or, rather, Rafferty walks and the man marches—to the steps leading up to the front veranda. The man stops and turns to Rafferty.

"Madame Wing has fifteen minutes," he says. "You will address her as Madame. What questions will you ask her?"

Rafferty thinks of himself as someone who rarely dislikes anyone on sight, but in this case he's willing to make an exception. "I thought I'd start with the Big Bang," he says. "Everything else did."

"If you do not tell me the questions," the man replies icily, "she will not see you."

"She called me, remember? I think she'll see me."

Jeeves's mouth works several times, like a man trying to generate some spit. His eyes go past Rafferty and then dart up and to the left, looking up the steps they will have to climb. Rafferty thinks, *He's frightened.*

The man's eyes come back to him, flint black. "Please," he says between his teeth. "Please tell me what you plan to discuss with Madame Wing."

Oh, well. "I plan to ask her about a maid who used to work here."

It is not what the man expected. His eyebrows go up the width of a hair. "A maid? You could have talked to me about that."

"You didn't write the letter of reference. She did."

The look he receives is not without a hint of pity. He shakes his head. "Then come."

The two of them go up the stairs and through a wide doorway into the house. The dark interior space slowly resolves itself into a series of long, high chambers with richly grained wooden walls. Teak floors gleam underfoot, slatted with ribbons of sunlight flowing through the louvers over the windows. Although the air is not hot, it is stuffy and close, as though the house has not been open to the breeze for years. It could be the air in the Pyramids, Rafferty thinks. He follows Jeeves like a good soldier into a smaller room with a single easy chair in it, directly in front of a standing sandstone Buddha that is probably a thousand years old.

"Sit here," the man says, stepping aside and indicating the chair, as though he does not expect Rafferty to know what it is.

"What about Madame?" It is the only chair in the room.

"Madame brings her chair with her." Jeeves leaves the room. Outdoors he marches; indoors he glides.

Rafferty takes a good look at the Buddha, at the calm face with its upturned lips and almond eyes, the long earlobes a symbol of spirituality. It is, he realizes, possibly the best Khmer carving he has ever seen, a prize for any museum in the world. On the opposite wall of the room hangs a broken piece of stone, perhaps six feet in length and four feet high, covered from top to bottom with bas-reliefs: the everyday life of the tenth century, not that different in most respects from life in the Cambodian countryside today. People long dead and turned to dust sit at tables and drink, play games, roast a pig over a fire, plant rice, push a wooden cart. Spaced evenly along the stone's ragged edges are the remnants of holes bored to seat the low-yield explosives that were used to break the fragment free. Rafferty cannot look at it without anger, wondering which of Cambodia's extraordinary temples was plundered to decorate this airless room.

The silence is pierced by a thin, insistent squealing from somewhere in the house. Rafferty backs away from the fragment of temple wall and seats himself in the armchair. The sound grows louder, and a woman comes around the corner and into view. She is tiny and angular, her sharp joints folded batlike into a wheelchair that is too big for her. The chair stops in the doorway, without entering the room, and the squealing stops with it.

She regards him without expression. For a moment he actually wonders if she is blind, simply directing her eyes where she knows the armchair will be.

"Madame Wing," he says, just to break the silence.

Her chin comes up a quarter of an inch, and all the planes of her face shift. Her eyes actually register him for the first time. She is thin to the point of being gaunt, the bones of her face as sharp as a cubist painting, the skull slowly surfacing beneath the flesh. The hands grasping the rubber wheels are all knuckles. The skin stretched over them has turned a peculiar bruised-looking purple.

"You came," she says with a hint of satisfaction. The voice, low and rough, scrapes Rafferty's ears. Despite the grandeur of her home, there is nothing refined about the way she sounds. She rolls herself a foot or so into the room. The wheelchair squeals again.

"You should get Jeeves to oil that thing."

She stops the chair's motion and regards him coldly. He has been regarded coldly before—he thinks of himself as an expert at being regarded coldly—but this is something entirely new. She looks at him as he might look at a snake coiled on his pillow. "His name is Pak, and you do not tell me what to do."

"Just a suggestion."

"Not ever," she says. Now that he can see her eyes more clearly, he wishes he could not. They are extraordinarily luminous eyes, but the light in them seems all to be reflected. They have the shine of an animal that can see in the dark. He can see the white all the way around the circles of her irises. "You have questions to ask me before I come to my business. Ask them."

*Her* business? Rafferty doesn't want any part of this woman's business, whatever it is. "You had a maid here," he says. "She may know something about a man I'm trying to find."

She draws herself up in the chair. It makes her seem both larger and heavier, despite her apparent frailty. "What man?"

"An Australian named—"

"No," she says, closing the subject. She sits back. "I know nothing of Australians."

"Actually," he says, "it's the maid you can probably help me with." He holds up the note from Bangkok Domestics. "You wrote a letter about her."

She extends a skeletal hand, a knot of knuckles and rings. It is absolutely still. Whatever health problems she may have, none of them causes her hands to tremble.

Rafferty begins to unfold the letter, but she gives the hand a peremptory shake, and he finds himself getting up to give it to her. "Sit," she says, the moment she has it. She does not look up to see if he does as he is told.

As she unfolds the letter, he gets a chance to look at her without having to face those unsettling eyes. Her hair, still mostly black, is pulled back into a bun so tight it looks like it hurts. The emaciated face is dark but not heavily lined, and Rafferty revises his estimate of her age. At first sight he thought seventy. Now he thinks she could be anywhere from fifty to sixty.

"*This* girl," she says at last, precisely refolding the letter. "She is of no account."

"She may have information I need."

She drops the letter into her lap. "Why should I care?"

"Not a reason in the world. You said you'd see me, so I thought—"

"I do not care what you thought. The girl was dismissed because she could not accept discipline. I have no idea where she went."

"How long did she work here before you fired her?"

The gaze she gives him says the question is an impertinence. "Seven weeks, eight weeks."

"If you fired her, why did you write her a letter of reference?"

"Why does that matter?"

"It's a natural question. The letter got her hired by someone else, and now that person is missing, and so is she."

Something very unpleasant happens to her mouth. "Are you suggesting that this might involve me?"

"It involves you to the extent that it brought me here."

"*I* brought you here," she says imperiously. "Not this stupid girl."

"And if I came, so will others. Who knows who they'll be?"

The hands drop to the chair's wheels as though she intends to leave the room. Instead she moves it forward several inches, squealing her way closer to Rafferty. When she is close enough to make him wish he could move the armchair backward, the squealing stops and the silence of the house once again presses against his ears, like water.

"And who do you think they might be?" she asks.

The intensity of the question unnerves him. "Could be anyone. The police, the Australian embassy."

She nods a tenth of an inch. Her lids drop slightly, hooding the eyes for a merciful moment, and then she turns to the carved stone on the wall. Her gaze travels left to right, like those of someone reading a newspaper. When she has finished, she says, without looking at him, "That's hardly *anyone*." Then she lifts her hands and claps once. The sound is still ringing in Rafferty's ears when Jeeves steps into the doorway.

"This horrible girl," she says, handing him the letter. "Bring the file."

Pak doesn't bow, but it's close. "Yes, Madame Wing." He is gone, and she shifts her eyes to Rafferty. The whites are a nicotine yellow. "The man is probably dead," she says, with no change in tone. "Everybody dies. It is the only thing we have in common."

Not many replies spring to mind. "Why *did* you write the letter?"

"She was making a lot of noise."

"But you knew she wasn't good at her job."

She looks puzzled. "What does that matter to me? At any rate, other people's households are not as disciplined as this one."

"Mine certainly isn't," Rafferty says. He is wondering who she thought might come knocking on her door, who it was who was not included in his "anyone."

She does not respond to his remark. She simply looks at him while she waits for Pak to return. The shining eyes do not shift or waver. Rafferty takes it as long as he can and then studies the bas-reliefs on the opposite wall. Life, action, argument, laughter, war, love. All in silent stone, as silent as this house. He can hear himself swallow.

Rafferty is on the verge of saying something, anything, to break the stillness when Pak appears with a file in his hands. He presents it to Madame Wing two-handed, as though it were on a cushion.

"You have a pencil," she says, opening it. Pak melts away into the hall.

"Tippawan Dangphai," she reads. "Twenty years old. Nickname . . ." She peers at the page as though the type has begun to square-dance.

"Doughnut," Rafferty supplies, pulling out his pad.

She shakes her head at the name. "From Isaan. The town is called—" She lets loose an avalanche of Thai syllables, which Rafferty does not even try to follow. He is not going to Isaan, no matter what. "This was her first position in Bangkok." She turns the page. "She still had mud between her toes," she says.

Rafferty is unsure how to react, but it might have been a joke. "What address did she give you?" Hoping it's not the Bangkok Bank.

"She was staying with a sister in Banglamphoo." She reads an address. "Have you got that?" The question is severe, as though she is daring him to say no.

"And you have no idea where she is now?"

"No." She closes the folder. "Now to my business." She rolls her chair backward and reaches behind her to close the door. The room seems much smaller. "Something has been stolen from me," she says.

Her face is suddenly white and pinched, her voice strangled. Rafferty is looking at pure, distilled rage. "You will find it."

"Afraid not," Rafferty says, getting up. "I'm pretty much booked up."

"When you find it, you will return it to me. You will not look at it."

"I'm not even going to find it."

She says, "Ten thousand dollars."

Rafferty sits. *Miaow's adoption*, he thinks.

"I had a safe buried outside. It had something in it that I need. You will find it, and you will find the man who took it."

"I don't know," Rafferty says, but he does. Ten thousand dollars would feed Rose's hopefuls until they find work. It would pay for Miaow's schooling for two years.

It would fund Hank Morrison.

"You will bring them both to me, the man and the thing he stole."

He takes another look at Madame Wing. The eyes settle it.

"The police—"

"I cannot go to the police. The thing that was stolen—" She hesitates for the first time since they began to talk. "It is private. I cannot trust the police with it."

"Then how do you know you can trust me with it?"

"You are one man," she says.

"And that means?"

She smiles at him. "You have one neck."

"Well, that's that," Rafferty says. He pushes his chair back.

"Twenty thousand."

"Madame Wing," he says, "you just threatened me."

"You can only threaten yourself," she says. "If you bring it to me unopened, you will have no problem."

"And how will you know if I've opened it?"

She puts the gnarled hands in her lap. "Your face will tell me." Then she says, "Twenty-five thousand." She settles back in the chair, completely relaxed.

"I don't work for people who threaten me."

"I did not intend to threaten you." She lowers her head. "Please forgive an old woman who has lost something very precious to her."

"Excuse an American expression," he says, "but you have impressive juju."

The chin comes up. "What is 'juju'?"

"Power. Like a kind of magic."

Madame Wing looks pleased. It is not a change for the better. "I had juju once," she says. "But that was a long time ago. Now I am old and helpless. Someone has taken something from me. He came here at night and stole it. Do you think this should be allowed? Do you think men should be able to steal things from old women who have nothing left but memories?"

Well, put *that* way. "Of course not."

"Thirty thousand dollars," she says. "That's as high as I will go. In cash. Half now and half when you bring me the thing that was stolen and the man who took it."

Fifteen thousand dollars. In advance. "I don't deliver people," Rafferty says.

"You will tell us where he is, then."

"What happens if I can't find it?" He is thinking in terms of being drawn and quartered.

She looks at him with those nocturnal eyes. "Then you do not receive the second payment. But I am certain you will find it."

"I have conditions."

She settles in. They've moved to negotiation. "They are?"

"If I find it, whatever it is, I'll return it to you or to whomever you choose, in a public place at a time I designate. You'll pay me then and there. I won't deliver the man to you unless I know you're not going to harm him. And, finally, I'll give it a week."

"Two."

Now it is his turn to wait her out. He forces himself to hold her gaze.

"One, then," she says. "I have conditions in return. I will require a daily report, on the telephone, since you are not comfortable coming here." Something about a light-year away from amusement flickers in her eyes. "The report will be detailed. You will tell me where you have gone, what you have done, whom you have spoken with. You will tell no one else at all, no one in the world, what you are doing for me. Is this acceptable?"

"I guess," Rafferty says. "Sure. It's acceptable."

"Good." She claps her hands again, three times, and the door to the room opens. Pak floats in, carrying a fat envelope, which he presents to Rafferty.

"Fifteen thousand dollars," Madame Wing says. "All hundreds, no counterfeits. You may examine them."

"Is there a price written on my forehead?" Rafferty asks. "What if I had stopped at twenty?"

She smiles, a new vista of awfulness. Her teeth are long and crooked, the color of mustard. "I would have clapped twice."

"What am I looking for?"

"An envelope. Not like the one I just gave you—bigger. Heavy brown paper, tied with twine. There is nothing written on it, but three old stamps have been pasted in the upper right corner. You are not to open it."

"You've made that point quite eloquently."

"The man you are looking for is a Cambodian. He will be between forty and fifty-five. He may be physically damaged in some way. He will be in Bangkok."

"How do you know all that?"

The eyes come up, hooded. "It is my life. Who would know better?"

"The safe was in that hole out there?"

She nods.

"How did he get in? You have guards—"

"He came on the river, at night. The guard at the dock was caught unawares and struck with a stone. The fool. He is no longer here, of course."

"I'll need to talk to him."

"He can tell you nothing. We talked to him for several hours. He did not see the man."

"I still want to talk to him."

She seems to be considering alternatives, but then she nods. "Pak will give you the address when you leave."

"How long ago did this happen?"

"Two nights."

"Were you here?"

"If I had been here," she says venomously, leaning toward him, "he would be dead."

Well, okay. "Two nights ago. Cambodian. How do you know he'll stay in Bangkok?"

She folds the gnarled hands, calm again, and looks at the carved stone. "He has to stay here," she says. "The robbery is only the beginning. He means to destroy me."

# PART II

# PLaCING the NaIL

## 17

## Horse Noodles and Horse Soup

Rafferty shouts directly into Arthit's ear, "Any Cambodians?" The drunk American sitting beside the music
system has found the volume control again, and walls are •
vibrating with the rhythm section of Bachman-Turner Overdrive, so
rarely heard and so little missed in the West.

The bar is jammed with male tourists drawn by the nearby sexual
supermarket called Nana Plaza. The tourists wear either T-shirts and
tropical shorts or the kind of la-la safari clothes Rafferty found in
Claus Ulrich's apartment. The Thais are dressed like human beings.
Arthit's brown policeman's uniform—stretched tight over the hard,
round belly he has recently stopped trying to fight—is conspicuous.
In one hand Arthit has a glass of Mekhong whiskey and in the other
a cigarette, a sure sign that something is wrong. As always lately,
Rafferty is afraid to ask what it is, afraid to blunder into the private
space Arthit and Noi have created around her illness, the disease that
has set slow fire to her nervous system.

"Cambodian safecrackers?" Arthit takes a handful of peanuts

and throws them in the general direction of his mouth. Most of them bounce off his shoulders and hit the floor. A miniature lunarscape of peanuts surrounds his feet. "Not that spring to mind. Cambos stick to the less-skilled trades. Smash-and-grab, mugging, chain snatching, picking pockets, hits. Especially hits. We've got truckloads of Cambodian hit men. There's a whole generation who got handed a gun at the age of ten or eleven and never really put it down."

"The killer kids." The executioners of the Khmer Rouge, back in the days of terror.

"Meanest little bastards in the world," Arthit says, chewing the one or two peanuts that somehow got into his mouth. "Conscience trained right out of them, kill without giving it a thought. Not children by now, of course."

"In their late thirties or thereabouts, right?"

"Say they were ten, and the Khmer Rouge got hold of them in, oh, 1975. That'd put them in their late thirties, early forties. But, you know, when they were thirteen or fourteen, they were beating people to death with hoes. And, of course, it was all over by 1979." In 1979 the Vietnamese, to their everlasting credit, invaded Pol Pot's Cambodia.

"Hold it." Rafferty pushes himself off the stool and crosses the room to the music system, which he turns down. The drunk American gives him a disbelieving glare and starts to get up from his chair, but Rafferty puts a hand on his shoulder and shoves him back into it. He points at Arthit, sitting mildly at the bar, and says, "Noise police." The American takes a long, sullen look at Arthit's uniform and buries his nose in his beer.

"So they're mostly thug-level," Rafferty continues in a normal tone of voice as he settles onto his stool.

"Not much opportunity for anything else," Arthit says. "Khmer Rouge closed every school in the country. For five years people raised rice and died. Most higher-level crooks are educated crooks."

"So who are the best safecrackers in Bangkok?"

"Oh, for heaven's sake." Arthit stubs out his cigarette as though he carries a grudge against it. "I'm a cop, not a database."

"But you can find out, can't you?"

Arthit lights up again and breathes directly through the cigarette. "This have to do with Claus Ulrich?"

"Maybe. I don't know yet."

"Spoken like a real policeman." Smoke plumes from his broad nostrils, making him look like a cartoon bull. "I know I asked you to do this, Poke, but don't get yourself into trouble, especially not with the Cambos. We'd hate to see anything happen to you."

"We" are he and Noi. He drains his Mekhong, puts the glass down on the bar sharply enough to draw a startled glance from the barmaid, and holds up two fingers for a double. She takes his glass and hurriedly begins to fill it. Arthit looks through her, at something private and internal.

"You got the pictures of my colleagues? The ones I faxed?" he asks.

The mention of the two resentful cops causes Rafferty more discomfort than he cares to show to Arthit. "Got them. Nice-looking guys, too. Do you know a Madame Wing?"

Arthit turns to him slowly, eyebrows high. "Rich lady, a general's widow, I think. One of the best old houses in the city. Guards, antiques, broken glass on the walls. Doesn't get out much. Nobody else gets in much."

"What kind of name is Wing?"

"I don't know. Sounds Chinese."

"If she's Chinese," Rafferty says, "she sure doesn't look it."

"So?" Arthit says. "Maybe Wing is her husband's name. Maybe she's an Eskimo. She keeps to herself." He drinks again and pitches some more peanuts at his face.

"Why don't you just drop them directly on the floor?" Rafferty asks. "Think of all the energy you'd save, not opening and closing your mouth like that."

"Don't be silly." Arthit pretends to chew, even though he missed. "Eating them this way demonstrates the kind of savoir faire that keeps me from being dreary. If you're finished with safecrackers and rich widows, what about Mr. Ulrich?"

"Nothing," Rafferty says. "That's the trouble. He's lived in Bangkok for twenty years or thereabouts, and he hasn't left a footprint anywhere. He's a cutout. The blank space is the only reason you know it was ever there."

Arthit puts a hand flat on the bar, fingers spread, as though he is confirming its solidity. "You're not looking in the right place. Nobody lives anywhere for twenty years without leaving a footprint. Friends, enemies, business associates, lovers, acquaintances, victims." A different finger taps the bar with each item on the list. "People do things to, or for, other people. That's the way it works."

"Well, I hope there's space in the new edition of *Believe It or Not*." Rafferty waves for a beer.

"You're drinking too much," Arthit says, hoisting his glass.

"Arthit," Rafferty says, putting a hand on his friend's arm and interrupting the drink's arc. "Thank you for calling Hank. I think he can help."

"Money," Arthit says, rubbing his fingers together. "Once Hank knows everything's okay, it's just a matter of money. Apply the grease to the wheel and the wheel will turn." He drinks.

"That's pretty much what Hank said."

Arthit starts to say something, thinks better of it, and then looks down at the bar. "Do you need a loan?"

"I'm fine, Arthit. And bless you for asking."

"If I'm offering you a loan," Arthit says, sitting back and resting his hands on his knees, "it probably *is* time to go home."

"How's Noi?"

"Life stinks," Arthit says. "But we'll get through it." He picks up the half-full glass and regards it. "Until we don't."


**THE BOY COMES** to the dinner table wearing one of Miaow's blouses. With a little electric jolt, Rafferty realizes that Superman has tried to dress up for dinner.

"Don't you look nice," Rose says brightly. The boy gives her the flicker of a smile and sits. He looks down at himself and plucks the fabric between thumb and forefinger. He draws two deep breaths. "Not pink," he says.

Rafferty forces himself to get into the act. "What did you do today?"

"Went to school," Miaow says into the silence. The boy is twisting the fabric of the blouse with great concentration. Rafferty is folding his fingers into his palms, one by one, beneath the table, counting as he waits.

"The street," the boy finally says, without lifting his face to them. Miaow's head swivels toward him, fast.

"*Okay*," Rafferty says. "Well. Hey." He can hardly believe that the boy spoke, and he does not feel equal to the challenge of a reply. He rejects three questions as too probing before settling on one. "Are you hungry?"

"Yes," the boy whispers. He is still studying the blouse as though he expects it to change color at any moment.

"Me, too," Rafferty says, feeling like the idiot father in a sitcom. "I could eat a horse. What have we got, Rose?"

"Horse," Rose says promptly. "Horse noodles and horse soup." The boy's eyes flick to her. "And horse ice cream for dessert."

Miaow laughs first, so loudly that Rafferty almost misses it when the boy joins in. Suddenly Rafferty is laughing, too, while Rose beams at all of them.

"I want the tail," Miaow says happily.

The boy says something to his blouse.

"What?" Rose asks. "What did you say?"

"The whinny," the boy says without looking up. "Give Miaow the whinny."

Miaow swats him on the head, and the boy ducks and raises a clenched fist. Rafferty freezes, but all the boy does is knock lightly on Miaow's part, three times. Rose laughs deep from her belly and begins to dish out the food. Both Miaow and the boy are blushing fiercely.

"Tomorrow," Rafferty says, eyeing the blouse, "let's go get you some shirts."

———

"HE'LL BE FINE," Rose says from the floor.

"What do we call him?" Rafferty asks. He has claimed the couch, since Rose doesn't want it. "I can't bring myself to say, 'Hi, Superman.'"

"Don't call him anything. Let him name himself. Maybe he wants to be Boo again." She yawns, making it look elegant. "He may get angry sometimes. It's not easy to quit using *yaa baa*."

"Did you use it?"

"I never smoked it, but I ate the pills like popcorn when I started dancing. The tourists choose the girls who look like they're having a good time. There are only so many times you can smile while you're dancing to 'American Pie.'"

"But you stopped taking it."

"I got tall," she says. "I grew three inches in my first year. Everybody else in the bar was short, so I stood out. I could just hang on to the pole and do the mermaid." She moves her hips back and forth in a sinuous curve, like someone swimming the butterfly stroke. "I stopped taking the pills, but it wasn't easy."

There is a silence. "You've been wonderful," he says into it.

Rose gives him a half smile. "I have always been wonderful. You just didn't notice."

"About the boy, I mean."

"He's a child," she says. "He can't help who he is. Maybe he's bad, you know? Some people are born bad. But probably something happened to him that killed part of who he was and left something else behind. Don't look at me like that," she says, although Poke is not aware that his expression has changed. "It happens to some people. Maybe it's something from their karma that suddenly falls on them, like a stone, and everything breaks. They still look the same, they still need to eat and sleep, but whatever their lives were tied to—whatever it was that gave them the chance to be good—it's gone. They lose their weight, they drift. They're empty. Sometimes they do terrible things to try to feel something again. They're like hungry ghosts."

"There seem to be a lot of those these days."

"There are always a lot of them. But a hungry ghost can sometimes be put to rest. And these people, maybe, can be given something new to tie themselves to. Maybe they can even remember who they used to be. If you can do that, you will make merit. It'll help you when you're reborn." She works a cigarette out of the tiny opening in the pack and lights it. When she looks up at him, she is smiling. "I have often thought you would be reborn as a goat."

"I've always figured I'd come back as a midsize sedan."

"You will be something that can be eaten," she says complacently.

"As long as the cook isn't English," Rafferty says.

She fiddles with the tip of the cigarette, touching it to the ashtray's edge to brush off the ash. Bangkok glitters through the sliding glass door behind her. "I am very pleased with what Mr. Morrison said about Miaow."

"Me, too."

"You will be a real family. That will be wonderful for her."

"Not quite." Rafferty swallows. He seems to have an orange lodged in his throat.

"Not quite what?"

"Not quite a real family." Heat creeps up his cheeks.

Rose's head comes up. She is as close to looking surprised as Rafferty has ever seen her. His face is burning and he can feel the pulse at his wrists. The moment stretches out, infinite to Rafferty, until she breaks it by stubbing her half-smoked cigarette into the ashtray.

"The boy will be wanting the couch," she says. "We should give him the room."

"You bet," Rafferty says, leaping up. "Poor kid's probably exhausted."

"And you need to sleep." She tosses her things into the big purse, as always in no discernible order.

"Not so's you'd notice," Rafferty says.

Her hands are still, but her face is downturned, shrouded by the fall of dark hair. "I heard what you said."

Sweat prickles Rafferty's underarms. "Thank God. I'm not sure I could say it twice."

"It needs a lot of thought."

"Are you saying you'll actually think about it?"

She raises her face to his, her features as smooth as stone. "How could I not honor such a suggestion with thought?"

"Hah," Rafferty says, unable to think of a single word in any language. Eventually he dredges one up. "So."

"So," Rose echoes.

"So I guess the important thing is not to . . . you know, change things while we think about it. Not break our usual routines."

"Such as what?"

"Such as we go into the other room and you get to start out on top. As long as it doesn't lead to any misunderstanding about who's really in charge."

She rises to her full six feet, lifting the purse as effortlessly as if it contained a quart of soap foam. "I think we both understand very clearly who's in charge," she says. She takes two steps toward him and brushes her lips against his, then turns to the bedroom door. With her hand on the knob, she turns back to him. "Definitely a goat," she says.

## 18

# Several Inventive Ways to Say "Stupid"

When Rafferty comes out of his bedroom, much earlier than usual, the boy is asleep on the couch. He has taken off Miaow's blouse and folded it so neatly it looks as if it just came from the laundry. He lies flat on his back with one knee upraised. The sheet he covered himself with is crumpled on the floor. Above the blue sweatpants, his hipbones protrude like parentheses, below a chest as narrow as a bird's. The ribs are clearly visible, the hollows between them as insubstantial as finger smudges on a wall. His belly practically touches his backbone. In the soft curves beneath his eyes, circles of weariness shade into the transparent gray of an old, old bruise. He has thrown one arm out, stretched above his head, and Rafferty is transfixed by the pale vulnerability of the boy's underarm.

He moans, and Rafferty tiptoes into the kitchen. The last thing they need right now is for Superman to wake up and find Rafferty looming over him.

He makes a cup of Nescafé. He loathes Nescafé, but it is quieter than grinding beans. Nescafé marks one of the visible points of difference between his world and Rose's. Twenty or so years ago, in one of the first invasions by a Western brand name, Nescafé shouldered aside the much more labor-intensive processes by which the Thais made some of the world's best coffee, replacing taste with convenience. One of the reasons Rafferty hates it is that it is a clear line of demarcation between the relatively leisurely pace of life in traditional Thailand and the hurry-up influence of the West. But Rose grew up with Nescafé. She adores it, hot, tepid, or iced. He has seen her eat a teaspoon of it, dry. No matter how many pounds of expensive beans Rafferty buys, she always makes sure there is a jar of Nescafé in his kitchen.

He takes a sip, rolls it around in his mouth like red wine, and revises his opinion. It's an interesting drink if you don't insist that it's coffee. An unpretentious little variant, he writes in his head, with no affectations of breeding. With his second cup, he silently toasts Rose, out cold in the other room. His mouth still feels warm where he kissed her as she slept.

The previous evening, after Rose dropped off to sleep, he had enjoyed a pleasant quarter of an hour studying her face, the upper lip with its upward curve in the center, the smooth swell of cheekbones, the slight flaring of her nostrils as she breathed. Then he had forced himself from the bed and spent a much less pleasant thirty minutes packing the small duffel bag he lifts now, with a grunt of effort. It contains his tools for the day: a slim jim for breaking in to cars, a crowbar, a heavy hammer, and a pair of bolt cutters. He doesn't know what he'll need the bolt cutters for, but it seems like the right kind of thing to take along. He closes the door softly and then remembers to double-lock it.

Thirty minutes later the bejeweled density of Ulrich's apartment overwhelms him once again. With the drapes drawn to shut out the heat, it has a tacky kind of Aladdin's-cave glamour, all shining surfaces and hidden treasures. He turns on the air con, listening to it kick reluctantly into gear. The air that flows from the vents smells like rust.

Lights on in every room, Rafferty decides to start with the furniture.

On his hands and knees, he checks the underside of each table in the living room. Nothing taped to them. Nothing in the curved drawers of the antique dresser except household clutter: keys, batteries, cleaning cloths, candles, paper napkins, old warranties and brochures—the kind of stuff nobody knows where to put. He pockets the keys, and then he pulls the drawers all the way out and looks beneath them. Nothing.

The cushions slide off the sofa easily, releasing a whiff of damp foam rubber. He puts them on the floor and presses down with his hands. Nothing hidden inside, or at least nothing bulky. He unzips the covers and peers between the fabric and the foam. No papers, no deeds, no travel documents. No million baht in hoarded cash.

After a strenuous hour, Rafferty has to admit that the living room is a wash, but at least the apartment is cooling down.

If the kitchen holds any secrets, they are culinary. Uncle Claus has amassed an impressive library of cookbooks, most of them well used if the punctuation marks of food are any indication. The size of his shirts becomes less of a puzzle. The cupboards set a whole new standard for predictability: The herb jars contain herbs, the tea bags contain tea, and the sugar jar contains sugar, which is being mined by a railroad train of ants. The freezer is empty except for some shrunken ice cubes. There are no diamonds hidden in a glass of water. There is no uranium hidden in a wine bottle, although some bottles of very good wine rest on their sides beneath the counter.

Two rooms down, nothing revealed.

On entering the bedroom, one burning question takes possession of him: How could anyone *sleep* here? The sheer volume of dust all the room's junk would gather oppresses him. If he were to sleep in this bed with its scarlet canopies, he thinks, he would have dreams that would give night sweats to a concentration-camp guard.

How had Claus Ulrich lived here? He was a big man. Didn't he feel cramped? There must have been times when he just felt like stepping out onto the balcony and screaming, "Give me space!"

Rafferty starts by stripping the bed. He lets the covers fall where they will; he's given up on the idea of preserving order. When he gets to the sheets, he learns that Uncle Claus is losing his hair. On and around the pillow are enough fine brown hairs to choke a small cat.

There is nothing else on the bed, nothing under the mattress.

Nothing beneath the bed, except for a single soiled sock, nothing taped to the underside of the box spring. The bureau drawers contain what men's bureau drawers everywhere contain: socks—including the laundered match to the dirty one under the bed—underwear, T-shirts, playing cards, male junk.

Except for a small collection of excellent, if flashy, watches: a gold Rolex, a Cartier tank watch, also gold, a platinum Ebel. Add them to the Vacheron Constantin on the table, they probably cost fifty thousand dollars or so. Would Uncle Claus have left these—so expensive, so portable—behind?

And did the maid leave before Uncle Claus did? Did they leave together? Is that why the sheets haven't been changed? Is that why the sock is still under the bed? Is that why the watches haven't been stolen? *The maid*, he thinks again. *The maid*.

He gives up on the bedroom as too depressing to survive for another minute and goes into the maid's room. It's been wiped as clean as a murder scene. Every drawer is empty. Every surface gleams. The light switches have been scrubbed. The scouring powder on the floor scrapes underfoot. So she cleaned her room but not Uncle Claus's. And she cleaned it very thoroughly.

The maid's small, perfunctory bathroom is more interesting. It, too, has been scoured like a hospital operating room, but the chipped and aging grout between the floor tiles nearest to the tub is stained unevenly, an unnerving rust brown. The concentration is heaviest near the tub, but there are also outlying islands of brown that probably represent splash patterns. Clarissa's apprehensive face comes into his mind, and he finds himself dreading what the stains might mean to her. He spends a few sober moments on his hands and knees, looking for anything he might have missed, and finds nothing but a rusted bobby pin wedged in the drain of the sink. He'll tell Arthit about the stains and get him to have them analyzed.

That leaves the room he actually came to search. He goes into the living room, retrieves the heavy bag, and lugs it into the office.

He sees it the moment he comes through the door, as obvious as a missing wall: All of Uncle Claus's software is gone.

The plastic storage tower that held the CD-ROMs is empty. The CD-ROM drive on the computer lolls open like a tongue. It, too, is empty.

"You dumb shit," Rafferty says aloud. He hadn't even thought about loading any of the disks into the computer, checking to see what they really were. He'd looked at the bootleg packages labeled WINDOWS, MICROSOFT WORD, EXCEL, PHOTOSHOP, and taken them at face value. There had been twenty to twenty-five disks. There may have been DVDs. Enough to hold gigabytes of information.

Uncle Claus's footprints.

For a long minute, Rafferty just stands there excoriating himself. He comes up with several inventive ways to say "stupid" and actually thinks about writing one of them down for future use in a book. Instead he tries each of the keys from the living room on the filing cabinet and then gives up and opens the bag he has toted with him.

Two strokes of the hammer drive the edge of the crowbar into the space around the upper drawer, and three good, back-wrenching pulls buckle the drawer in a rewarding fashion. It juts forward like a broken jaw. It is still locked, but he has opened it far enough to work it back and forth until the tongue of the latch comes free from the frame and the top drawer slides open.

As long as he is at it, he pulls it all the way out, giving him access to the middle drawer without having to destroy it. He sits on the floor with the top drawer in front of him and begins to go through it.

More bills and receipts, going further back than the ones in the desk drawer. He puts them in the duffel bag for review later. A photocopy of an international driver's license with Uncle Claus peering uncomfortably from the upper right. More unused letterhead for AT Enterprises. Two big manila envelopes. One of them contains Claus Ulrich's passport.

The other contains Claus Ulrich's passport.

Rafferty sits back on his heels. Both are current. One of them is for Claus Pieter Ulrich, a citizen of Australia. The other is for Claus David Ulrich, a citizen of Great Britain. Uncle Claus is two people.

At the rear of the drawer is a sheaf of American Express Travelers Cheques, already signed and countersigned. Anyone could cash them.

They are in hundred-dollar denominations, banded together in groups of twenty-five. There are eight bundles in all, two hundred individual checks. Twenty thousand dollars, as negotiable as greenbacks.

The heart medicine, the wristwatches, the money. The stains on the bathroom floor.

Wherever Uncle Claus has gone, he didn't choose to go there. In all likelihood, he didn't go anywhere.

Rafferty feels pity rise up in him. Ulrich was a man alone, a man like Rafferty before he met Miaow and Rose, a man trying to make whatever he could of the life he had been given. He was a man who had loved his niece.

The second drawer of the cabinet beckons, but that involves getting up, and for the moment Rafferty doesn't feel equal to the exertion. *Take three or four deep, slow breaths, put down the hands, push yourself upright,* he thinks as he does it. On his feet, he rests a hand on top of the cabinet to steady himself and peers down into the second drawer.

What he sees makes his day even darker.

The drawer is completely full, jammed to overflowing with videotapes in lurid packages. Reluctantly he reaches down, fishes one out. CINEMAGIC, it says on the spine. On the cover is a young Japanese woman, bound hand and foot with leather restraints. A ball gag has been forced into her mouth, secured by a strap that has been fastened tightly around her head. There are tear tracks down her face.

"Oh, hell," Rafferty says despairingly. Clarissa Ulrich's face swims up at him again. The apartment suddenly feels cold.

He pulls out four more: appalling variations on the theme of female torment and humiliation, all Japanese. The tapes look professionally packaged, meticulously lighted, produced with Japanese attention to detail: pain for sale.

The drawer is packed to the top rim. There must be fifty of the things.

He grabs a couple of cassettes at random and goes back into the one room he gave up on, the bedroom.

He finds the television in a teak armoire. The cassette player is below it. He turns it on, inserts the tape, and presses "play."

The tape has not been rewound. He hears the whistle and crack of a whip, followed by a muffled scream, before the picture tube brightens.

The young woman has been twisted forward and tied across the frame of a high-backed chair. She is naked. The man behind her lifts a knotted cat-o'-nine-tails and brings it down over her bare back with all his strength. The sound goes through Rafferty like a gunshot. There is no question about the damage being done. Her back begins to bleed.

Rafferty turns it off.

He wants to vomit.

The next tape is worse.

By the time he is back in the office, trying to pop the third drawer of the cabinet, he has managed to put it into some sort of skewed perspective. The man has an obsession with pornography of a particularly vile kind. After all, Rafferty tells himself, these aren't snuff films, just an appalling subgenre of professionally produced porn: Yes, it really hurts, but the participants are consenting adults. Japan being Japan, some of the actresses probably have fan clubs. Ulrich is undoubtedly long overdue for some serious psychiatry, but it doesn't necessarily mean that his fantasies carry over into his actions. One thing Rafferty has learned in Bangkok is that it's impossible to guess at anyone's sexual proclivities. Claus Ulrich, for all his disgusting peccadilloes, for all the violence he is doing to his own spirit, is probably harmless to others.

Then he works the third drawer open and sees the leather straps. The chains. The whips. The gags. The devices designed for insertion into a human body. His hand comes back involuntarily; he can't bring himself to touch them. He sits there, looking at this tangle of pathology and seeing disappointed eyes and a mass of flyaway hair, and he wishes he'd never heard of Clarissa Ulrich.

"GOOD LORD," SAYS the woman at the door. "What a decorative mix *you* are. Thai and what?"

"Irish," Rafferty says. "Filipino on my mother's side."

"How nice. Like a new cocktail or something. You know, you're always thinking Cointreau and *what*? But then you taste it, and it works." The woman is an American, in her early thirties, halfway through Hofstedler's Tragic Decade of Decline, and wearing it well. Her light hair is twisted into a loose knot, held in place by three or four random pins. She came to the door in a robe with a cup of coffee in her hand, reminding Rafferty how early it is. She has a comfortable, slept-in look.

Rafferty is too drained to force a reply. "Have you seen anyone go in and out of the apartment next door in the past few days?"

"My, my," she says. "A mystery."

"It's important. I wouldn't bother you otherwise."

"'Bother' is kind of a strong word." She leans forward slightly, and Rafferty catches a whiff of fresh bread. "Only the maid," she says. "Porkpie or whatever her name is."

"Doughnut."

"She came out of the apartment yesterday, about four. I practically bumped into her, right where you're standing. She was carrying a shopping bag full of stuff."

"This one," Rafferty says, showing her Doughnut's photograph. He forces a smile. The corners of his mouth feel like they weigh ten pounds each.

"That's her. First time anybody's been next door in weeks."

He leans forward to rest his weight against the wall. It brings him closer to her, but she does not step back. "When Mr. Ulrich was here, were you aware of anything strange going on?"

"Claus? Strange?" She blows on the surface of her coffee, and he can feel the breeze of her breath. "Claus Ulrich is the most boring man alive." She looks down at the coffee and back up at him. The gaze has a sleepy force behind it.

"People coming and going?"

"Only the maid. Popcorn." Her eyes crinkle just enough to register amusement, not enough to emphasize wrinkles. "Why do they call themselves things like that?"

"Because they can."

"I had a maid once, called herself Pun. This was a girl who wouldn't recognize a joke if it wore a T-shirt with JOKE written on it." She moves toward him very slightly and slips a finger through the hooked handle of the coffee cup. "So. As someone who's almost, sort of, halfway, second cousin to the Thais, what's your theory?"

This woman is not going to be rushed. "Thais have very long names. If they didn't choose short ones, they'd never get to the verb in a sentence. 'Pun' is short for 'Apple.' Girls like the word, and they choose the last syllable, but they can't produce the terminal *l*, so it comes out 'pun' instead of 'pl.' Okay?"

"Okay. A little silly, but okay. Your turn for a question."

"Were you ever in Claus's apartment?"

She looks past him for a moment, deciding whether to answer. "Once. I needed to borrow something."

"What?"

"Oh, who knows? A cup of sugar, isn't that what it always is?"

"Just curious?"

A sleepy shrug. "This is Bangkok. Boring or not, he could have been anybody over there, just on the other side of the wall. A random silly-nickname generator. Someone who performed human sacrifices."

"But he wasn't."

"Not with that furniture. If he was sacrificing anything, it was taste." She hoists the coffee cup and extends it in his direction. She gives him a lopsided grin. "You want some? I just made a pot." She blows coffee steam toward him. "It's hot."

"No, thanks," Rafferty says virtuously. "I have to get home to my kids."

Her eyes slide over his face. "It's hot every morning," she says.

**RAFFERTY DOESN'T EVEN** make it to the elevator. Instead he drops his bag to the floor and leans heavily against the wall of the corridor.

A wealthy foreigner, committed to a particularly furtive form of sexual expression, settles in Bangkok. So there, at any rate, is the reason for the lack of footprints Rafferty's been wondering about. For good reason the man keeps to himself, except for his erotic partners, who are undoubtedly professionals. He wouldn't find many volunteers. The Thais, overwhelmingly, take a simpler view of sex. They see it as fun.

Then the man disappears. Normally, you'd look for one of the partners. Maybe things went too far; maybe he violated the limits they set before they started the session. Rafferty doesn't know much about S&M, but he's certain that some sort of pact exists between the participants, some line that won't be crossed, some magic word to bring things to a halt. There has to be something to protect the one who is being done *to*.

Perhaps Claus Ulrich crossed the line, turned a deaf ear to the word. The session stopped being sex, however ritualized and however twisted, and became real violence. The partner became a victim. Maybe there was an injury, maybe worse. A grudge was held. The partner, or her pimp, or her friend, came back to settle things. Uncle Claus either fled—in a great hurry, obviously—or was taken. Or was killed there, leaving stains in the grouting of the maid's bathroom.

So what about the maid?

A young girl with modest skills, just down from the thin-dirt farms of Isaan. She gets one job in Bangkok, lasts for a few weeks— long enough to wheedle a reference—and quits. She immediately turns up at Claus Ulrich's, and he hires her because his maid of ten years or so has just been killed in a motorbike accident. Eight weeks later Claus Ulrich is missing.

A thought straightens Rafferty's spine. A really convenient time for the first maid to die, wasn't it?

He goes back and knocks again.

"You came back." She has brushed her hair so it falls to her shoulders. Rafferty liked it better the other way. She has put the coffee down somewhere, and her arms are crossed loosely across her chest.

"I was thinking about the maid," he says.

Something like disappointment flickers in her face, but she masters it and gives him a perfunctory smile. "What about her?"

"The first one, actually. I was thinking it must have upset Claus when she was killed. She'd worked for him for so long." He knows the answer from her face, even before he stops speaking.

"Noot? Killed? Don't be silly, she quit. Drove Claus up the wall, too. He offered her the world to stay, but she'd had enough. I mean, you've seen the place. Can you imagine cleaning all that every day?"

"Do you have any idea where she is?"

"This very moment, you mean?"

The question surprises him. "If you know."

"Sure. She's down in Mr. Choy's apartment—he's a Chinese gentleman? He's in latex. I mean as a business, not a wardrobe. It's 4-B. She's been working there since the day she left Claus."

The door to 4-B opens a few inches. The woman peering through the crack is small, wiry, and dark-skinned, probably in her early fifties. "Mr. Choy not here," she says.

"But you're Noot," Rafferty says.

She nods, her eyes fixed on him. He is willing to bet she has her foot against the door.

"I was just wondering why you quit your job working for Mr. Ulrich, upstairs."

Noot ponders the question for a moment and then gives him the brilliant smile Thais often use as a polite way of saying no.

She closes the door in his face and throws the lock.

## 19

## A Reassuringly Detail-Free Wall

The portable generator, which has been chugging away with a noise like a tethered helicopter, is suddenly silenced. The lights that were wheeled in blink out and give way to early daylight, dim enough in this narrow alley to turn the thing on the ground into something more reassuring, say, a bundle of rags. Sodden, muddy, twisted into heavy ropes and tossed onto the filthy concrete, disquietingly stained and reeking of urine. Just a bundle of rags, nothing worth a second look.

But Rafferty's first look, while the lights were still shining, was enough. It was enough to send him four or five automatic steps backward, enough to make him glad he had not eaten breakfast. The others in the alley, the ones who got here before the sun rose, are not so squeamish. Three uniformed policemen on hands and knees crawl around the bundle of rags, searching for bits of a puzzle that are too small to see from a standing position. One of them is studying the face that emerges from the bundle.

Dead, wet, and dirty, the man still looks surprised.

Rafferty has to turn away. Death and destruction have been too much in his thoughts lately. Faced with the real thing, in the cooling flesh, he wants to gag.

It is only 8:25 A.M.

"You'd better tell me about it, Poke." Arthit, wrapped in a long overcoat against what he probably thinks is an early-morning chill, has a paper cup half full of coffee in his hand and a stiffness in his face warning Rafferty that their personal relationship is not at the forefront of the conversation.

"Tell you about what? You called me here, remember?"

"The safecracker. Why were you asking about Cambodian safecrackers?

Rafferty takes another step away from the body and lets his eyes wander over the blank wall opposite, a reassuringly detail-free wall without a single window. "Well, Arthit, since you ask so nicely, what level of detail would you prefer?"

"Microscopic."

So he tells it all, beginning with the maid's reference from Madame Wing, right through the hole in the lawn and the empty safe and the missing whatever-it-is.

Arthit listens without so much as a nod. "And where have you gotten on it?"

"Nowhere. I was going to start after lunch."

"Well, you've just started." He lifts the cup in the direction of the body. "Meet Tam. Not Cambodian, but definitely a safecracker. One of our best." Arthit's tone is regretful. "Wasted here, really. Had the kind of skills he could have put to better use in Monaco or Switzerland, someplace with really serious safes."

"But she said he was a Cambodian."

"He was probably hired by a Cambodian."

"You think he's my guy. Why?"

Arthit dips a hand into one of the pockets on his outsize coat and comes up with a steamed dumpling wrapped in paper. "Hold this," he says, thrusting the coffee at Rafferty and peeling the paper back from the bun. When his mouth is full, he says, "See any mud in this alley?"

Rafferty doesn't have to look. "Only on the—on *him*, I mean."

"Very good." He repossesses the coffee. "So, to pursue the Socratic method further, where is Madame Wing's house?"

"The river, Arthit. And don't ask me what you get all over you when you dig a hole near the river."

"Wouldn't dream of it. If Socrates had known where to stop, he might not have had to drink that hemlock cocktail."

Four policemen come into the alley with a stretcher. Beyond them Rafferty can see the crowd of onlookers, see the dirt on their faces and the rips in their clothing. Klong Toey is Bangkok's port and one of its worst slums. The people craning their necks are poor and probably hungry, but they are alive.

"So this guy is muddy—"

"Tam." Arthit puts some force into the syllable, and Rafferty knows he is being reminded that the man had a name and people who called him by it. A life.

"Tam, then. Is that all? He's muddy?"

"No. He was working for a Cambodian. We've already interviewed his wife. One of the first cops on the scene recognized him, and somebody went to talk to her. Tam told her all about the assignment. He was going to make her rich. Thought he was going after the Saudi crown jewels."

The crook's chimera. "Can I talk to her?"

"Under normal circumstances you'd enjoy it. I'm told she's ravishing, real trip-over-the-curb material. I don't know why I never expect crooks to have good marriages, but she's devastated by Tam's death. So, sure, you can talk to her, but I don't know what you'll get. She never saw the guy." He wads up the paper wrapping from his bun and shoves it into his pocket. When his hand comes out, it has another bun in it.

"Anyway," Rafferty says, "what's the point?" He sees the second half of Madame Wing's fee fade into the distance. "I haven't got a job anymore."

One of Arthit's eyebrows comes up. Rafferty secretly thinks he practices in front of a mirror. "No? Why not?"

"There's been a murder, hasn't there? It's police business now."

Slowly and deliberately, giving it all his attention, Arthit nods. "Well, as you say, it's a murder. You'd certainly think the police would leap into it, wouldn't you?" He glances around the alley, at the stretcher bearers and the knot of cops gathered near the body. "Why don't you just step around the corner with me while we explore this further?"

Rafferty follows him out of the alley into the sunlight, and they take up a spot against the wall of a building that leans alarmingly toward the street. A thousand-watt glare from Arthit pushes the spectators back a respectful distance.

"Moving right along," Arthit says, picking absently at the paper on the second bun. "Maybe you can suggest to me the names of two or three police officers who would like to be the ones to find the link between the murder of a safecracker in Klong Toey and the rich and connected Madame Wing. Maybe you can even help us frame the delicate language in which we make the connection. Especially since it was almost certainly Madame Wing's own employees who carted the dead man away and dropped him in that alley, making her an accessory after the fact, at the very least."

"Why do you think that?"

"Our Cambodian obviously got what he wanted, because you've been hired to find it. Not much point in hauling a body across town when you're carrying something valuable. On the other hand, for a rich woman with a secret, Tam's body would be like hanging out a flag." He looks down at the bun and extends it toward Rafferty, who shakes his head, unable even to look at it.

"So if you can accomplish all that in a way that will advance the career of the lucky officer, as opposed to bringing it to a decisive halt, then you can definitely help me."

"You have a problem," Rafferty says sympathetically.

"I'm not so sure I'm the one with the problem," Arthit says, looking directly at him.

"Aahhh." Rafferty waves the bun away again, and this time Arthit draws his hand back. "So what you're suggesting—"

"I'm not suggesting anything," Arthit says. "I asked you for information, and you provided it to me. I, being possessed of a free and open nature, then shared some information with you. Upon reflection I've decided that the murder of a professional safecracker, however beautiful his widow, does not warrant an extensive commitment of police resources in these troubled times. We have the public safety to consider. We ate a fine breakfast, or at least I did, and we went our separate ways."

Rafferty needs to be sure. "You to police work, and I—"

"To do whatever you wish," Arthit says blandly. "Earning favors, perhaps."

There is a bustle of motion from the alley, and the stretcher bearers come out, their shoulders hunched against Tam's weight. One well-shaped hand hangs over the edge of the stretcher, bouncing with the bearers' steps. To Rafferty it looks like someone gesturing for attention.

"Got it," he says.

"Of course, given my concern for your safety," Arthit continues, "I will expect us to keep each other informed." He pushes himself away from the wall, slopping some coffee on the sidewalk. The coat looks very heavy on his shoulders.

Rafferty follows him to a waiting car, and Arthit slides in.

"Arthit."

His tone stops Arthit from closing the door. Arthit waits, taking a first bite out of the bun.

"I think there's blood in Claus Ulrich's apartment." He tells Arthit about the stains in the bathroom and then about the videotapes and the missing software.

Arthit's mouth twists as though the pork in the bun has gone bad. "You can buy the porn on Silom Road at night, right on the sidewalk. Illegal, of course, but so is half of everything people do in Bangkok. The stains are heaviest near the tub?"

"A few splashes farther out."

"Probably didn't cut himself shaving, then," Arthit says, and it suddenly occurs to Rafferty that his friend has seen many more bodies than he has. After peering beneath the polite veil of the social fabric long enough to write three books on the underbelly of Asia, Rafferty thought he had become hardened, but compared to Arthit he's a fluffy animal toy.

"It might not be blood," he says without much conviction.

"I'll get someone to check it. If we've got two dead people, you were probably right. There's a connection, and it's the maid."

"She does keep popping up."

"You're pretty good at this," Arthit says around a fresh mouthful of steamed bun.

"I don't know. I do know, though, that I'm not good enough at it to chow down while a dead man's lying six feet away. Gnawing away at that bun like that."

"Life goes on," Arthit says. He leans back against the seat and closes his eyes for a moment. "If there's one thing we've learned, all of us, in the last few weeks, it's that life goes on."

## 20

## Nothing Bad Will Ever Happen to Them

Tam's widow, Mai, is one of the most beautiful human beings Rafferty has ever seen. Her eyes—puffy now from crying—tilt upward above an extraordinary pair of cheekbones, smooth enough to have been shaped by running water. Her nose is delicate and finely formed. She wears her black hair chopped short to reveal a swan's neck and collarbones as refined as an angel's wings. The tilted eyes are a light brown with flecks of gold buried in them. She is the color of weak tea, with a hint of heat just beneath the skin.

"He was the sweetest man," she is saying. "He even loved my mother." The memory of his sweetness brings the tissue back up to her eyes. The floor of the neat little apartment, a concrete cube as brightly decorated as a doll's house, is littered with tight balls of Kleenex from the box on the table in front of her. The woman has been crying for hours.

"I'm sure your mother—" Rafferty begins helplessly, demonstrating all his skill with female grief.

"My mother is a dragon," Mai says. She wads up the latest Kleenex and throws it at the carpet. It rolls up against the television, and Rafferty sees, on top of the big, old-fashioned set, a color photo of her and Tam, framed in teak. They look young and radiant and secure. The world has just been waiting for their arrival to make it complete. Nothing bad will ever happen to them.

Through the window above the TV set, Rafferty can see the sloping corrugated-iron roofs that keep the rain out of a rambling cluster of squatters' shacks. The building in which Mai lived with Tam is a modest apartment house in aggressively unadorned Soviet cement, obviously put up ten or twelve years ago in the expectation that the neighborhood would somehow mysteriously gentrify. The occupants of the shacks, only a couple of dilapidated miles from the alley where Tam's body was found, have apparently not gotten the news, or perhaps the general or police captain who owns the land is waiting for a better offer before he calls in the bulldozers. The result is a representative square of the Bangkok patchwork: poverty, aspiration, and affluence, jammed side by side, kings next to deuces as though a pack of cards has been thrown into the air. Beyond the shimmering iron of the shacks' roofs, the broad brown ribbon of the Chao Phraya winds its way to the Gulf of Thailand.

"I *told* him to stop," Mai says. She puts a hand on top of her head, as though to keep it from exploding. "I told him to do something else. I begged him, told him we didn't need the money, it wasn't worth the risk. He was so proud of what he could do. 'Top two percent,' he kept saying. 'It's all in the fingers.' Like he was a magician or a violin player, not a criminal." She stops, blinks. "The Cambodian man was a violin player."

"He was?"

"Well, he said he was. That's one reason Tam took the job." She dabs at her eyes with the back of her hand. "Tam said they were both *artists.*"

"Did you tell that to the police?"

"I didn't believe it," she says. "I asked how he could play the violin with a hand that looked like a spider. Tam said he didn't even have fingernails. They'd been pulled out."

"Oh," Rafferty says, putting his own hands in his pockets.

"And his name, that was a lie, too. *Chon.* It's not even a real name. It sounds like something somebody made up who had heard Thai spoken on the radio." She has worked a fingernail into the seam of the couch cushion and is slowly slitting it open. A little bubble of foam rubber bulges out. "A violin player with a fake name. The Saudi *jewels.* How could he have been so stupid?" A sob catches in her throat and sends her free hand to the Kleenex box, but the one on top has failed to pop up, and she takes both hands and rips the box in half. Tissues flutter to the floor. "What am I going to *do?*"

"Do you—" He stops. "Do you have any money?" A fat fold of Madame Wing's fills his pocket.

The sob tails off into a sniffle, followed by a dab at her nose. "Money's no problem. I have a job. I've always had a job. What I don't have is a husband."

"Are there . . . um, are there children?"

"He was my child." She begins to weep again. "He was my child and my father and my husband. He *surrounded* me. I don't even know where I am anymore." She grabs a handful of tissues angrily and scrubs her face with them, then balls them up and tosses the wad, hard, at the window. "Are you married?"

"Not at the moment."

"Then you don't know anything," she says, not unkindly.

"I know I can find the man who did this to you."

She looks up at him, evaluating the worth of the offer. He has not taken a chair, although she offered him one. It seems impolite to do anything but stand in the presence of such sorrow. So there he stands, shambling and ill at ease, the duffel bag full of burglar tools sitting heavily at his feet like a sleeping dog. "It won't bring him back."

"No. Nothing will bring him back."

She exhales for what seems like a minute, so long that Rafferty half expects her to disappear. "Why bother, then?"

"Because it's wrong," Rafferty says. "Because he killed your husband and made you unhappy. Because somebody should make him pay."

She shrugs, and it seems to require all her energy. "He'll pay for it in a future life."

"I'd like to make him pay for it in this one. While I'm around to watch."

"Why? What does this mean to you? We don't even know you."

"I'm tired of death. And I'm sick of deaths no one can do anything about. Nobody can take revenge on a wave. It's just a wave. Even if you wanted to for some reason, you couldn't find the water that formed the wave, could you? It's disappeared back into the ocean. But a man isn't a wave." He realizes he has raised his voice and makes a conscious effort to lower it. "You can find a man."

She is still, toying with a new Kleenex. Then, slowly, she tears it in half. "If you say so."

"Do you know where they met?"

"In jail. Tam did something stupid, and they put him in jail. They were in the same cell just before he was released."

"How many in the cell?"

"I don't know. Eight, ten. What difference does it make?"

Rafferty pulls out his notebook. "It could give me a name. When was he in jail? When did he get out? Which jail?"

She closes her eyes, sealing herself off while she works through some private process. Then she sighs deeply and gets up from the couch.

"I'll get my journal," she says.

## 21

## Toadface and Skeletor

angkok, planted atop a river plain, is as flat as a piece of paper. The city slopes up slightly on either side of the river, but the incline is barely visible. The effluent-choked canals that once earned the city a highly misleading reputation as the Venice of the East flow between banks that rarely rise by more than three or four feet over the course of miles. Many of them now are too polluted and stinking to be navigated by anyone except locals in rough wooden flatboats.

In many great cities, the rich live within sight of water or on the heights. In Bangkok the water is likely to have wooden shacks built out over it with holes cut in the floor to serve as toilets. A river view here may mean nothing more than an extra ration of rats. Lacking hills to build upon, the city's rich create height with skyscrapers and then move to the top. An economic map of Bangkok would have to be constructed in three dimensions, with much of the money floating well above ground level.

On his way home from Mai's apartment near Klong Toey, Rafferty's *tuk-tuk* passes through a misassembled jigsaw puzzle of urban landscapes: one-story cement shops with sliding iron grilles across the front, the chromium glitter of nightlife areas, the occasional placid narrow street lined by trees and the high walls of the wealthy, much like those surrounding Madame Wing. Bright new steel-and-glass apartment houses share a property line with tacked-together wooden slums that look like collections of driftwood. Silom Boulevard, off of which he lives, is a hybrid: a Western-style shopping area packed with restaurants, modern department stores, and expensive boutiques, all reached by threading one's way through the little vendors' booths that crowd the sidewalk, most numerous where Patpong empties into Silom like, Rose might say, a poisoned river. A sharp left takes Rafferty onto his own *soi,* an aggregate of still-inexpensive apartment houses of which his own, the Lovely Arms, is perhaps the least expensive. But it's the closest thing to a home he's had in the years he's spent chasing himself across Asia to write his books and articles.

It's probably because he *does* feel so at home there that he fails at first to notice the two men in the corridor when he gets off the elevator. He's pulled out his keys before he registers their presence, and the day suddenly goes very sour indeed.

Two policemen, poised to knock two doors up from his, have turned to look at him. Rafferty tucks his keys into his fist so the points protrude, an impromptu pass at brass knuckles. He gets a better hold on the duffel bag, its weight suddenly reassuring rather than bothersome. There's no way around the fact that these are the cops whose faces and information Arthit faxed him.

"You," one of them says loudly. He's short and fat, with a toad-like face that reminds Rafferty of an Olmec head. Rafferty has no idea what the other one looks like, because he can't get his eyes any higher than the automatic the man has drawn.

"I *told* you it was 8-A," says the man with the automatic.

As the two of them approach, Rafferty spreads his feet slightly and bends his knees just enough to give him some spring, then wraps his hand more tightly around the duffel's handle. The one with the gun in his hand is thinner than his partner and dirtier, with a face so gaunt it makes Rafferty think of the cartoon character Skeletor. His uniform is smudged with dirt and spots of something that could be blood, hot sauce, or both.

"We're coming in," says the toad-faced one.

"Actually," Rafferty says, "you're not."

"We're the police," says the toad-faced one. "We'll go wherever we like."

Rafferty keeps his eyes on the gun. "At the moment you're just a couple of shitheads who are off the clock," he says. His voice is surprisingly steady. "And if anything happens to me, your own department will be up your assholes before you've had time to loosen your belts."

"Be nice." The fat one with the toad face is doing all the talking. "Just give us the money she gave you and we'll go away."

"She didn't give me any money."

Skeletor's gun comes up to focus its single eye on Rafferty's forehead, but the toad-faced man pushes it down. "Think about it," he says. He gestures at the door to Rafferty's apartment. "And remember that we know where you live. We know where your cop friend lives, too. Remember, his wife can't move very fast."

Rafferty feels the heat rise to the back of his neck. He lowers the duffel slowly to the floor, reaches into his shirt pocket, and pulls out his notebook, too angry to be frightened. He flips through it until he finds the page he wants and then turns it toward them. "Your home addresses," he says. "So if you invite me over, I won't need a map."

Toadface studies it, although Rafferty doubts he can read the English in which he wrote the information. The numbers should be clear, though. "Is this supposed to frighten us?"

"Of course not," Rafferty says. "But you should know that if anything happens to Noi, or if you try something with me that doesn't actually kill me, I'll be coming after you one at a time."

"This is a mistake," Toadface says. "A very big mistake."

"I'm good at mistakes." Rafferty closes the notebook. "I've made lots of them." He crosses the hall and pushes the button for the elevator. The doors open instantly. Rafferty says, "Get out of here."

Toadface takes a step toward him but stops dead when Rafferty's neighbor, Mrs. Pongsiri, bustles out of the elevator, a sheaf of papers tucked under one arm. Seeing the three of them, she halts, an expectant half smile on her face. Then she takes the papers out from under her arm and fans herself with them. "You have friends among the police, Mr. Rafferty?"

"Yes and no," Rafferty says. "These gentlemen are in the wrong apartment house."

"Bangkok can be so confusing," Mrs. Pongsiri says, her eyes bright with interest. The three men stand there as she watches them, still as figures in a display window. "Well," she says, "I wish you luck finding the right place." And she edges past Skeletor and down to the door of her apartment.

When they hear the lock thrown behind her, Toadface says, "You're the one who needs luck."

"All the time you had," Rafferty says, "and that's the best you could come up with? Bet you think of something better tonight." He presses the elevator button once more.

They stare at him so long that the doors open and close again, and Rafferty feels sweat prickling his scalp. Then the toad-faced one takes the other by the elbow and leads him to the elevator. The doors open, and the two of them step inside. As the doors slide closed, the one with the gun lifts it again and points it at Rafferty.

"Bang," he says. The doors close.

Rafferty lets the wall support him, not trusting his knees. His breath is shallow. It feels as if a steel band has been tightened around his chest. Not until it has eased, not until he knows he can walk a straight line, does he relax his grip on the keys, pick up the duffel, and go to the door.

He undoes the locks quietly and slowly pushes the door open, not wanting to awake the boy if he is still asleep.

The door bumps against something that should not be there, and Rafferty looks up to find himself being regarded by a dozen pairs of eyes. A hand comes around the door and pulls it the rest of the way open. A young woman had been sitting with her back to it.

From the couch Rose says, "Come in, we're almost finished."

"In many ways," says one of the others.

"Passing through," Rafferty says. Suddenly his voice is shaky. "I'll be out of the way in a minute." The women are regarding him with undisguised curiosity. So this is the *farang* Rose snagged, the brass ring so many of them hoped for when they worked the bars. One of them catches his eye, and, despite the fear, he feels himself blush. "Hello, Jit," he says.

"I forgot," Rose says, enjoying his embarrassment. "You know Jit already."

"Pretty well, too," Jit says in Thai. The women laugh.

"You forget me?" It is the woman who had been sitting against the door. Her face is scrubbed, unadorned by the garish makeup of the stage, and her age shows; she is ten years older than most of the other women in the room. It takes a moment for Rafferty to place her. "Fon," he says, wishing he were anywhere else in the world. "How are you?"

"Poor," Fon says, earning another laugh.

"Come the rest of the way in," Rose says. "For all I know, you'll recognize every one of them."

He closes the door behind him and forces a smile in the general direction of the group, scanning for, and failing to find, another familiar face. They sit easily on the floor in jeans and T-shirts. The air is thick with cigarette smoke. Looking more closely at them, he sees strain in some of their faces even though they laughed so easily. He knows that laughter does not necessarily mean that Thai women are happy. He has often seen them literally laugh while they're crying.

"We needed to talk," Rose says. Then she smiles and says, "And I thought it would give you a chance to see some of your girlfriends."

"Always a pleasure," he says, feeling like a minor character in a bad English play. "Where's the boy?"

"He said he was going out. Just out. But he drank a cup of coffee with me before he left."

"He's too young for coffee." The response is automatic, something his mother would have said.

"Coffee's pretty mild compared to some of the things he's already done. But the point was that he sat with me for half an hour. He even talked a little."

"About what?" Rafferty makes an erasing gesture, palms out. "Sorry. Later. Go ahead with your meeting."

"Come back soon, Poke," Fon says breathily in bar-girl English. "Miss you too much." Another wave of laughter.

In the bedroom Rafferty exhales heavily several times. Then he pulls the tools out of the bag, stops, asks himself what he is doing, and puts them in again. Normally they're stored in the kitchen, and it would take a fire to drive him back into the living room. He hoists the bag again and totes it to the closet, moving some clothes aside so he can put it behind them. *Where Ulrich's suitcase was,* he thinks. He rearranges the clothes to mask the bag and goes to the bed.

Built into the headboard, behind a sliding panel, is a small safe. He pulls a chain from around his neck, noticing that it is slick with his sweat. Dangling beside the Buddhist amulet Rose gave him for protection is a key. The safe's hinges squeal, so he opens the door slowly. Inside he sees the thick envelope containing most of Madame Wing's advance, converted into smaller bills, and an oil-stained cloth wrapped around something heavy. He removes the bundle and grasps one corner of the cloth, letting it unspool over the bed. The gun that hits the mattress is a Glock nine-millimeter, blue-black, with the forward-leaning lines that make so many guns look as if they are designed by small boys. Two spare magazines, already loaded, also tumble to the bed.

With a murder—perhaps two—plus a couple of renegade cops at the door, the gun seems like a sensible precaution. He is buffing it with the cloth when the door opens and Rose comes in with several sheets of paper in her hand. The sight of the gun stops her.

"Nothing to worry about," he says. He checks the safety and slips the gun into his pants.

"Of course not. We've got the boy on our hands, you're doing errands for the police, and now you're carrying a gun. And my business is falling apart. Other than that, everything's fine."

"What do you mean, the business is falling apart?"

She waves the hand with the papers in it in the direction of the living room. "Three of them are going back to the bars. One of them is Fon."

"Fon's too old to work the bars."

"Not the blow-job bars," Rose says. "They might not take her if she was dead, but as it is, she'll get work fast enough."

"This is about money." The blow-job bars are the most dismal of Bangkok's commercial sex venues, tiny, filthy holes where customers belly up to a bar with a curtain beneath it and a woman parts the curtain, kneels, and services them as they drink. He does not want to think of Fon in one of them.

"It's always money," she says. "Why do you think they work the bars in the first place?"

"Come on. All the guys hear the same stories: Mama's sick, Papa drinks, little brother has to go to school, the buffalo skinned its knee. You know as well as I do, half the time Mama spends the money on a color television set or a year-round Christmas tree because she likes the way it sparkles."

Rose's chin comes up. "So?"

"Not exactly life-and-death issues."

"To these girls Mama's color TV is the least they owe her. It's about family, Poke, not that I expect a *farang* to understand that. If a child can give something to the family, that makes merit, and it also makes Mama happy."

"So we're in a world where this makes sense somehow: blow jobs for a permanent Christmas tree."

She waves a hand as though she could scatter the words across the room. "It's not really about money. It's about failure," she says. "My failure. I can't get them work."

His irritation dissipates instantly. "Rose," he says.

She balls her fists, crumpling the papers. "Don't comfort me. I really couldn't stand to be comforted right now."

"You're just getting started," he says. "You can't expect it to work right away."

"They're *hungry*, Poke. And, worse than that, their families are hungry. Whether it's for food or a new leather couch. Say whatever you want, you have to remember there *are* brothers and sisters who need to go to school. Those kids are real. Papa's drinking problems are real. And in the meantime these girls are hungry."

"They can't work if they're hungry," Rafferty says. "How many of them are out there?"

"Thirteen. If Fon and the others haven't already left."

"Three hundred dollars each," Rafferty says, reaching for the wad in his pocket. "That's thirty-nine hundred dollars. Tell them it's an advance." He begins to count out the bills.

She watches him count for a moment, her eyes on the bills. "This money," she says. "This is why you're carrying the gun?"

"Mmmm. Yes and no."

She takes a step back. "Well, keep it. I mean, give it back. Put the gun away and let's just go back to the way we were."

"There," he says, finishing the count. "I can't give it back. The woman who's paying me is not someone I care to disappoint."

"Well, I don't want it. They'll never be able to repay it."

"Yes, they will. They'll be working in two weeks, most of them."

"Poke, you're not listening. I can't do this."

"That's part two of my plan," he says. "The advances are part one. Part two is to get you a partner."

"A partner." Her tone is flat, and she locks eyes with him, leans toward him, and takes a quick sniff. "Have you been drinking?"

"I'll explain it all later." He indicates the papers under her arm. "What are those?"

She has forgotten she had them. "They were on the floor. The paper tray on your fax is still broken."

"I'm going to ask the boy to try to fix it. Hank Morrison says the trick is to make them feel useful."

She hands him the papers, and he gives her the money. She glances down at it and shakes her head, and then she throws her arms around his neck and kisses him on the mouth. When she leaves the room, she is almost running.

Rafferty slips the remaining money back into his pocket. It is significantly slimmer than before. If his spontaneously generated plan for the partnership doesn't work out, Rose's business could leave him completely broke. He licks his lips, a little nervously, and tastes her lipstick, and the anxiety eases.

The faxed pages are from Arthit. The first is a Bangkok Police Department cover sheet addressed to LIEUTENANT PHILIP RAFFERTY, RCMP, probably using Poke's full name and giving him this entirely spurious rank for the benefit of the fax operators who actually sent the message. He scans the pages quickly and then reads them carefully.

Claus Ulrich lacks a police record and has never been mentioned prominently in the Bangkok newspapers. On the other hand, Immigration definitely records two Claus Ulrichs of the same age but with different middle names, one Australian and one British. Both passports have been scanned by Immigration multiple times over the past dozen years or so, coming from points of origin scattered around Southeast Asia—the Philippines, Laos, Cambodia. The most recent record of the British Claus Ulrich is a departure. Two weeks and three days later, the Australian Claus Ulrich reentered the country and has not left it. That was five months ago.

"So he's here," Rafferty says. "One way or another."

There is less hard data on Madame Wing—to whom Arthit gives the cryptic designation "unknown Chinese woman"—but the single paragraph is rich in implication. She had purchased the house in 1980 for the baht equivalent of $325,000, a tidy sum, especially since it was made in a single cash payment. The walls and gate—and, for all Rafferty knows, a moat full of crocodiles—were added almost immediately afterward with the appropriate permits, a euphemism for bribes. No police record, but several complaints of servant abuse have gone uninvestigated and eventually been dismissed. The source of her income is listed as "unknown."

It doesn't take much reading between the lines to see that Madame Wing is among the privileged few, those who are immune from police interference for anything short of mass murder. Arthit won't even put her name in a fax. Complaints are filed, but no one follows up. Either it's the weight of sheer wealth or she's connected. Or—third choice—she's paying through the nose.

If she were paying the police for immunity, though, wouldn't she have turned to them when her safe was burgled? Why involve a foreigner who doesn't even have official status in a matter that is apparently so important? Did the safe contain something even her protectors can't know about—something that would make the price of their services prohibitive?

That would have to be something, he thinks, with massive juju.

He draws a deep breath, wipes away the last of Rose's lipstick and licks it off his finger, and leaves the apartment to go terrorize somebody.

22

## I Go Where I Am Kicked

The bang the door makes when it strikes the wall is louder than the cannon in the *1812 Overture* and has even more impact than Rafferty had meant it to have. Its effect on the woman behind the desk at Bangkok Domestics is galvanic: She goes two feet straight into the air and lands standing. Now she waits, with her fingertips over her mouth and her back to the filing cabinet, keeping the desk between them.

"You lied to me." Rafferty grabs the desk by its edge and tilts it a couple of feet, spilling papers to the floor. He lets it drop with a loud thump that prompts a second instant levitation, this one backward as well as vertical, driving her all the way to the wall. "You told me Ulrich's maid was killed. That's *bullshit.*" The woman's eyes slide past him to the wall and search it frantically. "She's working downstairs. Probably a job you got her. You want to tell me why?"

A little defensive tug downward on the jacket of today's suit, a yellow the color of congealing butter. Her eyes drop to the spill of papers at her feet. "You have no right to speak to me like this."

Rafferty takes a folder from the desk. "Claus Ulrich is probably *dead,* do you realize that?" He slaps the folder onto the desk on the word "dead." "He's not some impoverished laborer, he's a *rich foreigner.*" Slap, slap. The muscles around her eyes bunch up each time, and her fingernails pick at a peel of skin on her lower lip. "He has an *embassy,* for Christ's sake." Slap. "What do you think they're going to do? How high do you think the cops are going to jump when they get the call? You think they're going to question you politely, maybe over dinner or something? What kind of trouble do you want to be in anyway?"

"I . . . I just," she says. She is watching the folder, hoping it stays in the air. "My business . . ."

"Your business is the least of your worries. This girl was stalking this man, and you knew it. And you *helped her get to him.*" Slap, slap. "Then, when I asked you what happened, you lied to me. Where do you think all this is going?"

"I . . . I don't know."

"Here's where it's going." He shifts to the left, as though he is going to come around the desk, and she dodges away. "If you don't want to see a picture of yourself wearing handcuffs in the *Bangkok Post,* you'll tell me what happened, and you'll do it right now."

Her fingers come away from her mouth to tug at a large button. She licks her lower lip where she picked at it. "She . . . ah, she paid me."

"Yeah, yeah, I already figured that out. Give me details."

Now the fingers have hold of each other, twisting as though she is trying to find new ways to bend them. "It's just that we—I mean, I—"

"She came in here a few months ago. With money." Another slap of the file.

"A lot." She swallows.

"What's a lot?"

The hand comes up with all the fingers spread to indicate five. "Five thousand dollars. Two hundred thousand baht."

Rafferty sits in the visitor's chair. "Sit down. *Now.* Keep talking."

The woman feels her way to her chair as though the room is

pitch-black and lowers herself into it very carefully. "She . . . well, she said she wanted to work for Mr. Ulrich. I explained that we don't do things that way. She said procedures could always be changed, and she began to put money on my desk."

"And?"

"And she . . . she said she was sure I could find a way. She had all this money in her lap, and she kept putting bundles of it on the desk."

"Business any good?" Rafferty asks, looking up at the photos of happier times.

"Terrible. We've been on the verge of closing forever. The economic crisis, and there are so *many* agencies now. Every month we say we can't go on, and every month we do anyway."

"So you needed the money," Rafferty says.

"Desperately. We still do."

"And here she was," he offers, "loaded with cash."

The blink he gets could be gratitude or just relief. "I told her she needed a domestic reference to get a job with Mr. Ulrich. I couldn't give her a false reference, because Mr. Ulrich was sure to check, do you see? And while she was sitting here, Madame—you know, *Madame*—called and said she needed somebody strong and stupid. Those were her exact words, somebody strong and stupid. And I said I might have the person for her, and I covered the phone and told the girl what Madame . . . uh, Madame Wing had said, and she said, 'I can be strong and stupid.' I told Madame Wing I had a girl for her, but she demanded to see three or four. I was trying to talk her out of it when the girl passed me a note she had written. It said, 'Tell her you're so certain this is the right girl that you won't even charge a fee.'"

"And Madame Wing went for it."

A nod. "She worked there a few weeks and got herself fired, which is easy to do in that house, and then she actually stood up to her and got herself a reference. I couldn't believe it," she says, shaking her head. "*Nobody* stands up to Madame Wing."

"But there was still Ulrich's first maid. Noot."

The woman shakes her head, in the negative this time. "Doughnut had already talked to Noot; that was how she got my name. Noot had wanted to quit for a long time. Mr. Ulrich is apparently . . . ah, peculiar. So I got Noot the job with Mr. Choy, who was happy to steal her. Mr. Ulrich is not well liked in that apartment house."

"Just so we're clear," Rafferty says, "you are in this up to your neck."

A wince, as though he had swung at her. "So after Noot quit, I told Mr. Ulrich the same thing I told Madame Wing. I'd send him one girl, and if he took her, there'd be no fee."

"Do you know where she is now?"

Her head is going side to side before he finishes the question. "No idea."

"Didn't you wonder why she was so eager? Didn't it worry you? She had obviously been watching the man, or she wouldn't have known who Noot was. She could have been up to anything."

"She's just a girl."

"So was Lizzie Borden. There had to be some kind of connection between them."

The woman looks down at her desk, possibly trying to work out who Lizzie Borden is. "I asked her about that. She said that Mr. Ulrich would understand it when it was time."

"I wonder if he did." Rafferty pulls the guest chair closer to the desk. The woman flinches. "Anything more? Anything at all?"

"No. That's all. That's everything."

"Okay, phase two." Rafferty takes out his notepad and writes a phone number on it and then slides it over to her. Then he reaches in his pocket and begins to peel off hundred-dollar bills. Her eyes are glued to the money.

"This is twenty-five hundred dollars," he says, dropping it on the desk. "You earn it by calling the woman whose number I've just given you and saying you'll get some of her girls work. There are thirteen of them. You get an additional twenty-five hundred dollars when they're all employed and you've worked out an arrangement with this woman so that she gets part of the employment fee and she can send you more girls in the future. She's going to be your main supplier."

"But the girls. Who are they? Where do they come from?"

"They've all been working in the hospitality industry. And they'll all have a reference. From me."

"I don't know," says the woman, her eyes still on the money.

"You know the old saying about the carrot and the stick?"

"An English expression. Yes."

"This is the carrot," he says, flicking the stack of money. "The stick is a real motherfucker."

**"ARTHIT?" RAFFERTY SAYS** into the cell phone as the *tuk-tuk* plods along Sukhumvit Road, congested as always. Robed Arabs glide along the sidewalk, so they must be near the Grace Hotel. "Tam's wife says the Cambodian was a violinist."

"So find him. Maybe you can get him to play 'Melancholy Baby.'"

"I need the names of the people who were in the jail cell with Tam. Surely only one or two of them were Cambodian. Names, mug shots, booking info."

"Fax it to the RCMP?" Arthit says in a much brisker tone. Someone has obviously come into his office.

"Attention of Lieutenant Rafferty."

"I think that should be 'Leftenant,'" Arthit says.

"The missing maid was a setup. Paid her way into Madame Wing's employ."

"Do you think she was involved in what happened at Klong Toey?"

"I don't know. *Somebody* was inside, because they knew where to dig for the safe. One neat hole, no false starts. I'm pretty sure it was the guard, though. I don't think Doughnut was there long enough to know anything about it. Also, anyone can see that the guard had something to do with it."

"Why is that?"

"One look will tell you. There's no way this happened the way he said it did."

"Noted, Leftenant." Arthit hangs up.

The *tuk-tuk* makes a two-wheeled left into a little *soi* and slows as Rafferty reads addresses. The building he wants is featureless gray concrete, six stories high, with windows no wider than archery slits. Washing hangs on poles protruding from the windows. One look tells Rafferty the building will not have an elevator. "Wait here," he says to the *tuk-tuk* driver, handing him two hundred baht. "I'll be out in ten, fifteen minutes."

The fired guard lives on the fifth floor. Rafferty is winded and sweating when he comes out of the stairwell into a narrow, uncarpeted hallway featuring grime-gray walls patterned with the prints of dirty hands. A single fluorescent bulb sheds light the color of skim milk. The veins on the back of Rafferty's hand stand out like a map of blue highways as he knocks on the door.

Nothing. He knocks, waits some more. No response, no sound from inside. No telltale darkening of the peephole positioned at eye level. He knocks a third time, just for form's sake, and then tears a page from his notebook and writes on it in a child's Thai, handwriting that Miaow would ridicule. What he writes is, *"Talk to me or I'll tell Madame Wing about the rock."* He puts his name and phone number at the bottom of the page, folds it in half, and slips it between the door and the jamb, at eye level so it will be seen by anyone who opens the door.

The *tuk-tuk* is at the curb, the driver asleep at the wheel. The shift in the vehicle's weight as Rafferty climbs in wakes him, and he blinks a couple of times and says, "Where?"

Rafferty pages through his notebook, finds the record of his talk with Madame Wing. There it is: the maid's sister's address, for whatever it's worth. But it's too late to go all the way to Banglamphoo. "Silom," Rafferty says. "Around Soi 8."

"You go all over," the driver observes conversationally, pulling away from the curb.

"I am a stone," Rafferty says mystically. "I go where I am kicked." He settles back. "Right now I'm being kicked to a department store."

## 23

## We Don't Need Any Stinking Police

In his entire life, Rafferty has never met anyone who hates shopping for clothes more than he does.

Until now.

The boy barely allows himself to be dragged from store to store. The sullen face has returned, accompanied by a stubborn silence. He seems completely indifferent to the clothing Rafferty suggests, and he nods assent only when the shirt being considered is blue.

"You really are being a pain in the ass," Rafferty says in English as the third shirt is bagged. The saleswoman looks at him, startled. "Not you," Rafferty says. "Junior here."

"Boys," the saleswoman says with the ancient wisdom of her sex. "Boys no like clothes."

"I know I didn't," Rafferty says.

"Your son?" the saleswoman asks. Rafferty is surprised by how fast the boy's eyes come up to his face.

"Sort of." The boy's eyes slip away.

"Handsome boy," she says, handing him the bag.

"He's handsome when he smiles," Rafferty says. "He smiles on Tuesdays." He gives the bag to Superman. "Come on, handsome."

On the escalator down, he turns to the boy and says, in Thai, "Enough for one day?"

The boy looks away. Then he nods.

"Enough for me, too. I hate to shop."

The boy says, "But—" and then thinks better of it.

"Look, it's dark outside," Rafferty says, gesturing toward the department store's street-level picture window. Cars with their headlights on dawdle on the boulevard, waiting for the light to change. It seems to be drizzling. "You want something to eat?"

A shake of the head. The boy's eyes are everywhere except on Rafferty.

"Well, fine," Rafferty says, suppressing a surge of irritation. "We'll go home, sit around, and chat some more."

A fine mist is falling, crowding the pedestrians on the sidewalk up against the buildings. Rafferty heads for the less sparsely populated curb so they can walk faster. The boy follows silently in his wake. Within a minute they are both wet.

Rafferty stops and puts out a hand. The boy looks at it and then slowly gives him the bag with the new shirts in it, as though he does not expect to get it back. Rafferty folds it over and hands it back. "Let's keep them dry," he says. The boy nods grudgingly and tucks the folded bag beneath his arm.

A scuffling sound behind him, and something hits Rafferty in the back, low down and hard. His knees buckle. His attention is devoted to the effort to stay on his feet when he sees a boy, a little bigger than Superman, snatch the bag and take off. Superman is after him in an instant. Rafferty follows in their wake, chasing children for the second time in four days.

The running boys turn into a narrow unlighted *soi*, one Rafferty has not explored. There is a corner five or ten yards up, and the boys round it to the right. There is a sudden grunt—Superman?—and Rafferty accelerates around the corner.

They are on him at once.

Several pairs of hands grab him and pull him further up the *soi*, away from the lights and crowds of Silom. He kicks out at one of them, and hands grasp the upraised leg and hoist it skyward, and then the other leg is seized and he is grasped beneath the arms. They carry him, kicking and struggling, into the darkness. Someone slams a fist against the side of his head, and Rafferty sees an interesting pattern of lights, and then the fist lands again, more heavily this time, and it also strikes the arm supporting his left shoulder, and the arm releases him, and he begins to fall.

*Four of them*, he thinks before he hits the pavement. Through the legs surrounding him, he sees a blue streak: Superman running out of the *soi*, the recovered shopping bag flapping behind him.

They begin to kick him.

They kick his ribs, his hips, his legs, working methodically and deliberately. There seems to be no anger in it, but they're putting their backs into it. He can hear them grunt with the effort. One man lifts a heavy shoe and tries to grind it down onto Rafferty's face, but Rafferty grabs it and twists it, and the man goes down, and Rafferty rolls through the empty space the man vacated and scrambles shakily to his feet. All four are in front of him. His head is spinning and his legs are rubber, but he backs quickly away until his back comes to rest against a wall. Without a word the men form a semicircle, cutting off access to Silom, and one of them, the one farthest to the right, reaches into his back pocket and comes out with a sock. The toe, filled with sand or buckshot, bulges heavily.

Not more than a minute has passed. No one has spoken a word. Panting, Rafferty searches their faces: not Arthit's renegade cops.

Two men feint to Rafferty's left, and as he turns to meet them the sock whistles past his ear and hits his right shoulder with the weight of a falling safe. His right side goes numb and he sags, knowing with the instinctive wisdom of bone and muscle that one more of those will finish him. As the men come at him from the right, he shifts his weight, leans against the wall, and plants a foot squarely between the legs of the shortest and nearest of them. The sap streaks down again, and Rafferty twists away, feeling the wind from the sap against his face as the short man he kicked drops, gasping, to the concrete.

It is important to keep the wall at his back. Everything he knows in the world has come down to this. It is important to keep the wall at his back.

The downed man is vomiting, knees curled against his chest. The one he had been paired with feints again on Rafferty's left, but this time Rafferty absorbs the punch, moving away to soften the impact and turning to try to intercept the sap. It lands on his forearm with a detonation of pain that threatens broken bones, and the man steps back and raises it again. Rafferty knows he cannot lift his right arm. The other men are coming in on him.

A blur at the corner of his vision. Before Rafferty can even question it, it turns into the boy, hanging with both hands onto the arm with the upraised sap, sinking his teeth through the shirt and into the muscle of the shoulder. The man with the sap grunts in surprise and then screams hoarsely as the boy's teeth break the skin and invade the muscle and bones beneath. He flails wildly, staggering back and trying to shake the boy loose, but every move he makes increases the depth of the boy's bite.

The other two men are staring in disbelief as Rafferty cups his left hand and brings the palm up with all his strength beneath the nose of the one nearest him, trying to drive the cartilage all the way back into the brain. The man makes a strangled, snuffling sound and staggers back, and Rafferty goes for the fourth man's eyes.

The man is ready for him. He brings his fist down on Rafferty's right shoulder, where the sap hit it, and Rafferty goes to his knees in a shallow puddle of water. The man above him draws back his leg for a kick, and Superman is suddenly clinging to it, pulling it back, bringing the man down facefirst. Rafferty rolls and snaps an elbow into the man's ear with all his remaining strength, and the man's head rolls around loosely. Suddenly Rafferty remembers the gun beneath his shirt, and he starts to reach for it.

"That's enough," a voice says in Thai.

Rafferty looks up to see the shortest of the men, the one he kicked.

He has an automatic in his hand, pointed at Rafferty's head. His other hand cups his testicles.

The man with the sap helps up the one Rafferty just elbow-punched. He seems only half conscious, his head hanging forward and his eyes unfocused. The one whom Rafferty tried to kill with the blow to the nose is bleeding heavily down his shirt and pants. Superman is sprawled on the concrete, facedown.

The man with the gun steps forward toward Rafferty, jacks a shell into the chamber, and touches the gun to Rafferty's temple. "Stop," he says. "Don't ask any more questions."

"About what?" Rafferty asks. The tip of the gun is unbelievably cold against his skin, so cold it seems to suck his body heat into it. "Are we talking about Madame Wing or—"

"That's the message," the short man says. "Don't ask any more questions." And he pulls back the gun and slams Rafferty squarely on the forehead with it.

The *soi* tilts and darkens, and Rafferty feels his head strike the pavement. He doesn't think he has lost consciousness, but the next thing he knows, he is staring down at wet concrete from a height of one or two inches. He puts his hands under him and pushes up, but they slide apart on the slick surface, skittering away from him, and he drops back onto the pavement. He changes strategy and gets his elbows against the pavement, forearms flat, and levers himself up to a sitting position.

The men are gone. Superman is several yards away, still facedown. He has not moved.

"Hey," Rafferty says, and then realizes he has not said it aloud. He clears his throat, swallows, and says, "Hey," again.

The boy is motionless.

Slowly, Rafferty rolls onto his hands and knees, trying not to move his head too quickly. His right arm will barely take his weight. Favoring the left, he crawls to the boy's side and puts two fingers against his throat, where a pulse should be.

The boy groans ands turns over slowly, his eyes open. He has blood on his chin and neck, and his forehead has been scraped raw against the pavement. He takes in the damage to Rafferty's face and looks directly into his eyes. Then, very deliberately, he smiles. It is a wolf's grin.

"No police on Silom," he says. There is blood on his teeth.

Rafferty finds himself smiling back. "We don't need any stinking police."

Simultaneously, the two of them begin to laugh.

Bleeding, laughing, and leaning against each other for support, they stagger toward home.

## 24

# The Sheer Volume and Variety
# of Japanese Porn

N
o more questions about *what*?" Arthit asks.

"Well, that's the issue, isn't it?" Rafferty moves the ice pack from his shoulder to the forearm the sap hit, which sports a swelling the size of a softball. "What am I being warned off of? I lit a lot of fuses in the past few days."

"Maybe you're complicating it," Arthit says. He leans forward to examine the swelling on Rafferty's arm. "Maybe it's only one story. Occam's razor and all."

They sit side by side on the couch in Rafferty's living room. Miaow is in her room with the door closed, nursing Superman, who retreated rapidly at the sight of Arthit's uniform. Rose bangs around in the kitchen, unbagging the ice she ran down to buy the moment she set eyes on Rafferty and the boy. She also sweet-talked a druggist out of some prescription painkillers, two of which are beginning to remap Rafferty's nervous system

Her alarm at his injuries was obscurely rewarding, almost worth the pain. Unfortunately, it was immediately followed by anger at his having put himself—and, by extension, all of them—at risk.

He closes his eyes to indulge a pleasant wave of wooziness. The couch undulates slightly. "I don't think it's one story, Arthit. Occam or not. I think that what happened between Doughnut and Uncle Claus is personal, just between the two of them. It's obviously not about money. She left behind fifty thousand dollars in watches alone. Nothing got stolen until Doughnut went back yesterday and bagged the software, if it was software. Whatever is going on with Madame Wing, it's something else. There's money involved, and it's something Cambodian."

"Swelling's going down nicely," Arthit says untruthfully. "Do you suppose someone could put some of that ice into a glass of Mekhong?"

"We don't have any. How about a beer?"

"What kind?"

"What have you got? Heineken?"

"Singha," Rose says from the kitchen, to let them know she is listening.

"How about a Singha?" Arthit says.

Rose looks up from the ice she is pounding. "One?" It verges on a dare.

"Two," Rafferty says.

A beat. "You shouldn't drink beer with that pain medication."

"Beer *is* a pain medication."

"I know cats with more sense than most men," Rose says. She throws open the refrigerator door, letting it whack the counter.

"So here's what I think, Arthit." Rafferty tries to get comfortable and fails. Even with the pills distributing millions of tiny pillows throughout his nervous system, a clenched fist slams the inside of his head every time his heart beats. "I went looking for Doughnut at Madame Wing's, and she hired me to find out about something else."

"I suppose," Arthit says, sounding unconvinced. "Four of them, you say?"

"With a sap and a gun. No match for me and the kid."

"And you've never seen any of them before."

"Well, they're not your two cops." He has told Arthit about the visit that afternoon. "They're just muscle. They didn't know anything besides what they said: 'Don't ask any more questions.' They were there to scare me, not kill me."

"*This* time," Rose says as she comes out of the kitchen with the Singha. The glance she gives Rafferty as she hands his to him is icier than the beer.

The beer is so cold it's thickening in the glass. The chill makes Rafferty's sinuses ache, and the fat, skunky fragrance fills his nostrils as he swallows. He feels better immediately. "What about my Cambodian?" he asks.

Arthit looks over at Rose, who is pretending not to listen, and lowers his voice. "You going to go on with this?"

"Sure," Rafferty says.

"I don't know, Poke."

"Well, I do. I can use that money. Miaow and I—"

"Obviously," Arthit says, "but it won't do her much good if you're dead."

"Everybody underestimates me." Rafferty takes another pull at his beer to accelerate the healing process. "It's my secret weapon."

"Up to you," Arthit says in the tone of someone who realizes that rational argument is not an option. "There was only one Cambodian in the cell." He reaches into his tattered leather briefcase and takes out a sheaf of papers, fastened with a clip. "Chouk Ran. Age fifty-one. Here legally. No prior arrests. Five feet seven, dark complexion, left hand badly mangled. Missing fingernails. He was staying in a flophouse when he was arrested."

"For what?"

"Shoplifting at Foodland. Put up a fuss when he got caught, so they called the cops."

"Shoplifting at *Foodland*?" Rafferty asks. "Come on. I know people who have been caught there. You give it back and slip the manager five hundred baht. They say thank you and good night. It's probably a line item in their spreadsheets."

"He wouldn't play. Had plenty of money in his pocket, too."

"What'd he take?"

Arthit grins. "An electric mixer. One of those things for cakes. In a box, no less."

"Not exactly something you can slip under a T-shirt. He just try to walk out with it?"

"Big as life."

"My, my," Rafferty says. "Either he really, really wanted to bake a cake or he wanted to go to jail."

"Good place to meet crooks," Arthit says.

Rafferty moves his head slowly from side to side and notices a novel blurring in the center of his vision as the room slides by. Pharmaceutical special effects. "Got a picture?"

"Of course." Arthit folds back the top sheet to show Rafferty a photocopy of a mug shot. The man has a dark shock of hair, stiff as a whiskbroom, that seems to grow sideways on his head; a straight, strong mouth; and the eyes of someone who has seen considerably more than he was prepared to see. He stares at the camera as though it were a gun pointed at his head.

"Not one of the guys in the alley," Rafferty says. The photo swims a little bit in front of him.

"Too much to hope for." Arthit hands the papers to Rafferty. "I have no idea where you got these."

"If you were this guy, Arthit, where would you be?"

"It depends on what he's doing," Arthit says. "But if what Madame Wing said is true, I'd bet he won't get too far from her."

"I don't think he'll get too close either," Rafferty says. He holds Arthit's gaze. "You haven't met Madame Wing."

THE SIZZLER, WHICH Superman chose since the meal is in his honor, is part of a little snarl of vehemently American fast-food mills on Silom that includes a Pizza Hut and a McDonald's. The boy wears one of his new shirts, the front geometrically adorned with a rectangle of creases where it was folded around the department-store stiffener.

He keeps sharpening the creases between thumb and forefinger, and Rafferty realizes it is probably the first new prefolded shirt he has ever worn. The scrape over his eye has turned into a broad calligraphy brushstroke of brown.

He looks very happy.

He eats two sirloin steaks, barely chewing. His glance keeps floating up from the carnage on his plate to Rafferty. Miaow watches him eat with openmouthed admiration, as though he had personally materialized the food before eating it.

Arthit has abandoned them, gone home to Noi.

"I'm going to walk back," Rafferty says when they hit the pavement. It is almost nine o'clock, and the vendors are crowding the sidewalk across the street.

"We'll all walk," Rose says. She has thawed some during dinner.

"No, Rose, if you don't mind." The children are not exactly appropriate to this particular errand. "I'm going to take my time, work out some of this stiffness. And I have some thinking to do." He reaches across them and punches Superman lightly on the shoulder. The boy's eyes go wide, and then he grins and feints a punch back. "Thanks again," Rafferty says.

When Rose and the children are half a block away, he crosses Silom. It seems to take a long time, and he recognizes that the pills are still at work. Walking a bit more deliberately than usual, he shoulders his way into the throng moving slowly in the narrow corridor between the rows of stalls. Watches, clothes, wood carvings, bootleg compact discs and audiotapes, hill-tribe artifacts, fake antiques, and silver jewelry gleam in the overhead spotlights.

The dark spaces are what he wants. Without Arthit's guidance he would have walked right past them and not given them a glance.

Dim little pools among the brightness. Just a card table with a man sitting behind it. On each card table are five or ten of the bright plastic albums that drugstores put snapshots in.

Rafferty stops at the first of the booths.

"Sit," the man says, pushing an overturned yellow plastic bucket toward him.

"Japanese," Rafferty says, and the man selects a stack of albums and shoves it across the table. Rafferty flips it open.

It is full of glossy color photos, five inches by seven, slipped into transparent sleeves just like pictures from a family holiday. Each photo is the neatly trimmed cover of a video box. Schoolgirls—or, rather, young women dressed in the Japanese schoolgirl uniform— peer up at him in improbably suggestive poses. Beaming girls wearing strategically positioned suds advertise videos set in "soaplands," the anything-goes Japanese version of the massage parlor. Close-ups of fresh-scrubbed faces promote the newest stars, most of whom look as though they've lived their entire lives on cotton candy and never uttered a nasty word. A year from now, these innocents will be dancing at Tokyo strip clubs that offer blow jobs in a little booth at the rear.

The second and third albums offer more of the same. "Anything special?" Rafferty asks.

The man counts down two or three more albums and pulls one out. Women with women, women with animals, women in the bathroom. Rafferty races through them in self-defense, but two pictures make him stop. Both feature women who have been tied up and handcuffed. He shows them to the man behind the table. "More?"

The man glances at the photos, and his mouth turns down. "Not have."

"Do you know this man?" Rafferty asks, showing him the photograph of Claus Ulrich. He gets a quick glance and a shake of the head.

"Thanks for the use of the bucket," Rafferty says, getting up. Too quickly: there is a little pop in his head and a sudden brightening of his vision. He has to put out a hand to remain upright.

By the time he has hit three stalls, Rafferty has learned to stand more slowly. He has also developed an unaffectionate appreciation for the sheer volume and variety of Japanese porn. The fourth booth is presided over by an imperious-looking woman in her early thirties wearing a great many silver bracelets. She is doing business as fast as she can; Rafferty has to wait for an unoccupied bucket.

"Japanese," he says, and as a shortcut he adds, "special."

"No problem." She reaches under the table and brings out a stack of albums almost a foot high. The bracelets jingle gaily. "Have everything," she says proudly.

And she does.

If asked, Rafferty would have said he had led a reasonably active and varied sex life, but what he sees when he opens the first album makes him feel twelve years old. Vegetables? Dead fish? Panty hose? Diapers? There seems to be nothing that is not the object of a fetish for someone.

He recognizes the first picture in the third album as the cover of one of the videos in Uncle Claus's secret drawer. Paging rapidly through the blur of four-color torment, spotting several more, Rafferty becomes keenly aware of all the people behind him. This is not how he wishes to be remembered. He hunches more closely over the album, realizes that it probably just makes him look even more furtive, and straightens up once more.

He closes the last album and pushes the stack back toward the woman, who gives him a disappointed look. "Have something more special," she says, and starts to reach beneath the table again. Rafferty brings up both hands, palms out. Whatever it might be that is "more special," he will fight not to see it. He pulls the photo of Uncle Claus from his pocket and shows it to her, and she gives him a big smile.

"*Khun* Claus," she says happily. "Number one customer. Every week four, five video."

Good Lord, a footprint. Rafferty switches to Thai. "How long has it been since you saw him?"

She gazes up at the phone wires, packed as always with a species of small birds that are distinguished by their extremely active lower digestive tracts. "Three months?" she asks thoughtfully. "Four?"

"Does that happen often? That you don't see him for so long?"

"*Khun* Claus travels," she says a bit grandly. "He lives in the world." She makes a gesture that is intended to sweep aside the borders of Thailand. "He comes, he goes."

"Well, thanks." Rafferty stands up, eager to get away from the table and everything on it.

"Three months," the woman says. Her eyes widen. "Do you think he was down there?"

"I doubt it." He starts to turn away, then thinks of one more question. "Did he ever buy other kinds of videos from you?"

She nods, eager to help. "Same kind." Then she motions him closer, and Rafferty leans in reluctantly, putting a hand out for balance. With this woman's standards, he does not want to hear anything she thinks needs to be whispered. She extends her hands to suggest handcuffs and says, "Sometimes boys."

**THAT NIGHT RAFFERTY** sits shirtless at his desk, icing his shoulder and drawing with a soft pencil on a drafting pad. The green-shaded student lamp on the desk is the only light in the room. The boy is asleep on the couch, his mouth open. He has, Rafferty notices, very good teeth.

A long time ago, he started to think of the books he wrote in terms of floor plans, working with pencil and eraser to explore the shape and balance of the manuscript without the distraction of words. Now he draws a floor plan of the mess he has gotten into, trying to create a geography of the situation.

The front door of his floor plan is opened by Arthit, who directs him to Clarissa. A line joins both of them to the two rogue cops. Clarissa points him down a hallway to the rooms that represent Uncle Claus, rooms that were furnished with secrets and violent pornography but are abandoned now. A short corridor leads him to Doughnut's room, scoured clean and locked tight, linked by two lines, the first leading downstairs to Noot, working for Mr. Choy, and the other pointing toward a box for Bangkok Domestics. Bangkok Domestics is connected to the dark, gothic complex inhabited by Madame Wing, from which two lines run, one leading to the dead safecracker Tam and the other toward a mutilated Cambodian named Chouk Ran.

If this were cosmology, the area surrounding all the neat little boxes would be the realm of quasars, dark matter, and the Great Attractor. Applying Arthit's suggestion of Occam's razor—the principle that says always to look for the simplest explanation—there *would* be a Great Attractor out there somewhere, pulling Doughnut, Uncle Claus, Madame Wing, Chouk Ran, and the others, known and unknown, toward a single point.

If that were true, the course of action would be relatively simple: Find the Attractor and ambush them on their way to it. Except that Rafferty doesn't believe in the Great Attractor in this case. He thinks he's looking at two separate orbits that just happen to share some space.

He rubs his stiff neck. Rose is asleep. Miaow is in her room.

His shoulder throbs. The pain pills have given up for the night.

He tears the page from the pad as quietly as he can and folds it into quarters without even knowing he is doing it. Then he drops the page into the wastebasket and gets up, pushing the chair back slowly. The boy doesn't stir as he passes, although Rafferty senses a coil of tension in the still form.

The security lock is in place on the inside of the door, which means it would take two kicks to knock it in instead of one. Rafferty goes into the kitchen and pulls five or six cans of tomatoes from the shelves. Rose buys almost as many cans of tomatoes as she does jars of Nescafé. He carries them to the door and kneels, pulling the gun from his waistband and laying it on the carpet, because it pinches when he leans forward. He stacks the cans on top of each other, leaning slightly away from the door at an angle somewhat less acute than the one that distinguishes the Leaning Tower of Pisa. If the door opens even an inch, the cans will fall to the floor, making enough noise to wake everyone in the apartment.

He checks the arrangement one last time and turns to see the boy up on one elbow, watching him.

"Burglar alarm," Rafferty says, feeling silly. "Kind of low-tech, but it's what we have."

"Good," the boy says with a nod. "Do you think they will come?" His voice is slightly hoarse, as though it does not get a lot of use.

"No. But it's better to be ready."

The boy's eyes go to the gun on the floor. "Can you shoot?"

"Enough," Rafferty says. "Listen, I want you to sleep in Miaow's room."

"Why?" the boy says immediately. He pulls back physically, shifting his weight to the other elbow.

"I want the couch. If anybody comes in, I want to be the one who's out here."

"You will need help." The boy has not moved.

"And you can come in as soon as you hear anything wrong. That way you'll surprise them, like you did in the alley."

"Okay." The boy gets up and wraps the sheet around him.

"Great. And tomorrow you can repair my fax."

"What's wrong with it?" The question comes quickly.

"I'll tell you tomorrow. Thanks for your help tonight."

The child thinks about it and then nods. "No problem." He trundles off down the hall, the sheet dragging behind him, and Rafferty goes into his bedroom to grab a blanket and a pillow.

He settles in and knows in ten seconds it's not going to work. The couch is too short for him. It's still warm from the boy. It has lumps in it. There's nowhere to put his knees. The room is too bright. His arm and shoulder throb. He knows he will never get to sleep.

When he wakes up, in broad daylight, the boy is sitting wrapped in his sheet, on the floor halfway across the room, looking at him.

## 25

## The Money Doesn't Matter

He writes, carefully, *"TEN MILLION BAHT."*

He had wanted to demand 25 million, but a quick calculation told him that it would be too bulky. Not manageable.

Anyway, the money doesn't matter.

The restaurant is as empty as before, but the waitress is awake. She greeted him as though he were a personal inconvenience, brought him his sweetened iced coffee silently, and retreated to her chair and a Thai movie magazine. The time is ten past four in the morning.

Chouk Ran—the man who called himself Chon—has placed a bright blue zippered bag on the table beside his notepad and pencil. He bought it on the street only two days ago, and the zipper is already broken.

He moves the bag aside with his elbow to give himself writing room.

*"You will need to buy two large suitcases,"* he writes. *"They will need wheels, because they will be heavy."* He pauses and reviews the

letter in his mind, where he has written and rewritten it many times. He reproaches himself for his failure of nerve, for the time he has wasted: There are only six days remaining to him before one of them must die.

*"Put the money in the suitcases. It should be in bills of 500 and 1000 baht. Tomorrow afternoon at four, a maid from your house will come out of the gate alone, with the suitcases. This is why they must have wheels. She will turn left, walk to the intersection, and get a taxi. She will put the suitcases in the trunk. I know your staff by sight, so I will know if she is not one of your maids. I will know if she is not alone. I will know if she doesn't get a real taxi. If she does not follow directions, you will lose the money and you will not get the envelope."*

He sips the iced coffee. The ice has melted, and the drink tastes watery. He tries to remember when he slept last.

*"She will carry the cellular phone I have enclosed in this package,"* he writes. He reaches into the blue bag and pulls out a small Nokia cell phone. He pushes the "power" button and checks the battery level, although he has done this three times already.

*"She will return in two hours or a little more. If you have done as I say, she will have the envelope with her. That will be the end of our business."*

He puts down the pencil and lights a cigarette. He lets the letter rest for a few minutes before he rereads it.

Her anger will be immeasurable. She will want to kill someone. He once saw her kill a four-year-old child because it was crying.

She will send the money. He is certain of that. As much pain as it causes her, she will send it. For the first time in her adult life, perhaps, she will have no alternative but to do as she is told. He tries to imagine the agony she will feel when she realizes she has no choice but to comply. Then he closes his eyes and tries to visualize how she will feel later, when she gets the suitcases back and looks inside.

He thinks that is the point at which she will begin to be afraid.

## 26

## Don't You Think Holiness Can Be Cumulative?

A small man, Heng has enough energy for three large ones. He bounces up and down on his toes as he listens, eager for the chance to reply. When he talks, he makes large, empty gestures that look to Rafferty like Nicolas Cage playing an Italian. Surrounded in his Khmer antiques shop by carved, immobile faces, his own face is never in repose. He goes through more expressions in ten minutes than Rafferty uses all day.

"I'm *completely* straight now," he informs Rafferty without being asked, his eyebrows bouncing up and down like a pair of bungee jumpers. "No more smuggling, papers all in order, keep a clean nose, observe all the international conventions. It's a new world we're living in, Poke, a global village. We're all citizens of the world. What goes around comes around."

When it is clear Heng has exhausted *Bartlett's Familiar Quotations* for the moment, Rafferty says, "Do you mind if I write that down?"

Heng pounces. "A Boswell," he says. "What every really *interesting* man needs. Have you ever stopped to think, Poke, how much good talk is wasted on just one or two people? Similes, metaphors, unexpected turns of speech, puns, insights, revelations, fresh perspectives? All of it gone, used once, *disposable,* tossed into the air like confetti, frittered away on a few people who probably won't even bother to remember. New ideas, perhaps even new religions, lost to the ether. Who was Samuel Johnson, anyhow? A blowhard with a Boswell. We need more of them."

"You're the only person I know who thinks the world is short of talk," Rafferty says.

"*Good* talk," Heng says, holding up an admonitory finger. Since the finger is in the air anyway, he waves it back and forth. "We're drowning in dull talk. No wonder our children are in trouble. Nothing to fire their imaginations. They hear dull talk all day long, this, that, blah, blah, blah, fact, fact, fact, cause, effect, pallid adjectives, the occasional timid speculation. That's why we live in the Age of the Concrete Slab. We might as well be mute as fish. There's no feeling for language, no appreciation for how it can be *stretched,* Poke, to weave that elusive net of words that can be thrown over, that can *capture,* the most ephemeral—"

"Heng," Rafferty says.

Heng stops. His eyebrows go up again, inquiringly this time, to demonstrate that he is listening with his entire being. For a moment Rafferty thinks he will cup his hand to his ear.

"This man, Heng," Rafferty says, holding out the photo of Claus Ulrich, which is becoming dog-eared with use. "Do you know this man?"

Heng takes the picture and scans it avidly, as though it is the first photograph he has ever seen and the technology dazzles him. He does everything except turn it over to see whether the image goes all the way through to the back. When he is finished, he reverently hands it back.

"I might," he says. He waits, bouncing a little.

It is the shortest sentence Rafferty has ever heard him speak.

"Well," Rafferty says, "why don't you tell me about it. Just a summary, Heng, sort of a caption."

"I said I *might,*" Heng says. Cataclysmic doubt floods his face.

"When and where might you have seen him?"

"It's a small community, Poke," Heng begins, but Rafferty holds up a hand.

"What's a small community?"

"People of taste," Heng says with nicely modulated awe. "People who can find room in their lives for the timeless. The things I offer, Poke, they trail behind them the perfume of—"

"He bought something from you," Rafferty says.

"Once," Heng says, unfolding a single finger in case Rafferty has trouble with lower mathematics. "Perhaps. But he might have come back many times."

"But if he did, he didn't buy."

"In a nutshell." Heng opens his arms to take in the extraordinary collection of objects that crowd his shop: statues, sections of carved temple walls, gilt Buddhas and monks, panels of carved wood, antique ivory. "But you speak of *buying.*" He allows a ten-percent tincture of disapproval to darken his tone. "These things belong to the world. They've been here for ages. How long can a statue of a god absorb the gazes of the faithful without *becoming* a god, Poke? Don't you think holiness can be cumulative?"

"Why didn't he buy again?"

"The small-mindedness of our times," Heng says, with a snap that verges on ire. "The idea that these treasures can be tricked out with pettiness like permits and provenances, pieces of paper pasted to the eternal. Like giving a mountain a nickname. 'There's a nice mountain. Let's call it Bill.'"

"The documentation costs money," Rafferty clarifies. "Prices have gone up."

Heng emits an admiring puff of air. "You have a gift, Poke. That's the writer in you."

"And Ulrich is cheap."

"Is that his name? Anyway, not my judgment to pass," Heng says virtuously.

"Do you know a Madame Wing?"

Heng's face slams shut. It is as though the plug has been pulled from the wall. "No," he says, not even circling his lips around the *o*. The lie is so transparent that Poke has only to wait.

"A woman, I suppose, by the title you give her," Heng says, looking extremely uncomfortable. He tries to bounce but succeeds only in jiggling. "Chinese, I presume? No, no, I don't know her. Never heard the name. Completely new to me, not a whisper of an association."

"But she's a collector. And—as you say—it's such a small community."

"I did?" Heng's eyes are darting around the shop as though he's afraid one of the antiques might contradict him. "Doesn't sound like something I'd—"

"Madame Wing, Heng. She's here. She's rich. She's got some of the best Khmer art—"

"Doesn't matter," Heng says, with renewed resolve. "I am telling you I haven't heard of her, and nothing you can say will change the fact that I am telling you I haven't heard of her."

Rafferty replays the sentence. "I understand you're *telling* me you haven't heard of her—" he begins.

"Yes," Heng says, nodding with some vehemence. "That's what I'm telling you. And that's what I *will* tell you, no matter how many times you ask, even if you try to help me identify her by telling me she lives by the river with a manservant named Pak."

"Got it," Rafferty says.

"No matter *how* many times," Heng repeats. "And please don't ask again. It makes me very nervous."

"Sorry. Back to Claus Ulrich."

"Claus Ulrich, yes," Heng says with evident relief.

"When was the last time you saw him?"

Up on the toes again. "If I saw him, it was months. Just months and months."

"Did he ever come in with anyone?"

"Solitary as a spider."

"What do you know about him?"

"If it's the same man, he's a bachelor. I always make it a point to find out. You wouldn't believe, Poke, the number of times a man buys something wonderful and the little woman makes him bring it back. Takes one look at it and sees—I don't know, a garbage disposal or a trip to some dreary European capital, all cobblestone streets, odd toilet paper, and strange electrical plugs."

"Must be heartbreaking. Anything else?"

"He has a niece in Europe or somewhere," Heng says, emphasizing the effort involved in dredging up the fact. His eyes almost disappear with the sheer strain of it. "He loves her very much. He talked about her several times."

"Did he?"

"Oh, yes." Heng leans forward and puts a hand over his heart, mirroring the traditional posture of compassion depicted on so many of the artworks surrounding him. "I had the feeling he lived for her."

Rafferty raises his eyes from the hand to Heng's own eyes, wide with fraudulent sincerity. "It's hard to tell what anybody lives for," he says.

**EVEN AT MIDDAY** the bar is dark enough to let people change their clothes in privacy.

"I have no idea where he is," Rafferty tells her. "But I know that the maid is involved somehow."

Clarissa Ulrich is wearing a different blouse, but her tolerance for the heat has not increased. Her face is red and wet, and when she barely glances at him as he sits down, he attributes it to exhaustion. They have taken Mac O'Connor's booth in the Expat Bar to get away from Hofstedler and the others, who are having their recurring conversation about playing a game of darts. In more than a year, Rafferty has never seen any of them actually pick up a dart.

"The maid?" she asks. "Are you sure?" She seems not so much exhausted as distracted, as though she is only half listening to him.

He tells her about the arrangement at Bangkok Domestics. She listens with her eyes closed, and when he is finished, she says, "This woman—this Doughnut—I mean, do you think Uncle Claus and she were—"

"It's too early to say. I have to tell you, your uncle Claus lived very quietly here. I've only been able to find a couple of people who actually knew him."

"Who?"

"A dealer in Khmer antiquities and a . . . uh, a bookseller."

She catches the hesitation. "You were going to say something else."

"No. I just wandered off there for a moment. Everything I learn only leads me to new questions."

She has a glass of tomato juice in front of her, which she has not touched. She moves it and puts both hands on the table, folded in a businesslike fashion. The tension flows from her in waves. "I need to talk to you about something."

Rafferty lifts his beer. "Talk away."

"This is more complicated than I thought it was going to be. I don't feel right asking you to go any further without . . . well, without discussing payment of some kind."

"Forget it. I'm having a good month."

"But I . . . I didn't know what I was getting you into. And I want to make sure . . ." Her eyes are everywhere but on him. "Please don't take this wrong. I want to make sure you don't write about this."

Whatever he was expecting, this isn't it. "*Write* about it?"

She picks up the tomato juice, slowly wipes the condensation away from the bottom of the glass with her forefinger, and puts it back down untasted. She centers it on the napkin. Then she centers the napkin in front of her. He wonders whether she is going to center the table. "I know you probably wouldn't. But it's important to me that Uncle Claus is—" She breaks off, and her face tightens into a mask of control. "That he's not slandered. His life shouldn't be trashed, just because he . . . he made mistakes, or had problems. He did too much good for that."

A silence falls between them. At the end of the bar, Hofstedler laughs, a sound like colliding echo chambers. "You've been to the apartment," Rafferty says.

"Last night." A tear snakes down her cheek.

"How did you— Oh, Jesus. I didn't lock the door, did I?"

"No," she says. She puts one hand around the glass of tomato juice as if to cool it. "Or the filing cabinet."

"I'm so sorry. I banged it up too much to close it." He feels personally responsible.

"Were you going to tell me about it?" she asks. She lets go of the glass and wipes her nose on the back of her hand.

"No."

"Thank you for that. I mean it, that's very sweet of you."

"It didn't have anything to do with you."

"No," she says. "No, you're right. It doesn't. It has nothing to do with who Uncle Claus was to me. He was never anything but wonderful to me." Then she is weeping, not delicately or discreetly, just great gulping sobs and a line of clear snot running down from her nose. She puts both hands over her face, and Rafferty reaches over and pats her shaking shoulder with a hand that feels as fat and heavy as a Smithfield ham. The fine, uncontrollable hair frames her hands like spun candy. It is a child's hair.

"I'm all right," she says after a moment. "Everybody has to grow up sometime." She takes the napkin from beneath her glass and blows her nose in it, then uses it to wipe her face. "People need to know the truth about things, I guess."

"I suppose," Rafferty says. It's not a doctrine to which he necessarily subscribes.

"Can I pay you, then?"

"No."

She nods, conceding. "Do you think you can find him?"

Rafferty considers it. "Yes."

She lifts his glass and takes the napkin, uses it to blot her forehead. "Do you know *what* you'll find?"

"Well," Rafferty says, "you want the truth, right?"

Her eyes come up to his. "Right."

"The truth is that I haven't got the faintest idea."

## 27

## I'll Never Drink Water Again

The man who stands in the door wears a pair of loose shorts in a dull pumpkin color that goes nicely with the yellowing bruises on his upper body and his face. He has bumps and cuts everywhere, his nose has probably been broken, and one eye is swollen tightly shut. Gashes—rips, really, they're too ragged to be called gashes—mark his face and shoulders in a violent calligraphy. The dark skin over his ribs is blotched with welts.

"You got my note."

The man nods and grabs his neck in pain.

"Pak did this?" Rafferty asks.

The man looks past him into the corridor to make sure Rafferty has come alone, and then he nods again. "Pak and some others," he says. Two of his front teeth have been broken. When he pronounces an *s*, he whistles.

"How long did they work on you?" Rafferty is speaking Thai.

"One hour, two hours, I don't know."

Rafferty steps in and closes the door behind him. The bruised man retreats. The apartment is the size of a large closet, hot, with an un-painted concrete floor and one tiny window. A hot plate in the corner serves as a kitchen, and a mat on the floor passes for a bed. Except for a sagging wooden table with a television on it, there is no furniture. Clothes hang from nails driven into the walls, which were painted aquamarine quite a long time ago. The ceiling is high and clouded with cobwebs.

"Did you tell them who the thief was?" Rafferty seats himself on the floor, cross-legged. After a moment of gazing down at him, the man sits, too, grunting with the effort.

He licks his lips and winces as though it stings. "I don't know who it was."

Rafferty lets it pass. "Did they make you help them get rid of the body?"

The man's good eye opens in alarm. "What body?"

"Tam's," Rafferty says, as if it were self-evident. "The safecracker."

"No body," the man says. He is looking at a spot above Rafferty's head.

"We'll get along a lot better if you just assume I know everything," Rafferty says. "I'm talking about the body you found in or near the hole they dug. The Thai man who had been shot, once, in the back. The guy who actually opened the safe while the Cambodian— What's his name?"

The man studies him with the open eye but says nothing.

"Chouk," Rafferty says, seeing the eye skitter away. "While Chouk stood over him."

"I don't know Chouk," the man says. His voice has a thin, rippling edge to it, as though he doesn't have enough breath to support it.

"Of course you do. You let him onto the property. Or maybe you know him as Chon."

"You should go," the man says, starting to rise.

"You should have made him hit you for real," Rafferty says, putting a hand on the man's shoulder and forcing him back down. It is pathetically easy to do. "What happened? Did he forget? Or did you go away while he was working and come back after he left?"

"He did hit me," the man says insistently. He leans forward and parts his hair to show Rafferty a nasty-looking wound on his scalp. "He hit me from behind, with a rock."

"Let's talk about the rock," Rafferty says.

The guard closes his eyes. "The rock?"

"Here's the way I figure it happened: You were on duty at the pier, vigilant as always. He pulled his boat in while your back was turned and tied it to the pier, and then he crept up the pier while your back was still turned, and then he went all the way across the lawn while your other back was turned, and he grabbed a stone from a row of them edging a flower bed, and then he crept all the way back down the lawn, while your back was turned, and hit you on the head with the rock. While all your backs were turned. Something like that?"

The man has paled. He opens his eyes and pats his bare chest, as though checking a pocket for cigarettes.

"You're not wearing a shirt," Rafferty reminds him.

"Cigarette," the man says. It is a croak.

Rafferty extends an empty hand and tilts it side to side to say he doesn't have any. "You want a glass of water?"

"Never." The man shudders. "I'll never drink water again."

"Pak didn't notice the rock," Rafferty says. "Nobody knows about it except you and me."

"I need to think," the man says.

"Want me to go down and get you some cigarettes while you work it out?"

"No. Yes."

"My treat," Rafferty says. He got up. "Just make sure you're here when I get back, because if you're not, Madame Wing is going to be very upset with you."

## 28

## The Ooh and Aah Phase

The guard was promised a million baht," Rafferty says.

"Did he get it?" Arthit is on a car phone that keeps fritzing in and out.

"Not yet."

"That might be good for us," Arthit says. "Unlikely as it seems, Chouk might try to make payment."

"Chouk came up to him in a restaurant one night, sat down, and started talking. Said he had it all worked out, had the plan in place. All he needed was the location of the safe and a couple of hours on the property."

"And the guard knew where the safe was."

"Helped to dig the hole. He'd worked there almost twenty years."

"He let these guys in after twenty years in the house? Doesn't say much for loyalty."

"Madame Wing isn't someone who inspires much loyalty."

Rafferty is lying full length on the couch, trying to find somewhere to rest his weight that doesn't hurt. Late-afternoon sun slants malevolently through the sliding glass door. Miaow has not come home from school yet, and the boy is off somewhere. Probably sharpening his teeth.

"You there?" Arthit asks.

"Just lolling around. It may be hard for you to imagine, Arthit, just how leisurely my life actually is."

"What could be in a cardboard envelope that's worth a million baht?"

"For all I know, it's her diary. This is not a woman with a sunny past."

"Does the guard have a way to reach Chouk?"

"He says not. Says Chouk will call him when the money's ready."

"Trusting soul, isn't he?" Arthit says.

"He's barely sentient."

"Are you going to tell Madame Wing about this?"

"I don't know," Rafferty says. "They really beat the shit out of him, and that was when they only *suspected* he was involved."

"So what's the next move?"

"We assume he's going to get paid."

"Why? Chouk's other little helper got killed."

"Whatever was in that safe, I think Tam got shot because he saw it. The guard got off the property and stayed off. He didn't see anything."

"So we watch the guard," Arthit says. "Wait for the payoff."

"Can you do that without attracting too much attention?"

"Sure. I'll assign Cho to it." Cho is Arthit's brother-in-law, a chubby, sweet-natured boy who took a degree in library science and then decided to be a policeman. The career move had been a mistake. "It's perfect for Cho. He can sit in one place and eat noodles in the car, and all he has to do is make a phone call when the subject starts to move. Does the guy move around much? If he's more mobile than, say, the average couch, Cho will probably lose him."

"At the moment he can barely make it to the bathroom. Who'll watch when Cho goes off?"

"I'll take care of that. I still have a fragile, if deteriorating, network of personal alliances at my disposal."

"I'm sorry about all this, Arthit," Rafferty says dutifully.

"Just keep your eyes open. My two colleagues probably aren't finished with you."

"No problem," Rafferty says. "I'll sic the boy on them."

THE MINUTE RAFFERTY hangs up, the phone rings. The screams of children in the background identify the caller as Hank Morrison before he can even say hello.

"Poke. Let's get together."

"What about the prospective parents?" Rafferty tries another position on the couch and rejects it.

"We're in the ooh and aah phase. It'll last a couple of days. You want to get this started?"

"More than anything in the world."

"When? I'll need at least two or three hours, Poke, one with the two of you and one or two with each of you alone. Not today, though," Morrison says. "I'm jammed. How about tomorrow afternoon?"

"Give me an hour after she gets home from school. Say, four, four-thirty. Is there anything I should bring?"

"Your passport, visa, whatever you've got. Something to show you're solvent—a year's worth of bank statements ought to do it."

"No problem." Thanks in part to the shudderiferous Madame Wing.

Morrison says, "Hold on," and Rafferty hears the phone hit the desk. A moment later the voices of the children are muted, and Morrison comes back on the line.

"Had to close the door," he says. He clears his throat. "Poke, don't take any of this wrong, okay?"

"Any of what?"

"Of what we're about to discuss. Is she a virgin?"

The muscles in Rafferty's shoulders go rigid. "I have no idea," he says stiffly.

"She's going to be examined, Poke. Medically, I mean. Most of the time, there aren't any snags, if only because there are so many ways a hymen can be broken accidentally, but any sign of repeated sexual activity—"

"As I said, I have no idea."

"You've never talked about it with her?"

"We've talked about everything in the world except that."

"Well, *I'm* going to have to talk to her about it."

"Good luck," Rafferty says, imagining the set of Miaow's mouth when she's planted her feet.

"You've got to tell her to answer me," Morrison says. "Tell her how important it is, that we could have problems if we don't know the truth. And that includes you, Poke. You've never touched her improperly, have you?"

"Hank, if it were anybody but you, I'd come over there and slice you from gut to gullet and put in a defective zipper."

"I have to ask you the question. I'll have to ask her, too."

Rafferty's heart is hammering in his ears. "If you have to, you have to."

"Poke, how emotional are you about the possibility that she's been abused in the past?"

"No more emotional than anyone else would be."

Morrison pauses. "Which is to say what?"

"Which is to say I'll kill anybody who messed with her."

"That's what I was afraid of. Look, I can either tell you what she says in our interview or not tell you. Which would you prefer?"

He weighs it for a moment. "Don't tell me. I want to hear it from her, when she's ready."

"What's your gut feeling?"

"I think, at the very least, people have tried." He tells Morrison about Miaow's defensive reaction when she is hugged too quickly or when she does not initiate it.

"Aaaahh," Morrison says. "It doesn't necessarily mean anything. Some of the most abused kids are also the most physically affectionate. They've learned it's the best way to manipulate adults."

"Well, that's not Miaow. Miaow manipulates adults by having the strongest will since Margaret Thatcher. Strong enough to talk me into putting up with Superman."

"On a temporary basis, I hope."

"Until I can figure something else out."

"Poke, you're not the first person to try to help that kid. He's had a lot of chances."

"Oh, please, Hank. Compared to who?"

"You can't think about these children in the same way you think about American kids. Compared to a lot of the little lost souls abandoned on the streets of Southeast Asia, *that's* compared to who."

"We're getting along fine," Rafferty says, and the door to the apartment opens and the boy walks in. He has the worst black eye Rafferty has ever seen, something straight out of the "Our Gang" comedies. The scrape on his forehead is a crust of brown, but his long hair is clean and neatly brushed. It falls over the damaged eye with a sort of Veronica Lake effect. He waves stiffly at Rafferty, as though the gesture is new to him, and Rafferty returns the wave.

"He's a good kid to have on your side in a fight," Rafferty continues, making a fist and pretending to hit himself in the jaw. The boy laughs. Rafferty tells Morrison about the attack the previous evening, making it sound like a random mugging. He smiles at the boy and gets one in return. Superman sits on the carpet, waiting for Rafferty to finish. He fidgets from side to side. He looks eager about something.

"Well, be careful of him," Morrison says. "Don't give him a chance to steal from you."

"I'm not worried about that. It's just stuff."

"That's either a noble statement or a stupid one. Bye, Poke."

Rafferty hangs up the phone and looks at the boy. The boy looks expectantly back at Rafferty, as though he is waiting for something. Rafferty feels his smile go stale, and he sees something like disappointment come into the boy's eyes. Finally, just the tiniest of gestures, the boy turns his head an eighth of an inch toward the opposite wall and lifts his chin.

Rafferty looks in the indicated direction. His fax has a paper tray attached to it.

"You fixed it!" Rafferty jumps to his feet and practically runs to the fax. The paper tray is in place, firmly anchored and ruler straight. He turns to the boy.

"I fixed the ring, too," the boy says shyly. "Now it only rings twice before it answers."

"This thing has been broken for months."

"Easy," the boy says. He is looking at the carpet.

Rafferty starts to hug him and then slaps his hands together instead. There are probably twenty ways to handle this, and nineteen of them are wrong. He goes through at least seventeen of them mentally before he says, "How much do you know about garbage disposals?"

**SOK POCHARA IS** having an unusual day.

He has been driving the cab since 6:00 A.M. His first fare, a *farang* man, threw up in the backseat, reminding Sok that it is rarely a good idea to pick up someone who is flagging you on all fours. After Sok cleaned the cab, he picked up the fat twins, two men in their forties who looked exactly alike, dressed exactly alike, and talked exactly alike. They could barely squeeze into the back of the cab. When he dropped them off, they split the fare exactly and tipped precisely the same amount, which is to say zero. They were followed by a ladyboy in an all-white wedding gown with sparkles on it who was weeping uncontrollably and who jumped out of the cab at a stoplight without paying him. The cab is still sweet with his/her perfume when he picks up the girl with the two big suitcases.

*Airport*, he thinks as he pulls to the curb, barely beating out two other cabs. He loads her luggage, as heavy as he is, into the trunk, gets back into the cab, and says, "Where?"

"Anywhere," she says. "Just drive."

"That could get expensive," he says, and she reaches forward and drops a thousand-baht bill on the seat beside him. "I'll drive," Sok says.

Half an hour passes. Sok decides to see how many times he can cross the river without covering the same ground twice. The meter says 820 baht when the girl's cell phone rings.

"Hello?" she says. Then she listens for a long minute. Then she says, "I understand," and leans forward and says to Sok, "Stop here."

Sok pulls to the curb and starts to get out to help her with the suitcases, but she says, "Wait," and hands him another 500 baht. "Stay here," she says. "In a minute you'll see me talking to a man. When we finish, he'll get into the cab, and you take him anywhere he wants to go. When he gets out, he will take my suitcases with him."

*Another one,* Sok thinks. *Maybe I should be doing construction work.*

Within seconds, a cab pulls up to the curb in front of them, and Sok watches as a man gets out. He is short and dark, and there is something wrong with one of his hands. He waves his cab away with the bad hand, and when it has disappeared in traffic, the young woman gets out of Sok's cab. The man gives her a big envelope and comes toward Sok's cab. He gets in and says, "Drive."

Sok lets him out in Pratunam twenty minutes later. The man melts into the crowd, pulling the suitcases.

An hour after that, Madame Wing tears open the envelope and sinks her nails into the maid's eyes.

## 29

## Send Me Number 57

Madame Wing does not telephone to demand an update that night. Rafferty calls anyway to report that he has identified the Cambodian man, but Pak says she is too busy to come to the phone. "Nothing else is happening," Rafferty says.

"According to you," Pak says mysteriously, and hangs up.

"Why do I have the feeling," Rafferty asks Rose, "that things are being kept from me?"

Rose is settled at Rafferty's desk, doing her business accounts. She has a pencil in her hand, another behind her ear, and a hank of hair between her teeth, usually a prelude to some frustrated pencil chewing. Twice a week she writes down in a ledger every baht she has earned and every baht she has spent—for food, rent, shampoo, soap, clothing, pink plastic hair clips, donations at the temple, money sent to her family, and—finally—her business expenses: *tuk-tuk* fares, advances to the women, new T-shirts and jeans for their interviews, cell-phone charges. The exercise does little for her mood.

"When I think of all the money I threw away when I was dancing," Rose says, studying the numbers on the page, "I could scream."

Rafferty looks at the familiar terrain of her profile, at the play of light on her hair, at her straight back and at the smooth skin over the curve of her neck. At the carefully ironed shirt she wears tucked in to her jeans because the bottom is frayed and it embarrasses her. "I haven't heard you scream in a while."

"Since you gave me that money, I have nine thousand baht in the bank," she says, ignoring him. "A little more than two hundred dollars. Do you think I should send some of it home?"

"Save it for a rainy day," he says in English.

"Poke," she says gently in Thai, "it rains nearly every day."

A wave of longing, mixed with something like loneliness, washes over him. "All the more reason," he says, also in Thai.

"I'll send them five thousand. Half and a little bit. That will make them happy."

"You make a lot of people happy, Rose."

She says nothing. Rafferty can almost see the words hanging in the air between them. He feels the same breathless awkwardness he experienced in junior high, when he first asked a girl for a date. The stillness in the room presses in on him like water.

"Rose—"

"Don't confuse me, Poke," she says. She closes the ledger with a soft pop. She still has not turned to face him.

"I'm not trying to confuse you."

She waves the words off. "But you are. You're making me think too much. And don't tell me I said I'd think about it. I *am* thinking about it." The chair's hinged back creaks when she leans away from the desk, as though she wants to be farther from the ledger and the numbers it contains. Her right hand tightly grips the arm of the chair. "We were fine until you started. We got along, we laughed, we didn't . . . we didn't ask questions. I was comfortable here. Now you want to change everything—adopt Miaow, bring the boy in, marry me. You *do* want to marry me, don't you?"

"Well, I . . . yes. Sure. That's why I asked."

She leans back some more and then straightens. For a moment he thinks she is not going to answer him. "Getting married is much more complicated than just sleeping with me."

"Why?" He thinks he knows some of the answers, but they have to talk about them sometime.

She breathes out sharply in exasperation and turns to him. "How far is it from me to you right now?"

This is not what he expects. "I don't know. Six, eight feet."

She throws the pencil onto the desk. "It's a million miles, Poke. And more than miles. It's what we believe, what we've done, who we are. What we need to do."

"If it's that far," he says, trying to make light of it, "we should get started early."

She claps her hands, just once, to get his full attention, and he feels his shoulders straighten. "*Listen* to me. You're a fine-looking man. You're sweet. You have a good heart. Any woman in her right mind would be happy you asked. I don't know, Poke. Maybe you should ask one of them." She gets up and walks to the sliding doors and then past them, the city lights framing her.

"That's silly, Rose. This isn't a raffle. I don't want anyone except you."

"And I suppose I want you." She stops in midstride and gives him both eyes in a gaze that seems to focus about four inches beneath his skin. "But that may not be enough."

Rafferty wants to stand, too, but he is afraid to. The connection between them is suddenly so tenuous that almost anything could sever it: a disturbance in the air, a beam of light coming in through the window. And, fragile as it is, it's a bridge he has to cross. "If that's what we have, it's what we have," he says. "And I'll do whatever it takes to make it enough."

"I know you'll try. But can you do it? I don't know. And I don't know whether I can either."

Rafferty starts to reply, but the words are carried away by a cold breeze that seems to blow straight through him. He can feel his heart contract. He has made a tremendous mistake. He's been so focused on

Miaow that he hasn't taken the time to look at all of this from Rose's perspective.

Or even to recognize that he doesn't have the faintest idea what Rose's perspective is.

The room, with all its familiar features, suddenly feels like someplace he's never seen before. An unknown place in an unknown country.

His hands are in mid-air before he knows consciously what he is going to do. He brings his hands together, palm to palm in a gesture of prayer, to make a *wai*. He raises the *wai* face high to express respect and says, "Forgive me."

Keeping her eyes on his, she turns her head slightly to the left, as though she might be able to see him more clearly this way. She looks wary. After a moment she says, "I have forgiven you many times. What am I forgiving now?"

"I'm an American," he says. "As much as I love you, as much time as I've spent here, I'm still an American. And I've made the classic American mistake."

She doesn't even blink. "Which is?"

"To think that everybody is really just like us, even if they don't act that way. Or that they *want* to be like us, they *would* be like us if they could just shake off all the stuff that makes them seem different." He is choosing his words anxiously, picking one, discarding others, knowing how limited his Thai is, how unequal to this challenge. He hadn't worried about it until this moment, convinced that the most important part of the conversation would be heart-to-heart. But now he knows he doesn't understand Rose's heart either.

"If it's really a million miles from me to you," he says, "please help me to cross it."

Rose pulls her head back fractionally, less than an inch, as though she has been struck by something very soft. Her hands go into the pockets of her jeans, and she stands there, considering, while Rafferty holds his breath. Then she says, "I believe in ghosts, Poke. Do you?"

"I don't know."

"I believe that trees and stones have spirits living in them. I believe that people have light inside them, even the worst people. I believe that the lives we are living now lead us to our next life, and the lives we led before led us to this one. Do you believe in your next life, Poke?"

"I don't know how I'm going to get through my current one."

"No, you don't," she says. "And that's a problem for me. I have problems, lots of problems, that you can't see, Poke, and some of them are about you. I see things in your life and mine, and Miaow's, that can't just be *fixed*." Her hair has fallen forward, and she pulls her hands from her pockets, slips them beneath the long fall of hair, and throws it back over her shoulders, a gesture he has always found compellingly beautiful. "You see a problem and your response is to fix it, like it's a broken air conditioner, or forget about it. I can't do that. That's not how life works for me. The things we do, the things we don't do, they carry forward into other lives. Lives that come after this one. And they affect other people's lives, now and in the future."

Rafferty's head feels like it weighs fifty pounds. He lets it drop forward so his chin almost rests on his chest. "Give me an example."

"My life before I met you." Her voice is defiant.

Poke had expected this subject, but not in this context. "I know all about that."

"Do you? I don't think you do. You know about it the same way you'd know the story of a movie you watched." She raises her hands to her shoulders and brings them straight down, putting herself inside an invisible frame. "She danced, she went with men, she quit. End of story, except that you get to feel good about yourself by putting it all in the past, by saying it doesn't matter anymore. But it *does* matter."

"I know this is probably the wrong thing to say, but it doesn't matter to me."

"Do you understand the damage I did to myself? Do you know what I have to carry with me? That I danced up on that bar night after night with my rear end showing, so men could say, 'Send me Number 57,' like I was a sandwich? That I went to their hotels, no matter what they wanted—whether they wanted to make a pornographic video, or have me pee on them, or give it to me in the ass? I *did* that, Poke, I did all of it. I *took money* for it. I could have walked out of those rooms at any time, and I didn't."

She stops herself and draws two deep breaths. Her shoulders slump, and suddenly she is sitting on the coffee table in front of the couch. She picks up a pack of cigarettes, works one out, flicks the lighter, and looks at him over the flame.

"There's nothing I can do about that," Poke says, "except to love you and to understand why you did it."

"Yes," she says. She inhales hard, brightening the coal at the cigarette's tip enough to cast a red glow on her cheekbones. "You do understand that. I did it for my family."

"And that makes merit," Poke says. He has both hands on the edge of the table, leaning forward with enough force to whiten his knuckles. "That has to mean something. It has to . . . I don't know, cancel out some of . . . some of the other stuff."

"I'll carry it with me as long as I live," she says. "And beyond." The cigarette dangles loosely from her fingers, forgotten. "And I bring that damage into your life. Into Miaow's."

"We need you," he says.

"You think you do. And you think I'll be good for you and you'll be good for me, and that will fix me, just like adopting Miaow will fix her, just like you want to fix the boy. That's good of you, Poke. It's generous. It comes from a warm heart. But we're not air conditioners. We are who we are because of who we've been, in this life and in the past. It's too deep to tinker with, and you can't see that, even though to me it's a wall fifty feet high." She rediscovers the cigarette, puts it to her lips, and lowers it again without taking a drag. "And it will be here, that damage, in this house."

And then she's up again, walking away from him. "You think you understand about my family," she says without looking back. "You know I worked the bars because of my family. But if I did that for them, Poke, what else will I do?"

"You'll take care of them. I'll help you take care of them."

She turns to face him. "We have ten dollars left," she says. Her voice is so low he has to strain to hear it. "Miaow is hungry. My little sister up north is hungry. Who gets the ten dollars?"

Rafferty pushes the table so hard it slides away from him. "We're never going to be down to ten dollars, Rose. You can't take an insurance policy against the entire future."

"I would send the money to my sister," Rose says. "Without a minute's thought. Is this a problem?"

After a moment too long for Rafferty to measure it, he says, "Yes."

"Well, that's what you would be getting, Poke. You would be getting my damage, my mama and papa, and my brothers and sisters, too. You would be getting *my priorities*. And I would be getting the knowledge that I might harm you, and even Miaow."

"How much harm would you do to Miaow if you left?"

She shakes her head, and for a second he thinks he misunderstood something she said. "I'm not talking about *leaving*. You said you wanted to marry me. That's different than playing house. That's joining souls, Poke. The threads they'll tie around our heads will join my soul to yours. I do you the honor of taking that seriously." She holds up a hand, palm out, to stop him from replying. "Don't you think this is difficult for me? Don't you think it would be easier for me to pretend that none of this matters? I could just say yes, Poke, and bring you into a world you'd never understand. You wouldn't even know who was sleeping next to you. Most girls who came out of the bars would say yes in the amount of time it would take their hearts to beat. And then they'd clean out your bank account and leave you in the middle of the night, and I know lots of girls who would think I'm crazy for not doing that."

"They're not you."

"No, they're not. But what they would have done to you might be better for you than marrying me."

He leans back, suddenly aware that he looks like someone who is about to spring. "I'm listening to you. I'm trying to understand what you're saying. Do I get to talk?"

She gives him a half smile. "I've never known you not to."

"Okay." He folds his hands, looking desperately for the words. "So here's me. I'm not the greatest bargain in the world. I've spent most of my life looking for something easy, something that might be fun for an hour or an evening. I've been the guy in the hotel room, remember? Ask Fon. I'm not proud of that. I'm not proud of much I've done. I've wasted a lot of my life." He grabs a breath. "This life anyway." Rose lowers her head to hide another smile. "Maybe the best thing I can say about myself is that I try not to hurt other people. I don't always succeed, but I try."

"That counts." Rose has leaned against the edge of the desk, her back straight. Holding her left shoulder with her right hand. To Rafferty it looks like a defense.

"And you . . . well, you're one of the best people I've ever met. You're good and generous and truthful and beautiful. I could look at you for the rest of my life without my eyes getting tired. Maybe you're right, maybe I don't see most of what you see. Maybe I'm lost, maybe I'm sleepwalking. Maybe you could wake me up."

Rose draws a long breath and blows it out, turning slowly to the glass doors. She could be counting the lights in the windows. "A while ago, you said 'I can try,'" she says. She looks back to him. "I can try, too."

"I promise to keep my eyes open. I promise to listen. I promise not to think I can make everything right by fixing your intake valve or something. But I don't promise not to try to make things right. That's part of the way I love you."

Rose brings both hands to her mouth. The gesture stops him.

"I haven't said I love you," Rose says. "I should have said that first. I do love you. I love you enough to try to do this right or not do it at all."

"We *can* try," Rafferty says. "We can try together." For the first time, he feels confident enough to stand.

"There's one more thing," Rose says. "And, Poke? I don't expect us to solve all these things tonight. But I want it all said. I don't want to leave anything under—what is it you say?—under the couch."

"Under the rug." He is aching to hold her.

"All right, under the rug." She brings her hands together in front of her, loosely folded. "I'm someone who is changing her life. I'm the person, the only person, who takes care of my family. I'm someone who has been used and lied to, and lied to again, for years. I've met the experts."

"I know."

She holds up both hands. "Right now, Poke, I'm balanced on top of a high wall. If I walk exactly right, I'll be fine. If I take a wrong step, I'll fall. What happens to me is not important, but what happens to my family if I fall is very important. But, Poke? You're balanced on top of a wall, too. I don't want to be . . . to be what you trip over."

"I'll walk carefully. And I'll look out for you, too."

"Then listen to me now. I won't talk about this again." Her eyes close slowly, and when she reopens them, she is looking at a spot on the floor, midway between them. "I danced on that stage a long time. There were a lot of men, hundreds of men. To them I was Number 57." She brings her eyes up. "Your wife. Number 57."

"My wife. Rose."

"We'll meet them," she says. "They're everywhere in Bangkok." She extends a hand, mimicking an introduction. "'This is my wife, Number 57.'" She widens her eyes in mock surprise. "'Oh, I see. You've already met.' It'll be you and Fon all over again, except that the girl will be me. Your wife."

"Do you honestly think I'd feel that way?"

"Or suppose Number 58 comes along."

"That's not going to happen."

"No," she says, pulling her hair back again. "It probably won't. You're an honorable man."

"Then is that it?"

She sighs. "Poor baby," she says. "That's it. But promise me you'll think about it, Poke. About all of it."

"Fine, but I'm going to ask you to think about something, too."

"What?"

"Miaow."

She puts long fingers to her eyes and rubs them gently. Without looking at him, she says, "I think about Miaow all the time. Almost as much as I think about you."

"I know you do."

She gives him the smile that starts with her eyes, slowly finds its way to the corners of her mouth, and always makes his legs wobble. "You know what I think about, do you? Then what am I thinking right now?"

He grins back at her. "You're thinking about kissing me."

"You *are* paying attention. How about it?"

"A kiss is a viable option," he says in English. He takes a step toward her.

The telephone rings.

"Wait a minute," Rafferty says to the phone without picking it up. He wraps his arms around her, feels the long, strong back, the deeply rounded gully of her spine. She tilts her head, and their lips meet. The tip of her tongue traces the shape of his lips and then darts into his mouth. He tastes her sweetness and breathes in the faint fragrance of her skin. Her cheeks are dusted with baby powder.

She steps back, her face flushed. "You'd better get that now, or you won't get it at all."

Rafferty picks up the phone. In the background he hears a shrieking that sounds like a thousand rusty hinges, like a convention of crows, like nothing human.

"You must come," says Pak. "You must come *this minute.*"

## 30

## Madame Is in an Excitable State

He can hear her screams even while he is talking with the guard at the gate. Pak meets him halfway up the drive, dripping sweat, with panic widening his eyes. They head toward the house at a run.

"What is it?"

"She will tell you." Pak is out of breath. He has to fight to get the words out. The back of his jacket is soaked with perspiration.

The front door stands open, light pouring out into the night. Pak leads him to the right, toward the screams. "You must be patient with her," he says over his shoulder. "Madame is in an excitable state."

"Thanks for the bulletin."

They enter the small room where he first met Madame Wing. She is crumpled in her wheelchair with her knees drawn up to her shoulders, looking as angular and insubstantial as a swatted spider. A blanket covers the lower half of her body. Two enormous male servants are in the room, their heads bowed, as Madame Wing pours her fury on them, a shrill stream high enough to make dogs howl. When Rafferty comes in, she breaks off and gives him a glare that is intended to nail him to the wall.

"*You*," she spits. "What have you been *doing*? What earthly good are you? Your mother should have aborted you."

"I'm fine, thanks," Rafferty says. "And you?"

"*Idiot*. You took my money and you have done nothing. I placed my faith in you—"

"And I identified the man who robbed you in less than twenty-four hours. By the way, his name is Chouk Ran."

"A lot of good that does. A *name*." She almost chokes on the word. "What use is a fucking *name*? I need *that man's skin*."

*The hell with it,* Rafferty thinks. *Take the fifteen K and walk.*

She strikes at the arms of her wheelchair with the gnarled hands as though she could beat the truth out of it. "He made a *demand*," she snarls. "He had the effrontery to make a *demand*. If you had done your job—"

"When did the demand come?"

She breaks off, her mouth open and quivering. She swallows loudly enough to be heard across the room. "Early this morning."

"Excuse me? Did you say early this *morning*?"

"Are you deaf as well as useless?"

"No, I'm just having a little trouble believing my ears. I thought you said it came early this morning—"

"That *is* what I said—"

"—and, see, that doesn't make sense, because I know you would have called me. Since I'm working on this for you, remember? It would have been stupid not to call."

Pak inhales sharply behind him.

Madame Wing stares at him with something like disbelief. Finally she says, in a tone so cold he can almost see her breath cloud, "You were not needed."

"Apparently I was. Or am I missing something? He made a demand, and you met it, and he kept what he stole from you. Something along those lines?"

"Mr. Rafferty—" Pak begins, but Madame Wing silences him with a look.

"Yes," she says. She is watching him, the dark eyes flat and still as a snake's.

"What did he want?"

The steel returns to her voice. "Ten million baht."

"And you sent it to him. Who took it?"

Her mouth twists as though she would spit at his feet. "A maid," she says.

"Bring her."

"That is not necessary."

Rafferty is suddenly so angry his throat is almost blocked. "How about this? How about bring her or I leave?"

She blinks as though she has received a blow to the face. "Leave?"

"Go home. Send your fucking money back and let you deal with this yourself."

For a moment Rafferty thinks Madame Wing will fly out of her wheelchair and straight at him, but instead she settles back and, in a voice like a grinding knife, says to Pak, "Get her."

"Did he send you anything?" Rafferty asks when Pak is gone.

"Oh, yes," she says. "He sent me something." She reaches beneath the blanket on her lap and withdraws an envelope. She holds it out, and he crosses the room and takes it from her. Her hand is shaking for the first time. In the envelope are three sheets of cardboard, very much like the ones that came in the shirts he bought for Superman.

"And I'm correct in assuming that this was not what he stole."

"Do not bait me, Mr. Rafferty. Better people than you have tried."

"I'm not afraid of you. Whoever you are, you're not used to people who hit back."

She coils herself deeper in the chair, but before she can reply, she suddenly registers that the other two servants are still in the room. "Out," she snaps. They practically collide in their eagerness to leave.

"Did Chouk pick up the money himself?" Rafferty asks before she can launch into whatever she was going to say.

She is looking at him as though she is trying to guess his weight. "It would seem so."

"How did he do it?"

Grudgingly at first and then with mounting fury, she tells him about the taxis and the cell phone.

"It sounds like he's alone," Rafferty says, working it through. "There's nothing he would have needed a partner for. He gets into a taxi and pays it to wait on the boulevard for two or three hours before the maid is supposed to come out. He's looking for a setup. He writes down the plate numbers of the cars that seem to be idling around, if any are. Then, when the maid gets into her taxi, he follows for an hour or so to make sure there's no one behind him, and then he calls her and tells her where to stop."

"What could you have done about it?"

He studies the bas-relief for a moment, not really seeing it. "Well, off the top of my head, I would have been in a private car with a driver, a few blocks away. The maid would have had two cell phones, one I could call on and the one he gave her, so he would never get a busy signal. She would have called me the moment she was in the cab, so I could hit the street just as she pulled away. I would have changed cars once or twice so I wouldn't be spotted, and called her to find out where they were so I could direct my driver. I suppose there's a small chance that they might have made the exchange when I wasn't around, but not much of one."

After a moment she says in a withering tone, "Pak did not think of this."

"Yeah," Rafferty says, "and neither did you."

He hears people enter the room behind him and turns to see Pak, trailed by a plump maid with a blunt-chopped schoolgirl's haircut, no more than eighteen or nineteen years old. She wears a black skirt and white blouse, and she is hanging her head. It is not until she lifts her chin that he sees the quivering jaw and, above it, the bandages.

One eye is completely swathed in white adhesive, with the puffy edges of a cotton pad peeping out from beneath it. The bandages continue down both cheeks, all the way to her jawline. One slants white across her nose. Above the bandages on the left side of her face are two long, red gouges, scored deep into the defenseless tissue and stained with iodine. Her eyes skitter toward him for an instant and then drop to the floor.

Rafferty turns to Madame Wing, feeling the tightness come back to his neck and shoulders. "Did you do this?"

Madame Wing's chin comes up, and the corners of her mouth pull down. "And if I did?"

"Then you're an appalling old bitch." Pak lays a hand on his shoulder, and Rafferty pivots quickly and knocks it off. "Don't touch me again unless you want a lot of stuff to get broken." To Madame Wing he says, "Who the fuck do you think you are, the empress dowager?"

"*Mr. Rafferty,*" Pak says.

"I'm going to work this out," he says, his voice ragged with anger, "but not because of you. Because a Thai safecracker named Tam got killed by your Mr. Chouk, and he had a very sweet wife whose heart was broken by it. And thanks for telling me about the dead man. You can pay me or not, I don't give a shit. I never want to lay eyes on you again." He wheels around and says to Pak, "Get out of my way."

"Stop, Mr. Rafferty," Madame Wing says. "Please stop."

"I don't brake for assholes."

"You want to solve this, don't you? For whoever it was. Then you have to see what else he sent me."

He turns back to her in spite of himself. "What?"

"You'll be interested," she says acidly. "Follow me."

She wheels herself past Pak, past Rafferty, and through the door, the wheelchair making its trapped-animal squeal. Rafferty tracks her down a long hallway into a spacious, formal room. On the floor of the room are two large, open suitcases. At first Rafferty thinks they are full of rags. Then he looks more closely and inhales so sharply he starts to cough.

"Ten million baht," Madame Wing says. "Shredded."

He hears a rustle of paper behind him, but he can't stop looking at the shredded money, ten million baht cut into narrow, worthless strips. "He also sent this," Madame Wing says.

He tears his eyes away from the suitcase to see her holding out a sheet of cheap notebook paper. It is written in a language he cannot read, just a few short words, a single line of flowing script.

"What does it say?"

She looks up at him with those luminous nocturnal eyes. "It says 'I want the deed to your house.'"

He looks back at the spirals of paper, worthless now. Trying to measure the amount of hate in the gesture. Against all his instincts, he realizes, he wants to know more about that hate.

He says, "Give me the deed."

# PART III

# HaMMERSTRiKE

## 31

## Nobody Has to Know Everything

For the second day in a row, Rafferty is up at six. After months of trying to get up early and failing, he has found the remedy: Sleep on a lumpy couch in the apartment's brightest room. He is at the kitchen counter, working on his second cup of coffee, when Miaow comes briskly into the living room. Her school clothes are primly immaculate, seams plumb straight, her face shining with the effect of the cold water she uses to wake herself up. Her hair is so precisely in place it looks like she arranged it one strand at a time. Rafferty's joints grow weak at the sight of her.

She is preoccupied, all business, and he has a sudden vision of what she will look like as an adult: She will look like a corporate vice president. She stops at the couch, notices the blanket Rafferty dropped when he got up, and goes through a small pantomime of exasperation. She does everything but shake her head. With an expression of sorely tried patience, she picks up the blanket and refolds it into sharp-cornered quarters. When she has placed it neatly at the head of the couch, she turns and sees him for the first time. Her eyebrows chase each other toward her hairline.

"Good morning, Miaow."

She looks at him, then at the clock on his desk. "Am I late for school?"

"No. I'm early. I want to talk to you about something."

She purses her mouth, bringing Mrs. Pongsiri to mind, and angles her head slightly in the direction of her room, the direction of Superman. "A problem?"

"Not about him," Rafferty says. "And not a problem, really. A good thing."

He watches her cross the room and climb up onto the chair beside him. He suddenly realizes he has no idea what her morning routine might be. A pang of guilt pierces him: What kind of father *is* he? "Do you want some milk or something? Cereal? Eggs?"

"An orange," she says. "And a Coke."

"Coke? At this hour? And an orange?"

"That's what I eat," she says patiently. "Every morning."

"Breakfast is the most important meal of the day," his mother says in his voice.

"Is that why you're just drinking coffee?" She makes a grimace. "Coffee." She says it the way she might say "mucus." "*Bean drink.* Hot bean drink. And you give *me* a hard time."

"I'm a grown-up. I don't need breakfast."

"And you hate it," Miaow says.

"There's that," he acknowledges.

"I hate it, too. This is my breakfast. A Coke and an orange. Unless we have grapes."

"I see." He has run out of things to say, so he gets up and grabs an orange and a can of warm Coke. "It's a pretty awful breakfast," he says, pouring the Coke.

"I know," she says, closing the subject.

"Ice?" The question is ridiculous and he knows it.

She doesn't even look up. "Oh, *please.*" She manages to pack into the words a remarkable amount of world-weariness for someone who's only eight.

"I have to say *something*, Miaow. It's sort of my job."

"I'm used to being alone in the morning," she says with a tinge of grumpiness.

"Me, too." He sits across the counter from her on the living-room side, so he can see her face. The two grumps share a companionable silence as she peels her orange. Its sharp fragrance invades his nostrils. He can hear the Coke fizzing in the glass. He feels inexplicably happy. How could he have missed this for so many mornings?

"What are we supposed to be talking about?" she says with her mouth full.

"I want you to stay with me," he says.

She looks up at him, chewing. "I *am* staying with you."

"No. I mean forever. Permanently." After what he went through with Rose, he has no idea how Miaow will react. He can feel his heart bumping its way around inside his chest as though it's gotten lost.

She looks quickly away, her face closed. For a long moment, she works on chewing her orange. Then she says, "Okay."

Rafferty makes a firm decision that he will not burst into tears. He concentrates on the orange, half peeled on the table, on how the light strikes the jeweled sections and the fine white threads, and then he says, "Up until now we've been kind of breaking the law. I want to adopt you. Officially. Do you know what that means?"

She still has not looked at him. "Sure," she says. "It means you're really my . . . um, my father. Instead of just pretend."

"That's right." He has difficulty getting the words out, and she darts him a glance at the sound of his voice, then looks away again. He clears his throat and says, "That's what I want."

"Oh," she says to the refrigerator. Then she says, "Me, too."

*Oranges smell like happiness*, Rafferty thinks. "We have to go talk to a man today. He's a nice man named Hank Morrison."

"Khun Hank," she says. "All the kids know him."

"Do they like him?"

"He helps." Her enthusiasm is somewhat reserved.

"Well, we have to go talk to him today, after school. He's going to ask us questions, about how we live here and about what happened to you before you came here."

Her shoulders rise protectively. "What kind of questions?"

"About everything," he says.

She looks him full in the face and then, slowly, lowers her eyes until she is gazing at the surface of the counter. With a coiled index finger, she strikes the half orange, sending it spinning.

Rafferty waits until the orange wobbles to a stop. "He'll ask you some questions I've never asked you. I want you to promise me you'll tell him the truth."

"He doesn't have to know everything," she says. "Nobody has to know everything."

"He has to know everything."

Her face sets. "No." She strips a thread from the orange and rolls it into a tight ball between thumb and forefinger, then flicks it—hard—across the room at the refrigerator. Her spine is rigid.

"It's to help us. He has to ask the questions, or the police won't let me adopt you."

She pushes her chair back stiffly, ignoring the half-eaten orange. "I'm going to be late for school."

"So you'll be late. What're they going to do, chop you up and fry you?" He puts a hand flat on the counter between them. "Listen, Miaow, I can make you a promise. I promise he won't tell me what you talk about if you don't want him to. But you have to talk to him."

She looks down at her lap, evaluating the weight of the promise. "We'll see," she says, and Rafferty hears his own equivocation, refined over a lifetime, coming back at him, from a child he has known only a few months. As he watches her shoulder her book pack and close the door behind her, he wonders what other dubious gifts he may have passed on.

———

**ULRICH'S DRAPES ARE** open. Someone has been here. Rafferty pauses at the door, holding it open, listening. It is not difficult for him to imagine someone else standing absolutely still in one of the rooms, listening as well. After a minute or so, he figures the hell with it and goes in. He picks up one of the small stone apsarases, hefts it like a club, grabs the gun with his free hand, and does a quick search. He is alone.

The place is hot again. As little as he wants to touch them, he has come to look for manufacturers' marks on the whips and restraints in the bottom drawer of the cabinet; they might tell him where they were bought. He is dreading the moment he has to pick them up. The instant he enters the office, he stops as suddenly as he would if he had walked into a glass door.

Uncle Claus's CD-ROMs are back.

Not all of them, he sees, as he nears the desk. There are three empty slots in the storage tower. The others have been returned, presumably by whoever removed them in the first place, which—according to the woman next door—had been Doughnut. Considering all the trouble she took to gain access to Claus Ulrich's life in the first place and the care with which she erased her presence when she left, it must have been important to her to return to take these things away, and equally important to bring them back.

He sits down at the desk and turns on the computer. While he waits for it to go through its internal checklist, he opens the first of the CD cases, which says WINDOWS 98.

The disk inside is home-burned from a blank available everywhere in Bangkok, ten disks for two to ten bucks, depending on the gullibility of the buyer. Written neatly near the center, in black permanent marker, is the notation "*AT Series 400–499.*"

AT Series. AT Enterprises, the letterhead in the drawer. He opens the next case, watching the irritating hourglass on the computer screen and asking himself for the thousandth time why they couldn't have programmed the damn thing to actually fill with sand so you'd have some idea how far along you are. How difficult could it be? The second disk is in a box that says COREL WORDPERFECT, but it too is home-burned. The notation says *"AT Series 600–699."*

He opens all the cases, arranging the disks by number. When he's finished, he has a pile of jewel boxes on the floor and thirteen disks spread out across the desk, beginning with AT Series 0001–0099 and ending with 1500–1599. Missing are 500–599, 700–799, and 800–899.

The computer is ready at last. He slaps the 0001–0099 disk in the drive and looks at the directory.

The files are, as promised, numbered AT 0001 through AT 0099. They are .jpg files, which means pictures. His heart sinks at the information. He does not really think he wants to look at these.

And until he sees the first one, he has no idea how right he is.

**CHOUK HAS ASKED** himself a hundred times whether he should make the payment he promised the guard. He knows the risks, knows it is one of the few times he will be exposed. For the first time since he intercepted the maid to take delivery of the money, he will have to arrange a meeting. Madame Wing will be far more vigilant, now that he has returned her money, shredded into scrap, and made his second demand.

How he wishes he could have been there when she opened the suitcases. Perhaps the guard knows how she reacted. That alone would almost be worth the risk of paying him.

Why had Tam looked at the photos? He has talked with Tam incessantly in his head since that night, trying to explain why he pulled the trigger: the risk that Tam would turn on him, that he would go to Madame Wing. No one can be allowed to prevent Chouk from completing his work. He has made promises to too many people who are now long gone.

But still, Tam had loved his wife, and she probably loved him in return. Chouk has ruined two lives.

It is fitting, he thinks, that Tam had known him by a different name. Chouk no longer knows who he is; he is as hollow as a ghost. All that remains is the course he has set. Motion is everything.

He is no longer Chouk Ran. He is just whoever it is who is doing this.

And she will pay for that, and for all those she destroyed.

But still, the bits of him that remain are troubled. He killed Tam, and if he does not pay the guard, he will have abandoned both of the people who helped him. He could not have done what he has already done without their aid. Even though they did it for money, not because they believed in his mission.

He looks around the rented room he has slept in for two nights. Unlike the flophouses, here there are no rows of bunks; it has a door and walls to keep people out. He needed the privacy to handle the money. The large shredder he bought at the office store gleams in the corner. He should probably change rooms, but he can't face the work of moving the shredder. He had no idea how heavy it would be.

With a strong feeling he is doing the wrong thing, he goes down to the street to find a pay phone.

A CHEAP HOTEL room. It could be any of a thousand hotels, anywhere in Southeast Asia. Cold light comes through a small window. It is probably raining.

The bed is narrow, with a garish red coverlet. The floor is dirty linoleum. There is no rug or other furniture except an attached bed table and a large, old-style phone with a dial.

A number hotel, maybe.

In 1982.

Uncle Claus's camera had an automatic date-stamp function, and he occasionally forgot to turn it off. The picture on the screen is dated 9-16-82.

The little girl hog-tied on the bed was somewhere between eight and ten on September 16, 1982. The ropes bite into her wrists and ankles, and her defenseless stomach is bare and streaked with red.

She is crying.

The series began with photos of her wearing the clothes of poor Southeast Asian children everywhere: T-shirt, shorts, sandals. She had been smiling in the first few shots. She stopped smiling when her clothes began to come off. She started crying when the hot red wax dripped from the candle onto her bare chest.

After he has looked at fifteen or twenty pictures, Rafferty gets up and goes to the bathroom and vomits into the toilet. On his way back to the computer, he stops at the filing cabinet and, for the first time, forces himself to pull out the restraints, the leather straps and gags and handcuffs and the collar with the spikes set into its edges that are designed to cut into the neck and chest.

They are *tiny*.

He returns to the screen and searches further through the pictures, feeling the fury rise in him, mixed with a swelling terror. He has difficulty forcing himself to keep his eyes on the screen, and he jumps to his feet and steps back, believing for a moment he will pass out, when he gets to the picture of the child with the electric iron on her chest. Her right arm is thrown over her eyes, her mouth wide in pain. Her ankles had been cuffed together so she couldn't kick in self-defense.

*He* was in some of the pictures, too, a naked fat man with his face crudely blacked out with Magic Marker. He held a camera remote in one hand, with a button at one end of it. He depressed the button to snap a picture whenever he was satisfied with the level of monstrosity being inflicted on the bright red bed.

There are almost *sixteen hundred* of them.

Rafferty feels the sickness and the fear rise up in him again, but he forces them away and then lets the fear back in, lets it drive him forward despite his revulsion as he keeps looking, opening one disk after another, paging through the photos as quickly as the computer will allow, looking at nothing but the faces and paying special attention to the later ones, the 1300, 1400, and 1500 series, some of which are date-stamped within the past three to four years. The most recent image with a date stamp, AT1548, was taken in 2003.

He is looking for Miaow.

*This* is something she would never talk to him about. She would never talk about it to anyone. If it is here, if *she* is here, he has to know it before they meet with Hank Morrison in—what? Three or four hours? He has been here, in this hell, for hours.

If she is among these tiny victims he needs to know it, before he forces her to tell this story to Morrison. Face after face, scream after scream, he searches for her.

And finds Superman.

He is one of only four boys. Uncle Claus definitely preferred to torment girls. He gave special attention to the boys, however. They presented a different set of anatomical possibilities. What he did to Superman passes Rafferty's understanding so completely that it seems like the work of a different species.

Sixteen hundred photos. At least forty children.

By the time Rafferty turns off the computer, he could kill Claus Ulrich himself.


**THE PHONE RINGS** deep in the pocket of Rafferty's jeans, hard to fish out in the cramped backseat of a *tuk-tuk*. He doesn't even hear it at first. He is trying to lose himself in the heat and light of the day, trying to leave the morning and its bright, terrible screen behind. It is a window he wishes he had never opened.

He wrestles the phone free on the fifth ring and surveys the traffic in front of him. If they don't get a break, he is going to be late meeting Miaow.

"Poke," Arthit says. "There's a lot happening. The stains in the bathroom are blood."

"Good."

"Excuse me?"

"The man was a pig. No, that's not fair to pigs. I'll tell you about it when I see you."

"And another thing. The address for Doughnut's sister was real, but she's moved. A while back, one neighbor says. But, Poke? The blood changes things. I've got two patrolmen talking to everyone in the building. She must have told someone where she was going."

"That's great," Rafferty says. He has to force himself to pay attention.

There is a pause, Arthit undoubtedly evaluating Rafferty's tone. "Are you okay?"

"Peachy. By the way, the Cambodian definitely got Madame Wing's attention." He tells Arthit about the note and the suitcase.

"Ten million baht?" Arthit sounds like he is trying to swallow a whole chicken, perhaps alive. "*Shredded?* That's a whole new kind of hatred."

"Let's hope it was only nine million and he kept a million to pay the guard." Rafferty heaves a sigh that seems to come from the navel. "For now I guess the thing to do is to find the sister."

"If we get something, where will you be?"

"Adopting a child," Rafferty says.

## 32

## One Room for Me

aking the chain from around his neck, Rafferty unlocks the cabinet and puts the CD-ROMs, minus their bootleg cases, inside. They fill the space. He does not return the gun.

A sport coat he never wears conceals the bulge at his waistband. In the mirror he sees himself pale-faced and drawn, overdressed and already perspiring.

He flops heavily down on the couch to wait, wondering how he can face Superman. For that matter, he's not sure he can look Miaow in the eyes. What he has seen is such a horrific violation of the most basic human trust that all adults should be ashamed.

*Some people deserve to die,* Rose had said. What blight destroyed Claus Ulrich so completely? Did he grow around something vile and alien, like a knot in a tree? *Clarissa,* Rafferty thinks, with a sudden surge of nausea. Clarissa's loving Uncle Claus. He leans forward to rest his face in his hands, trying to rub away the images he has just seen and the image of Clarissa's face.

He knows the popular Western psychology: Everybody is a cloud of inner children and warring adults. Rafferty has met sadistic police-men who loved their kids, corrupt lawyers who took care of their aging parents. He has come to expect the beast beneath the skin and to respect those who keep it under control. Rose had talked about karma, about people whose reality was stripped from them by some tremendous event, cutting them adrift like ghosts, forcing them to seek their reality in sensation.

No matter how you explain it, Rafferty has never met anyone whose character was as deeply fractured as Claus Ulrich's.

Had he taken care of Clarissa as penance? Was it his way of prov-ing to himself that he was still human? Was Clarissa the one thing that allowed him to sleep at night, the thing that prevented him from putting the gun into his mouth? Or did he not even connect the two? Was his spirit so completely sundered that he felt nothing but sexual excitement when he was brutalizing those children, nothing but greed when he was selling the pictures, nothing but love when he was with Clarissa?

The reason for the multiple entry stamps for Cambodia and Laos in Uncle Claus's passport is now clear: He was hunting children.

And the way the apartment is furnished suddenly makes sense: all that ornate clutter, all that distraction, all those *things* competing for attention. No clear vistas. Put Claus Ulrich in a bare Japanese room and he would probably have cut his stomach open.

Judging from the occasional date stamps, the missing disks, 500–599, 700–799, and 800–899, contained pictures that were taken eigh-teen to twenty years ago, during a two-and-a-half-year period when Uncle Claus had been especially active. The most recent photo in the 500 series had been dated 1986, and the earliest dated shots in the 800 series had been taken in January of 1989. The 900 series ended in April of that year.

Rafferty is certain he knows why those three disks were not in the apartment.

It gives him no pleasure to have solved the puzzle. He feels as if he weighs five thousand pounds. He knows that the hours he spent in front of that screen have changed him for the worse, and he hates

Claus Ulrich for it as much as he has ever hated anybody in his life.

Empty, bleak, overdressed, and exhausted, he slumps onto the couch to wait for Miaow. The gun feels cold near his heart. For the first time in years, he wishes he knew how to pray.

**HANK MORRISON'S REFUGE** for Bangkok's discarded children occupies a half block of baking pavement surrounded by dirty chain-link. In the center of the pavement, two knots of kids collide noisily in the shade of a squat concrete building that has been painted a squint-inducing shade of buttercup yellow. Oversize Disney characters decorate the walls. As he half drags a reluctant Miaow across the asphalt, Rafferty notes that there are three pictures of Goofy.

Morrison is a tall, slender man with theatrically steel gray hair and sky blue eyes, surrounded by the kind of creases that always identify actors as pilots in the movies. He has a rigid military bearing that may be due to a bad back; he bends stiffly to extend his hand to Miaow.

"And this is Miaow," he says. To his credit, he doesn't slow down and overact the words, as many adults do when they first address a child. If he is surprised at the glare he gets in return, he doesn't show it.

"Why don't you guys sit down?" Morrison goes behind a beat-up desk and hauls out his chair to make things a little less intimidating. Miaow and Rafferty claim territory on a narrow orange couch made of vinyl. Miaow sits rigidly, her spine at a perfect ninety degrees, but Rafferty leans back to demonstrate how relaxed he is and feels his sweat-soaked sport coat squish beneath his weight.

"This isn't going to take long," Morrison says. He is speaking Thai for Miaow's benefit. He smiles at her again. "And it isn't going to hurt a bit."

Miaow gives a short sniff.

Morrison bends forward. "Are you unhappy to be here, Miaow?" His Thai is accented but serviceable, much better than Rafferty's.

"Not talk," Miaow says in English. Her words land on the floor between them like stones.

"We're going to have to talk a little," Morrison says, still speaking Thai. "That's what we're here for."

"Talk no good," Miaow says, sticking to English. Rafferty looks at her, puzzled. It is the kind of pidgin she spoke eight months ago. She's moved far beyond it now.

"You don't have anything to be afraid of," Morrison says. "All we want to do is fix things so you can stay with Poke until you grow up. You want that, don't you?"

Miaow doesn't speak. Rafferty is looking at her, but he can feel Morrison's eyes dart to him. He returns the man's gaze and gives a tiny shrug.

"The two of you *have* discussed this, haven't you?" Morrison asks.

"Sure. She's just nervous about what you're going to ask her."

"Is that it, Miaow? Are you worried about what I'm going to ask you?"

"Talk about Poke okay," Miaow says in the same stubborn pidgin. "Talk before Poke no good."

"Her English—" Rafferty begins, but Morrison warns him off with a look.

"That's fine, then. Let's talk about Poke. Do you like living with Poke, Miaow?"

She chews her lower lip, folds and unfolds her hands, and squirms on the hard couch. After what seems like an eternity, she nods.

"And, Poke, do you like having Miaow live with you?"

"I love Miaow," Rafferty says.

"Do you think Miaow loves you?"

"I hope so. But she'd have to tell you that."

Morrison looks at Miaow expectantly. Miaow opens her mouth and closes it again. Then, moving stiffly, she reaches over and puts her hand in Rafferty's. She turns her head and regards him soberly. Something inside Rafferty shivers and then dissolves.

Morrison sits back in his chair with a suppressed sigh. He crosses his legs and relaxes. "Tell me about Poke's apartment, Miaow."

Miaow looks surprised at the question. She closes her eyes for a moment as though she is searching it for a trap. "High," she says at last.

"Really." Morrison sounds impressed. "How high?"

"Eight floors." She raises her right hand as high as it will go and keeps it there. "Eight floors above the street. No dirt."

"Well, well. How many rooms?"

Miaow's eyes go to the wall as she visualizes it. "Four."

"Let me guess," Morrison says, beginning to count on his fingers. "You have a living room, and a kitchen, and Poke's bedroom, and—and—"

"My bedroom," Miaow says. "I have one room for me."

"You're a lucky girl. Lots of kids don't have their own room."

"Lots of kids don't have a *house,*" Miaow says severely. Rafferty begins to relax. "We have a bathroom, too. Our own bathroom. It has hot water. We can use it and Rose can use it, but nobody else gets to use it, no matter how bad they have to go, unless we say they can."

"Would you let me use it?" Morrison asks.

"If you said please." She adjusts herself on the couch. "Then, maybe."

"Who is Rose?"

For a moment Miaow looks confused, as though it is impossible that there should be someone who doesn't know Rose. Then she says, "Poke's girlfriend." She looks up at Poke and says, "Same-same mama for me." Rafferty involuntarily says, "Ohh," and wishes Rose had heard her.

Morrison pulls his chair a few inches closer. "Tell me one thing you like about Poke."

Miaow looks up at Rafferty again and then down at the center of his chest. "He never yells at me. Not even once."

"Tell me one thing you don't like about Poke."

She gives it a moment's thought. "His clothes. He doesn't have any pretty clothes."

"I do too," Rafferty says immediately.

"Do not."

"Do too."

Morrison's eyes go back and forth between them.

Miaow grabs a handful of Rafferty's sport coat and gives it a tug hard enough to pop a button. "You don't have *any* pink shirts except the one I bought you."

"You bought Poke a shirt, Miaow?"

A decisive nod. "All of his are ugly."

"I've noticed," Morrison says.

"Two against one," Rafferty says bitterly.

Miaow barks a laugh and elbows him, surprisingly hard, in the ribs. "Same as Rose and me."

"Tell me about your room, Miaow."

"It's pink," Miaow says. "Poke bought me a pink rug, too. And I have two beds, on top of each other, like a building—"

"Bunk beds?" Morrison asks.

"And I can hang pictures anywhere I want, and there's a really little room that's just for my clothes. A room just for *clothes*. And I have almost enough clothes to fill it, and they're new clothes, too. They smell good. And if I don't want anybody to come in my room, I can close the door."

"Do you lock it?"

"No. I use the frowny face when I don't want anybody to come in. When it's okay for people to come in, I use the smiley face. I made them," she adds, in case Morrison is confused. "They're really cardboard, but I drew faces on them."

"And you sleep there all alone."

"Except for Superman," Miaow says, and Morrison's eyebrows leap half an inch.

"It's temporary," Rafferty says, but Miaow is already talking.

"He used to sleep on the couch, but now Poke sleeps there. With a gun. To protect us."

"Really," Morrison says icily, and Rafferty's cell phone rings.

"Ummm," Rafferty says, and answers the phone.

"People keep beating him up," Miaow says happily.

"Arthit?" Rafferty is aware of Morrison's very level blue eyes on him.

"We've got her," Arthit says. "We've got an address, I mean."

"Is anybody home?"

"How would I know? We found a neighbor lady who knows where the sister moved. They might still be together."

"Is your man still on the scene?"

"Sure. He just called."

"Have him watch the door. He shouldn't talk to her, unless she tries to leave. He can't let her leave."

"Poke," Morrison says, flagging for attention.

"Where is it?" Rafferty asks, pulling out his notebook.

Arthit gives him an address.

"I'll get there as fast as I can." He hangs up and finds Morrison regarding him questioningly.

"I have a problem," Rafferty says. "Start with Miaow, okay, Hank? I'll be back by the time you're finished."

"This is an important meeting," Morrison says. "It's not something we can start and stop again. You should have cleared the afternoon, Poke."

"I did, Hank. This is something I can't help. It's an emergency."

"Emergencies. Sleeping in the living room with a gun. This is not what I wanted to hear today."

"Miaow will explain it. Is that okay with you, Miaow?"

Miaow looks from him to Morrison. "I guess."

"Hank, it won't happen again. All this stuff is temporary. I'm trying to help somebody, and it just—"

"I'll let Miaow tell me about it." Morrison is obviously disconcerted. "But if you're not back here in ninety minutes, Poke, we're going to have a problem."

Rafferty rises, adjusting his jacket to keep Morrison from seeing the gun. "I'll be back. This is an emergency. Only this time, Hank. Seriously. Once in a lifetime."

As he leaves the room, he hears Miaow say, "He's always like that."


"I DON'T KNOW where she is."

Doughnut's sister walks with a limp so severe it almost looks like a parody, dragging a flopping foot behind her like a stone. She grips the

furniture as she goes, looking for balance. The living room is arranged
so there is something solid for her to hold on to every three or four
feet. She wears a loose, shapeless black dress, ankle length, and a wide
black plastic bracelet on her left wrist. Her face puts her somewhere
in her thirties, but they have obviously been hard years. Strands of
gray are already woven through her hair.

Rafferty is standing in the doorway, since she did not invite him
in. "But you can get a message to her."

She makes an equivocal gesture with her right hand: *Maybe,
maybe not.* Her left hand is holding on to the back of a chair.

"This is important," Rafferty says. "To your sister and to you,
too."

A dubious shake of the head. "So what is it?"

"I want you to tell her this: I understand why she kept the three
disks from Claus Ulrich's apartment. Tell her I know what happened
to Claus and why, but no one else does. There are no police involved. If
she talks to me, I'll try to make sure that no police *become* involved."

Her eyes had widened fractionally at Ulrich's name, but now the
impassive face is back in place. "And if she doesn't?"

"Then there may be cops. *I* figured out what happened. How long
do you think it would take them?"

She brings her left hand up to clear an errant wisp of hair from her
eyes, and the wide bracelet slides up her arm. Rafferty sees the deep
white scars crisscrossing the inside of her wrist. There are at least a
dozen of them: She had hacked at herself frantically. She realizes what
he is looking at and lets her arm drop. The bracelet slips back into
place, masking the scars.

"You'll tell your sister."

"If I see her."

"Here's how she can reach me." He writes his name and phone
number on a page in his notebook and tears it out. She tugs the bracelet down and reaches for it. "You'll give it to her."

She folds the paper in half without even looking at it. "If she gets
in touch with me."

"Of course," Rafferty says. "If she gets in touch with you."

---

**MIAOW'S EYES ARE** swollen and red, but the smile she gives Rafferty is the broadest he has seen all day.

"You two getting along okay?" Rafferty asks.

"She's quite a girl," Hank Morrison says. He is sitting next to Miaow on the couch, which in itself is a good sign. "You're a lucky man, Poke."

"I know."

"Hey, Miaow," Morrison says. "There are some kids outside, and I'll bet you already know a few of them. Why don't you go out and see?"

"I want to be here," she says.

"Not now. Poke and I need to talk alone, just like you and I did."

"Are you going to talk about me?"

"We might say how *wonderful* you are," Morrison says. "We might talk about how smart you are and how well you take care of Poke. But mostly we're going to talk about Poke."

Miaow visibly loses interest. "I already know about Poke."

"So you don't have to listen."

She turns to Morrison, face set. "But you're not going to talk about—"

"We both promise," Morrison says, and Poke holds up three fingers and then crosses his heart for emphasis.

"Promise so hard you'll die if you break it."

"I do," Morrison says.

"Me, too." Poke watches her slide down off the couch and walk to the door. "I promise, Miaow," he says again.

"Don't break it," she says to him. "I don't want you to die."

"I wouldn't dare die. You'd kill me."

"You're silly," she says severely, pulling the door closed behind her.

"Whew," Morrison says. "You weren't kidding about her will-power."

"She's going to rule the world."

"She's been through a lot. It's a miracle she's so . . . I guess the word is 'intact.'"

"*She's* a miracle," Poke says. "I never knew I could love anybody so much."

"Well, which do you want first, the good news or the bad news?"

"Up to you."

"The good news is that I haven't got any reservations at all about the way things are between the two of you. I'd stake all my experience that you've got a normal, loving relationship, and that's nine-tenths of the battle."

"What's the other tenth?"

"That's the bad news. I'm not happy with what she's told me about the situation at home, Poke. From what Arthit said, I thought you were a writer, some kind of academic or something. What she's been describing to me sounds like something out of a Schwarzenegger movie."

"It's just that—"

Morrison leans forward. The lines around his eyes no longer soften the blue of them. They're as cold as Freon. "You're sleeping in your living room with a gun because you're afraid some goons are going to kick the door in. The goons who beat you up a few days ago. Does that sound like a stable environment for a kid?"

"It's not as if this happens much, Hank."

"You're carrying a gun right now."

"Shit," Rafferty says, tugging automatically at his jacket. "I didn't think you'd seen it."

"You're wasting my time," Morrison says. "You've got a wonderful kid there, and you're living like a juvenile delinquent. You can't even sit through the meeting without running off to get into a sword-fight or something. Why would I help you adopt her when you might just make her an orphan again?"

"It's not that serious."

Morrison sweeps a hand toward his desk. "This is how serious it is. Those papers are the forms you have to fill out to move forward with this. Two minutes after you and Miaow came into this room, I decided to ask you to fill them out today. Well, I'll tell you what, Poke. I'm going to put them back in the drawer until you've convinced me that you're capable of giving that little girl a stable environment."

"Hank," Rafferty says. "This situation—it started out simply and got very bad very quickly. I began by trying to help a young woman whose uncle disappeared here in Bangkok, and I wound up stumbling over the worst, most violent child pornography you can imagine." Morrison's face goes absolutely still, and he sits even straighter. "I can't drop it, Hank, but I don't really think we're in danger. I haven't met a lot of child pornographers, but I doubt they'd hurt anyone their own size."

"These pictures," Morrison says slowly. He stops and sits forward, as though he has cramps. "You said violent." Rafferty nods. "Are they of Asian kids?"

"Yes."

"Mostly ten, eleven, twelve? Mostly girls?"

Rafferty feels a wave of discomfort. "And a few boys."

Morrison takes a breath deep enough to empty the room of air. "Tied up, being tortured?"

Rafferty meets his eyes. "My turn to ask a question. Why do you know about this?"

"Poke." Morrison puts out both hands, palms forward, a gesture that says *Stop.* "I work with these kids. I've worked with them for twenty years. There isn't much that's happened to them that I don't know about." He gets up, not going anywhere, just moving to move. "How could I do this job if I didn't try to understand their lives?" He stops pacing and puts his hands on his hips, looking down at Poke. "These pictures. Do they have a title?"

Rafferty can't think of any reason not to tell him. "The AT Series."

"My God. Is this man in Bangkok?"

"If he's alive, he's in Bangkok."

"But he may not be alive?"

"I'm glad to say, Hank, that I think, actually, he's not."

"Hallelujah, it's Christmas," Morrison says. "But then what are you looking for?"

"The person who probably killed him. And, if I can find them, the names of anybody he might have shared his hobby with."

"Where'd you get the pictures?"

"Out of the guy's apartment."

Morrison's mouth opens, and he closes it again. "I don't know why I'm so surprised. I always figured the fucker was based here."

"For about twenty years," Rafferty says.

"I know some of these kids," Morrison says. "They've been torn into tiny pieces."

"Hank," Rafferty says, and his tone brings Morrison's head around. "Superman was one of them."

**AS THEY CROSS** the orphanage playground, Miaow reaches up and takes Rafferty's hand. He gives hers a slight squeeze and gets back a grip that makes his knuckles crack.

"I love you, Miaow," he says.

Miaow squeezes even harder.

Rafferty's emotions are a skein of conflicting feelings: revulsion at what he saw on Ulrich's computer, a mixture of pity and horror caused by the sight of the scars on the wrist of Doughnut's sister, a hatred of Claus Ulrich so intense it vibrates in his chest. Against those are the exhilaration he feels about the interview and Morrison's reluctant reconsideration of Superman in light of the fact the boy was one of Ulrich's victims. He might be able to help him after all.

And Morrison had let him fill out the forms. On this front, anyway, Rafferty thinks, everything may work out. The idea makes him so happy he laughs out loud, and Miaow looks up at him, grabs his arm with both hands, and presses her head against his hand.

For Rafferty, time stands still.

## 33

## A Whole New Standard for Awful

*If I had a to-do list,* Rafferty thinks, *it wouldn't have a single thing crossed out.*

In two days he's made no progress at all. Arthit hasn't found a scrap of data on Doughnut in any of the city's databases. The battered guard from Madame Wing's hasn't set foot outside his apartment. Chouk Ran has not contacted Madame Wing.

Doughnut has not called.

The forgery of the deed to Madame Wing's house has been made and one copy sent to her, but nothing has happened to bring it into play.

When Rose comes home from Bangkok Domestics with the news that two of her women have gotten jobs, but also reports that the woman who runs the business had treated her with contempt, it is almost a relief for Rafferty to pick up the phone and methodically take the woman apart. When he is finished, Superman is regarding him with raised eyebrows that signal something like admiration.

While Miaow was at school, Rafferty played Tetris on his computer with Superman and suffered one humiliating defeat after another. The boy could see patterns faster than Rafferty could blink. It wouldn't have been so bad if the kid hadn't laughed, an irritating roosterlike sound, every time Rafferty made a mistake.

"Not so long ago," Rafferty said in English, "I'd have given anything to hear you laugh. Now I'd give anything if you stopped."

The distraction of the computer gave Rafferty the time he needed to be able to look at Superman without seeing the battered, violated boy in the cheap hotel room. By the fourteenth straight loss, Rafferty could meet the boy's eyes.

While Rafferty stewed over the lack of progress, the boy fixed the garbage disposal, the toaster, the stuck window, the light switch in Miaow's room, the light leaks around the air conditioner, and the combination mechanism on Rafferty's suitcase, which had been permanently locked. He also eradicated the stain on the carpet, to Rose's obvious pleasure.

Rafferty and Rose did not discuss their situation, but there was a lightness to her—in her bearing, in her voice—that made Rafferty smile at inappropriate moments. Superman took to imitating him, which Miaow found hilarious.

On the third night, Rose went home to clean her own place, and without her to provide moral and nutritional guidance, Rafferty took the kids to McDonald's, and they ate their recommended allowance of fat for the decade. On the walk home, he told them the story about the Three Little Pigs, changing it so it ended with a recipe for roast pork. Superman thought the new ending was funny. Miaow didn't.

Rafferty talked them through the crowded sidewalk, improvising a plan to write a fairy-tale cookbook: soap-flavored bread crumbs that children could drop behind them in the woods without the birds eating them, a low-calorie gingerbread house, a wolf's stew with boiled grandmother. Superman made a few contributions, but Miaow walked silently between them. When Rafferty laughed aloud at something the boy suggested, she moved around to Rafferty's other side, so he was in the middle. Accepting the hint, Rafferty let his hand drop lightly onto the back of the boy's neck. Superman gave a tiny start and stopped talking in midword, but he did not move away, and a moment later he picked up where he'd left off.

Rafferty felt like he'd just won a marathon.

They got home and settled happily in the living room, although it felt a little emptier without Rose. Miaow began to cut out the figures from her drawings and paste them together in new combinations, and Rafferty suffered a few more grueling defeats at Tetris. At nine o'clock he put the kids to bed and curled up on the couch with his gun.

He decided he'd had a wonderful day.

SURFACING ABRUPTLY FROM sleep, he answers the wrong phone first, saying hello to the dial tone while the cell phone continues to bleat from across the room. The only light is the city's diffuse glow through the sliding glass door, and he barks his shin on the corner of the coffee table on his way to grab the phone.

"Hello." He squeezes his eyes shut, trying to focus his attention.

There is a silence. He thinks he can hear traffic in the background.

"Hello," he says again. "What time is it anyway?"

After a moment a woman's voice says, "Three."

It is an unfamiliar voice, self-possessed and pleasant but reserved, as though its owner is unsure whether to say anything more. Rafferty has to relax his hand on the phone. He is gripping it tightly enough to snap the hinge.

"Hello, Doughnut," he says.

At first he thinks she will hang up, but then she says, "Why did I keep the disks?" To his surprise, her English is excellent.

"Because you're on them," Rafferty says. He grabs a breath and makes the leap he has been considering ever since "You and your sister."

He hears a short, reflexive grunt, as though someone has poked her in the gut. "You looked at the others."

"Yes."

"Did you *enjoy* them?" She drags out the word as though it exerts friction in her throat.

"They're the worst things I ever saw. They set a whole new standard for awful."

"You had to be there," she says. "You want to talk to me. Talk."

"Face-to-face."

"Why?"

"I want to see you. I need to see who you are."

"I'm a girl," she says. "There's nothing unusual about me."

"Oh," Rafferty says, "I think there is."

A siren goes by in the background, and a moment later he hears it in the street below. She is very near.

"I'll call you," she says. The line goes dead.

Rafferty tiptoes down the hall and looks into Miaow's room. Both children are out cold, the boy snoring softly in the top bunk. His sheet, as always, is on the floor. Rafferty covers him gently and goes into his own room to get dressed.

Silom Road is dark and deserted and insubstantial, the bustle and energy of the day long behind. Shop windows are dim. The neon signs are just drab squiggles in glass. The few lighted windows are five or six stories up, where apartment dwellers face their own sleepless nights. He walks several blocks, looking for a pay phone, before he decides that the quality of the connection made it more likely Doughnut was using a cellular. He keeps walking, aimlessly now, covering another block or two before a *tuk-tuk* pulls optimistically to the curb, although he has not signaled it.

"Where?" the driver says, gunning the motor happily. He is chubby and cheerful-looking, with a fat mole on his chin that sprouts black hairs long enough for knot practice. The Buddha's belly below the handlebars is tightly sheathed in a T-shirt covered in children's handprints in bright primary colors.

*When the Buddha sends you a tuk-tuk*, Rafferty thinks, *it's probably a sign that you should go somewhere.* "That way." He indicates the direction in which he is walking and climbs in. The driver pops the clutch, and Rafferty's back slams the back of the seat.

As he accelerates, the driver catches Rafferty studying his face in the rearview mirror and gives him a grin that is extremely rich in gums. "Where we go, boss?"

"Suppose I killed somebody," Rafferty says, watching the man's grin slip. "Where would I put the body?"

He gets a quick lift of the head: The answer is obvious. "Klong Toey. Everybody use Klong Toey."

"But the police would find it if I left it in Klong Toey."

The man purses his lips. "River," he says.

Rafferty says, "But where? Somebody would see me if I dropped it over a bridge."

"Small *soi,* not so many houses. Better than a bridge."

"Show me."

"How many place you want to see?"

"How many can you show me?"

A shrug. "Ten, fifteen."

"How do you know where they are?"

"Police find a body," the driver says. "Everybody comes to look. They need *tuk-tuks.*"

"Okay, show me the best place. Near Pratunam."

Within twenty minutes Rafferty has seen six places, all within an easy drive from Claus Ulrich's apartment, from which a weighted body could have been dropped into the Chao Phraya unobserved. He and the driver sit musing, the little two-stroke engine popping away, as the river glides by, its waters a thick reddish brown, opaque with silt carried down from the north. There could be a sunken city two feet beneath the surface, Rafferty thinks, and no one would ever know it. Cup water in your hands and you couldn't see your palms.

"He was a very big man," he says aloud, without realizing he is speaking.

"Wrap him in a big sheet," the driver suggests. He became voluble when he realized Rafferty could speak Thai, and he has entered completely into the spirit of this hypothetical murder. He twists the hairs growing out of his mole as inspiration strikes. "Dye it black so you can carry it at night."

"That's good, but getting him here . . . She's just one woman, and I don't think she's a big one."

The driver pulls a packet of Krong Thip cigarettes from his shirt pocket and fires one up. "Cut him in pieces."

The stains on the bathroom floor. "Make four or five trips carrying an arm, a leg? That's a lot of back-and-forth. Somebody would notice."

"Boyfriend," the driver proposes instantly. "Kill fat husband, get help from skinny boyfriend."

"Could be." Up until now he has always seen Doughnut acting alone. On the other hand, there were the four men who beat him up in the *soi*.

There is a pause while they both think, and then the driver says, "Good man, bad man?"

"Very bad man."

The driver's face glows red from the coal on his cigarette. "So no problem. One bad person dead. Plenty left."

This is an argument Rafferty has been getting a lot of. "Let's go home." He is suddenly light-headed from lack of sleep. He has a disorienting sensation of motion, as though the river were still and they were gliding sideways.

By the time he walks into the apartment, it is four-thirty. The kids are still asleep, Superman's sheet once more on the floor. He picks it up and covers the boy again, and Superman stirs and his eyes half open. Rafferty is startled by how fast he moves. Within less than a second, he is curled against the wall, knees drawn up protectively, glaring at Rafferty. His teeth are bared.

"No problem," Rafferty says. He takes a step back. "You dropped your sheet."

The boy looks down at the sheet and then up at Rafferty. The tautness slowly goes out of his face, and he nods. He covers himself and stretches out again but keeps his eyes open and fixed on Rafferty's face.

"Go to sleep," Rafferty says, in what he hopes is a fatherly tone. He leaves the room and closes the door all the way so Superman can hear the latch click home.

He makes a silent cup of Nescafé and sips at it. Grim as sin. The Nescafé performs the desired sabotage on his central nervous system, and Madame Wing makes an unexpected appearance in his mind's eye.

What had she looked like when she was younger? She is thin in a way that says she has never been fat: she has the gauntness of someone whose appetites have nothing to do with food. She would have had those terrifying eyes even then, set into a face that was young and old at the same time; she would never have shone with the soft flush of youth. Even at eighteen, he thinks, she would look like someone who had never been out of doors, who had never shared a secret, who had never lost her heart. She has the face of an animal with multiple sets of teeth.

*A whole new kind of hatred,* Arthit had said. Collect ten million baht, shred it, and return it, just to cause her pain. The pain more important than the profit.

Claus Ulrich had probably inspired a new kind of hatred, too.

He is assuming Ulrich is dead.

Suppose he's not, though. Uncle Claus has demonstrated a talent for living inconspicuously, although his weight makes him a conspicuous man. But if a ghost were to appear from his past, a grown and dangerous version of someone he never thought could be a threat to him, someone he saw as a passive object, to be tormented at will— what would he do? Wouldn't a man like Claus Ulrich have a bolt-hole handy in case someone like Doughnut *did* appear? Or would he even recognize her? Twenty years in the same city is a long time, no matter how reclusive you are. He could have encountered dozens of them by now, grown up beyond recognition.

But they would remember *him.*


FIVE CUPS OF coffee later, Rafferty is still on the couch, Miaow has left for school, and the phone finally rings. He grabs the receiver, expecting it to be Doughnut. Instead it is Arthit.

"Get a motorcycle taxi," he says. "Take your cell phone. Your guard is on the move."

## 34

## An Unusually Spiritual Attitude in a Thief

The motorcycle hits a pothole, and Rafferty is momentarily weightless. Then, as he hits the seat, he emphatically isn't.

"We're turning," Rafferty's motorcycle driver shouts into the wind blowing over his shoulder. "Hang on."

For a long, stomach-sinking moment, Rafferty has the sensation of being almost parallel to the surface of the road as the tires squeal, slide sickeningly, and grip again. Then they are upright, and he focuses on the spots of light doing a Busby Berkeley number behind his closed eyelids. The cell phone pasted to his ear is slick with sweat.

"How far from Sukhumvit Soi 28?" Rafferty asks his driver.

"Three or four minutes."

He opens his eyes in time to see the gray iron wall of a truck's side inches from his elbow.

Rafferty has promised the driver two thousand baht for speed, an exorbitant sum, and the bike is at full throttle. Rush-hour cars and trucks hurtle by in a blur or loom massively in front of them, slipping past at the last possible second by a few slim inches. He has a vision of himself spread across the roadway like peanut butter. A blind man could follow them by listening to the horns.

He forces himself to look past the traffic and focus on a more distant blur that resolves itself into shop fronts: tailors' shops, jewelry stores, a coffin maker, a watch shop called Lovely Hours, a sign that says, in English, WE HAVE ALL KINDS GRIT. In other words, a typical Bangkok block. "Can we go any faster?"

The driver starts to turn his head and thinks better of it. "You're joking."

"He still hasn't looked back," Cho says through the cell phone.

"We're almost there," Rafferty says. "Just keep him in sight." They hurtle past a sedan, children's startled hands and faces pressed to the windows watching the crazy *farang* and his driver trying to kill themselves.

"Wait, wait," Cho says on the phone. "They're slowing down. They're . . . um, they're pulling over to the curb."

"Is he getting out?" Rafferty asks Cho.

"No. Just sitting there."

Rafferty's stomach takes an anxious dip. "Maybe he spotted you."

"I don't think so. Hold it. A motorcycle taxi stopped next to the cab. The passenger is getting off it."

"What's he look like? Does he have a bad hand?"

"Yes, the left. He's getting in the car. He's got a blue bag with him. Like a bowling bag or something. Oh, my golly," Cho says, a librarian to his fingertips. "They're moving."

"Sukhumvit coming up," says Rafferty's driver. The bike downshifts and slows. "Hang on. Turn."

Once again the bike yaws wildly, and Rafferty is flying sideways through the air, gripping the seat between his knees with all the strength he possesses. When they are vertical again, the driver says, "Sukhumvit," as proudly as if he'd named it himself. The road stretches wide and congested in front of them, the sky crisscrossed with more electrical wires than any city would seem to need.

"What *soi*?"

"Thirty-two," Cho says, and Rafferty's driver says, "Sixteen."

"This is interesting," Cho says musingly. "That's really inter—"

"Cho, I swear—"

"The motorbike is staying right behind the taxi."

"Get closer. I don't want him getting back on that motorbike. Run over the goddamned thing if you have to. What color is the car, Cho?" The motorcycle is zipping between lanes of relatively slow-moving cars, their rearview mirrors whipping past like chromium hands snatching at the bike.

"Red, a red taxi with a dented . . . um, left back fender."

"First numbers on the plate."

"Um . . . three, two."

"Three-two!" Rafferty shouts to his driver. "Red taxi, license plate starts with three-two."

"Got it!" the driver calls.

"Yeah, well, remember it."

"No, I *got* it. Up there." And Rafferty looks ahead and sees Cho's car loafing along in front of them and, in front of that, the taxi.

Rafferty reaches into his pocket and pulls out a laundry receipt, a Kleenex, a paper clip, two stamps that have glued themselves together, a used movie ticket, one of Rose's bobby pins, and—finally—his money. When he looks up, they are directly behind the bike that is following the red cab.

He slips the open phone into his shirt pocket and waves a fan of thousand-baht bills in front of the driver for about a tenth of a second. "Get next to him."

"How close?"

"Close enough to smell him."

The bike accelerates until they are within a foot of the motorcycle taxi that brought Chouk to the payoff. Its driver glances over at them, sees how close they are, and starts to yell a caution, and Rafferty pulls the Glock out of his pants and waves it. At the same moment, a head turns in the cab's backseat, and Rafferty sees Chouk's face for the first time.

Instead of peeling off in panic and fading into traffic, the other motorcycle driver guns his engine and cuts around to the rear door of the cab, between the cab and the cars parked at the curb. Chouk is staring back at them wide-eyed. He jerks a thumb at Rafferty and shouts something at the guard, who shakes his head and raises both hands in what looks like an angry denial. Chouk continues to shout, and suddenly he reaches over with his good hand and snatches back the blue bag.

"Stay right where we are," Rafferty tells his driver. "Don't get any closer."

The other motorcycle driver is yelling at the window of the cab, some kind of urgent question, but Chouk does not seem to know he is there. The guard has lunged toward him and grabbed one of the bag's straps, and the two of them struggle back and forth in a constricted tug-of-war, slamming against the cab's doors. Chouk plants a foot high on the back of the driver's seat for leverage and brings the ruined hand down on the guard's shoulder, and the guard jerks back and drops the handle of the bag.

Chouk turns his head away to check the position of the motorcycle, and the guard reaches down and then brings his arm up, and something glints in his hand. He strikes Chouk in the right side once, pulling back quickly. Then he does it again.

Chouk's head snaps back as though he has been hit by a train. He turns slowly to look at the guard, his face a mask of astonishment—mouth open, eyes enormous, his neck corded with fear or pain, or both. Then, moving in slow motion, he turns away again and puts out his right hand. He is going to open the door of the car.

The guard reaches over and grabs the blue bag.

"Get between them," Rafferty says.

The driver's back stiffens. "You're crazy. There's not enough—"

"Get between them. I don't care if we hit the car."

"Well, I do."

Rafferty moves the gun forward so the driver can see it. "Get between them."

"Getting between them," the driver says.

He cuts to the left and aims for the sliver of daylight separating the cab and the motorcycle. Then the bike surges forward, and there is a protesting scrape of metal as the bike's handlebar digs a long gouge in the cab's rear fender. The friction pulls the front wheel around, and for an instant Rafferty thinks they are going down, but the driver reaches out with his hand and pushes them off the side of the cab, and they wobble once and then bump against the other bike.

The other driver has his lips peeled back in fury, and he reaches down into his coat pocket. Before the hand comes up, Rafferty lifts his right leg and kicks the bike's gas tank. His own driver swears, and their bike swerves again into the side of the car, but the other bike careens away, its rider struggling to right it, and then it sideswipes a parked car and the front wheel turns ninety degrees. The last thing Rafferty sees is the bike cartwheeling, its rider in midair, already tucking his knees to try to somersault when he hits the street.

"Up to the driver's door!" he shouts.

The bike leaps forward again. Rafferty's driver is still swearing, a long, unbroken string of invective. When they are opposite the front window, Rafferty reaches over and taps it with the gun. The taxi driver's head snaps around, and he sees the gun and hits the brakes so fast that the two men in the rear are thrown forward against the back of the seat in front of them. The instant the cab comes to a stop, the far door opens and the guard darts into traffic on foot, carrying the blue bag. He vanishes between cars.

Chouk does not move. He stares through the window as Rafferty approaches. He looks indifferent, even sleepy.

Rafferty pulls the door open and points the gun at him, and Chouk, who had been leaning on the door, unfolds slowly out of the car and hits the street facefirst. Rafferty steps back, then looks around and sees the staring crowd gathering on the curb, the fallen man at his feet with a pool of blood spreading beneath him, and Chouk's motorcycle driver limping toward them with a wrench in his hand.

Rafferty yanks the cell phone from his pocket. "Goddamn it, Cho," he shouts, "get up here and arrest me!"

**NINETY MINUTES LATER** Poke's friend Dr. Ratt comes out of the apartment bedroom with blood on his white sleeves.

"He's lucky," he says, heading for the kitchen as he peels off his latex gloves. "The knife hit the ribs. No punctured lung, no arterial damage. Just sliced muscles." He turns on the water and pours liquid dishwashing detergent on his hands. "I sewed him up. He's low on blood, ought to have a transfusion."

"What happens if he doesn't get the transfusion?"

"He'll be pretty weak."

"Weak is a good idea," Rafferty says.

"*Poke,*" Nui scolds, emerging from the bedroom in her latest silk nurse's uniform. This one is salmon-colored.

"This isn't Albert Schweitzer, Nui. He killed a man earlier this week."

"Really?" Dr. Ratt's tone is skeptical. "He's awfully sweet to be a killer."

"He also stole a bunch of money."

"How much?" Nui handles the finances for her husband's mobile medical practice.

"Ten million baht."

Dr. Ratt whistles and Nui says happily, "Then he can pay us."

"Not exactly. He shredded it."

Dr. Ratt pauses and lifts a soapy hand. "He . . ."

"Shredded it. Then he sent it back."

"What was the point? The emptiness of materialism?" Nui asks. "This is an unusually spiritual attitude in a thief."

"Actually, I think he was trying to piss somebody off."

Dr. Ratt shakes water from his hands. "Who was the man he killed?"

"Paper towels are under the sink," Rafferty says. "The man who helped him in the robbery."

Dr. Ratt drops from sight beneath the counter and resurfaces with a roll of paper towels. "Let me play this back. This man, who is really extremely nice, Poke, even cultured, robs someone, kills somebody else while he's committing a robbery, and then shreds the . . . the . . ."

"Loot," Nui supplies.

". . . the loot, and sends it back?"

"I know," Poke says. "It doesn't make a lot of sense to me either. He and I need to have a chat."

"You lead an interesting life, Poke," Nui says. "*We* don't know anybody who's shredded ten million baht. How's Miaow?"

"She's an angel."

"And Rose?" Her long, sleepy eyes come up to his. There is more than casual interest in them.

"Ah, well," Rafferty says, and realizes he is blushing.

"Whoops," Nui says. "Perhaps I'm intruding."

"Nui, when there's something to know, you'll know it. How badly injured is he?"

"Nothing life-threatening. It'll be a week to ten days before he can get around comfortably. He's going to have very limited movement in his right arm for a while. What in the world happened to his left hand?"

"One of the things he and I are going to discuss."

"What it looks like," Dr. Ratt says, "is that somebody yanked three of his fingernails with a pair of pliers and then put the hand on something flat and hit it a couple of times with a sledgehammer."

"Yikes," Rafferty says.

"Most of the bones are broken in several places. There was obviously no kind of medical attention. I've seen injuries like it—" He stops, looking embarrassed.

"Where? Where have you seen injuries like it?"

"Beggars," Dr. Ratt says. He is blushing at being caught in a good deed. "I treat beggars one day a week."

"Why would beggars—"

"They're Cambodian beggars. Old enough to have been in the Khmer Rouge prisons."

"Jesus freaking Christ," Rafferty says. He sits heavily on the couch.

"Excuse me?" Nui always wants to learn new English.

"It's an idiom Americans use when enlightenment strikes." He puts his hands to his head and massages his temples. "It's always enlightening to realize you're an idiot."

## A Matter of Information

The boy slows the moment he comes through the door, looking at the spots of blood that dapple the carpet like a spill of bright red coins. He follows the trail with his eyes to the closed door of the bedroom, and then he turns questioningly to Rafferty. He seems more curious than alarmed, as if blood falls into the category of the everyday.

"We have a guest." Rafferty is in the kitchen, pouring bottled water into smaller bottles and spilling quite a bit of it. "He's asleep. He was hurt pretty badly, so let's all be quiet."

"Your friend?" The boy glances again at the blood. He is wearing the last of his new shirts. He has worn each of the others two or three times, until the fold marks from the store disappeared. The sharp-edged rectangle across his chest makes him look like somebody who is shoplifting a book.

"Not a friend. He killed somebody." The boy's eyes kindle with interest. "He's handcuffed to the bed, and I want you to stay out of there."

"Just because he killed somebody doesn't mean he's a bad man," the boy says in a reasonable tone.

"It doesn't make him a good one either. It's hard to think of a solid reason for murdering someone."

"I can think of lots of them," the boy says.

"Well, keep them to yourself."

"What happened to him?"

"He ran into a knife that someone was holding."

"Knives are no good. They only work up close. And they're messy." He kicks at a blood spot as though he expects it to skip across the carpet. "Have you ever killed anybody?" The boy's tone is conversational, but his eyes have the same kind of intensity Rafferty saw in the garage, the first time Superman looked at him.

"No."

"Think you could?"

Rafferty's silence stretches so long that the boy shrugs and starts to turn away. "I don't know," he says at last.

"Okay." The boy swivels his head toward the closed door. "You call the police?"

"Not yet."

"Good." He turns and starts down the hall to Miaow's room.

"Wait." The boy stops at the sound of Rafferty's voice but doesn't look back. "Why did you leave Phuket?"

Rafferty has been speaking Thai, but the boy reverts to broken English. "You say what?"

"You wouldn't tell Miaow why you left Phuket. I want to know."

Superman turns and regards him soberly long enough for Rafferty to think he will speak, but then he turns and continues down the hall. The door closes behind him.

Rafferty grabs one of the small bottles of water and follows the trail of blood into his bedroom.

Chouk's eyes open as Rafferty comes in. If he is frightened, it does not show in his face. He looks like a man who woke up in a strange place and is waiting until he remembers where he is.

"Are you thirsty?"

Chouk smiles. It is, as Dr. Ratt said, a sweet smile. "Thank you. I'm afraid you will have to hold the bottle." His ruined hand is cuffed to the frame of the bed, and the right arm is motionless beneath the covers. Dr. Ratt taped it to his side, mummy style, to keep him from tearing the damaged muscles.

"No problem." Rafferty raises the bottle to Chouk's lips and tilts it, and the man drinks half of it in one long series of gulps. When he is finished, he lifts his chin, and Rafferty removes the bottle.

"I didn't know I was thirsty." Chouk's voice is soft, even refined. He speaks Thai fluently but with a distinct accent. He sounds like a university professor.

"You lost a lot of blood."

"Ah, well. Not enough, apparently."

Rafferty grimaces. "A little melodramatic."

Chouk's eyes come to his, blank as the windows of an abandoned building. Whatever was once behind them has moved on. "I hope not. There has been more than enough melodrama in my life. There has been more than enough of practically everything." He smiles again, but the expression in his eyes does not change. "And so *much* of it was given to me by one person."

"Madame Wing."

He nods approvingly, a teacher pleased by the performance of a particularly bright student. "Are you working for her?"

Rafferty gives the question the thought it deserves. "I don't know."

Chouk rolls toward him, forgetting the cuff, which tightens and makes the bed creak ominously. "Either you're working for her or you're not."

"I *was* working for her. Am I working for her now? It's all a matter of information, isn't it? We make our choices depending on the information at our disposal. I'm sort of wondering what your information is. I can't say I like her much."

Chouk takes it in, looking at nothing. "Is she paying you a lot?"

"Yes."

"Well, there's no way I can compete there."

"No. You were pretty decisive about that."

Chouk laughs. "And I just gave away my last million."

"You seemed to have second thoughts in the cab."

"I thought he'd led you to me."

"He did, but he didn't know it."

"I should have guessed. He's not the hardest man to fool."

"If he were any dumber, he wouldn't have thumbs."

A shake of the head, so tiny it is barely a movement at all.

"So you can't give me money," Rafferty says. "Tell me about Madame Wing instead. But listen, you have to know that I'm going to turn you over to the cops no matter what you say."

Chouk settles back on the pillows and regards him out of the corners of his eyes. "Because I shot Tam."

"He had a wife."

"I know. He said her name before he began to work on the safe. *Mai.* He said it like a prayer. I have regretted shooting him every minute since it happened. Since I did it, I mean. It didn't *happen.* I pointed the gun at him and pulled the trigger. It felt at the time like I had no choice, but of course I did." His head drops back onto the pillow, and he draws several short breaths.

"Because he saw what was in the safe."

Chouk's black eyes come to him and lock on his, and something flickers in them. "Do you know what was in it? Did she tell you?"

"No."

"I thought not. She'd have to kill you. Are you curious?"

"A man was murdered for it. A terrible old woman paid you ten million baht for it. Of course I'm curious."

"Yes," Chouk says listlessly. His brief flare of interest seems to have burned itself out. More than anything, he looks exhausted. "You'd think it was something important, wouldn't you?"

"Isn't it?"

"To a couple of people. For most of the world, it's not worth five baht. I suppose it was important once, a long time ago, when someone could have done something about it. The worst thing is, there was probably no reason to shoot Tam at all."

Chouk turns away. "I'm going to jail," he says. It sounds like he is trying the idea on.

"Afraid so."

"It doesn't matter. I couldn't finish now anyway."

"Finish what?"

"Reducing her to ash," he says mildly. "Making her feel as much pain as possible and then reducing her to ash."

"What did she do to you?"

"What did she do to me?" His eyes close slowly, and his lips curve into the ghost of a smile. "What didn't she do? I could tell you a story, but it would only be a story, about a lot of people you don't know. People who wouldn't be real to you, a time that wouldn't be real to you. I can show you, though. And I will. You should know who you're working for." He jerks against the chain connecting the handcuffs to the bed. "Unlock these and I'll show you."

"Can't."

"It's not here," Chouk says, his voice urgent for the first time. "It's in my room. The thing that explains Madame Wing."

"Sorry. You're here for the duration."

"What would I escape to? I can't use my good hand anymore. I couldn't finish even if I were free."

"You'll heal."

"It'll be too late by then. It had to be done by day after tomorrow."

"Why the day after tomorrow?"

"Later," he says. "After you see."

"Just out of curiosity, what were you going to do with the deed to her house?"

Chouk's smile is broad and sudden. "I was going to make it out to Vinai Pimsopat and send it to him. Anonymously, from a grateful constituent."

Rafferty laughs. Pimsopat is a notoriously venal politician, even by Southeast Asian standards, a short, fat, black hole into which enormous quantities of government funds disappear. His nickname in the press is "The Scoop."

"She'd have had a hard time getting it back."

"It would have cost her another ten or twenty million baht. Most of all, it would have frightened her."

Rafferty says, "Where's your room?"

"Not far. We can get there in twenty minutes."

"Not you. You're not supposed to move around yet."

"And you're probably not going to wander off and leave me here, so who can go?"

Rafferty gets up and goes to the door and pulls it open. "We'll send Superman," he says. "After all, he's faster than a speeding bullet."


"ON APRIL SEVENTEENTH, 1975, the Khmer Rouge marched into Phnom Penh," Chouk is saying. His voice is weak but steady. "We all stood in the streets and cheered. Cambodia was going to belong to Cambodians again. Our country had been sold out from under us. Lon Nol didn't care about the people; all he wanted to do was milk the Americans for more money. The Americans had decided that the central Vietcong headquarters were in Cambodia, even though there *weren't* any central Vietcong headquarters. So America sent the bombers." His ruined hand describes an arc until the handcuff stops it and then lands next to a plate containing half a sandwich. Rafferty had fed it to him until he shook his head. "A lot of Cambodian people died. Men, women, old people, children. The Americans were killing us every day of the week, dropping fire out of the sky on nuns and babies, and the government just sat there with its hand out saying 'No problem, send money.'"

"While people died."

"The Americans gave the Khmer Rouge the only thing they'd been missing: an enemy everyone could hate. The Khmer Rouge moved in, and Lon Nol ran like a rabbit." He takes a shaky breath. "What I remember most clearly is how young they were. The soldiers. They looked like children. Some of them actually *were* children, of course, and we'd learn more about that later. The way the Khmer Rouge used children, I mean." He squeezes his eyes closed and shifts his weight, easing the strain on the bandaged arm.

"Do you want to rest?"

A tightening of the mouth, a dry swallow. "I want to talk."

"Your call."

"Phnom Penh was a beautiful city, with broad boulevards and graceful buildings and trees everywhere. It had shade, the river, the flat plain, with its one hill and the temple on top of it." He is looking at the opposite wall, and his eyes and voice are soft. "I loved the city then. I played violin in the symphony orchestra. I taught music. I had—" He stops and swallows. "A wife. Sophea. Two children. Two girls. Eleven and thirteen."

A tear slides down his cheek, but he seems not to notice. He doesn't even blink his eyes against the moisture. "So they came. We cheered for them. We invited them into our homes and fed them. We had victory parties. Two days later they began to empty the city.

"They said everyone was going to work the soil." Chouk is speaking so softly Rafferty has to lean forward to hear. Superman has been gone more than an hour. It is getting dark in the room. "It took them three days to drive everyone out, even the sick people in the hospitals. Six hundred thousand people in three days. We were each allowed to carry as much of our lives as we could squeeze into one bag."

He puts his head back as far as he can, stretching the long muscles in his neck. "The bag was a trap. On the way out of the city, the soldiers stopped and searched everyone. Anybody who had packed a book was killed. Anybody with soft hands—'office hands'—was killed. Anybody who wore spectacles was shot or beaten to death." He closes his eyes and rolls his head slowly from side to side. "My family stood in line with soldiers on either side, holding one another's hands, with our bags packed full of books, some of them in English. I had my violin. We were waiting to die." He is breathing rapidly and shallowly, as though he were once again lined up, waiting for his bullet.

"This can wait," Rafferty says.

"When it came to be my family's turn, an officer stepped forward and stopped the soldiers from opening our bags. We were led to one side and told to wait. I later found out he'd been a subscriber to the symphony. He'd seen me play the Beethoven Concerto in D. He'd enjoyed it. The soldiers took us back to the city, back to our own house. They put guards all around us, as though we had anywhere to run when the whole country was being turned into a prison.

"So we were still in Phnom Penh when the bombing started. They blew up the banks, the libraries, the churches, the hospitals, anything with ties to the West. There were going to be no foreign influences in the Year Zero. That's what they called it, the Year Zero, the glorious new beginning." He stops and opens his eyes. "Could I have some water?"

Rafferty raises the bottle to Chouk's lips. One swallow, two, and then Chouk lifts his chin: enough. "*Glory,*" he says. "It was about glory. We—Cambodia, I mean—were going to return to our days of glory, the days of Angkor, when Khmer kings ruled most of Southeast Asia." The sound he makes might be a laugh, or just something caught in his throat. "Of course, the days of Angkor were a thousand years ago. That was Pol Pot's great leap forward—ten centuries into the past."

"I wasn't aware there were a lot of violinists at Angkor."

Chouk's grin is quick and white, with no more humor in it than the laugh had. "They were such hypocrites. The fat boys—Pol Pot, Nuon Chea, Ieng Sary, all of them—had been rich kids. They went to school in Paris. The people, the ordinary people, were sealed off from the West—from books and ideas and even medicine. But the fat boys liked music."

"And that saved you."

"In a manner of speaking, I suppose it did." He starts suddenly and looks around the room at the darkness, as though he is just noticing the passage of time. "Where's the boy?"

"Probably stuck in traffic. It's rush hour."

"It shouldn't be taking him this long."

"He'll be here." Rafferty prompts the man back to his story. "You met Madame Wing in an interrogation center."

"'Met' is an interesting choice of words. You could say I walked into her, in the sense that people sometimes walk into an airplane propeller. You could say I was thrown into her, like a tree into a chipper. 'Met' is a little on the soft side. But I don't want to talk about her yet. We'll talk about her when the boy gets here."

"I want a beer," Rafferty says. In fact, he needs to escape the room: the thick, dark atmosphere and the darkness of Chouk's past. They combine to exert a pressure that makes him feel like he's been buried alive. "I'd offer you one, but it'd probably knock you out."

"I don't drink."

"Hang on." He goes out into the equally dark living room, snapping on lights as he goes. The illumination does nothing to lift his mood. A detour takes him to Miaow's room, where she is bent over a schoolbook, copying something down. The tip of her tongue is pasted to her upper lip.

"Hello, Miaow."

"Hello, Poke." She does not look up from her work. "Where's Boo?"

The old name seems appropriate for the first time. "On an errand."

"Who are you talking to?"

"Someone who doesn't feel well. I'll tell you about it later."

She squints down at the book. "What does 'spontaneous' mean?"

He hates this kind of question. "Um . . . sort of unplanned. You know, if you were a witch and you decided all of a sudden to turn me into a toadstool, that would be a spontaneous decision."

"You're too nice to be a toadstool," she says without looking up.

"Thank you, Miaow."

"I'd turn you into a mushroom."

"Great," Rafferty says. "I could be your pet mushroom. You could buy me a little hat."

"Mushrooms already have caps," Miaow says, dismissing him.

One-upped by an eight-year-old. There is something sane and warm in being one-upped by an eight-year-old. In the kitchen he pops a beer, draws a deep breath for strength, and goes back into the bedroom. On the threshold he hesitates and then decides against turning on the lights. Chouk rolls toward him, his face thrown into relief by the light coming through the door until Rafferty pulls it closed behind him.

"You were in Phnom Penh," Rafferty says, sitting on the edge of the bed.

"Not for long. A few weeks. Then we were sent to the country-side. We grew rice. We dug ditches. We dug graves." He pauses and swallows. "A great many graves. The killing never stopped. And the interrogations went on day and night.

"There were already interrogation centers all over the country, for those who didn't plant rice fast enough, or grumbled about being worked sixteen hours a day, or starved with insufficient enthusiasm. Or people they should have killed the first time around but missed. People like me."

"How did they find out who you were?"

"Somebody talked." He takes a breath and holds it, then releases it. "Somebody always talked." He turns to Rafferty, and his eyes glint in the darkness. "It might have been one of my daughters. They in-doctrinated the children twenty-four hours a day."

Rafferty says the only kind thing he can think of. "But you don't know that."

"And I don't want to know. I think it would kill me."

"So you were betrayed. What happened?"

"I was special, because I'd had some status before the revolution, so they sent me to Tuol Sleng. In the middle of Phnom Penh, they took over a high school and turned it into something new: an inter-rogation and murder facility for Khmer Rouge who had betrayed the revolution. Of course, nobody had betrayed the revolution. It was just craziness, paranoia. They used Tuol Sleng to torture confessions from people Pol Pot was afraid of, or just tired of. The basic idea was simple. Bring people in, torture them until they signed a confession, and kill them. Seventeen thousand people went in. Seven came out."

The room is almost completely dark. The sound of traffic from the street is like an anchor to the life of Bangkok, going on all around them. "What were they supposed to confess to?"

"Anything. Collaborating with the CIA. Sympathizing with

Vietnam. Listening to Thai pop music. Eating weeds in the forest. One person confessed to not watering his houseplants. Whatever it was, people were tormented until they said what they were told to say, and then they were taken to the killing field at Cheung Ek in trucks and put to death. Beaten with hoes, usually, or chopped with machetes, because the revolution was short of bullets."

"Did they do that to your hand?"

"This?" Chouk looks at Rafferty as though he hasn't been listening. He lifts the hand as far as the chain will allow. "This was just a way of saying hello. It's trivial. They wouldn't even have bothered with it if they hadn't known I was a violinist. They did it to hurt me inside and also, I think, because they just hated beauty. Beauty frightened them. They beheaded every Buddha at Angkor. This hand could finger the melodies of Beethoven and Bach, so they destroyed it."

He gazes at the ruined hand regretfully but remotely, the way someone might look at a house that burned down years ago. "They did it with a hammer and pliers in one of the interrogation rooms. Classrooms, they had been, with blackboards and windows so the children could see the sky while they learned. They put an iron bed frame in each room and wired it to a hand-cranked generator. In one corner they put the knives and the bolt cutters and the pruning shears and the whips made out of heavy copper electrical wire, and the iron rods they used to break the long bones. They placed these things in the corner opposite the door so they were the first thing the subject saw when he came into the room. To the left of the door was a little table with a chair in front of it for the interrogator to use. The table and the chair were so neat, so *clean*. In some ways they were the worst things in the room. We were chained to the bed frame, filthy and stinking with our own piss and shit, and the table and chair were so clean. The interrogator sat there and made notes while his assistants did their work. They worked around the clock sometimes, in shifts. You could hear screaming all day and all night. For some reason it was worst at night."

The door to the bedroom opens, and Superman comes in, framed in light, holding a file folder. His eyes are enormous, stunned, like someone who has just survived a disastrous accident and doesn't know why. He moves quickly to Rafferty and thrusts the folder at him as though it were an animal that bites. Then he turns to the bed and spits on Chouk.

"*No,*" Rafferty says, rising to take the boy by the shoulder. "He didn't do anything."

"You haven't looked," the boy says. "Kill him."

Rafferty is still standing. "You've got it wrong. Now beat it. Go sit with Miaow. And don't talk about this. I'll explain it after dinner." He takes a napkin from the sandwich plate and wipes the spittle from Chouk's face.

"Not hungry." Superman has not taken his eyes off Chouk. He purses his lips, and Rafferty thinks he will spit again, but instead he stalks from the room, slamming the door behind him.

"A warrior," Chouk says. "Is he yours?"

"Apparently." Rafferty turns on the bedside light, squinting against the glare, and begins to open the folder.

"Wait," Chouk says. "Before you look at it, let me tell you what it is."

He shifts a little in the bed. "Just in case anyone still doubted that Pol Pot was insane, he declared war on Vietnam. This was the country that had just defeated America. They were better armed than the Russians. The war lasted two weeks, and then the Vietnamese came."

"And bless them for it."

"We were already in Tuol Sleng by then. When a subject was sent to Tuol Sleng, his family went with him. So my wife and children were there, too." He stops, and his eyes go to the folder. "My wife and children," he repeats.

"Tuol Sleng was a summer camp for monsters, but they were precise monsters. The precision took the form of exhaustive files on every prisoner who entered the prison: the charges against them, the forms of torture used during the interrogation, the confession, and the date of death. We were all going to die, of course. It was like the Red Queen in *Alice in Wonderland*: sentence first, verdict afterward. Every prisoner was photographed, sometimes just before they were killed. The highest-ranking prisoners were photographed dead, as proof for Pol Pot and the other fat boys. There were thousands of photographs."

"I've seen some of them."

"A man named Duch headed up the operation, but the interrogators did most of the work. The head female interrogator was called Keck."

The two men look at each other, and Rafferty says, "Madame Wing."

"We had been there a week when she killed my wife and daughters. She killed my oldest daughter first, in front of my wife. She was trying to make my wife say I was a CIA agent. Tiara was a beautiful girl, so she began by cutting off her nose. She did it with a razor, and she made my wife sharpen the razor. She told my wife, 'The sharper it is, the less it will hurt.'"

He is looking at the blanket now, and tears are falling from his downturned face. "She murdered them all. She saved my wife for last and killed her with me in the room. She made it go on for two days. I was shackled hand and foot while she worked. There was nothing personal in it as far as Keck was concerned. It was what she did, eight hours a day. She took pleasure from it, but it wasn't personal. They could have been anyone, as long as they had nerves and tears and blood and bone. I could have been anyone, as long as I loved them, as long as it hurt me to watch. It wasn't enough to maim us, to kill us. First they had to drive a nail through our hearts."

Rafferty draws a couple of deep breaths. "Why are you alive?"

"Pol Pot's war against Vietnam. The Vietnamese invaded Phnom Penh, and the guards and interrogators ran. They had just started on me. I guess you could say I was lucky. After my first session, they returned me to the group cells. As soon as the Vietnamese entered Phnom Penh, the interrogators killed everyone in the interrogation rooms, and then they went to get the files. When the Vietnamese arrived, they found bodies everywhere and seven of us alive. In one room there were two filing cabinets full of photos. One drawer was empty. It had held pictures of the interrogators at work. Keck emptied it. I saw her leave with it." He glances down at the folder in Rafferty's lap. "With that."

"This is hardly a drawer's worth."

"I don't know what happened to the rest. She may have thrown them away. She may have sold them, one at a time, to the people who were in them. Those are the pictures of her. You can look at them now."

The folder opens too easily for what it contains.

The first thing he sees is Keck's eyes. They look out of a gaunt younger woman's face. The flesh beneath the skin has been burned away by the rage that animates the face. The eyes could be looking at a barren landscape, a blasted tree, the face of the moon. They have no time for anything living.

The other pictures are unendurable. Flesh tears, bones snap. Keck's long fingers slice and probe. The luminous eyes look down as from a great altitude, as though the living beings she is driving mad with pain are as distant as ships slipping below the horizon.

Rafferty looks at the top sheet and closes his eyes. While they are still closed, he shuts the folder. When he opens his eyes, Chouk is studying him to assess his reaction. "Why would she keep these?"

"The same reason people keep photos from their school days, or of their families. It was the best time in her life. She was happy."

"How did you find her?"

He shakes his head. "It was easy. It took some time, but it was easy. She had been stealing money for years, taking everything people owned—cash, gold, art, everything—and promising them freedom. Then she had them killed. She put it all in Thai banks, millions and millions of baht. With that kind of money here, I knew she'd buy a house. She needed the security of a house, someplace she could hide in, someplace with open space around it, where she could see people coming. Where she could have guards. So it had to be a house, a big house. With walls. She needed a prison. From one prison to another." He sighs. "I searched the city records. Not that many expensive houses are registered in women's names. I found about forty that had been bought fifteen to twenty years ago. Out of those, only a dozen were walled off. I went to those one at a time, waiting outside until I saw a woman of the right age. She drove out of the ninth house I watched, the second day I was there. I knew her the moment I saw her."

"The eyes," Rafferty says.

"Of course."

"Did she see you?"

"It didn't matter. She wouldn't have recognized me anyway. I was one of thousands. When she was finished, she forgot us instantly. We were interesting only while she had us chained to the bed frame."

"Well, shit," Rafferty says. "It's a shame you didn't get her before I found you."

"Nothing to be done," Chouk says. "I took too long. This is what I deserve. It wasn't right for me to want her to suffer that way."

"Yeah, but it's not what *she* deserves. Why not give the pictures to the cops or send them to the newspapers?" He knows the answer as he asks the questions.

"The papers wouldn't print them without proof the woman in them was Madame Wing. The police would just go to her and demand more money. There's no way to prove who she is, and she's got enough money to satisfy even them."

"A little while ago, you said it was too late for you to finish. What did that mean?"

"I made myself a promise," he says. "Two days from now is the twenty-seventh anniversary of my wife's death. I vowed that one of us would be dead by then." He lifts the chained hand and lets it drop again. "And now look at me." The tears start to flow again. "So she lives to a ripe old age."

Rafferty automatically picks up the plate and the empty bottles. His mind is working so fast he doesn't know what his hands are doing. "Well," he says, "let's not leap to conclusions."

36

## As Poisonous as a Krait

Dinner is pineapple pizza, brought back from Silom by Superman. During the time he is gone, Miaow sets the table, filling a vase with cutouts of flowers she has colored on heavy paper, which seems to be a special touch for the boy. The flowers give the table a bright, cartoonish touch, although Superman barely seems to notice them. He keeps his eyes on the table. But he eats.

Rafferty moves aimlessly from room to room in a fog of fury, arguing with himself and losing. It's not so much, he tells himself, that what he has in mind will probably result in Madame Wing's death; it's that he will be having others do the dirty work. Rafferty has always believed that bad deeds, if they must be done, should be done personally.

But he can't just let her walk away.

While they are eating, Arthit knocks at the door. He comes in wearing his plaid trousers, eyes the pizza, and accepts a slice. While Rafferty is getting him a beer, he appears in the kitchen door.

"Thanks for coming," Rafferty says.

"I was coming anyway, even if you hadn't called. My two colleagues, the ones who were helping Clarissa spend her money, put an interesting file on my desk this afternoon."

"This is exactly what I need to hear right now," Rafferty says, opening a second beer. He is gripping the can so hard that it crumples as the top pops, and beer sloshes over his hand. He stares down at it and then licks it off.

Arthit is watching him with interest. "It's a complaint against you. Alleging that you're keeping children here for immoral purposes."

Rafferty lets the counter take all his weight. "I'll kill them. I mean it, Arthit. I'll kill both of them."

"No you won't." Arthit looks at the beer in his own hand but doesn't drink. "Not yet anyway. They told me you had two days to pay them off or they'll file the complaint officially."

"Two days. There seems to be something magical about the day after tomorrow. How much?"

"Fifty thousand dollars."

"*Fifty?*"

"They think big."

Miaow comes into the kitchen with a plate containing a second slice of pizza for Arthit, looks at their faces, and leaves, still carrying the plate.

"So back to Plan A." Rafferty lowers his voice. "I kill them."

"We have two days to come up with Plan B," Arthit says. "When you called, you said something about a market for fugitives."

"Is there one?"

"This is a vague area. Talking about it puts me in a difficult position, Poke. Normally, of course, what one does with fugitives is turn them over to the police."

"This particular fugitive has the police in her pocket."

Arthit looks past Rafferty for a second and then right at him. He takes his first pull on the beer, a good long one. "Is this somebody we've discussed before? Lives on the river?"

"It is."

"And you can verify her fugitive status?"

"Can I ever."

A pause long enough for Arthit to be doing addition in his head. "Do you have a name? Other than the one I already know?"

Rafferty watches Arthit's eyes. "Keck."

For a moment Arthit has no reaction. Then he says, "My, my. One of the top beasts."

"I've got pictures."

"I'll bet they're lovely."

"If you're going to look at them, you'll be glad you didn't have that second slice of pizza."

Arthit drops his eyes to the can in his hand and then lifts them to the ceiling. "I need to think." He goes to the kitchen counter and pulls out a chair. "Join me?" he says.

"Always a pleasure." Rafferty sits opposite him and watches him think. Looking at the sallow skin, the lines of strain around his friend's eyes, he feels a sudden surge of affection. He reaches over and clumsily pats the back of Arthit's hand. Arthit grabs his hand for a second, then releases it and straightens, all business.

"If you have the pictures, I assume that you also have the person who stole them, since they were obviously in the safe."

"Assume away."

"Okay, three things. First, I wasn't kidding about this being dangerous for me. It's beyond illegal. I can't be involved in any way. It could end my career, such as it is. More important, it could endanger Noi. Her medical bills are eating me alive. If I were to lose my job—"

A wave of shame washes over Rafferty. "Forget it. I shouldn't have asked. I wasn't thinking."

Arthit raises a hand. "And I wasn't finished. That was the first thing. The second thing is that you're going to need agents, for want of a better word, agents who can shop her. She's not a Nazi or a Serbian war criminal. People like that you can turn over to a number of organizations, even governments. But no one is hunting for Khmer Rouge executioners. The Cambodians would probably pay you *not* to find her. Many of the ranking members of Hun Sen's government were KR not so long ago. Someone like Keck could tell stories that would be intensely embarrassing."

"So?"

"So that means the clients, such as they are, will be individuals. There should be plenty of those, but they'll have limited funds."

Rafferty shakes his head. "I don't care about the money."

"No, but your agents will."

"You said three things. What was the third?"

"You're going to think I'm crazy."

"If I were going to think you were crazy, Arthit, I'd have started long ago."

"It's about your agents. You need to consider the skills they'll have to possess."

This is going somewhere, although Rafferty doesn't know where. "Maybe you could save me the effort. Since you already seem to know."

"Righty-oh." Arthit holds up a handful of fingers and ticks them off one at a time. "They need to be connected to the criminal underground. They need to know Bangkok extremely well. They need to be familiar with the protocols of delivering prisoners. They need to be greedy. And they can't be afraid of a little violence."

Rafferty's mind is going off on an extremely unattractive tangent. "I'm getting a bad feeling about this."

"Think of it," Arthit says, "as two birds with one stone."

"I take it back. You *are* crazy."

"It would save them face. It would give them a little money—not as much as they want, but enough to salve their wounds." He drinks again. "It would kill the report on my desk."

"It would bring those two assholes back into my life."

"You're not paying attention. *It would kill the report on my desk. It takes care of this vile woman. Poke. Just once in your life, as a favor to me, be rational."

"They're not smart enough. This is no ordinary old lady. She's as poisonous as a krait."

"You need greedy and brutal, and you're getting greedy and brutal. You supply the smart." He drums his fingers on the table, waiting. "Shall I set up a meeting?"

From the living room, Rafferty hears Miaow and Superman talking. "Fine," he says brusquely. "But I'll call them, not you." Then he looks again at the man seated across the table: tired, rumpled, homely, wearing awful trousers. "Arthit," he begins, but Arthit raises a hand.

"You're my friend," he says.

"There'll come a time."

Arthit picks up the can of beer and sloshes it experimentally, hears nothing, and puts it down with a disappointed expression. "And what about our murderer? Do you plan to notify me officially at any point?"

"Eventually."

"When?"

"As soon as he's better," Rafferty says.

"What? Is he down with the flu or something?"

"Iron poisoning."

"Not lead?"

"Nothing that technologically advanced."

"And you're tending his wounds?" Arthit cranes his head in the direction of the living room. "My, my. You're running a regular little hotel here."

"Arthit," Rafferty says. "The people she'll be sold to . . ."

"What about them?"

"They're not likely to wish her well."

Arthit picks up the beer can and peers through the hole in the top, then looks back up. "That's a safe assumption," he says.

## 37

# The Hinges

He matches the phone numbers to the faces in the file Arthit gave him and chooses the toad-faced one, the one who seemed to be calling the shots during their single encounter. While the phone rings, he surveys his little domain: two homeless children tucked away in one bedroom, a murderer chained to the bed in the other, sweetheart temporarily displaced. A tomato-soup-can burglar alarm stacked beside the door. His dream home.

A child answers the phone.

Rafferty has a sinking feeling he's been experiencing a lot lately. The last thing he wants to do is begin to think of Toadface as an actual human being. "Can I speak to your father, please?" he asks in Thai.

"Sure," the child says. Then she shrills, "Papaaaaaaa!"

*Papa.* Just what he wanted to hear.

"Hello?" Toadface says.

"This is Poke Rafferty."

"That was fast." The man's tone is fat with satisfaction.

"Yeah, well, don't get ahead of yourself. Clarissa hasn't given me any money, and I couldn't raise fifty thousand dollars if you gave me a year."

"And you've only got two days. Doesn't sound like we've got much to talk about." Rafferty hears a child's question, and Toadface says, "In a minute, sweetie." His voice is completely different.

"That's one way to look at it," Rafferty says. "Two days from now, I don't come up with the money and you go ahead and destroy my family. And I lose a child I love, and you get zero. Nothing. Not a baht. Think about it. Does that sound like a worthwhile objective?"

The child asks another question, but it goes unanswered. It is repeated. Finally Toadface says, "Have you got something else in mind?"

"I do," Rafferty says. "And you guys are perfect for it."

**RAFFERTY IS PICKING** up the tomato cans when the boy comes into the room. He immediately begins to help.

"We don't need these anymore?"

"I don't think so. Everybody who wants to kill us is busy."

Miaow has gone to her room. She seems upset about Chouk's presence, especially the information that he is handcuffed, and Rafferty wonders whether she'll turn it into a bulletin for Hank Morrison at their next meeting. The boy is wearing his new blue sweatpants and the pink T-shirt Miaow bought Rafferty as a gift. It's too small for Rafferty, but on the boy it hangs like a poncho.

"Let's put these away for Rose," Rafferty says. The boy follows him into the kitchen.

"The policeman who was here," the boy says. "Is he your friend?"

"One of them. I actually have several."

A pause as the boy works something through in his head. "You like him, even though he's a policeman."

"I like some crooks, too."

"Huh," the boy says, unconvinced.

Rafferty closes the cabinet door and heads back to the living room, the boy trailing in his wake. He sits at one end of the couch, leaving room for Superman, but the boy sinks into a cross-legged stance on the floor. He fluffs the rug with the palms of both hands, something Rafferty has watched him do dozens of times. "Soft," he says.

"That's the point."

He opens his mouth, thinks about it, and strokes the carpet as he would a puppy. At last he says, "Too bad the world isn't soft."

"Ah," Rafferty says with a twinge of unease. They seem to be having a talk.

"Do you know why it isn't?"

Rafferty gives the question some thought. "You mean, why is it softer for some people than for others?"

"Yes."

"I have no idea."

The boy doesn't even blink. "Who does?"

"Oh, well," Rafferty says. "Lots of people have theories. Priests, politicians, philosophers. I think they're all guessing, though."

"What's your guess?"

"Dumb luck," Rafferty says, glad Rose isn't there to hear him.

"That just makes me angry." The boy's jaw comes forward, bulldoglike.

"Then believe something else. Karma, reincarnation, Cosmic Lotto. Being angry's just going to make things worse."

A shrug, too weary for a child his age. "Like it matters if I'm angry."

"Right now you're dry, you're wearing clean clothes, you just had that awful pizza with all the pineapple on it. You've got a bed to sleep in tonight. You've got friends."

"Because you *gave* it all to me," the boy challenges. "Tomorrow if you change your mind, I'll be on the street again. How do you think that feels?"

"Better than being there tonight. And I didn't give it to you, we all did. Why do you think we did that?"

The boy looks down at the carpet. He makes scissors from his fingers and pretends to trim the nap. He shows Rafferty nothing but the top of his head. When he speaks, Rafferty can barely hear him. "Phuket," he says.

Rafferty had thought he had used up his evening's supply of apprehension, but there it is again, dead center in the middle of his chest. "Right," he says. "Phuket."

The boy looks up at him and then away. "You won't tell Miaow."

"I won't tell anybody. Look, there are lots of things I've never asked Miaow. I figure it's her business to tell me when she wants to. It's the same with you. It's your story, and you tell it to her when it's time."

"I'll never tell it to her."

"Your call."

He plays with the carpet again. "It was a man," he says.

Immediately Rafferty thinks of Ulrich. He breathes a couple of times to make sure his voice will be steady. "What happened?"

"I went down there because the police were looking for me here. And I wanted to be someplace where I didn't have to be, you know . . ." His voice trails off. "Where I didn't have to be Superman." He tugs the carpet hard enough to lift it from the floor. "I wanted to stop taking *yaa baa*."

"Good for you."

"And I met a man. He saw me on the street and talked to me. He was an American, like you, and he . . . he seemed to like me. Not just for sex. He took me to movies. Real movies, in theaters, not videos. He bought me things." Rafferty remembers the boy's sullenness during their shopping expedition and, with a pang of shame, the irritation it had provoked. "He let me stay with him. I slept and slept. I stopped taking pills and smoking. When he wanted me, he gave me whiskey so it wouldn't hurt so much." He lifts his head and looks in the direction of the hallway that leads to Miaow's room. "It still hurt, really, but I said it didn't. I got to like the whiskey." He seems to lose the thread for a moment, gazing down the hall. "I began to think he loved me," he says. "His name was Al."

"What happened?"

"He ran out of money. One day he had money, and the next day he didn't. They were going to throw us out of the room. So one night Al brought home two men and told me they had paid to fuck me, and I was going to fuck them, or he was going to kick me out. I thought about going, but I had seen the money. I fucked them."

"I'm sorry," Rafferty says.

The boy shrugs the sentiment away. "That night, after the two men left, I waited until Al was asleep. Then I got dressed and opened the dresser and took the money. And then I crawled across the bed and bit Al's ear off."

His eyes are locked on Rafferty's. "He bled a lot," he says, still watching. When Rafferty doesn't avert his gaze, the boy looks away. "I ran. All the way back to Bangkok."

First Chouk's story, now this. Rafferty shuffles through a dozen replies and finally says, "You didn't deserve any of that."

"Then why did it happen?" The boy's voice scales so high it almost breaks on the last word. His eyes are enormous, and Rafferty sees them for the first time as what they are: the eyes of an eleven-year-old boy. "Why did it happen to *me*? Why not somebody else?"

"Wait," Rafferty says. "This is a big question. Give me a second here." He leans back against the couch and rolls his head slowly around to get the stiffness out of his neck. "Okay. Listen to me, even if I make some mistakes, right?"

"Fine," the boy says.

"Nobody can really answer that question. Why am I lucky? I don't know. I've never gone hungry, I've got both arms and legs. You've had a shitty life, and I don't understand that either. Rose would say it's karma, but I don't understand much about karma. So do I know why you had to be the one that man treated that way? No. I can't explain how the guy handcuffed to my bed could have gone through what he went through either, so I'm a complete bust. By the way, you were wrong about him. He wasn't one of the ones who did all that. He was one of the ones it was done to."

Superman ducks his head awkwardly, and Rafferty knows that it is all the apology the boy will make.

"Anyway," Rafferty says, backtracking, "you're here now. Al's not. Who knows? Maybe he died of blood poisoning. Maybe the tsunami got him. But you're here. And you're wrong about why you're here. We didn't just give it all to you. If you hadn't been a good kid, I'd have bathed you and debugged you and thrown you back on the sidewalk, no matter what Miaow said."

The boy mumbles something to the carpet.

"Say what?"

"Not good. Me."

"Oh, shut up," Rafferty says. "I know enough about you to know you're a great kid. So you bit a guy's ear off." He can hardly believe he's saying the words. "He had it coming. It wasn't your fault. You're smart, you're tough, you're self-sufficient, you're brave, you can fix anything. . . ." He runs out of steam, hearing the hollowness of his words.

The silence stretches between them, and the boy offers him a way out of it. "I fixed the lock on Miaow's closet door."

This is real news. "Really? It's not permanently locked anymore? She can close it?"

"No problem." The boy glances up at him. He is on safer ground. "What did you do when she closed it before?"

"Took it off the hinges," Rafferty says, happy to have a question he can answer.

The boy lowers his face and makes a sound that could be a snicker. "The *hinges*," he says.

"See? You can do things I can't. I can do things you can't. That means we can do things for each other, doesn't it?"

A dismissive shake of the head. "Yeah, yeah." The boy puts a hand down in preparation to get up.

"Hey. You started this. I'm not exactly an expert on life, but you asked me a question and I think you ought to sit here until I finish making a fool out of myself."

The boy doesn't respond, but he remains seated.

"Look, the world is softer for some people than others. That's the way it is. Some people don't have enough to eat, some weigh three hundred pounds. And you, you got a really shitty deal. Okay, that's too bad. We all agree, it's just terrible. It absolutely keeps me awake nights." His tone brings the boy's head up sharply. "So what can you do? You can't change the world, you know. It's too damn big. So what does that leave?"

The boy says nothing, just sits cross-legged with both palms pressed to the carpet, his fingers splayed like those of a runner about to start a sprint.

"I hate to give advice, so I'll tell you a story instead. It's a Tibetan Buddhist story. A young monk goes to the wisest man he knows, the abbot of his temple, and asks the same question you've just asked: Why is the world so hard and sharp? Why does it have to hurt my feet? And instead of answering, the abbot asks the kid whether it would be better if the world were covered with leather—have you heard this?"

The boy shakes his head.

"Okay, so the young monk says sure it would. It'd be a lot better. And the abbot asks the kid whether he knows how to cover the world with leather, and the kid says no, of course he doesn't, because he's a smart kid, a realistic kid. There's no way he can cover the world with leather. 'Fine,' says the abbot. 'Can you cover your feet with leather?'"

Superman's eyes lift slowly to study the wall above Rafferty's head. After a long moment, he nods once. "Then what?" he asks.

"Then we're going to get you into a school," Rafferty says. "And you're going to hate it sometimes, because you're just going to be a kid, not someone who runs things, but you're going to stay there because you belong there. Nobody's giving you anything. You'll earn it by being a good, smart kid and by showing up every day and by staying away from *yaa baa* and glue and whatever the hell else you were stuffing into your system. And if you screw up, you know what? There's not going to be a net. You're just going to fall. We can help you, but only if you want it. If you don't want it badly enough to pay for it, there's nothing anybody can do."

"You can do this? You can get me into a school?"

"No problem." Rafferty replays his conversation with Morrison in his mind. "I think."

"You'll try?"

This is not something to take lightly, and he pauses long enough to feel the boy's eyes on him. "I promise."

"Why?" He still has his hands braced on the floor, as though he is ready to bolt from the room.

"Because Miaow loves you. Because you helped her."

The boy looks away, out through the sliding glass door at the lights of Bangkok. His body is very still.

"And because I think you're a terrific kid," Rafferty adds awkwardly.

The boy says, without turning, "And you don't want anything?"

"I want you to work. I want you to do whatever you have to do to put leather on your feet so you can step on the sharp stuff without hurting yourself."

The boy gets up, all in one motion. Rafferty can remember being that limber, but not for quite a while. Superman puts both hands in his pockets and stares at the floor. Then he takes a slow step and then another, toward the hallway. At the last moment, he detours toward the couch. Without looking at Rafferty, he pulls one hand from his pocket and reaches out and touches him on the shoulder lightly, just brushes him with the backs of his fingers.

As he goes down the hall, Rafferty hears him say, "The *hinges.*"

# PART IV

## the HEaRT

## 38

## She Gets Sold to Someone
## Who Wants Her Dead

I n the bland light of a restaurant, Toadface and Skeletor look more like regular cops and less like something that escaped from one of Raskolnikov's nightmares. They even have nicknames: Toadface is Chut and Skeletor, for some reason, calls himself Nick.

"Khmer Rouge," Chut says without enthusiasm. Nick, in defiance of the no-smoking ban recently imposed in Bangkok restaurants, lights his second cigarette in five minutes. Rafferty doesn't like the smoke, but at least it keeps the man's hands above the table.

"*Big-time* Khmer Rouge," Rafferty says. "Should be worth a lot."

Nick snorts a stream of smoke, nicotine disdain, and Chut says, "Shows what you know."

Rafferty feels a surge of homicidal anger and waits it out. "Okay, well, you guys are the experts. But a lot of people would like to see her dead."

"That doesn't make them millionaires." Chut looks down at

Nick's pack of cigarettes and pushes it halfway across the table and out of reach, and Nick speaks the second word Rafferty has heard him utter. He says, "Hey."

"So get a pool together. Everybody chips in. Show some fucking creativity."

Chut puts two hands on the tablecloth and, with some difficulty, laces his fat little fingers together. "And you think this lets you off the hook."

"What I think is that Clarissa brought about six thousand to Bangkok and you guys got more than half of that. She's been living here ever since—what? About ten days? Figure it out. She's got maybe fifteen hundred dollars left. I'm offering you this person on a silver platter. Should be worth ten times that."

"What's her name?"

Rafferty waits until the waitress puts two bowls of rice and some fish in front of Chut and Nick and a couple of scrambled eggs in front of him. He continues to wait until she has returned to pour coffee for him and Chut. Nick is drinking something that looks a lot like a tequila sunrise.

"You get the name, plus the address and a floor plan of the house, when we have a deal," Rafferty says. "You *can* find customers?"

Chut says something with his mouth full. Rafferty can't catch the words, but the gist seems to be "piece of cake." The man swallows, and says, "Just for the hell of it, what's the deal?"

Rafferty takes a deep breath. This is not a position he ever expected to be in. "One: She gets sold to someone who wants her dead. Two: Your problem with me is over. Three: I get one-fifth of whatever you sell her for." He has a use in mind for the money, especially since Madame Wing won't be making her second payment.

Nick laughs. It starts out like a snake's hiss and turns into a cough. Chut says, "You've got balls, I'll give you that."

"I got off on the wrong foot with you guys," Rafferty says. "Not my fault, not your fault. I'm just trying to make it right."

"And pocket a little money." Chut picks up his bowl in both hands and drains whatever liquid was at the bottom. "One-seventh," he says. Rafferty pushes back his chair and starts to rise. "Okay, okay. One-fifth."

"Done." He sits again, gives them Keck's address, and describes the layout of the house and grounds. Then he hands over a plan of the first floor, drawn from memory. The thin one, Nick, listens with his eyes closed, his upper lip grasped between his teeth. Chut takes notes in an elegantly leather-bound booklet. Rafferty finishes and waits for questions.

When one comes, it comes from Nick. "How do you know you can trust us for the money?"

"Oh, please," Rafferty says, getting up again. "You're Bangkok's finest."

**ON THE SIDEWALK** in front of the restaurant, he watches until the two of them are out of sight, trying to rationalize away the uneasiness he feels about having ordered someone's death as casually as if it had been on the menu. When he turns, he bumps against someone. Looking down, he sees the dark little man from the *soi*, the one who had hit him with the gun. Behind him are his three teammates. One of them—the man whose nose Rafferty tried to drive into his brain—is wearing a raccoon's mask that resolves itself into two black eyes that look borrowed from a cartoon. A long swelling, big enough to hide a baguette in, runs across his forehead, just above the eyebrows.

"Someone needs to talk to you," the little man says. His right hand disappears into a small leather tote bag, secured by a shoulder strap. Protruding an inch or two from a hole cut into the side of the bag, a few inches from Rafferty's belly, is the barrel of a gun.

Rafferty says, "It took her long enough."

## 39

## Just a Flower Seller

The fragrance of the flowers is so overpowering, Rafferty thinks, that it ought to tint the air—perhaps salmon, with halos of pink around the naked bulbs dangling from the bare electrical cords high overhead. The perfume seems thick enough to foam around his feet as he pushes his way through it, with two of the men in front of him and two behind.

There are obviously people here and there, but none in sight. The rows of flowers are too high, the aisles between them too narrow. He can hear voices occasionally, the energetic back-and-forth of bargaining, frequent bursts of laughter.

The five of them stop in front of a volcano of orchids taller than Rafferty. The small dark man, who has been directly behind Rafferty, steps forward and puts out a hand. He looks almost apologetic.

"Skip it," Rafferty says.

"Those are the rules."

"Make new ones."

The man takes the gun from his bag, shows it to Rafferty, then drops it back in and zips the bag tightly shut. He walks several yards away and places the bag on a display table beneath a spray of exotic flowers that look like they evolved to snatch bats in midflight. Then he comes back and raises his arms to shoulder height, inviting Rafferty to pat him down. "Do you want to check us? Lift your shirts," he says to the others.

"Skip it. So I can see you haven't got guns? You'll have one when I give you mine, won't you?"

"Look around," the small man says. "This is a public place. Everybody in Bangkok who wants flowers is here."

"Compromise," Rafferty says. He slides the automatic free of his trousers, pops the clip, and hands the clip to the small dark man. Holding the gun between thumb and forefinger, he lets it dangle harmlessly in the air. "That's the only clip," he says. "Trust me."

"I don't actually have to." The dark man hikes his pant leg to show Rafferty a small automatic tucked into an ankle holster and then he grins like a small boy doing a magic trick.

"On the other hand," Rafferty says, bringing the barrel of the gun up beneath the man's chin, "there's still the one under the hammer. Jesus. Every time you think mankind has evolved, you get slapped in the face with a dead fish."

"Tell me about it," says a voice from behind him. A woman.

"Soon as he gives me his gun."

She sighs. "Do you really think we'd bring you here to kill you?"

"It doesn't seem efficient. If I know anything about you, it's that you're efficient."

"You came all this way," Doughnut says, with the sorely tried air of someone forced to state the obvious. "We might as well talk."

"The clip," Rafferty says. "These things cost money."

The man slowly hands it over, watches with total concentration as Rafferty slips the clip back in and secures the automatic beneath his waistband. Then he nods, and Rafferty turns to face Doughnut.

At first glance she is completely unremarkable, someone he would pass on the street and not remember a moment later. He would put her in her forties, but he knows she can't be. The photos on the missing disks were taken toward the end of the eighties, and she must have been ten to twelve at the time, like the other children in the AT Series. She can't be much older than twenty-nine or thirty. After what she has lived through, he thinks, she should look eighty.

Shoulder-length hair, painstakingly parted and brushed, frames a round, somewhat flat face with the low nose and full lips of Isaan. Her skin is dark, unlightened by makeup, its duskiness emphasized by a fine white scar that runs the length of her chin, the result of a slicing wound. She wears the prim pastel clothes of an office lady, a bank teller, someone with a job in the safe world.

The eyes don't look at the safe world. They are black, the purest, deepest black, and they seem to be set several inches behind the face, like those of someone holding up a costume mask and peering through it. Someone with a lot of practice at estimating arm's reach and staying outside it.

She submits patiently to his gaze and then gives him a perfunctory smile that tells him he's looked long enough. "Just a flower seller."

"You're just a flower seller," Rafferty says, "in the same way Joan of Arc was just a farm girl."

She turns without a word and leads him down the aisle, the four men trailing behind, Joan of Arc's soldiers in T-shirts and plastic flip-flops. They make two turns, and Rafferty has no idea what direction they're going in.

"Here," Doughnut says. They have reached a rickety structure, roughly square and no more than ten feet on a side, framed in unfinished lumber. Chicken wire nailed to the uprights turns it into a cage of sorts. A table, four feet square and topped with scarred plywood, tilts alarmingly in the center of the cage. Flowers stretch away in all directions, sullen smears of color. Doughnut opens a plywood door and stands aside. "Okay?"

"And if it weren't?" She follows him in without answering. "Your office?"

"Might be, might not be." She closes the door and takes the seat nearest it. Rafferty takes the seat opposite and sees that the open door concealed a television set wired to a VCR.

"So you're Poke," Doughnut says when she is settled. She beats a quick tattoo on the tabletop with her fingernails. "And you think I'm going to tell you my story."

"It's me or the police." He places a hand on the table, and it dips a couple of inches and rocks up again. One leg too short.

She leans back and puts one arm up, over the back of her chair. "Why would I be afraid of the police?"

He sits opposite her. His chair rocks, too. "Because you killed Claus Ulrich."

Doughnut looks like she is stifling a yawn. "You can prove this?"

"I don't have to. You were there. You disappeared. You left bloodstains. You were in the pictures. For the cops that's a royal flush: means, motive, opportunity."

A golden box of Dunhill cigarettes appears on the table, along with a slender silver lighter, either a Mark Cross or a good knockoff. "The police don't actually need anything. They just manufacture what they don't have." She flips the box open, one-handed. "Why would my story interest you?"

"Because a nice lady came all the way from Australia to learn what happened to Claus, and I told her I'd find out."

She lights up and plumes smoke from her nostrils. "The famous niece, I suppose." She rolls the tip of her cigarette gently on the plywood surface of the table to remove a film of ash. The corners of her mouth go down, her first overt display of emotion. "So she asked you. And you always do what you say you'll do?"

"It makes it easier to get up in the morning."

The four men are arrayed behind her, tallest to shortest, as though they've lined up for a photo, peering in through the chicken wire. She turns to see what he is looking at and waves the men away with the hand holding the cigarette. They melt like gnomes into the flowers. Several moments pass, measured in exhalations of smoke. "Let's see," she says at last. "I have a question for you first. Do you think murder is a crime?"

After the week he has had, there is only one truthful reply. "I used to."

She gazes at the cigarette, turning it in her hand so she can read the gold writing on the filter. "If I killed Claus Ulrich, was that a crime?"

"I saw the pictures," he says.

"So what you're saying is, I tell you my story and then wait while you decide my fate."

Rafferty shifts in the hard chair. "I'm not really comfortable with playing judge."

She smiles slightly at the evasion. "But that's what you're doing."

"I think I'd like a cigarette." He hasn't smoked in almost a year.

She extends the pack and the lighter. "This makes you nervous?" She is very calm.

"I'd smoke used toilet paper to get rid of the smell of these flowers."

"Too much of anything will make you sick," she says. "Unless you're already sick, of course." She watches him light up. The lighter is a real Mark Cross. He turns it over and sees the initials "C.U." engraved in a flowing script, fancy as a minaret. "It was his," she says.

Rafferty turns the lighter over in his hand. "You left an awful lot there. Money, watches, all sorts of stuff. Why take this?"

"I didn't want anything he'd touched. But he *used* this." Her gaze floats over his left shoulder, unfocused. "Do you remember the red candles?"

"I'll remember them my whole life." The flame haloed in the photographs, the spills of hot wax across the children's abdomens.

"So will I. So will Toom." She meets his eyes and gives him the perfunctory smile again. "My older sister. Toom."

"How did he get his hands on you?"

She regards him for a moment as though he is a distance she will have to cross, and then she sighs. "My mother sold us when I was ten and Toom was twelve," she says. "A lady came from Bangkok and promised my mother she could find us good work in the city. Washing dishes in a restaurant, she said. When we got bigger, we could be waitresses, with uniforms, two for each of us. She showed my mother a big color picture of the uniform. How I wanted to wear those clothes. I still remember exactly what they looked like." She draws a finger down the scar on her chin, and Rafferty would bet she doesn't know she's doing it. "The lady told my mother we could make two or three hundred dollars a month in the restaurant. My father didn't earn two hundred dollars in a year. She offered an advance on our salary. Is any of this new to you?"

People are beginning to move past them, choosing the blooms they will sell in the shops, in the streets. They glance incuriously at the two of them, just a *farang* and a Thai woman, having a conversation, probably bargaining over the price of flowers. "I know about it in the abstract, as something that happens. As a personal story, it's new."

"I'm aware it's not original. The same thing happened to the other girls in the house."

"What house?"

She shakes her head impatiently. "The one that wasn't a restaurant. Everything that happened to any of us happened to all of us."

Rafferty tries to keep the revulsion out of his voice. "You were ten."

"Almost eleven. And it hurt more than I could believe. But not for long, at least, you know, not down there. I didn't stay eleven for long either. It was interesting. In no time at all, I was older than my sister. Even though she was twelve. She was the one who kept crying. I was the one who decided, as you Americans like to say, 'Fuck this.'"

"You tried to escape?"

"Of course. The first time I didn't even get out of the building. They used wet towels on us. No marks, you see. Customers don't like scarred girls. They hit us until their arms got tired, and then they gave up. Just locked us up. Toom hadn't tried to get away, but they beat her anyway, just to show me what would happen if I did it again."

There is heat inside Rafferty's chest. "Who were they?"

"Two Chinese men. Lee and Kwan. They were brothers and they owned the house, the restaurant, everything. They owned us. After they beat Toom, I decided to wait. I realized I *could* wait. I learned to live through things. To look at the ceiling, as long as they left me on my back. When they didn't, I looked at the wall, or the floor, or the pillow, if I was someplace fancy enough to have pillows."

"How long did this go on?"

"A year, three months, and two days. I was marking the days on the floor under the bed with a pen I had brought with me from my village. My mother had bought it for me so I could write down people's orders in the restaurant. I was going to smile at them and nod and write down their orders *exactly right.* They were going to love me."

She closes her eyes for a moment. When she opens them, she is gazing at the cigarette in her hand. "Then Claus came along."

Rafferty can see no change in her face, but she has sunk the fingernails of her left hand into the edge of the table. There are bands of white around the knuckles. He waits.

A deep drag, two jets of smoke. "He didn't look any worse than anybody else until I realized that the other girls were hiding. They had disappeared through the doors. Behind the sofa. One of the girls who couldn't get out of the room pissed her pants right there."

"He took you."

She shakes her head. "Actually, that time he took her. Her mistake. He liked piss." She sees him looking at her hand and relaxes it. "He liked pretty much everything, as long as it hurt or humiliated us. I figured out later that what really interested him was hurting us *inside.* It wasn't enough that we'd bled and been burned and pissed on. We had to feel like we were shit. We had to want to stop living. Some of us tried to."

The scars on Toom's wrist, Rafferty thinks but does not say. Something Chouk Ran said comes to mind. "He put a nail through your heart."

She looks at him, startled. "Yes," she says. "And the person who got up from that bed was never the same again." She passes her fingertips over her cheeks as though she was spreading makeup. "But I didn't know that until he took me." She drops her hand to the table, slides open the pack of cigarettes and extracts one, lights it off the butt in her hand, and drops the butt to the floor. "And I'm not going to talk about it. I promised myself, after I finished with him, that I would never talk about it again. Never think about it again. It was all I'd thought about for most of my life, do you realize that? Most of my fucking life I've been thinking about Claus Ulrich. Anyway, you saw the pictures of the others. There was nothing special about me. It all happened, and it all hurt, and it all took forever, and that's all there was to it, except that he took me again and then again. He was thinking up new things. That's what I thought at the time anyway. It wasn't until years later, when I opened his filing cabinets and saw the videos, that I realized he wasn't even a creative pervert. He just imitated the stuff he imported from Japan."

Her hair, there is something about her hair.

"Such a dull, ordinary man," she says. "You expect beasts to be different, but they're not. They're as boring as everybody else."

"You can't tell anything about anybody," Rafferty says. "You, for instance. Looking at you, no one would ever guess what you've survived." He is studying her hair, the perfection with which it has been brushed. Something stirs inside him.

"Then he took both of us," she says. She watches him for a reaction. "Sisters. Some men like sisters, you know? They like them— together. He made us do things to each other. Sex things. Then . . ." She falters. Looks down at her lap. He sees that the part in her hair is straight enough to have been cut with a knife.

Like Miaow's.

The perfection of Miaow's part is one of the ways she proves she can control things. He mentally waves the image away, but it persists. "Then what?"

"Then this," she says. "This is something you haven't seen."

She swivels in her chair and turns on the television set. It blossoms into electronic snow until she pushes a button on the remote. "He took a few of these," she says, waiting for the picture. "But the camera was too bulky, and he couldn't work it with a remote, so he had to stop playing with us to make the video." The familiar room blinks onto the screen. "But he took this one because it was special."

The image is mercifully low-resolution, the product of a cheap video camera from more than twenty years ago. A small naked brown girl, barely recognizable as Doughnut, is on the red coverlet. Her wrists have been tied to her ankles, which are separated by metal cuffs with a two-foot rod between them. The bindings open and lift her legs and arms, leaving her splayed and helpless on her back.

A slightly larger girl, also naked, enters the picture from the left. She is already crying.

"Toom," Doughnut says.

Toom sits on the bed next to Doughnut and gently reaches over to smooth her sister's hair, which is plastered with sweat to her face. The camera jumps, and Toom yanks her arm back as though Doughnut were a live wire. Then, jerkily, the camera moves in on the two girls. Doughnut has her eyes closed, and her face is vacant, almost otherworldly, but Toom watches with enormous eyes as the camera advances on her.

A hand comes into the frame, holding a lighted cigar. The hand is shaking, and Rafferty realizes that the camera is shaking, too. Claus Ulrich is excited.

Toom waves the cigar away and hangs her head. The hand disappears and comes back without the cigar, and then it moves too fast for the camera to track and backhands Toom across the face. Toom's face snaps around, the short hair flying, and she is knocked sideways across Doughnut. Doughnut's eyes remain closed. When the hand re-enters the frame, it has the cigar in it again.

Without opening her eyes, Doughnut says something to her sister. This time, very slowly, Toom takes it. With the cigar pressed between the first and second fingers of her right hand, she does the best she can to make a very high *wai* to her sister, who has opened her eyes.

Doughnut smiles at her.

"Turn it off," Rafferty says. His voice is a rasp. He has looked away from the screen, but he doesn't even want the images in his peripheral vision.

"It goes on for quite a while," Doughnut says, snapping the set off. "Although at the time it seemed much longer."

Rafferty reaches reflexively for another cigarette, catches himself.

"So, two nights later, I broke a window and went out through it. Cut myself here." She swipes at the scar on her chin. "I had to do it, for Toom. She hadn't stopped crying since she hurt me. I thought she was going to cry herself to death. I couldn't help her while I was inside, so I got out. My first night out, I met Coke on the street."

"Coke?"

"The short one," she says, indicating the vanished men with her chin. "He was little, but he liked me, and he helped me. And he had something I needed."

"What?" Coke and Doughnut.

"A gun." She brings the black eyes up to his, as though to make sure he is listening. "I had to get Toom out, so I needed a gun. I didn't know they had cut her to get even with me for escaping. Cut her here." She raises a leg and draws a quick line across her Achilles tendon.

The flopping foot. "Who did?"

"The two Chinese men."

"I'm surprised you didn't go after them, too."

Doughnut stubs out her half-smoked cigarette on the tabletop, being very careful to fold it over neatly before she drops it on the floor. She looks down at it and twists her shoe on it, killing it dead.

"Well, sure," Rafferty says. Despite his mounting revulsion—at what he has seen, at what she has done—he can't help seeing her as Miaow grown up, a Miaow for whom things had gone differently, things over which she had no control. The plain brown face, the dark hair, the knife-edge part. He realizes she is talking.

". . . finally, Lee, the one who liked to beat the girls, drove her out and took her to a number hotel, and I got off Coke's motorcycle and walked into the parking lot, just as Lee got out of the car. I shot him there, and we took Toom. When I saw her foot, I decided to kill Kwan, too." She lets her chin fall onto her chest, the first time she has betrayed anything like exhaustion. "And I did, about eight months later." She sounds as calm as someone describing what she had for dinner. "A week after my twelfth happy birthday. Then I went off with Toom and Coke, and we made a life."

As she describes it, it had not been a conventional household. Coke robbed people and sent Doughnut to school with the money he stole, while Toom kept house. Doughnut learned English and computer skills and thought about Claus.

"How did you find him?"

"I didn't. I just saw him on the street. Big as ever. Just walking along, like a real person. You want to hear something funny? I was terrified." She brings her right hand to her heart and taps, twice. "*Terrified.* He was exactly the same. He looked at me like I wasn't there, and I realized he didn't know who I was. I smiled at him." She fiddles with the package of cigarettes and then pushes it aside. "I think that was the hardest thing, that smile, that I ever did. He nodded and walked right past. So I turned around and followed him, and then I knew where he lived. Easy. I could hardly believe it."

"I think I know some of the rest of it," Rafferty says. He tells her what he has learned about Noot and Bangkok Domestics and Madame Wing. "So you got in, and there you were. In that apartment. Just you and Claus."

She nods. Then she reaches up and smooths her hair.

"How did you stand it?"

Her fingers find the cigarettes again, and she takes one out without looking at it. "No problem. It was almost fun. I was nice to him. I cooked and cleaned and took care of him like he was a big, fat, ugly, smelly baby. He stank of meat. He had hair on his back, like a monkey. He poured sweet stuff all over himself because he smelled so bad. I told him he was handsome. Why do men always believe they are handsome? I made him *love* me. He called me his little *sugar doughnut.*" She spits the English words like hard seeds, as though she expects them to bounce on the table. "I wanted him to love me. I wanted him to think I loved him. Like Toom loved me, like somebody sometime must have loved all those girls he hurt. It was *necessary* for him to think I loved him."

"Because it wasn't enough just to kill him."

She places the unlit cigarette between her index fingers as though she is measuring it and looks at him over it. "Would you think it was enough?"

Rafferty does not answer, just regards the small, dark, harmless-looking girl sitting opposite him in her pastel clothes. Looks at the clean, cropped nails; the bright, childish plastic bracelet; the meticulously brushed hair. Looks at the child tied to the bed. Doughnut. Who could have been Miaow.

She returns his gaze impassively and lets the cigarette fall to the table. "Well, it wasn't. First he had to trust me. Then he had to love me. Then he had to do something good, just once in his life."

"He already had," Rafferty says. "Clarissa. The niece."

She moves her head to one side, dodging the words. "For *me*. He had to do something for me, so he could feel good about himself. Feel good about being alive."

"Jesus," Rafferty says.

"So I borrowed money from him. I told him my family needed it, which was true. I gave him some time to feel what it was like to be good, to be proud of himself. I gave him a week, thanked him every day. Told him he had saved my mama's life by buying medicine for her. He was so proud of himself that he went on a diet. Then I fell in my bathroom. I screamed. He ran in to help me. Feeling like a hero. I'd thought about where to do it while I polished all that furniture. I needed him to be in the bathroom."

"For cleanup." He is watching her eyes, trying to see the person behind them. Only when she catches him and glances down does he see a crack in the surface, a vulnerability in the shell.

She does not look back up. "He lifted me off the floor and sat me on the edge of the tub, and I shot him in the leg. Then I shot him in the other leg."

"You were close to him."

"I wanted to be close. I would have liked to have been inside him, so I could know how much it hurt. After he fell down, I shot him again, very low in the stomach."

"Ouch," Rafferty says.

"I stood in the tub, waiting to make sure he couldn't move. His eyes were open, looking at me like I was something he'd never seen before. Something he'd never imagined. I suppose I was. A girl hurting *him*. I suppose it was something new."

Rafferty thinks for a moment about what he wants to say. "You can live a long time with a stomach wound."

"And I let him. I told him all about it. Everything he had done to me." For a moment she seems puzzled, and she looks back up at him with something like an appeal in her eyes. "He didn't *remember* me. He had me confused with another girl. I'd thought about him every day for years, and he didn't remember me. But when I talked about Toom, about us being sisters, *then* he remembered. You know what he said?"

Rafferty discovers that he doesn't really want to know. He lifts a palm.

"He said, 'Those were good pictures.' So I shot him in the head."

She slumps back in her seat. "I was tired," she says. "I didn't mean to let him go that fast."

Rafferty reaches across the table, picks up the cigarette she dropped, and lights it. Feels the good poison course through him, killing him a little but not quite enough. "Have you ever cried about all this?"

Her chin comes up and her lips thin, and for a second Rafferty thinks he is seeing the face Ulrich must have seen in his last minutes. "About what happened to you, what happened to Toom. Did you ever take the time to cry over it?"

"Toom cried," she says flatly. "One of us had to be the dry one. One of us had to do something about it."

"Then what *do* you feel? Now that it's over."

She stretches across, takes the cigarette from his mouth, and puts it between her lips. "I feel like I made a mistake."

It is not the answer he expects. "You do?"

"I should have waited. I should have let him lose some more weight on his diet. Take it from me. If you're going to shoot somebody and you have to get rid of the body, choose someone thin."

"I'll keep it in mind."

"But I couldn't wait. Do you want to know why?"

"I think I do," Rafferty says. "He had packed a bag. He was going somewhere, wasn't he? Somewhere where he could get hold of some kids."

"I'm impressed," she says, not sounding particularly impressed. She looks down at the cigarette. "I miss him, in a way," she says thoughtfully. "He gave me something to do."

"Can I have the cigarette back?"

She passes it over to him, shaking her head. "I didn't know I'd taken it."

"Anybody left?" he asks. She glances up at him, eyebrows raised. "Are you at the end of your list, Doughnut, or is somebody left?"

Another shake of the head, without much behind it. "Finished."

"What about the lady who brought you to Bangkok?"

"That was only business. If I kill everybody who does business, there won't be anybody left. No. They were different. They needed to die."

Rafferty sucks deeply on the cigarette, replaying the remark in his head. Then he hands the cigarette back to her. He gets up, feeling light-headed and profoundly doubtful about what he is going to do. "Okay."

She looks startled, something he didn't know she had left in her. "Okay?"

"Okay. That's it. I asked, you told me. The end."

She studies his face. "Do you mean that? No police?"

"The way I look at it," he says, "this wasn't murder. It was self-defense. It was just a little late." She sits there, immobile, and her eyes drop again, and some of the rigidity leaves her shoulders.

He goes to the door behind her and turns back, looking at that perfectly controlled hair. "Doughnut," he says, and she brings her head around and gazes up at him, looking younger and more open from this perspective. "You swear you're finished, yes?"

She nods. "Yes," she says. She touches her heart with her index finger. "Promise." Then she smiles at him. "If I weren't finished, you'd be carried out of here with the dead flowers."

## 40

## He Could Probably Unlock Buckingham Palace

Clarissa Ulrich says, "I'm going home."

"I'm sorry, Clarissa," he says. The telephone is slippery in his hand. Superman turned off the air-conditioning while Rafferty was gone, and the apartment is stifling. He has been home half an hour, too exhausted to get up from the couch and start the air flowing.

"Sorry about what?"

"Sorry I couldn't do anything that helped. Sorry about what I did do. The filing cabinet." He hasn't told her about Doughnut, and he can't imagine that he will.

"I suppose I had to find out about him sooner or later," she says bravely. She sounds to Rafferty like a child who has survived a trip to the dentist, although he knows the comparison's not fair, that she has been permanently damaged, to use Rose's word, by what has happened to her in Bangkok. "Not much point in believing he was a good man if he wasn't."

The urge to offer comfort is overwhelming. "He was good to you. That counts for something."

"He was a man." Her voice seems to sour and curl at the edges. "That's about all he was."

There is a silence, which Rafferty uses to get to his feet and turn on the air-conditioning unit. It belches once and starts spewing hot air, rich with Bangkok exhaust. He stands in front of it, letting it hit him in the face. It smells better to him than the flowers. He never wants to smell another flower.

"I'm not necessarily finished, Clarissa," he says, although up to that moment he had figured he was.

"Please," she says. "You've been very sweet, but I don't need anything more. He's dead, or he might as well be. And I'm alive, and I have to figure out what to do about that. He's not coming home, not ever." Her voice is thin as a ribbon. "I shouldn't have come in the first place."

"You had to. You owed him that."

He can almost hear her shrug, see the expression on her face. "I guess."

"When do you go?"

"Tomorrow night. I couldn't get on a flight any sooner. Apparently there are lots of people who want to get out of here." A short laugh, more like a cough. "Can't imagine why."

"Well, maybe I can do something by then. Don't leave without calling me, okay?"

"What? What could you possibly do?"

Good question. "I'm still checking on a couple of things." One possibility occurs to him as he says the words, but it will require yet another favor of Arthit. At least this one won't threaten Arthit's career.

"I'll call," Clarissa says, "even if it's just to say thanks," and she hangs up.

Rafferty throws the telephone at the couch, harder than he means to, and then has to go pick it up and make sure it still has a dial tone. It does, but that doesn't make him feel any better. He puts the phone on the table and goes into the kitchen for a beer. It's still early for a drink, but what the hell. He's just let a triple murderer walk away without so much as a slap on the wrist and allowed her only innocent victim, Clarissa, to go home with her life shattered. He's about to put a good man in jail. He's inveigled his best friend into something that could endanger both his job and his wife. He's sending a woman—a dreadful, unforgivable woman, but a human being nonetheless—to her death. A beer sounds right. Give him a little perspective.

Chouk looks around when Rafferty stalks into the bedroom. The television is on, the screen full of writhing snakes. The Discovery Channel has come to Bangkok. He downs the beer in four long gulps, picks up the remote, and kills the TV, wishing there were a button that would make it explode. "Today," he says.

"As good as any other," Chouk says.

Rafferty scoots Chouk over as far as the constraints will permit. Then he unlocks the cabinet and shoves aside the stack of CD-ROMs from Claus Ulrich's apartment. The tidy pile collapses. Behind them is an envelope. He takes it out and drops it on the bed, relocks the cabinet, and hangs the chain with the key on it around his neck.

"The cop who's coming is okay," he says shortly. "You can trust him."

"I have to go to the bathroom," Chouk says.

"Yeah, I'd imagine you do. We're through with these things anyway." He goes around the bed, fumbling through his ring of keys until he finds the one for the cuffs. With the key in the lock, he pauses. "The kid didn't undo these, did he? He could probably unlock Buckingham Palace."

"No. He just brought me the food and fed it to me, and took the little girl to school," Chouk says. Rafferty unsnaps the cuff and lets it dangle from the bed frame. "He's a nice kid."

Rafferty straightens, feeling his back tighten and creak from sheer accumulated tension. "'Nice' may not be the precise word."

"Nice is for rich people," Chouk says, flexing his ruined hand to the limits of its mobility. To Rafferty it looks like a spasm. "The rest of us do the best we can."

Rafferty tears his eyes away from the hand. "Are you even remotely interested in what's going to happen to you today?"

"No." Chouk sits up stiffly. Dr. Ratt has untaped his arm from his side, but the ribs are still tightly wrapped. The white bandages make his torso look darker than mahogany. "Be right back." He takes tentative steps, heading for the bathroom.

Returning to the kitchen, Rafferty tosses the beer toward the trash can, misses, and kicks it with all his strength. It bounces off the wall and hits him in the shin, and he jumps into the air and lands on the can with both feet, mashing it flat. Then he kicks it again, and it slides under the stove.

"And fuck you, too," Rafferty says to it. "Stay there." He pulls open the refrigerator. "More perspective," he says, taking another beer. The doorbell rings.

Rafferty shifts the can of beer to his left hand and, just in case, pulls the gun with his right. He positions himself in front of the door, holding the gun at gut-shot level, and says, "It's not locked."

Arthit pushes the door open and looks from the gun to the beer. "Not a difficult choice," he says, taking the beer.

"You're early," Rafferty grumbles, heading back to the kitchen.

"Good morning to you, too. I would have brought you a Danish, but I thought it might endanger our relationship with Scandinavia."

Only two beers left, a Singha and an Angkor, from Cambodia, that Rafferty doesn't recall buying. He takes the Singha. The toilet flushes.

"Our boy?" Arthit says, leaning against the kitchen counter.

"Let's not be breezy," Rafferty says, ripping the tab off the can. "I can handle just about anything except breezy."

"I treasure these moments," Arthit says, and drinks. "When I look back on this part of my life, these little talks will be marked in yellow highlighter." He drinks again, crumples the can, and tosses. The can hits the wastebasket, a slam dunk, and Arthit regards Rafferty expectantly.

"Would you like my last beer?"

"Sure," Arthit says. "What else are you going to do with it?"

"Aren't you on duty or something?"

"The law never sleeps."

"Maybe not, but sometimes it sits for long periods of time with its eyes closed and its mouth open."

"Gosh, I hate to cut this short." Arthit pushes himself away from the counter. "There's never enough time in the day, is there?"

"Wait, Arthit. I've been talking with our murderer, and I think we can do this without getting you in trouble with the folks who are protecting Madame Wing."

"That's the nicest thing you've said all day." Arthit folds his hands in front of him, looking patient.

"It's very simple. You arrest him for Tam's murder and everybody just leaves Madame Wing out of it."

Arthit nods slowly, like someone who is too polite to disagree. "A ten-million-baht ransom, paid and shredded, a safe dug up in the back-yard of a rich and powerful woman, something taken out of it that was apparently *worth* ten million baht, a guard who got paid off to let the thieves in—none of that's likely to surface. Not worth a mention."

"Totally extraneous," Rafferty says. "Didn't even happen. They were planning a crime, and they got drunk down near the river, which is why Tam was covered with mud. They got into a fight, and Chouk shot him."

"So it was a spat." Arthit clears his throat. "A falling-out among thieves."

"He was drunk. He's been regretting it ever since. That's why he's coming forward to confess, as you cops like to say. This is true, by the way. He wants to atone for what he did."

"And you can keep it that way?"

"Yeah. He'll play, and who else is going to volunteer informa-tion? Madame Wing? She's not going to be talking to anybody. Look, it's everything you could want: You get to arrest someone for Tam's murder—someone who actually *did* it, no less—there's lots of nice evidence, and you don't have to be the cop who links Tam's murder to the rich widow and all her inconvenient connections. They didn't even get around to the robbery. He just confesses and goes to jail."

"Does he have money for jail?"

"He will."

There is a pause long enough for Arthit to take his own temperature. "Poke," he says at last, "tell me you're not supplying it."

"Okay, Arthit, I'm not supplying it."

Arthit starts to say something, but he is cut off.

"Is this the one?" Chouk asks from the living room.

"Chouk, this is Arthit," Rafferty says, "and vice versa. You know which is which." A wave of dizziness overtakes him. "Why don't you two boys chat while I get rid of this beer?"

When he has finished vomiting the beer into the toilet, he washes his mouth out with Listerine and brushes his teeth hard enough to make his gums bleed. His mouth still tastes foul. He grabs the envelope from the bed and goes into the living room, where Chouk and Arthit have claimed the couch.

"Here." He pitches the envelope to Chouk. "That's fifteen hundred U.S. I'll have more in a couple of days."

"I can't take this," Chouk says, not touching it.

"It's Madame Wing's," Rafferty says. "The rest of it will be Madame Wing's, too. In a manner of speaking."

"You're going to want money in jail," Arthit says to Chouk. "It makes a big difference. A cell by yourself, maybe a carpet, a girl every now and then." He gets up and pulls the wrinkles out of his trousers. "Let's leave Mr. Sunshine here and get you to jail, where people are pleasant."

**WHEN THEY ARE** gone, Rafferty sits absolutely still at his desk for the better part of fifteen minutes. He does a quick survey of his life and comes up with three shining exceptions to the landscape of flat tires, tin cans, and free-floating injury he's been inhabiting since his talk with Doughnut: Rose, Miaow's adoption, and the progress with Superman.

The moment Superman enters his mind, the phone rings.

"Poke?" Hank Morrison says. "Is this a good time?"

"Depends on you. Is there anything new?"

"I think I've got a guy at a school who'll take Superman," Morrison says. "But he's a little iffy. I think some shock therapy will push him over the edge. Do you still have those pictures?"

"Until I figure out how to throw them away. They're not something you toss in the trash."

"Well, e-mail me a couple of the ones with the boy in them. Nothing too hair-raising. I want to convince him, not give him a heart attack."

"Jesus, Hank, that means I have to look at them again."

"Up to you," Morrison says. "But it'll help."

"Hang on a minute." Rafferty gets up, phone in hand, and forces himself to go into the bedroom. The closed door to the safe looks far too benign, considering what it's hiding. Rafferty reluctantly puts his hand on the key hanging around his neck.

"Okay, Hank. Look for them in a few minutes, and for Christ's sake don't let anyone else open your e-mail."

"Thanks, Poke. I'm pretty sure this will do it."

Morrison hangs up, and Rafferty works the chain off his neck and opens the safe. The CDs slide out in a long spill across the surface of the bed. He flips open the cases as though they contained venomous snakes and finds the two he thinks the boy's photos will be on, then carries them back into the living room.

It takes him five or ten dreadful minutes to find what he's looking for. He chooses two from relatively early in the sequence, before the bestiality reached its crescendo, and mails them off. Then he closes the lid of the computer in self-defense and carries the cases back into the bedroom. As he gathers up the ones on the bed, he decides the best way to dispose of them will be to give them to Arthit and let the police destroy them. He feels slightly lighter as he relocks the safe.

Back in the living room, he realizes he wants to tell somebody about Hank's possible breakthrough. Miaow is in school. Arthit is at work. Superman isn't reachable, and Rafferty wouldn't tell him anyway without the matter being resolved. That leaves the person he really wants to talk to, and he dials Rose's cell number.

"Hello?" Her tone is brisk.

"How long has it been since I told you I love you?"

"Ah," she says, a bit coolly. "What a nice surprise."

"It is not. You've known it forever."

"Yes. I suppose I have."

"You're a world I want to enter," Rafferty says.

"And I'll hold the door."

"There's something I want to tell you."

"Something good?"

"I think so."

Rose covers the mouthpiece of the phone and says something. Then she says, "Can it wait?"

"Sure," Rafferty says. "You're somewhere where you can't talk."

"Absolutely correct."

"At Bangkok Domestics?"

"Actually," she says, "I'm at Peachy and Rose's Household Agency."

"Peachy?"

"The canned kind, I think. By the way, your last conversation was extremely productive. Just a complete about-face. You may recall that there had been a certain prickliness."

"On Peachy's end."

"Yes. Oh, and I remember having said something to you recently about keeping a cool heart. Well, a hot one works occasionally, too."

"Peachy and Rose, huh? That has a nice ring."

"And two more situations have been found for members of the labor pool. Turns out some people actually *prefer* attractive maids."

"I know I would."

"Oh, good," Rose says sweetly. "We can send you someone you already know. You won't even have to learn her name."

"Rose, our Cambodian guest is gone. You can come home."

"Hmmm. That means the bed is free?"

He is up and pacing, feeling better than he has all day. "Why not come right now? We'd have the place to ourselves."

"I'd love to." She lowers her voice. "You have no idea how much

I'd love to." Back at a normal volume, she says, "We're meeting with a designer about the new letterhead and business cards, and then I've got two interviews to supervise."

"The demands of success," Rafferty says.

"A good businessperson puts business first."

"I guess she does."

"A good businessperson also pays her debts," Rose says. "And, of course, the interest. Have *you* got a payment coming."

He finds himself grinning at the phone. "I'll change the sheets."

"Hardly seems worth it." Rose lowers her voice again. "We'll probably have to throw them away when we're done."

## 41

# Individually They Would Be Harmless

With nothing to do and a recently emptied stomach, Rafferty discovers he is ravenous. He hasn't eaten since the breakfast with Chut and Nick. By now, he thinks, they should have some buyers lined up.

He kills ninety minutes at a restaurant called Banana House, eating as much chili as the waitresses dare to serve a foreigner, since all Thais secretly believe that *farang* live on mayonnaise and warm milk. He sits back in the chair, burps fire, and thinks about the past few days.

Chouk is in jail, partially provided for. Action is being taken to close Madame Wing's long-overdue account. Clarissa Ulrich is poised for her heartsick flight home. Rose is designing the graphics for her new business. Hank Morrison is knee-deep in adoptive parents. Miaow is at school until three.

Doughnut is making a life, he supposes, either selling flowers or not. Whatever it is, he hopes it will be less interesting than the one she has had so far.

On his way out of the restaurant, Rafferty finds himself at a complete loss. The day stretches in front of him, hot and featureless as the Gobi, although he's never seen the Gobi. He's pretty sure it's hot and featureless, though, and if it's not, it must be a miserable excuse for a desert.

Well, the boy might be back by now.

It takes him just twenty minutes, a world record, to get home. With no need for hurry, the Bangkok traffic moves like lightning. He nods out in the back of the *tuk-tuk* and revises his plans as it lurches to a stop at the curb. He'll sleep until the end of the world, or maybe a little longer.

His sleepiness vanishes at the sight of his apartment door. It is wide open.

The boy, he thinks, the boy doesn't like air-conditioning. But even from the hall, he can see that something—everything—is wrong. He has the gun in his hand as he goes in.

The first thing he registers is the long slash in the couch, the stuffing exploding from it onto the floor like the cotton snow in the Christmas windows of Bangkok department stores. Yellow streaks across the wall announce the places where raw eggs shattered against it. The coffee table is on its side with one leg snapped off. The carpet where the boy likes to sit has been sliced and torn to expose the gray concrete beneath.

*Why can't the world be soft?*

*The boy.*

Rafferty runs down the hallway to Miaow's room and throws open the door. No one there, everything where it should be. The bunk beds are made. The pink T-shirt she gave him is the only thing out of place, wadded tightly on the floor. He picks it up, and it flutters to the carpet in pieces. It has been cut into ribbons.

And suddenly he *knows,* and his stomach shrivels until it is the size of a walnut and heavy as an anvil. He hurtles back through the hall, into the living room, and stops, his heart plummeting. The laptop is open, its screen bright and terrible.

*The boy,* he thinks. *He was going to play Tetris.* And then Rafferty realizes that he e-mailed Morrison, got up, and left the disk in the computer.

He hurries into the bathroom and, for the second time that day, he throws up.

**HE NEEDS SEVERAL** frantic minutes to find the telephone number. He has had it for months on a pad next to the phone on the chance he might need it, but nothing is where it should be, and in his panic he picks the pad up and throws it aside and then chases it across the room, kicking things in front of him.

The boy glares at him from the computer screen on his desk. His hands are cuffed behind him, his feet separated by a pole like the ones that forced Doughnut's ankles apart. His eyes are wide and dry, glittering through his tangle of hair: Even then he had refused to weep.

That picture, on this screen, in this room. That disk in the computer. The boy's last chance to trust, and he finds that evil here.

*I should have known. I should have known.* The disk is on the floor, warped and blackened, partially torched with, Rafferty guesses, a disposable butane lighter, one of the dozens Rose has left behind. He dials the number on the pad and waits, swearing at each ring. The battery on the computer dies, and the screen goes black. A small mercy.

"Hello?" says a male voice on the other end, and Rafferty waits for a moment, struck dumb at the possibility he is making a disastrous mistake. If he talks to Miaow, she'll know something is wrong, and she'll demand to know what it is. He can't explain yet, doesn't know how to frame it, especially at this stage in their relationship. *Adoption,* for Christ's sake.

"Hello?"

On the other hand, if he doesn't say something, the boy will go get her. He will want to rescue her. From Rafferty, from what he thinks Rafferty is. It can't be risked. Whatever happens, Rafferty has to talk to her before the boy does.

It takes him less than two minutes to get through to the person he needs to talk to and make the arrangements: Miaow is to be kept there after school for an hour, or two if necessary, released to no one but him under any circumstances. She is not to be allowed on the playground. If she wants to know why, she is to be told he will explain it to her later.

When he's had time to think of something. After he's made things right with Superman.

He pulls the computer off the desk, yanking out the power cord, and throws it across the room.

As he runs onto the Silom sidewalk, all he can think is, *At least I probably know where the boy is.*


**HE SEES HIM** instantly.

The boy stands with his back to the street, pressed up against the chain-link fence that surrounds the school, watching the playground. He is once again all in blue—in the first clothes Rafferty bought him. Two very dirty smaller boys flank him, keeping lookout. Despite the tinted windows of his taxi, darkened against the heat of the day, it is all Rafferty can do to keep from shrinking out of sight.

Twenty or thirty feet away, a group of kids play with typical childlike violence, doing their level best to blind and maim each other, apparently immune to the noon heat. Miaow is not among them.

"Around the block," Rafferty says.

"Okay." The cab swings right, narrowly avoiding an oncoming van, and shoots up the street, hugging the middle to bypass the traffic in the lane nearest the curb. Cars and pedestrians scatter.

"Slower." Rafferty is studying the side of the school, which takes up much of the block. No sign of Miaow. No other boys loitering, waiting for something to happen.

"All the way around?" They are at the corner.

"All the way." A stretch of shop fronts intervenes, the sidewalks crowded with pedestrians. A few children, none of them Miaow. *Be inside, be safe,* he wills silently.

As they make the next right, Rafferty hands a wad of bills over the front seat. "Back to where we saw those three kids. Slow down, but don't stop. I'll get out while you're moving."

"Up to you. You have insurance?"

"There's no such thing as insurance."

The driver makes the last right, and Rafferty jumps out of the cab at a run. He is no more than ten yards from Superman when one of the smaller boys spots him and yells, and Superman glances over his shoulder and takes off, the other boys scattering in his slipstream. They head in different directions, apparently a standard drill, but Rafferty stays behind Superman, watches the long hair flowing in the sun as the boy lopes down the sidewalk, easily, effortlessly outpacing him.

He wills his legs to pump faster, feeling Doughnut's cigarettes clawing at his throat. Chain-link blurs past. Superman takes the right that Rafferty's cab took, glancing back, running straight into the traffic. Rafferty follows, already gasping with the effort, as cars swerve to avoid him, their brakes a high screech like a diamond on glass.

A *soi* opens up on the left, and Superman streaks into it, lengthening his stride as though shifting gears, and Rafferty knows he will never catch the boy. He thinks for a despairing instant about giving up, but the boy leaps onto the curb and catches his foot, staggering for a moment, and Rafferty closes the gap by a few yards before the running boy gets his feet under him again. A shot of hope courses through Rafferty's veins, red and hot. He finds speed he didn't know he had.

Then he has to negotiate the curb himself, and he looks down to keep from stumbling, and when he looks up, the boy is gone.

He slows, irresolute, scanning the street. Two turned heads, adults, form a kind of wake that tells him which direction the boy took, and for the second time in a few days, Rafferty runs into an underground garage.

And thinks instantly, *This is a mistake.*

He hears feet scuffing behind him, five or six people by the sound of it, and he runs farther into the gloom of the garage, putting distance between him and them, trying to see Superman. The light coming through the door behind him dims and then brightens again, and he looks over his shoulder to see eight or ten children, none of them any older than Superman, crowding through it and separating into two groups. There are already four others, the first feet he heard, circling off to his right. He thinks, *Coyotes.*

"*Boo!*"

No answer, but something strikes his shoulder, sharp as a knife, and a stone clatters onto the concrete at his feet. Another missile whistles past his head, a chunk of cement as big as a child's fist, and bangs into the door of a car. Then an impact on his right elbow, and his arm goes numb. More cement.

He calls the boy's name again. Knowing it will do no good, knowing the boy will not answer. Knowing he has to get out of the garage. He turns to see more than a dozen of them, all small, between him and the door. Individually they would be harmless. He starts toward them, thinking he can break through the line, and they charge.

They swarm over him, a storm of hands and feet, knees and elbows, climbing him, hitting him high and low, taking him to his knees. A small hand comes up with a stone in it and slams it down across his cheekbone with an impact that ignites a sudden flare of red light, blossoming and vanishing like a pound of flash paper. For a blind moment, he sees nothing, feels the hands tearing at him, feels the bright radiating pain of a bite on his upper arm, and then something hammers his shoulder, high up, where the muscle is still sore from the fight in the *soi,* and he manages somehow to get a leg under him. Nails rake his face, aiming for the eyes. Kicks rain on his ankles and shins. He tries with all his strength to shake the children off, a bear besieged by a pack of dogs, and the back of a hand swipes his mouth and skids off wet skin. He is bleeding.

Fierce gasps as they jockey for position, the smell of dirt and sweat, kicks and blows drumming on his back and thighs, a hand grabbing at his hair. Another stone, in the small of the back this time, just missing the spine, and Rafferty strikes out for the first time with all the force he can command and connects with something solid, hears the high cry of a child, and his assailants retreat just enough to give him room.

He gets his numbed hand down to his waist and brings it up with the automatic in it. He knows he cannot use it, and he hopes they don't know it, too.

He is on his knees. The children take a step away, ringing him, two deep. He can hear their panting, smell their breath. Their eyes are on the gun, but he cannot cover them all at once even if he could bring himself to fire, and again something slams into his back, savagely enough to knock the breath out of him. Then again, in a different place, but still only inches from the spine.

A shouted word, and the blows stop. He turns slowly, keeping the gun close and low, and sees Superman emerging from between two cars. The boy walks toward them deliberately, his eyes narrow, fixed on Rafferty's. Rafferty tries to say something and fails.

The children part to let Superman through. He looks down at Rafferty, who is still kneeling, and extends a hand. There is only one thing Rafferty can do to demonstrate faith.

He hands the boy the gun.

Superman hefts it, as though considering its weight.

"Let me explain," Rafferty says. A rock grazes his ear, and then there are children climbing his back, beating at him, and he goes down beneath them. The world is a concrete floor and a crowd of dirty shoes. Pain ignites along his spine.

The shot almost blows out his eardrums.

The children back off, and Rafferty looks up to see Superman brandishing the gun, aiming it in the general direction of the kids. "Leave him alone," the boy says.

The gun clatters to the floor in front of Rafferty's face. The clip lands next to it.

"You can have it back now," Superman says with contempt, and the children turn and walk away. Sauntering, not running. At the door to the garage, the boy turns to look at him. "I'll be back," he says. "For Miaow." Then they are gone.

Rafferty is still for a long while. Getting to his feet requires a set of careful stages, moving one thing at a time. It seems to take an eternity to limp blinking into the bright day. The children are gone. He mops the blood from his face and flags a taxi, bleeding, stinking with fear, and aching in every joint. He ignores the driver's eyes in the mirror. When the elevator doors open on his floor, he has to lean against the hallway wall for another long moment before he can force himself to cross the hall and open the door of his apartment, where he finds himself looking into the bottomless eyes of Madame Wing.

## 42

## There Are People Who Should Die

Toadface and Skeletor flank her wheelchair like a pair of mismatched tutelary figures guarding a throne. Madame Wing raises her chin.

"You stink," Madame Wing says.

"Yeah, but I can take a shower," Rafferty replies shakily. "What are your options?"

She perches in the chair, more batlike than ever, sharp knees drawn up to her chest. The inevitable blanket covers her legs, but her feet protrude from the bottom edge. She has prehensile feet—long, thin toes with narrow, yellowish nails that extend far enough to curl downward, long enough to break if she had to walk. They are the ugliest feet Rafferty has ever seen. It gives him a cold twinge of comfort that she has had to live with such hideous feet.

Skeletor—Nick—leaves her side to circle him, keeping his distance, and shuts the door. He positions himself with his back to it.

Rafferty leans against the wall, his joints too loose and his bones too heavy, his body too big and bulky to move. Pain radiates out from a dozen places where he was hit. "This isn't exactly what I had in mind," he says.

"Change of plans," says Toadface.

"So I see." Rafferty draws a deep breath and blows it out. "How you doing, you merciless old bitch?" he asks Madame Wing.

She knocks the insult away with a knot of knuckles. "Where is the man who took my money?"

"You'll never know." He can't tell the truth. He knows she can reach Chouk in jail, as easily as stretching out a hand and slapping him.

"Oh," she says comfortably, "I think I will."

"Yeah? What's the plan? You going to kiss me?"

She almost smiles. "We're going to wait," she says.

"For what?"

Madame Wing slips a hand beneath the blanket and comes out with a piece of paper. He can see the bright colors through the back of the sheet even before she turns it around to face him. It is one of Miaow's new drawings, a family group of four: Rafferty, Rose, Superman, and herself. It seems to him to have been months since she drew it. "Until the children come home," she says.

There is a hot pressure in Rafferty's chest that he recognizes as terror. "They won't come home," he says.

"Really." She is undisturbed. "And why not?"

"The boy's gone," he says. "Miaow won't leave school until I go get her."

"The school called," she says. "About three minutes ago, because you hadn't shown up. And one of these gentlemen told them to put her in a taxi and send her here. And they will. The Thais are not careful people. They put too much faith in the future."

"It's too late for you," he says.

"Is it?" There is not a trace of interest in her face.

"The pictures. They're already at the *Bangkok Post*. They'll be on the Internet by this time tomorrow."

"I'm sure they'll be popular." She drops Miaow's drawing to the floor. It lands right side up near the wheel of her chair, the bright, cheerful picture facing Rafferty. "The *Post* won't publish them. The laws of libel are almost the only laws the Thais enforce. What do they show? A young woman. She could be anyone."

"You underestimate your ugliness."

Her whole head snaps forward, quick as a cobra. "You have no idea what I've survived," she says. "Do you honestly think *you* can make an end of me? You, with your cheap apartment, your sad little life. I am as far beyond you as the stars."

"Those whom the gods would destroy," Rafferty says, "they first give weak dialogue."

She does not even pause. "You will disappear so completely that no one will even bother to look. Who would miss you? Especially since the child will be gone, too." She rests the terrible hands on her knees, a bundle of brown twigs, the nest of some predatory bird.

"You guys really on board for this?" Rafferty asks. "You going to hurt a kid?"

"If necessary," says Nick.

"And you," Rafferty says to Chut. "You have a daughter of your own."

Chut starts to reply, then stops. He looks away.

"She paying you a lot?"

Nick says, "A lot more than we could have gotten from selling her."

"The only person in the world who can identify me is the man you are hiding," Madame Wing says. "Tell me where he is, and we'll let the child live."

"I wouldn't shit on you if you needed the ballast."

"Be as brave as you like. Do you know how many thousand times I've been through this? It's always the same. I can predict every stage you'll go through. First you'll refuse to tell us anything. Then you'll lie. When the lies don't stop us, you'll tell us what we want to know. Then, at the last, you'll say anything—*anything*—to make us stop. You'll tell us where your mother is. You'll beg us to hurt the little girl instead of you. Do you think there were no brave men and women in Cambodia? There were thousands of them. Do you know how many of them refused to talk to me in the end? None of them. Not one."

"I know what 'none' means."

"Save yourself the pain," she says, settling back in the chair. "In the end it will be the same anyway, except that you will have suffered and the child will die. Where is he?"

"On an airplane."

Her eyes widen and narrow again. "A lie. I'm not going to bargain any further. I've given you all I'm going to give. A quick answer from you and we'll be gone before the child arrives. Once she comes through that door, she's dead, I promise you."

Rafferty turns to stare at Chut, who averts his eyes. "These guys haven't got the stones for it."

"It's remarkable," she says complacently, "how many people turn out to have the stones, as you say. There was no shortage of willing hands in Tuol Sleng. It's like heroism. You have no idea what people can do until they do it. One of my best helpers was a boy who cried at sad movies."

"He's on a plane," Rafferty says again. "On his way to Hong Kong."

A tightening of the skin over the bones of her face. "Using what for money?"

"Obviously, yours."

Madame Wing looks at the others. "Does anyone here believe that?"

"He's working for free?" Nick says. The thin lips twist. "I don't think so."

"Listen," Rafferty says. "He's gone. He can't hurt you now. Killing me is just going to complicate your life. The police—"

"The police?" She waves a twisted hand at Nick and Chut. "The police are already here. They've been taking care of me for years. The police are not a problem. The *problem* is that you're not taking this seriously enough. Nobody really believes they're going to be hurt. They think we'll stop at some point before it gets awful." She leans toward him, boring in on him with those light-gathering eyes. "But we don't." She turns to the skeletal Nick. "Remove his trousers."

Rafferty starts to move, but Nick raises his hand, and it comes up with the automatic in it. The man's eyes are unsteady, flickering toward Chut and away again, but the pistol does not waver. It points straight at Rafferty's belly. "Take them off," Nick says.

"You can't actually shoot me," Rafferty says to Madame Wing with more certainty than he feels. "You want information."

Nick snaps a round into the chamber.

"Of course he can shoot you," Madame Wing says, and then she says to Nick, "Aim at the knees."

"Wait," Rafferty says. "You guys—listen, I'll give you the deed to her house. It's worth a hundred times what she's paying you."

Chut looks at Nick and then at Madame Wing.

"It's a forgery," she says.

"Afraid not," Rafferty says. "I sent you the forgery."

He has the brief pleasure of seeing the rage flare in her eyes, but then she wills it away. "We'll get the deed, too, after you tell us what we want to know." She tucks the blanket over her feet. "And, just for that, we're not going to wait. We'll get started and let the child walk in on us. Surprise her." She reaches beneath the blanket again, and when she brings her hands up, they have a thin black zippered case in them. "Which airline?" she says, unzipping the case.

"I don't know."

"What flight number? What time did it leave Bangkok?" The case is open now. A row of straight razors gleams against the black leather, arranged precisely from large to small. "Get him moving," she says. "I want him on the couch." She pries a razor from the case with her knotted fingers and opens it. It has a curved back, and there are nicks in the sharp straight edge. "This one isn't as sharp as I'd like it—no, as *you'd* like it to be. Tell me the flight number, and I'll use a sharper one."

"I don't know the flight number."

"Assuming he's even on a plane, which I don't believe for a moment. The couch," she says to the man with the pistol in his hand. "Get his trousers down and get him on the couch."

Nick walks around behind Rafferty and punches him between the shoulder blades. Rafferty takes two steps toward the couch, the man following a step behind, and there's a sound at the front door.

The knob turns, the clicking noise audible to them all. The door begins to open.

Rafferty raises a heavy boot and brings it down on Nick's instep. The man gasps and takes a quick jump backward, and Rafferty drops to his knees, rolls with the momentum, and comes up with the automatic in his hand, swinging the barrel around toward Nick, who is backing up fast.

The door opens, and Rose comes in.

She stands there, blinking for a moment, and Chut moves behind her and closes the door. Suddenly there is a gun in Chut's hand, too. All Rafferty can hear is his own breathing.

"Put down the gun," Madame Wing says. "You can't kill all of us. Chut, if he doesn't drop the gun, shoot the woman."

Chut brings his gun around to Rose and licks his lips. "Sort of a standoff, isn't it?" he says.

"Actually," Rafferty says, "no." And he draws the deepest breath of his life, swivels, and shoots Madame Wing twice.

At first he thinks she is trying to get out of the room. He hears the metallic animal squeal of the wheels as the chair rolls back, and then she throws up a hand and the chair tips backward and goes down, partially folding sideways as it falls. The blanket flies into the air and settles, in what seems to Rafferty to be slow motion, over Madame Wing's face. She coughs, and her left foot kicks once and then collapses against the edge of the lopsided chair.

"You're the one who said it," Rafferty says to Rose. He has to swallow twice. "There are people who should die."

Nick and Chut stand with their guns dangling at their sides, pointed at the floor, looking like men who have lost a winning lottery ticket. Rose comes slowly the rest of the way into the room, ignoring the two of them completely. Avoiding Rafferty's eyes, she stands over Madame Wing until it is clear she is not going to move. "I'm smoking a cigarette," she says to no one in particular, and then, very suddenly, she sits on the floor. She turns her head so she is not facing Madame Wing and begins to ransack her purse.

Chut has opened his mouth wide to clear the sound of the shots in the small room.

"You've still got your buyer," Rafferty says. He sits on the couch, which seems to be a very long way down, so far he thinks for an instant he has missed it. His body folds forward until his hands touch the carpet. He lets the gun fall from his fingers. He hears a match strike, and Rose's smoke tickles his nostrils. "There really is a buyer, isn't there?"

"Yes," says Chut, looking regretfully down at Madame Wing.

Rafferty leans back against the couch and closes his eyes. The room tilts, wheels around him, and rights itself. "Then get her out of here and sell her," he says. "And if she's gone before my daughter gets home, I'll give you the deed to her house."

## 43

## A Cynic Is Someone Who's Been on the Train Too Long

Arthit says, "Give me the phone."

Rafferty hands it over with gratitude. Clarissa has kept her promise to call to say good-bye, and he has been unable to think of a single thing to tell her.

"I need to talk to you about your uncle," Arthit says after identifying himself. He does not look at Rafferty. He is speaking his best English, British-clipped and stiff as a pig's bristle. He wears a polo shirt that Claus Ulrich's catalog would probably call "color-free" and a new pair of plaid trousers, bright enough to light a ballroom.

Rafferty can hear a question on Clarissa's end, and Arthit says, "He was working for us. He was a very valuable asset."

Privately Rafferty thinks Arthit has been reading too much John le Carré, but he leans back on the slashed couch and keeps his opinion to himself. An hour with a household cleanser that stank of ammonia has deleted the smear of eggs from the wall, and a throw rug covers the wet spot from which he'd scrubbed Madame Wing's blood. He'd gotten up from the mutilated bed around four in the morning, the third time he'd dreamed about killing her, and moved the rug from the kitchen.

That leaves only the rest of the apartment to clean up. Sitting uselessly on the floor, he begins to gather the couch's stuffing.

"As you probably know, the commercial abuse of women in Asia is a serious problem, a failure of international policy. Cultural issues enter into it as well, the relative value to Asian society of men and women." Arthit's eyes are closed. He seems intentionally to be choosing the driest language available without actually resorting to footnotes, but Rafferty gives it a second thought and decides it's probably brilliant. Anything more personal would not be half so convincing.

"So for us to have someone who was European, or at least Australian, who was mobile, who could cross borders . . ." He waits again, as Clarissa talks. Rafferty can't make out the words, but her voice is pitched high.

"Of course," Arthit says. "He was invaluable. Once he'd established his cover, buying all that awful pornography, he could position himself as a serious customer. He could gain their trust, something none of us could have hoped to do.

"We made arrests," Arthit says. He is sitting sideways on the ravaged sofa, gazing at the spot above it where the egg smear used to be. "I can say without hesitation that one Chinese gang has been put completely out of business, at least indirectly because of your Uncle Claus." This is not only a clincher, Rafferty thinks; it has the added merit of being true. In a way.

"Yes, my dear," Arthit says, his eyes flicking to Rafferty. "He was a hero, of sorts. And what happened to him—well, it probably didn't happen in Thailand. We think he was most likely in Laos when they got to him. We may never know exactly."

He listens again. "It's my pleasure," he says. "No one wants to think badly of someone we love after they're gone. There's no way for them to explain." His eyes find Rafferty again, and he shrugs. "Yes, yes. So please don't be too harsh on us. And have a good flight." He hangs up.

The two of them sit in silence for a moment, Rafferty with both hands full of cottony stuffing. Arthit looks out through the balcony window at the darkening sky, slowly going a sullen lead gray. "I guess the sun has called it a day."

"And who has a better right?" Rafferty asks, and immediately regrets his tone. He jams the stuffing into one of the slits in the couch, picks up some more, and drops it again, trying to exhale several liters of mixed emotions. "Thank you, Arthit."

Arthit pats his belly. "You said something about dinner."

"I did, didn't I?" Rafferty gets up stiffly, feeling battered and drained and older than he intends to be at death. "I thought we'd cook it out on the balcony."

"Probably a good idea, since I'd hate to think of you anywhere near a stove. You'd probably end up with your head in the oven. What's on the menu?"

"Man food," Rafferty says with a relish he does not feel. "Steaks."

"With what?"

"What do you mean, with what? They're big steaks."

"Where are Miaow and Rose?"

"At Rose's. Being girls together. And staying out of Superman's way." He doesn't add that Rose left to intercept Miaow after the shooting without speaking to him. It seems to take him fifteen minutes to get to the kitchen. He opens the refrigerator and pulls out the steaks, two of Foodland's biggest, cut specially for the occasion. "How do you want yours?"

"Just breathe on it a couple of times," Arthit says, hitching his blinding trousers by way of preparing to rise. "I'll bet there's a beer somewhere."

"Heineken. Just for you."

"It is manifestly a perfect world," Arthit says.


"THE VICTIMS WERE guilty," Rafferty says. "And the murderers were innocent."

Arthit drains his fourth green bottle. "I hate when that happens."

They are sitting on folding chairs on the balcony, looking out over the Bangkok night. Most of Rafferty's steak is still on the plate, sheened over with cold fat. The coals, coated with powdery ash now, are settling into the hibachi. Rafferty reaches over with the barbecue fork and pokes them, producing a small explosion of sparks. He leaves the tines of the fork buried in the pile of coals, as he used to do when he was a child in California, trying to heat the tines until they glow.

"And the boy?" Arthit asks.

"Gone. But he said he'd be back, to get Miaow."

"Then you'll have another chance with him, won't you?" He glances over at Rafferty, assessing the damage to his face. "The apartment looks terrible," he says.

"Really? I had it redone just for tonight."

"You look terrible, too."

"I ran into a door."

"That's a lot of damage for—"

"It was a revolving door."

"If it's any comfort, there are a couple of police generals who look worse," Arthit says, ignoring Rafferty's evasion. "Since Madame Wing's body was pulled from the river, they look like someone just cut their pay in half, which is probably accurate. Confusing world, isn't it? Even someone as wretched as she was will be missed."

"Confusing doesn't begin to describe it. It's like learning that all the maps were just made up at random, that they don't correspond to anything. Directions are a polite fiction. There's no such thing as north. Did you know, Arthit, that we 'orient' maps to the north because early mapmakers arbitrarily put Asia at the top of their maps? We've been going in the wrong direction for centuries. For all we know, that goddamned wave wanted to hit California."

"I've always thought a sense of direction was overrated," Arthit says, "since everything's pretty much the same everywhere."

"Well, I thought I had one. Take Madame Wing. I oriented myself toward her for a time because that's where I thought Doughnut was. Typical Bangkok two-step: Start out in one direction, sidestep, and suddenly you don't know who you're dancing with."

Arthit slides his eyes over at Rafferty and then out at the black Bangkok sky. A thin, high layer of clouds obscures the stars, making heaven as blank and featureless as a faulty memory, or the proverbial clean slate. The night is hot and still. "That thing about the Orient. Where'd you learn that?"

"A book."

"Gosh. Reading a lot lately?"

"One corker after another." Rafferty straightens his legs in front of him, looking down at his bare feet, almost the only unmarked parts of his body. "One of the nice things about books," he says, "is that they have endings."

Arthit says, "In case no one has told you, Poke, life has an ending."

"A KID WHO'S vanished back to the street," Rafferty says. "A very nice murderer in jail. A missing Australian who will apparently remain missing throughout the rest of this geological age, whatever they've named it. *His* murderer missing. Not exactly a tidy resolution."

Arthit glances at him and then away again. "The pseudonymous Doughnut. Disappeared, has she?"

"Without a trace."

"If she'd left a trace, Poke, she wouldn't have disappeared. She'd just be temporarily occluded."

"It's a good thing I like you," Rafferty says, "because if I didn't, you'd be unbearable."

"One thing that might interest you. Your two friends on the police force both resigned this morning."

"Well, they weren't really cut out for the job, were they? Did they give any explanation?"

"Real estate," Arthit says. "They're going into real estate."

"I thought it took capital to get into real estate."

"Well, apparently they have some." Arthit picks up the bone left from his steak, gives it a once-over, and drops it back onto the plate. "There are some things it's good not to look into too closely."

Rafferty is watching ash glaze over the glow inside the coals.

"Everybody, especially everybody in the West, thinks the guilty are guilty and the innocent are innocent," Arthit says. "Okay, so there are a few people who are just plain guilty. Madame Wing is a good example. Then there are an approximately equal number of people who are just plain innocent. I know three or four, and so do you. Everybody else is somewhere in the middle, trying to muddle through it all. After spending most of my life as a policeman, I still believe that most people are as good as they know how to be."

"Based on what evidence?"

"Little things, big things. On the big side, say, Angkor or Chartres."

"You could just as easily say those are ego. The old big-buildings-equal-big-dicks theory."

"No." Arthit puts his beer down and picks up Rafferty's. "They're aspiration. Spirit carved in rock. An enormous attempt over hundreds of years to express something that people feel deeply but don't know how to talk about. Something that's in the center of most of us, turned into millions of tons of stone. Ego—well, Albert Speer's designs for the Third Reich, those were ego. Ego pure and simple. The Brandenburg Gate, the Chrysler Building—those are aspiration."

"I don't know. More evidence."

"My wife's eyes," Arthit says. "Miaow's face." He reaches over and punches Rafferty on the thigh, harder, Rafferty hopes, than he intended to. "Friendship."

Rafferty grasps the handle of the fork. It has grown warm to the touch. "You got me," he says.

"You're such an unconvincing cynic," Arthit says. "I don't know why you even bother to try."

"I've been hearing that a lot lately."

"You know what a cynic is?"

"Yes, Arthit. A cynic is a disappointed romantic."

"A cynic is someone who's been on the train too long."

"The train," Rafferty says, and waits for it.

"I've always wondered why people travel by train," Arthit says. "Trains invariably pass through the shabbiest, most wretched parts of cities. To someone who lived his entire life on a train, the world would seem to be long stretches of emptiness occasionally interrupted by patches of ugliness. Once in a while, you need to get off the train and see what the world's really like."

"Yeah, yeah."

"You've been on an unusually long train ride—"

"All *right,* Arthit. You don't have to hammer it into my skull."

"Oh, I don't know." He slaps Rafferty's empty bottle against his palm. "Westerners seem to have difficulty with metaphors. I've often wondered whether it has something to do with the frontal lobe. Your heads are shaped so oddly."

"Tell it to Isaac Newton."

"You're going to adopt a child, Poke," Arthit says in a tone of gentle reproof. "You're going to be in charge of her universe, at least until she's old enough to take charge of it herself. You need to work on your worldview. And hers, too, since it's not the same as yours."

"I'm learning about that."

"And Rose's." He plucks at the crease of his pants. "How does she explain all this?"

"Hungry ghosts."

"See? Nothing even close to what you've probably come up with."

"Do you believe in them?"

"Hungry ghosts? Oh, yes indeed. The world is full of them."

"Then how—" Rafferty begins. "Hell. Okay, the world is swarming with hungry ghosts. How do I protect my wife and child? War and famine and pestilence and random malice, I'm comfortable with those. You can see them and smell them. I sort of know what to do about them. But this other stuff . . ."

"Don't be silly. You're making a family. You'll *love* them. You'll do things for them. You'll hold them when they need it and let them hold you when you need it. You'll listen to them when they try to educate you. Life is stronger than death when there's love in it. And along the way you'll change. Nothing changes a really putrid worldview like doing something good for someone who needs it."

"You big cream puff."

"I *do* have a soft center," Arthit says, "and I'm proud of it."

A cool wind suddenly materializes, brightening the coals and soothing Rafferty's raw and battered skin. "My God," he says. "A breeze."

Arthit lifts his face to it and breathes deeply. He closes his eyes. "If life were any better," he says, "we could sell tickets."

**FOR THE SECOND** night in a row, sleep won't come. After two hours or so, he simply settles back and lets the feelings bombard him. They pummel him from every direction, riddling him, blowing holes in his consciousness like cosmic rays, except that the particles seem to be the size of basketballs.

Even with the air-conditioning at full, he is perspiring. When the sheets on his bed become damp, he gets up and moves back to the couch. He fits into its new lumps and valleys as though he's been sleeping there for years and gazes out through the sliding door. A high, thin fog has settled over the city like ash, like the settling coals on the balcony, probably cold by now. Something seems to have burned out inside him, too.

He doesn't know whether it's something he can ever light again.

He is mentally rewriting his relationship with the boy, playing an especially agonizing game of "what if," when he hears the whispers at the door. He reaches automatically for the gun, realizes it's not there, and gets up, wrapping the sheet over his shoulders. Before he can make it to the door, it opens.

Rose and Miaow are standing there, pale as ghosts in the fluorescent light of the hallway.

"We couldn't sleep," Miaow says.

And Rose says, "Neither of us." She clears her throat. "Could sleep," she says. Then she adds, "With you here alone." She has a plastic bag in her hand.

Rafferty wants to say something, but he finds that he can't. He steps back, inviting them in.

Miaow steps forward, her eyes wide at the ruin of the apartment, but Rose hesitates, looking down at something beside the door. "Do you have a guest?"

"Where's Superman?" Miaow asks. She points her chin toward her room. "Is he—"

"We have to talk about Boo," Rafferty says. He steps forward and rests a hand on her shoulder, and her warmth travels up his arm and straight to his heart. "About all of it. Tomorrow." Rose has stooped down to pick something up, and when she rises, she has in her hand a pair of shoes—battered, worn out, scuffed, and beaten. The soles flap loose like a clown's. Shoes, Rafferty thinks, as some of his new happiness drains away, that were probably retrieved from a trash bin and then carefully placed at his door.

"What are these?" Rose asks. "They're not yours."

"No," Rafferty says, the word finding its way around the sudden weight in his chest. "They're not." Miaow's head comes up sharply, and her eyes pierce him.

"Then why are they here?"

"Aaaahhh," Rafferty says. He drops to his knees and hugs Miaow, and although she stiffens for a moment, she exhales and settles against him and lets her head fall onto his shoulder. He kisses the knife-straight part in her hair and looks back up at Rose. "I guess someone's decided to go barefoot."

"Well," Rose says, bewildered, the shoes dangling from her fingertips. "In that case—" She starts toward the kitchen, toward the trash.

"Wait." Miaow pushes herself away from Rafferty and goes to Rose, her back straight and her shoulders high. The long braid perfectly bisects her back, as though she has willed it into order. She extends a hand, and after a moment Rose gives her the shoes. Miaow goes to the open door and puts the shoes just outside, touching the edge of the mat. She turns to Rafferty, her face soft and unguarded.

"In case he changes his mind," she says. She closes the door.

## 44

## Path of Light

This will do until we go to the temple tomorrow," Rose says, on her knees on the carpet. One by one the items come out of the bag. Sixteen small candles, just clear glass cups about two inches high, into which white paraffin has been poured. Six sticks of incense and six burners. Rose lights four of the sticks, rises, and places them in the corners of the room. Then she places two more, one on either side of the door.

A clear plastic bag full of water, secured by a rubber band. A new bowl, shallow and white except for a lotus painted in very pale green on the bottom. A small ceramic figure of the seated Buddha.

Miaow is asleep, or at least in her room. Rafferty doubts she will sleep well tonight. Wondering about the boy.

"*What* will we do until tomorrow, Rose?"

"Sssssssshhhhhhh." Seated again, she dips a hand into her bag and comes up with a lighter, which she uses to light two of the candles. The light they emit is different from the electric light in the room, calmer and warmer.

"Open the door," Rose says.

Rafferty says, "The door."

"There has to be a place," Rose says, "for her to go."

"Right," Rafferty says. "A place for her to go." He gets up and opens the door to the relative dimness of the hallway.

"You don't want her here," Rose says, lighting two more candles. "Believe me."

"Not to look a gift horse in the mouth or anything, but is this why you came back tonight?"

"Of course it is." She lights two more candles. "Well, it's one reason. Turn off the lights. No, wait." She gets up, bowl in hand, studying the carpet, then stoops to pull aside the throw rug from the kitchen. "Here," she says. Even from the door, Rafferty can see the scrubbed spot where he tried to wash the last of Madame Wing from his life.

Rose kneels slowly and places the bowl in the center of the spot. "Now," she says. "The lights."

Rafferty hits the switch. The candles make pools of light on the carpet and glow softly on Rose's skin.

"Take two of the candles and put them by the door," Rose says. "One on each side." She lights two more and puts them on either side of the scrubbed spot on the carpet, about eighteen inches apart. Rafferty does what he is told, and Rose places two more lighted candles about a foot closer to the door, slightly farther apart than the ones that define the spot.

"In my village," she says, placing two more candles another foot closer to the door, "every New Year we cleaned the houses." She lights two more candles and puts them still nearer the door, a bit farther apart. "We shook out the carpets and washed the walls and swept the street."

"Starting the New Year clean," Rafferty says.

She places two more candles, then makes a small adjustment in the two she had put down last. Rafferty can't see any difference, but she cocks her head to one side and studies it, then leaves it alone. "At the end of the day, we lit candles in paper bags and put them along the street and then off across the fields to the forest."

"And the point was . . . ?"

"It was a path," she says. All the candles are in place now, illuminating a strip of carpet that begins at the wet spot and gradually widens to the door. "Come here," she says. She sits on one side of the wet spot and slips a fingernail beneath the rubber band that seals the bag of water. Intent on the task, which she is doing slowly and very deliberately, she lifts her head a fraction of an inch to indicate the place on the opposite side of the spot. "Sit."

He sits. He can feel the flesh on his legs shrink away from the dampness beneath his knees.

She has worked the rubber band free of the bag now, holding it carefully by the open end so not a drop of water spills out. She lifts her face to his. He can see the tears standing in her eyes.

"We couldn't leave you alone with her," she says. "Miaow and I. We both love you. And we know you. We know you'll just go on stepping over this spot. Waiting for it to dry. And it will never dry. And you won't know she's here."

He wants to say that she's not here, but all he can really hear is, *We both love you.* He nods his head, uncertain of his voice.

"Tell her you're sorry," Rose says.

For a long moment, a moment subdivided by the flickering of the candles, Rafferty isn't sure he can say it. Then he whispers, "I'm sorry."

Rose's eyes never leave his. "Tell her you don't blame her for the karma that trapped her, that made her do such terrible things. Tell her you know she had light inside her. Tell her you wish her spirit well."

Rafferty gets through it somehow. When he says he knows she had light inside her, he realizes he is crying.

"Put out your hands," Rose says. "Over the bowl."

He does as he's told, palms up, and she slowly pours the water over them. She puts down the empty bag, picks up the small Buddha, and holds it over her heart. She closes her eyes. "Now tell her she's free."

IN THE HALLWAY outside, Mrs. Pongsiri steps from the elevator and pauses at the open doors. She sees the shoes beside the door, the path of light, the two people kneeling at the end of it, the water being poured. Then the man, her neighbor Mr. Rafferty, says something, and at the same time the candles flicker as though a window has been opened, and something cold blows against—no, through—Mrs. Pongsiri. She takes a step back, feeling the skin pucker on her arms.

At the end of the path of light, the man and the woman bend toward each other until their foreheads touch. Their eyes are closed.

# Note

The AT Series exists. It is just as described. The photographs were taken in Southeast Asia, probably in Thailand. There are hundreds of them. As far as I know, the man who took them has not been identified.

Tuol Sleng still stands in Phnom Penh as a monument to the thousands who spent their last days in torment there. At the time of this writing, exactly one of the Khmer Rouge who brutalized and killed more than a million Cambodians is behind bars; the only other murderer to be jailed died in captivity. Hundreds of other Khmer Rouge leaders remain free and even prosperous, in the Pailin region of Cambodia and elsewhere.

The story about the young Buddhist monk who learns to cover his feet in leather is beautifully told in the Tibetan film *The Cup*.

The economics of Patpong and Nana Plaza persuade most of the women to remain in the bars. The bar workers who are most successful, to look at it from one perspective, can make more money in a week than their parents earn in a year. There are no physical restraints and no pimps in the usual sense of the word. The women can refuse to go with any customer, although they are fined if they don't clock out a certain number of times each month. Some women, like Rose, leave while they are still young enough and attractive enough to keep working, but they are in the minority. The women who walk away return willingly to relative poverty in the faith that they can make a life elsewhere. Hundreds, even thousands, of girls come down each year from the impoverished northeast to take their places.

## Acknowledgments

This book needed, and got, a lot of help, and it seems only fair to say thanks.

I write largely in restaurants and coffeehouses, and I'd like to express gratitude to the people at Lollicup in West Los Angeles, the Novel Café in Santa Monica, and the Cow's End in Venice, all in California; the Tip-Top in Bangkok; and especially the terrific staff of Pose Café in Phnom Penh, Cambodia. These people made me feel welcome and kept me fed and caffeinated while I wrote this story and then wrote it again. And whenever I needed a face, I could just look up and steal one.

When I was first learning my way around Bangkok, my home was a hotel, the Tawana Bangkok. The care they took of me was personal and unforgettable. It's a pleasure to thank them.

Aural energy was provided, via an overworked iPod, by Bob Dylan, the irreplaceable Marvelettes, the Shins, Shonen Knife, Lyle Lovett, Arcade Fire, Delbert McClinton, Rufus Wainwright, Sufjan Stevens, Missy Elliott, and the Flaming Lips, among others.

Several people were especially helpful in taking the book apart and helping me put it back together. Stan Cutler, a fine writer, read the first draft and offered invaluable and tactful practical advice based on a lifetime of writing and a genetic surplus of humor. My agent, Bob Mecoy, made truly architectural suggestions that turned the story inside out and upside down and—when the dust had settled—revealed a whole new world for Rafferty to explore. Thanks, Bob. And Marjorie Braman at Morrow looked at the story's resolutions and challenged some of them, to good effect.

Amphornnet Phanphunga Pridgen made some valuable suggestions about Thai interior life and contributed greatly to the scene that closes the book. Pritsana Chomchan reviewed the entire manuscript from a Thai perspective, something I was obviously not capable of doing myself, and helped keep that aspect of the book on track.

And finally, my wife, Munyin Choy, listened to the whole thing read aloud several times and—as always—not only held open the door to my creative impulses but also showed me where that door was in the first place.

# THE FOURTH WATCHER

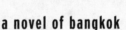

a novel of bangkok

## TIMOTHY HALLINAN

Available in hardcover in July 2008 from

WILLIAM MORROW
*An Imprint of* HarperCollins*Publishers*

1

## Three-Card Monte

Poke Rafferty has been on the sidewalk less than five minutes when he spots the tail.

Three of them, all male. One ahead, two behind. Tak-
ing their time, no telltale urgency. All relatively young and dressed to
fade: one white T-shirt, one red T-shirt, one long-sleeved black shirt.
Pants of that indeterminate color produced by years of hard launder-
ing, a sort of enervated second cousin to beige.

The clothes aren't much help, but they're all Rafferty has: no conspicuous physical anomalies, no scars, no rap-inspired dreadlocks,
no tattoos, no bleached hair. He's looking at a trio of standard hands
dealt out of the Thai genetic shuffle—short and slim-waisted, with the
black hair and dark skin of the northeast. Three everyday guys, out on
a choreographed stroll, doing a pretty slick version of the Barre rota-
tion: changing places at random intervals, the man in front casually
crossing the road to the far sidewalk and drifting back, replaced moments later by one of the pair behind. A rolling maneuver, like a deal in
three-card monte.

The guy in the black shirt is what Arnold Prettyman calls "the Flag." He's wearing reflective shades, he walks funny, it's too hot for long sleeves, and it's too sunny for black, even at 10:30 A.M. So either Rafferty is supposed to notice him or he's not very good.

Prettyman's First Law of Espionage, drummed into Poke's head over the past couple of weeks: Always assume that the other guy is good.

So. Take score. Moderate foot traffic, average for an early weekday morning in an upscale Bangkok shopping district. Stores just open, offering lots of nice, big, reflective display windows, useful to both the stalkers and the target. The sun is still low, so shadows are long, which can be either helpful or deadly around corners. The usual blast-furnace, wet-blanket Bangkok heat, heat with an actual *weight* to it that frequently takes Rafferty by surprise even after more than two years here. It changes the way he dresses, the way he breathes, and even the way he walks. The way everybody walks. It shortens the stride and makes it pointless to waste energy lifting the feet any higher than absolutely necessary; all the effort goes into moving forward. The result is what Rafferty has come to think of as the Bangkok Glide, the energy-efficient and peculiarly graceful way Thai people have of getting themselves from place to place without melting directly into the sidewalk.

Unlike the other two, whose glides are so proficient they might as well be ice-skating, the guy in the black shirt moves like a man wearing cast-iron boots: heavy steps, a lot of lateral hip action. He looks like Lurch among the ballerinas. The man has, Rafferty finally recognizes, a clubfoot, so put a check in the physical-anomaly column after all. The clubfoot is housed in a black architectural structure half the size of a *tuk-tuk*, the three-wheeled taxis so ubiquitous in Bangkok. So here's Black Shirt, a/k/a *Tuk-Tuk* Foot; him, Rafferty can spot.

Okay, he can spot him. So what?

Thought One is to lose Black Shirt first. Reduce the opposition numbers and then worry about the others. Thought Two is to stay with Black Shirt and try to lose the others, on the assumption that he can spot Black Shirt anytime.

*But.*

The men who are following him probably expect him to proceed from Thought One to Thought Two. Of course, they might know he'd realize they'd expect that, and they'd revert to Thought One. That's what Prettyman would probably do in this situation.

Or is it? And is there a Thought Three that hasn't even come to him?

Rafferty feels a brittle little arpeggio in his forebrain, the opening bars of the overture to a headache.

A long time ago, he learned that the best course of action, when you're faced with a difficult problem, is to choose one solution, at random if necessary, and stick with it. Don't question it unless it kills you. Okay. Lose Black Shirt and keep an eye on the other two.

The flush of comfort that always accompanies a decision recedes almost immediately at the thought of Prettyman's Second Law. There are usually more than you can spot.

Moving more slowly than the flow of foot traffic, forcing the trackers to lag awkwardly, Rafferty passes the entrance to a five-story department store, one of the newly cloned U.S.-style emporiums that have sprung up all over the city to serve Bangkok's exploding middle class. He pulls his followers out of position by moving an extra twenty steps or so past the polished chrome of the revolving door, as yet unsmudged with shoppers' fingerprints. Then he stops and searches the glass for reflected movement while he pretends to be fascinated by whatever the hell is on the other side of the window. He counts to five, turns away, takes two steps in the direction he's been moving in, then decides that whatever was in the window—on second glance it seems to be women's shoes, of all the stupid fucking things—is indispensable after all. He reverses direction abruptly, seeing the pair behind freeze at the edge of his vision and then scramble to separate, and goes back to the store entrance, moving quickly and decisively, trying to look like a man who's just spotted an irresistible pair of high heels. Pushes at the revolving door.

Cool air like a faceful of water.

He finds himself in the cosmetics department, where a hundred mirrors point back at the door he has just come through. In the closest one, Rafferty watches White T-Shirt come through the revolving door, snap a quick, disbelieving look at the mirrors, and keep right on going until he's outside again.

Rafferty is practically the only customer in the store. Half a dozen hibernating saleswomen gape at him. One of them shakes herself awake and says, in English, "Help you, sir?"

"I've got a terrible problem with . . . um, tangling," he says, tugging at his hair and keeping his eyes on a mirror that frames the two men talking in the street behind him. White T-Shirt with his back to the door, Red T-Shirt displaying dark skin and a pimp's thin mustache. Lots of gesturing.

"You hair okay," says the woman behind the counter. She employs the unique Thai-style selling technique; the chat is more important than the sale. "You hair pretty good." She squints dubiously. "Maybe too long, *na*? Maybe cut little bit *here*."

In the mirror Rafferty sees Red T-Shirt lose the argument on the sidewalk and push the revolving door. "I'll come back tomorrow," Rafferty says, shoving off from the counter. "Before I brush." He walks quickly through the cosmetics department and boards the store's central escalator.

Standing sideways as the escalator's sole passenger, he watches Red T-Shirt do some broken-field running between the counters to catch up, and then Rafferty turns and takes the rest of the steps two at a time.

Turn right at the top of the escalator, move at a half run through a voluptuary's forest of mannequins wearing impractical underwear the colors of extinct tropical fruits. The women's-underwear department borders the housewares department, a broad expanse of gleaming white marble and porcelain meant to awaken kitchen envy in female shoppers. Rafferty stops at the first of a long line of gleaming stainless-steel sinks, complete with a homey assortment of washed dishes in a drying rack, and grabs the squeeze bottle of detergent, hoping it's not just a prop. It is reassuringly heavy. Without looking back, he pops the top and spews a long zigzag of clear, thick liquid on the tile floor as he retreats up the aisle. At the far end, he waits until Red T-Shirt has found his way through the glade of underwear. Once he is sure the man has seen him, Rafferty turns and breaks into a full-out bolt.

He is rewarded by the distinctive sound of running feet behind him, then a cry of despair followed by a clamorous crash as some display or another goes down. A glance over his shoulder shows him Red T-Shirt at the bottom layer of a heap of broken dishes, flailing to get his hands and feet under him on the slick floor as shopgirls come running from all directions.

The down escalators take Rafferty in easy stages to the basement, which is positively arctic. Housewives on the verge of hypothermia paw listlessly through piles of bargain clothes. At the far end of the sale area lurks an ersatz McDonald's, complete with its own frightening clown. Beyond the bright plastic tables, their chairs bolted gaily to the floor, a set of tiled steps leads up to the sidewalk, and Rafferty takes them in two springs.

Hot air again. Hot pavement through the soles of his shoes. Traffic noise.

Lots of pretty women wearing bright colors. No White T-Shirt; he's almost certainly watching the entrance. No Black Shirt. Red T-Shirt is probably flat on his back picking slivers of crockery from his hair.

Rafferty slows, debating the wisdom of turning the tables and grabbing one of them for a brief conversation. He is weighing the pros and cons as he makes a right into a side street and the little man with the black shirt and the clubfoot steps out of a doorway, smiles apologetically, levels a small black gun at Poke's head, and shoots him square in the face.

## The Fourth Watcher

From his perspective half a block away, where he appears to be entirely focused on choosing a spray of vaguely reptilian orchids from a sidewalk vendor, the fourth watcher—the one the other three don't know about—tracks the movements of the gun. He stiffens as the little man in the black shirt brings his hand up, takes a useless step forward as Rafferty stumbles back, watches openmouthed as the trigger is pulled.

Not until he is walking away, his orchids tightly wrapped in newspaper, does he permit himself to laugh.

## The First One She's Had in Years
## That Isn't a Street Fake

The first thing Peachy notices is that the man counting her money is perspiring very heavily, almost as heavily as a foreigner. Like many Thais, she finds it perplexing how much *farang* sweat, although Peachy, who has persisted in regarding herself as a lady through a lifelong roller coaster of social ups and downs, would never use a word as common as "sweat." During one of the brief periods of prosperity her family enjoyed when Peachy was growing up, they hired a British governess named Daphne. Almost forty years later, what Peachy remembers most vividly about Daphne is her hatred of the word "sweat." "Horses sweat," Daphne had said, sweating generously in the Bangkok summer. "Men perspire. Women *glow.*"

So the bank teller fumbling with the bills for her payroll is *perspiring,* in defiance of the glacial air-conditioning, which is cold enough to raise little stucco bumps on Peachy's bare arms.

In fact, the teller's shirt it so wet it's transparent. Peachy has seen horses sweat less profusely, even after one of the races to which she used to be . . . well, addicted. If there's a more polite word for "sweat,"

Peachy thinks, counting silently to herself as she watches the stack of thousand-baht bills grow, there should be a more polite word for "addicted" as well. "Habit" is a bit weak, considering that the horses cost Peachy practically everything she owned. She managed to hang on to her business only because a *farang*, an American, had handed her an irresistible, absolutely life-changing wad of money that she couldn't refuse even though it came with a mandatory partner. Together, she and Rose, the partner by command, have rebuilt the business until they have actually begun to show a profit. But the horses had cost her dearly, had cost her much of what she had taken for granted in life, had cost her—

Had cost her, in fact, much more than she is prepared to think about now, especially when she should be watching this very nervous man count out her money.

The teller's hands are shaking, too.

His eyes come up to Peachy's and catch her regarding him. He smiles, or tries to smile. It looks like the smile of a man who wants to prove he can take bad news well. *Cancer? No problem.* The smile is impossible to return. Peachy begins to feel distinctly uneasy.

"Forgive me," she says, leaning forward slightly and politely lowering her voice. "Are you feeling all right?"

The teller straightens as though someone had plugged his stool directly into a wall socket, and his eyes widen into an expanse of white with the irises marooned in the center. Peachy involuntarily thinks about fried eggs. "Me?" the teller asks, swallowing. "Fine, fine. And you?"

Peachy takes a discreet step back. The man smells of something, perhaps illness or even fear. "Fine, thank you."

"It's just . . . you know," the teller says, blinking rapidly. He makes a tremulous gesture at the stack of white-and-brown bills in front of him. "Lot of, um, um, money," he says.

"We pay the girls today," Peachy says, and then replays the sentence in her mind. "They're *housemaids*," she clarifies. "We run a domestic agency. Bangkok Domestics." Although she's grown fond of Rose, she still can't bring herself to call it Peachy and Rose's Domestics.

The teller tries to square the bills into a neat pile, but his hands aren't steady enough, and he gives up and shoves them under the glass partition like a pile of leaves. "You must be doing well."

"It's getting better," Peachy says. Although the bills all seem to be brand-new, they look damp and a little bit sticky, as though they had been absorbing moisture in the perspiring man's pocket. She doesn't, she realizes, actually want to touch them. Below the counter she un-snaps her purse—Gucci, the first one she's had in years that isn't a street fake—and holds it wide. Then, using her expensive new finger-nails and hoping she's not being rude, she sweeps the money off the counter and into the purse. "Bye-bye," she says in English, turning away.

THE BANK TELLER'S eyes follow her all the way across the lobby: a woman in her late forties, wearing clothes that could provoke buyer's remorse in a seventeen-year-old. He resolutely refuses to look out through the picture window at the front of the bank, where he knows the man will be. Watching him.

He looks up to face his next customer.

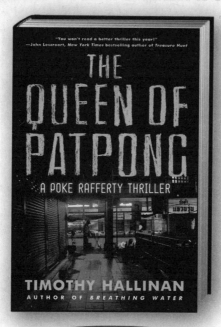

# POKE RAFFERTY THRILLERS BY TIMOTHY HALLINAN

### THE QUEEN OF PATPONG

ISBN 978-0-06-167227-9 (paperback)
**An Edgar Award Nominee for Best Novel**

"Hallinan takes his Poke Rafferty series to the next level with this taut, offbeat and fast-moving thriller that focuses on Bangkok's red light district and sex trade."
—*Kirkus Reviews* (starred review)

"You won't read a better thriller this year!"
—John Lescroart, *New York Times* bestselling author

### BREATHING WATER

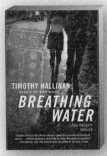

ISBN 978-0-06-167225-5 (paperback)

"Cleverly crafted, masterfully written, characters and dialogue rooted in reality, *Breathing Water* offers fascinating insights into the dark side of crime in another culture."
—Steve Martini, *New York Times* bestselling author

### THE FOURTH WATCHER

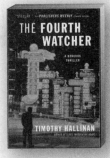

ISBN 978-0-06-125726-1 (paperback)

"Stellar. . . . Smooth prose, appealing characters, and a twisting action-filled plot make this thriller a standout."
—*Publishers Weekly* (starred review)

### A NAIL THROUGH THE HEART

ISBN 978-0-06-125722-3 (paperback)

"*A Nail Through the Heart* is a haunting novel that takes place way out on the fringe of the moral landscape. It's fast, bold, disturbing, and beautifully written. Hallinan is terrific."
—T. Jefferson Parker, author of *California Girl*

Visit www.TimothyHallinan.com and www.AuthorTracker.com
for exclusive information on your favorite HarperCollins authors.

**Available wherever books are sold, or call 1-800-331-3761 to order.**